SOME SUNNY DAY

Annie Groves lives in the North-West of England and has done so of all her life. She is also the author of *Ellie Pride*, *Connie's Courage* and *Hettie of Hope Street*, a series of novels for which she drew upon her own family's history, picked up from listening to her grandmother's stories when she was a child. She is also the author of *Goodnight Sweetheart*, based on wartime recollections of Liverpool from members of her family who come from the city. For further information on Annie Groves, visit her website at www.anniegroves.squarespace.com

Visit www.AuthorTracker.co.uk for exclusive updates on Annie Groves.

By the same author

Ellie Pride
Connie's Courage
Hettie of Hope Street

Goodnight Sweetheart
The Grafton Girls

ANNIE GROVES

Some Sunny Day

HARPER

Harper
An imprint of HarperCollins*Publishers*
77–85 Fulham Palace Road,
Hammersmith, London W6 8JB

www.harpercollins.co.uk

This paperback edition 2007

First published in Great Britain by
HarperCollins*Publishers* 2006

Copyright © Annie Groves 2006

Annie Groves asserts the moral right to
be identified as the author of this work

A catalogue record for this book is
available from the British Library

Set in Sabon by Palimpsest Book Production Limited,
Grangemouth, Stirlingshire

Printed and bound in Great Britain by
Clays Ltd, St Ives plc

ACKNOWLEDGEMENTS

I would like to thank the following for their invaluable help:

Maxine Hitchcock, my lovely editor, who is so truly inspirational

Yvonne Holland, for her patience and skill

Everyone at HarperCollins who has contributed to the publication of this book

Teresa Chris, my agent, for her wisdom and her generosity

Tony, for patience above and beyond the call of duty

My writing friends and fellow members of the RNA who have been so generous with the details of research sources for my WW2 books

I would also like to thank all those who lived through WW2 and have so generously contributed their first-hand experiences to online research sites. Reading their stories brought the reality of war home to me.

To all those who lived through WW2
– and to all those who did not.

PART ONE

June 1940

ONE

''Ere, Rosie, you live down in Little Italy with the Eyeties, don't you? Only it's just bin on the wireless that that Mussolini of theirs has only gone and sided with ruddy 'Itler, just like it's bin saying in the papers 'e would. I heard about it when I took Mrs V.'s parcels to the post office for 'er.' Nancy, rushing into the small sewing room at the back of Elegant Modes, announced the news with malicious relish. 'Fascists, that's what they all are, living over here, spying on us. If you ask me, the whole lot of them want locking up.'

'That's not fair, Nancy,' Rosie Price objected, her brown eyes brilliant with emotion, and her cheeks flushing as she put down the dress she was holding and determinedly faced the other girl. 'Most of the Italians in Liverpool have been here for years, and I know for a fact that a lot of the boys from the families near us were amongst the first to join up when war was announced.'

Nancy tossed her head and eyed Rosie resentfully.

Until Rosie had started working at the dress shop on Bold Street just after Christmas, *she* had been the prettiest girl there and had grown used to the other girls both admiring and envying her. Mrs Verey, who owned Elegant Modes, had even asked Nancy to model the dresses now and then if a customer couldn't quite make up her mind.

Mrs Verey bought her stock with her regular customers in mind. For daytime there were smart tweed suits for the winter with neat little fur collars, to be worn with pretty knitted twinsets, and blouses trimmed with lace; for the summer, short-sleeved cotton and silk dresses and good navy-blue light-weight coats. She also carried a range of truly beautiful evening frocks, in silks and satins, with full panelled skirts flaring out from tightly fitted bodices. Most of the frocks came with matching wraps and pretty little evening bags. These dresses, like the wedding dresses she also sold, were kept in special glass-fronted wardrobes in their own special 'salon'. And since Rosie, with her tiny waist and her curves, her thick, naturally curly dark hair, and the dimples that softened her cheeks when her mouth curved into a smile, had come to work at the salon, it was she who Mrs Verey chose and whose inherent style the other girls were now trying to copy.

Rosie loved the expensive fabrics of the clothes Mrs Verey sold and searched the stalls in St John's market for offcuts and bargains – pretty pieces of lace and unusual buttons with which to dress up her own clothes. She favoured neat, simple styles rather than frills and ruffles, preferring to buy plain things she could put her own stamp on with some pretty trimmings: a lace collar, or a contrasting belt. Mrs Verey had said approvingly, 'You've got a proper sense of style, Rosie, and no mistake. That's something that can never be bought.'

'Well, *you* might be all pally with them, Rosie, but there's a lot of folk in Liverpool who are a bit more patriotic,' Nancy announced sharply. 'My dad was saying only the other night as 'ow we don't need the likes of Eyeties and Fascists over here eating our rations and that.'

Rosie had no idea why Nancy kept picking on her the way she did. From her very first day at the shop, Nancy had gone out of her way to be unkind to her and get her into trouble. Rosie could still remember how, on her first morning, Nancy had told Rosie to iron a fragile satin dress satin side up, which would have ruined the garment completely if one of the other girls hadn't stopped her just in time. When Rosie had said innocently that she was following Nancy's instructions Nancy had claimed that Rosie must have misunderstood her. But it hadn't been until later in the week when Ruth, one of the girls, had overheard Nancy telling Rosie that Mrs Verey wanted her and that she was to go down to the showroom right away, that Rosie realised that it wasn't kindness that was motivating Nancy to take an interest in her but quite the opposite.

'Rosie, you just tek no notice of anything Nancy tells yer to do, wi'out checking wi' one of us first,'

Ruth had warned her. 'We all know that Mrs Verey doesn't allow us girls to go down into the show-room in our workroom clothes, and looking untidy. I reckon Nancy has a mind to get you into trouble so that Mrs Verey decides to get rid of you. She's allus bin a bit like that, has Nancy. She's got a real nasty streak to her, if you ask me.'

Now Rosie tried to avoid Nancy and not get drawn into arguments with her. She didn't want to risk losing her job, not whilst she was still only a trainee assistant, to give her job its proper name. Rosie's working day was filled with a variety of jobs that included making sure the floors were kept free of dust, especially in the workroom, learning how to press the delicate fabrics, making sure that clothes that had been tried on by customers were put back properly in the correct place, and just occasionally, under the stern eye of one of the more senior girls, being allowed into the shop to serve those customers who had come in for some small item such as a pair of stockings or some handkerchiefs. But now she couldn't just stand there and let Nancy get away with saying what she had.

'That's not fair,' Rosie repeated. 'Some of the families, like the Volantes, the D'Annunzios, the Santangellis and the Chiappes, have been in Liverpool for fifty years and more.' Although she wasn't Italian, Rosie had grown up amongst the immigrant Italian families who inhabited that part of the city known as 'Little Italy', the heart of the

Italian community in Liverpool. Rosie knew how proud Liverpool's Italians were, both of their roots in the Picinisco area of Italy, poor farming country between Naples and Rome, and of their English home from home. The first immigrants, men in the main, driven out of their home country by poverty, to look for work to support their families wherever they could find it, had worked hard, saving what they could to send home, and returning there in the summer to help tend the family farms. As soon as they were able to do so, they had brought to Liverpool their wives and children, and a tradition had built up of the Italians marrying within their own community and adhering as much as they could to the ways of the old country.

The Italian immigrants had always been made welcome and were able to find work because they possessed wonderful artistic talents. Rosie had been told how in the early days of their arrival, in Lionel Street, a number of Italian families had converted their cellars into little workshops where they made beautiful and intricate figurines and statues, sometimes working in marble. These skills were passed down from one generation to the next. Those unskilled men amongst the earlier immigrants had been prepared to undertake almost any type of work to support their families. One of their occupations was knife sharpening, and Rosie had often heard how proud the Gianelli and the Sartorri families were of the fact that from humble beginnings they had developed commercial businesses within the city, offering their knife-sharpening services to hotels and restaurants.

As new immigrants arrived from Italy, those who were already established welcomed them, taking them in as lodgers and helping them to establish themselves in turn, so that a closely knit community began to develop. Ever watchful for an opportunity to earn a living, one man, Vincenzo Volante, set up in business hiring out handcarts and larger carts for transporting barrel organs. Vincenzo could speak several languages and so he took on the responsibility of helping the newcomers who could not speak English.

As la Nonna, the grandmother of Rosie's best friend, Bella, had told Rosie with great pride, the Italians coming from the homeland were extremely gifted artistically and musically, and soon the streets of Little Italy were warmed by the songs of the old country and the laughter of its people.

Those who pushed their barrel organs around the city entertaining the public, quickly realised that there was a market for the ice cream they had enjoyed at home in Italy, and so certain families set up small businesses in their homes making ice cream. Raphael Santangelli in particular was famous for his ice-cream business, starting from humble beginnings in Gerard Street, and selling his ice cream first from handcarts pushed around the streets, and then, as the business became more successful and he could afford them, via three-wheeler ice-cream carts. Now the Santangellis were well known and respected, and their motorised ice-cream vans were seen everywhere in the city. La Nonna was very proud of her own family's distant connection to the Santangellis, to whom she was a cousin several times removed. She had boasted to Rosie, though, that her own recipe for ice cream was just that little bit better than that of the Santangellis, owing to a 'secret' extra special ingredient she had learned at her own grandmother's knee and which she only intended to pass on to her daughters on her deathbed.

The Chiappe family was also famous for its ice-cream business. They had a well-known ice-cream shop near the Gaiety Cinema in Scotland Road, and another branch at 8 Feather Road, owned by Angelo Chiappe, who was a great friend of Bella's father. In the winter, when no one wanted to buy ice cream, the sellers sold roasted chestnuts instead.

Many Italian men found work in the catering trade in Liverpool's hotels, and in 1939, when Romeo Imundi had retired from Romeo's, the grocery store owned and run by the Imundi family on Springfield Street, the whole community had turned out to wave him off back to Picinisco.

Knowing what she did about the length of time the Italian families had been established in Liverpool, and just how much they had contributed to the city in different ways, and how much they cared about it and about one another, it shocked and disgusted Rosie to hear Nancy speaking so nastily about them, and she was fully prepared to say so. Nancy, though, wasn't prepared to listen.

'They're still Eyeties, though, aren't they?' she insisted.

'Don't pay no mind to Nancy, Rosie,' Ruth said quietly as Rosie carefully hung up the dress, ready to start work on it in the morning. 'I dare say Nancy's had her fair share of Gonnelli's ice cream and Podestra's chips in her time.'

Rosie managed a small smile, more out of politeness than anything else. It made her so angry when she knew how hard the Italians worked to hear them being run down so unfairly.

'Nancy's being so unkind, Ruth,' she replied fiercely. 'You should have seen how proud the Italian folk in our street were when their boys joined up. St Joseph's Boxing Club was practically empty, so many of the boys who go there had enlisted. The Fuscos a few doors down from us lost their only son at Dunkirk,' she added quietly. Her eyes clouded at the thought.

The whole country was still in shock over the dreadful news they had all heard about the British Expeditionary Force, the very best of the country's experienced soldiers. Trapped when Hitler had swept into Belgium and then France, the British soldiers had been forced to retreat to the French beaches of Dunkirk. Thousands of them had died there and thousands upon thousands more would also have perished or been taken prisoner had it not been for the brave men who had risked their own lives over and over again to sail across the Channel to bring their fellow countrymen safely home.

Rosie had seen the newsreels, showing that valiant rescue operation. She had seen too the heart-wrenching celluloid images of the haggard, grey-faced men in their uniforms, heads bent in shame and defeat. Mr Churchill's stirring words, though, had raised everyone's spirits and given the fighting men of Great Britain back their pride, as he had turned defeat into pride that so many brave men had been saved. But the terrible events of Dunkirk had left a shadow over the whole country, along with the fear of Hitler's threatened invasion.

Just thinking about the war made Rosie feel so afraid. And not just for herself. Her father was a merchant seaman, sailing under the 'Red Duster', as the Red Ensign was nicknamed. All through the winter, merchant ships had made their way across the Atlantic in convoys, bringing much-needed supplies to the country, but the loss of life and shipping had been severe, and Rosie could never relax when her father was at sea.

Although the dress shop closed at five o'clock, the girls in the sewing room were expected to work on until six. Normally Rosie, who as a trainee was mainly working on alterations to start with, loved her work, adjusting pretty clothes in beautiful material, coming up with interesting trimmings and using her skill as a seamstress to excellent effect, but tonight she was anxious to leave so that she could hurry home and find out more about the news Nancy had referred to. Their Italian neighbours had been reluctant to talk about

11

the likelihood of Mussolini joining Hitler. All of them still had family back in Italy, and Rosie, knowing how close-knit Italian families were, could only imagine how anxious they must be feeling.

The shock of being at war, and most especially the Dunkirk evacuation, was at the forefront of everyone's mind and had brought a sombreness to people, but it had also brought a resoluteness, Rosie recognised, as she stepped out into the early evening sunshine and headed for home. Rosie's parents rented a small house in Gerard Street. Like the children of their Italian neighbours, Rosie had attended Holy Cross school and worshipped at Holy Cross itself.

It wouldn't take her very long to walk home, and although her stomach growled hungrily as she drew level with her favourite chippy, she refused to give in to the temptation to go in, telling herself as she turned into Springfield Street that she'd come back later after she'd seen Bella and get herself a tuppenny dinner. It wasn't likely there'd be dinner on the table, after all. Her mother, Christine, wasn't the domes-ticated sort, and Rosie had learned from a young age that when her father was at sea she had to look after herself. Rosie expected that right now Christine would be round at the Grenellis', smoking and laughing with the men, whilst Maria bustled around her kitchen making dinner for everyone. Sometimes Rosie found it hard to understand what her un-domesticated, often hard to please mother had in common with gentle, homely Maria, and why Maria put up with a friend who was as difficult and selfish as Rosie knew her mother to be. As a little girl she had often wished secretly that Maria was her mother, loving the way she would sweep her up onto her lap and cuddle her, something Christine never did.

Her mother practically lived at the Grenellis' when Rosie's father was away at sea. Rosie imagined that Christine, who had left her large family of brothers, sisters and cousins behind when she had left Preston to come and live in Liverpool as a young wife, missed them so much that she naturally preferred the hustle and bustle of her neighbours' house to the solitude of her own home. Rosie knew how her father had fallen in love with her mother at first sight when he had been visiting a fellow sailor who lived in that town, and how he had refused to take no for an answer and had finally persuaded her mother to marry him. She had often complained to Rosie, though, about how lonely she had felt when she had first arrived in Liverpool, knowing no one there but her new husband, who had promptly returned to sea, leaving her on her own. It had been the Grenellis – especially sweet-natured, gentle Maria – who had taken pity on her and taken her under their wing, inviting her into their home and offering her their friendship.

Rosie suspected that it was because of that friendship, and her reluctance to be parted from such long-standing and kind friends, that her mother had refused all her father's attempts to persuade her to move out of the Gerard Street area, with its small shabby houses, and up to a bigger and smarter house on Chestnut Close between Edge Hill and Wavertree where his widowed sister already lived. Her father was a hard worker and, unlike many other seamen, neither drank nor gambled away his wages, so they had the money to go, but her mother wouldn't even entertain the idea of moving.

Rosie had grown up hearing her parents arguing about it, and then pulling the bed covers over her ears to block out the sound. She often felt guilty for loving her father so much more than she did her mother. But her mother treated her sometimes as though she resented her rather than loved her. It wasn't that she was ever actively unkind to her, Rosie admitted; her mother simply wasn't like that. But neither was she the kind of mother who openly showed tenderness and love for her child, and Rosie had learned very young not to go to her mother for cuddles. If she did, Christine was more than likely to refuse to pick her up, telling her instead to go away.

Things were better between them now that Rosie was almost grown up, and these days Rosie found herself behaving towards her mother as though *she* were the child, and in need of looking after, as well as taking over most of the domestic responsibilities.

The love she hadn't got from her mother, though, she certainly had received from her adoptive Italian family. Maria had no children of her own but her comfortable knee and warm arms had always been there for Rosie throughout her childhood. And whilst her mother had often spoken critically and sometimes even unkindly to her friend about her plumpness and her homely ways, Rosie loved Maria deeply. She had sensed too, in that way that children can, that Maria loved her. It had been Maria she could remember singing lullabies to her and telling her stories, Maria to whom she had wanted to hurry after school so that she could tell her about her day.

Giovanni and Lucia, Bella's grandparents, had first come to Liverpool as a very young couple, with the encouragement of other family members already living in the city. Both Maria and Sofia had been born in Liverpool, although Giovanni had insisted on them marrying young men from his and Lucia's old village. Maria and Sofia had both been new brides at the same time as Christine, and Rosie's first memories were of being in the Grenellis' busy, aromatic kitchen, playing with Bella whilst the grown-ups worked and gossiped around the kitchen table. Rosie soaked up the Italian language like la Nonna's famous ciabatta soaked up the pungent olive oil that was lovingly sent from Italy four times a year. La Nonna, as the whole family called Lucia, could speak English but she preferred her native tongue and, especially whilst cooking or eating, the rest of the family followed suit. Over the years, sitting on the floor, listening attentively, wide-eyed and enthralled, Rosie learned the history of the Grenelli family from la Nonna.

Rosie had been so entranced by la Nonna's

stories that she had asked her school teacher, Miss Fletcher, to show her where Naples and Rome were in the dusty, slightly worn pages of a school atlas, and had then lovingly traced the whole country of Italy from that map, marking out first the cities la Nonna had named, and then the Picinisco area itself. When she had seen what Rosie was doing, Miss Fletcher had helped her to chart a dotted line all the way from Picinisco across the sea to Liverpool. Then when this had been done, under Miss Fletcher's guidance, Rosie had transferred the tracing onto a clean piece of white paper, carefully marking out the cities of Rome and Naples in different coloured pencils before drawing in Picinisco itself. When she had proudly given her map to la Nonna she had been rewarded with tearful delight and a good many hugs and kisses.

La Nonna had so many stories to tell about the old country and the old ways of life, and about the hardship her people had endured in their journey to Liverpool. Rosie had listened to them with delight, drinking in everything she was told, and imagining for herself how it must have felt to go through such a frightening upheaval. With the acceptance of the young, Rosie had seen no difference between herself and Bella, feeling as at home sitting on the floor listening to la Nonna as though she were her own grandmother, and the stories she was hearing were stories of her own family.

Indeed, from a young age Rosie had been more familiar with the names and family relationships of

Bella's extended family, in Liverpool and in Italy, than she was with her mother's extensive but seldom seen siblings. As an only child, she relished the close network of the Grenellis, the support and love they showed for one another. It would have been a lonely life otherwise, especially when her father was at sea.

Perhaps it would have been different if they had lived nearer to them or if her father had been part of a large family, but he only had his elder sister, Rosie's Aunt Maude and her husband, Henry, whom they had seen so rarely that, after his death when she was twelve, Rosie could barely remember what he looked like.

That her mother and her father's sister did not get on had always been obvious to Rosie, even when she was little. Whenever her mother spoke about 'your Maude' to Rosie's father, she did so in a scathing, slightly high-pitched and angry tone of voice that always made Rosie's tummy hurt, especially when she saw her father looking so sad and sometimes cross.

As she got older Rosie was told by her mother that her Aunt Maude was a snob who had never wanted Christine to marry her brother. And in fact on more than one occasion her mother had told Rosie that part of the reason she had married Rosie's father had been 'to show that snotty bitch what's what'.

The trouble had started, apparently, when Rosie's father had taken his new fiancée to Liverpool to introduce her to his sister.

'Acted like I was a piece of muck wot had got stuck to her shoe, she did, trying to show off wi' her la-di-da way. If you ask me she never wanted yer dad to marry anyone. Mothered him she had, you see, Rosie, him being the younger and then him going spoilin' her by giving her half his wages and allus bringin' her stuff back when he came ashore. Of course she didn't want him getting married and her gettin' her nose shoved out of joint. Stands to reason. But your dad's that soft he couldn't see that. He thinks she's perfect and she bloody well isn't. I'll bet that husband of hers were right glad to die and escape from her.'

Her mother had always been fond of making outrageous statements of this nature but Rosie had always dreaded her making them when her father was at home in case it sparked off one of their increasingly bitter rows.

'Then you coming along didn't help,' her mother had informed Rosie bluntly, 'especially when she saw how your dad took to you. She and that husband of hers never had no kiddies of their own and you'd have thought she'd have bin glad to have a little 'un in the family, but not her. Hates you almost as much as she does me.'

Her aunt certainly didn't like her very much, Rosie was forced to admit. Whenever her father took her to visit, her Aunt Maude's manner towards her was always cold and disapproving. There was none of the warmth in her aunt's house that there was in the Grenellis', even if there was

18

more money. Not that the Grenellis were poor. Giovanni had worked hard for his family, and both his sons-in-law worked in his ice-cream business: small, plump Carlo, who was Sofia's husband and Bella's father, with his twinkling eyes and lovely tenor voice, and tall, good-looking Aldo, who spent his spare time like many of the Italian men at St Joseph's Boxing Club, or in the room at the back of Bonvini's shop with his fellow *paesani*, playing cards, and who was married to kind Maria. In the winter the men of the family, all skilled musicians, earned a living entertaining cinema queues and playing at Italian weddings and christenings.

The first thing Rosie noticed as she turned the corner into Springfield Street was the strange silence. The street was empty of the children who would normally have been playing under the watchful eye of their grandmothers. The caged singing birds, trained by some of the Italian families who had brought them from their homeland, were absent from open doorways and the doors themselves were firmly closed where normally they were always left open for friends and family. There were no voluble discussions on the merits of rival products from the women, no occasional mutters of deeper male voices belonging to the card players in the smoke-filled, wine-scented room at the back of the shop. And, most extraordinary of all, the shops themselves were closed – even Jimmy Romeo's, as the grocery shop owned by the Imundi family was fondly known. Rosie stared at it in bewilderment. Jimmy Romeo's *never* closed. On halfdays when other shops locked their doors and hung their signs in the window, and proud fathers walked with their sons to meet up with friends, Jimmy Romeo's remained open for the men to play their favourite card games of *scopa* and *briscola* in the back room, and exchange banter. The street seemed almost alien without the familiar sharp smells of cheese, sausage, olives, coffee and garlic wafting through the open doorways. Something, not fear exactly, but something cold and worrying trickled down Rosie's spine like the ice cream Dino Cavelli had deliberately dropped down the back of the taffeta dress Maria had smocked so carefully and lovingly for her to wear for her eleventh birthday party. Dino's parents were close friends of Bella's, *comparaggio* in fact, the name Italians gave to those very close friends they had honoured by inviting them into their family. As was the tradition, Dino's parents had been *compare* and *comare* at Bella's parents' wedding, and were also Bella's godparents, just as Bella's parents were Dino's. Rosie often envied Bella the security of the traditional Italian network of friends and family that surrounded her, although Bella complained that she found it restrictive and would love the freedom to go out with girlfriends that Rosie enjoyed.

Dino was a tall handsome young man now, and Rosie didn't mind admitting that she rather enjoyed his flirtatious teasing whenever they happened to meet. Like her own father, he was in the merchant navy, and it always gave her a small *frisson* of excitement to see him walking down the street towards her when he was back on leave. So far she had resisted his invitations to go to the pictures with him, knowing all too well that he would not have dared to put such an invitation to an Italian girl. It was well known that young Italian men might enjoy a bit of dalliance with English girls but when it came to marriage they were too worried about their mamma's feelings to do anything other than marry the girl of her choice – and she would always be a good Italian girl.

Not that she wanted to marry Dino – or indeed anyone right now. It was impossible for her to think of falling in love and being happy when the country was at war and so many dreadful things were happening. Her father was the kind of man who believed in protecting his family from the realities of what it meant to sail across the Atlantic, knowing that Hitler's U-boats were waiting to hunt down and sink the merchant vessels that were bringing the much-needed supplies of food, oil and other necessities back to Liverpool. He might not say to them that each time he sailed he knew that every day he was at sea could be his last, but Rosie knew the truth. In February his ship had been late getting back into Liverpool, because one of the other vessels sailing with it had been torpedoed and sunk with the loss of most of its crew. Rosie had inadvertently overheard her father talking about it with some of the other sailing men from the area.

No, her father might not talk much to her about

the dangers he and the other merchant seamen faced, but that did not mean that Rosie was not aware of them. She had felt indignant on her father's behalf when she had learned that if a merchant ship was lost then the seamen were paid only for the number of days they had been on board it. If a ship was torpedoed and the men had to abandon it, they were paid nothing at all for the days, sometimes even weeks, it might take them to get back to port and find another berth.

Rosie had heard her Aunt Maude berating her father for not getting a shore job where he would be safe and better paid, but as easy-going as her father was, when it came to his work he could not be shifted. He had salt water in his blood, he was fond of saying, and the life of a landlubber was not for him.

Rosie crossed Christian Street into Gerard Street, a small smile curling her mouth as she thought of her father. The smile instantly disappeared the moment she heard angry raised voices, followed by the sound of breaking glass. Half a dozen or more men had suddenly appeared at the far end of the street, some wielding heavy pieces of wood, and yelling out insults and threats as they smashed in the window of an ice-cream shop. As Rosie watched, paralysed with fear, more men joined those attacking the shop, and then several started to march up the street, one of them stopping to throw a brick through a house window, whilst others banged on doors and called out insults. Above the yells of the attacking mob and the sound of glass being trodden underfoot, Rosie could hear a woman screaming and a baby crying. Rose Street police station was only five minutes away. If she ran she could be there in less, Rosie decided, her heart bumping against her chest as she hurried off.

Fortunately she didn't need to go all the way to the police station, because she met several policemen coming towards her. One of them was their local bobby, Tom Byers, whose son had been at school with Rosie and Bella.

'There's a gang battering down Gonnelli's ice-cream shop,' Rosie told him breathlessly. 'I could hear a baby crying . . .'

'You get yourself off home, and make sure you stay there, young Rosie,' Tom told her grimly, straightening the chinstrap of his helmet, his usually friendly face looking very stern. 'It isn't safe for you to be out with these young hotheads on the loose, creating trouble for decent honest folk.'

'What's happening to . . . ?' Rosie began, but the noise from the mob was growing in volume and the policemen had already started to hurry towards it.

But instead of going home, Rosie scurried down to the Grenellis', going round to the back door as she always did and calling out as she knocked on it.

'It's me – Rosie.' She couldn't bring herself just to walk in unannounced. even after all these years and countless admonishings from the Grenellis to do so.

The door was opened immediately, and Rosie was almost pulled inside by Bella's grandfather.

'Did you see what's happening, Rosie?' Bella asked her anxiously from the back of the kitchen. 'We heard shouts and breaking glass.'

'It'll be them crazy mad *Inglesi* who was down here earlier full of drink, yelling that we're all Fascists,' Sofia, Bella's mother, always sharper-tongued than her gentler sister, Maria, answered tersely.

'Well, you can't blame 'em for what they're thinking, not with bloody Mussolini doing what he's done,' Rosie's mother announced, putting out her cigarette and almost immediately lighting another one as she leaned against the wall, constantly stealing quick furtive glances towards the door.

Despite the fact that it was June, the room seemed unfamiliarly shadowed in some way, and shrouded in an atmosphere that was a mixture of confused helpless anger and growing apprehension.

Rosie's father was always saying what a beautiful girl her mother had been, and she was still good-looking now, Rosie admitted, although privately she couldn't help wishing that her mother wouldn't dye her brown hair such a brash blonde, nor wear such a bright red lipstick. She had seen the way other people looked at Christine and it made her feel both angry and protective. Her mother made no secret of the fact that she liked a good time: she loved dancing, and Rosie had often heard her asking Maria if she minded if she borrowed her Aldo so that she could go down to the Grafton for a dance.

No one was thinking about dancing now though, as the sounds from outside grew louder and ever closer.

'We'll be all right,' Carlo tried to reassure them. 'It will be those with shops they'll be going for.'

'How could anyone do something like this?' Rosie protested.

'They're doing it because we're Italian,' Sofia told her. 'If I was you, Christine, I'd take meself home. It'd be much safer for you and your Rosie there, that's for sure. After all, you aren't Italian, are you?'

Inexplicably there was a mounting tension between her mother and Sofia that Rosie didn't understand and for the first time she felt uncomfortably like an outsider to their close-knit family group.

'I saw Tom Byers on the way here and he said it was just a few hotheads, and that they'd soon have it sorted out,' she offered, in an attempt to give some reassurance and dissolve the tension, but as she spoke the noise from outside became so loud that she couldn't even hear Bella's response.

Giovanni and Carlo exchanged anxious looks and, as always in times of great emotion, Giovanni reverted to Italian, gesticulating wildly as he spoke.

'I don't understand what's going on,' Rosie repeated, trying not to wince as she heard the threatening sound of shouted abuse mingling with that of breaking glass. It was so loud now, as though a full-blown riot were taking place: angry voices, the sound of blows, breaking glass and police whistles.

'It's because Mussolini is joining Hitler, Rosie,' Bella explained to her, raising her voice so that she could be heard above the din.

'I know about Mussolini but why should that mean—'

'Some people look for any excuse to make trouble,' Sofia told Rosie. 'They think that because we are Italian we are now their enemy. They forget that our children play with their children, that we have sons who are wearing the same uniforms as theirs. It's all right, Mamma.' She tried to comfort Lucia, who was looking anxiously at the door and crossing herself, whilst saying that she wished she had never left Italy.

'You'd better go next door, Carlo, and make sure that Giovanna is all right,' Sofia instructed her husband. 'She'll be on her own with the babies because Arno's gone over to Manchester to see his brother. Tell her she's welcome to come here if she wants. And if you see any police about, ask them what they're doing, letting this happen.'

Despite the gravity of the situation, Rosie couldn't help smiling slightly as she listened to Sofia bossing her husband around.

Carlo had almost reached the back door when the sound of someone banging loudly on it made them all gasp.

They each let out a breath when they heard Aldo's voice calling out, 'Maria, it's me, Aldo. Let me in.'

Maria opened the door, but it was Christine who was first at Aldo's side, leaning weakly against his broad shoulder and saying weepily how afraid she was. Almost comically opposite in looks to his brother-in-law, Aldo was tall, and broad-shouldered, lithe, with a dark, smouldering gaze and a dismissive way of treating Maria that made Rosie feel for her.

'Aldo, Carlo's just going round to bring Giovanna back here. You'd better go with him, in case she needs some help with the *bambini*,' Sofia instructed her brother-in-law.

Although no one ever said anything – like all Italian families, they were intensely loyal to one another – Rosie suspected that Sofia was not over-fond of her sister's husband.

'There's no point,' he answered her dismissively, causing Maria to pale and Sofia to suck in her breath.

'It's too late? They've been hurt?' Maria exclaimed in distress. 'Oh, Aldo . . .'

'Did I say that?' he answered irritably. 'They're fine. Giovanna's brother was at the club. He walked up the street with me.' The women exhaled a collective sigh of relief. Rosie, as ever, automatically fell into the familiar pattern of echoing the huge sigh and expressive gestures of the others.

'Here, Mamma, drink this,' Maria was instructing la Nonna whilst she hurried to get a small glass and pour her some of the special restorative 'cordial' that came all the way from 'home' and which was normally only served on very special occasions or when someone was in need of a tonic. 'Rosie *cara*, help Bella to make us all some coffee, will you?' Maria called back over her shoulder.

Rosie needed no second instruction. It felt so comforting to go through the routine she and Bella had learned together as little girls. Rosie could still remember how proud she had been when she had been allowed to serve la Nonna and Grandfather Grenelli the first cups of the coffee she had made all by herself.

These days there was no need for her to concentrate or worry as she ground the beans, releasing their wonderful rich dark aroma into the kitchen, and then waited for the kettle to boil. The Grenellis preferred to use an old-fashioned range rather than a modern stove, and Rosie admitted that there was something comforting about the warmth it gave out.

The giving of a medicinal cordial followed by the family gathering round the cordial drinker to offer comments on his or her condition, whilst they drank coffee was a part of Rosie's growing up and she took comfort from it now.

When her father was at home Rosie always drank tea because she knew it was what he preferred, but secretly she preferred coffee. Here in the Grenelli household she was more Italian than English, whilst at home she was very much her father's daughter. She had, she knew, inherited his calm temperament, and his abhorrence of any kind of flashy showiness. They shared the same sense of humour, laughing over silly jokes on the wireless on programmes such as *ITMA*, which had her mother complaining that they were both daft. The delicacy of Rosie's bone structure came, her father had always claimed, from his side of the family, along with her warm smile. Rosie cherished the closeness between them, and even though she envied Bella the closeness of her loving family, Rosie wouldn't have changed her dad for anyone.

As Maria handed her husband the coffee Rosie had just poured, he told them, 'And Giovanna's brother is taking them back home with him. I saw the police helping them out the back way.' As always, Aldo barely acknowledged Maria, taking the coffee from her without bothering to thank her and then turning back to Rosie's mother, who was still clinging fiercely to his arm, to say, 'Don't worry, Chrissie, there's nothing to be afraid of now. The police have moved the rioters on.'

La Nonna muttered something to Sofia that Rosie couldn't catch, but which caused Maria to shake her head gently.

'Trust you not to be here when Maria needed you, Aldo,' Sofia told her brother-in-law scornfully.

'I couldn't get back. We had to stay where we were for our own safety, until the police had rounded up the troublemakers. It weren't just winders they were battering, you know,' Aldo answered her defensively. 'When I came up the street there was a man lying in the gutter who the mob had left for dead. Police were waiting on an ambulance to tek him to the hospital.'

'And with you, of course, your own safety always comes before that of anyone else, especially poor Maria,' Sofia snapped.

'Sofia, please,' Maria protested. 'It is not fair to blame Aldo. He is not responsible for those who are rioting.'

'Isn't it time you went home, Christine?' Sofia said to Rosie's mother sharply. 'You aren't Italian, after all,' she repeated, 'and you'll be safer behind your own front door.'

Again a charged look passed between her mother and Sofia, which Rosie couldn't interpret.

Christine gave a small shrug. 'Walk us 'ome, will you, Aldo?' she demanded. 'I don't fancy walking back on me own, not with all them fellas running riot.'

A strange, almost prickly silence filled the small room, broken only when Maria bowed her head and said softly, 'Yes, Aldo, you must go with Christine and Rosie, and make sure they get home safely. May the Blessed Virgin keep you safe, Rosie,' she added, her words muffled against Rosie's hair as she hugged her tightly and kissed her.

Tears burned the backs of Rosie's eyes as she returned the hug and then followed her mother and Aldo, who was already opening the back door.

The street was now quiet, its silence making the devastation that lay before them all the more shocking. The road was scattered with broken glass and doors that had been ripped off their hinges. Rosie's stomach lurched when she saw the bright red streaks of blood on the glass. She hoped fiercely they belonged to the men who had done the attacking and not to those who had been attacked.

'Jesus, it looks as though bloody Hitler's bin bombing the place,' Rosie heard her mother whisper to Aldo, as she clung tightly to his arm. Rosie, though, hung back, reluctant to take hold of his other arm. For some reason she was unable to understand, Rosie had never felt entirely comfortable in Aldo's company. In fact, when she witnessed the way he treated poor Maria, she couldn't understand how her mother could make such a fuss of him and, even worse, openly flirt with him in front of Maria herself. But she knew better than to take her mother to task for her behaviour. Christine made her own rules and didn't take kindly to being criticised, plus she had a keen temper on her when she was angered. Rosie had heard the arguments between her parents when her father had attempted to reason with her. On more than one occasion Rosie had witnessed Christine throwing whatever came to hand at her husband, including the crockery, before storming out, slamming the back door behind her and leaving Rosie and her father to pick up the broken shards.

They had almost reached their own front door, which was several doors down from the Grenellis'. Their house, unlike those of the street's Italian families, looked uncared for, the step dusty and undonkey-stoned, and the paintwork dull instead of the bright blues, reds and yellows favoured by the Italians, which, like the window boxes of summer bedding plants in their equally rich colours they loved so much, were reminders of the warm, vibrant Mediterranean they had left behind. Stepping into the streets of Little Italy was like turning a corner into a brilliantly vivid special place where all the colours seemed brighter, the song birds sang more sweetly, the laughter echoed more happily, and even the air itself, scented with the rich smells of Italy, seemed warmer. But, best of all, the whole area, or so it seemed to Rosie, was imbued with a special atmosphere of love.

Set against this backdrop, her own home seemed unwelcomingly drab. No carefully tended window boxes of flowers adorned her mother's windowsills, the sound of singing and laughter never wafted out onto the air from open windows, no appetising smells of delicious pasta and soups wafted from her mother's kitchen, unless Rosie herself was making them, which wasn't very often because her father didn't like 'all that foreign muck', so when she cooked for him Rosie stuck to the traditional English dishes.

Christine modelled herself on her favourite screen actresses, like Rita Hayworth, who were known for their glamour rather than their domestic virtues, rather than on a respected Italian mamma like la Nonna.

'Rosie, run over to Currie Street and fetch us a fish supper from Pod's, will yer?' Rosie heard her mother demanding. She was still leaning on Aldo's arm and had handed him her door key, intimating that she felt too weak to unlock the door herself. But not so weak that she didn't want her supper, Rosie reflected wryly as she hurried off towards Podestra's, hoping that the chip shop had escaped the vengeance of the rioters.

Podestra's fish-and-chip shop was normally only a few minutes' walk away, but tonight, with the glass and other debris littering the streets, it took Rosie over twice as long as usual to pick her way through it in the ominous silence that hung as heavily on the air as the dust from the destruction.

Sickeningly, through one of the windows that had been broken in she could see where furniture had been smashed to pieces, the horsehair spilling out of a sofa through the deep knife cuts slashed into it, whilst a child's hobbyhorse lay broken on the floor beside it. Despite the warmth of the evening, Rosie shivered, wondering what had happened to the family whose home it was, and praying that they were unhurt.

Although Rosie's mother was a Catholic, her father was staunchly Church of England, which was yet another bone of contention between her parents. Rosie had been christened as a Catholic at her mother's insistence, but Christine was not a devout churchgoer, and sometimes Rosie suspected that her mother had only insisted on Rosie becoming Catholic to annoy Rosie's father. It had been pious Maria who had encouraged Rosie to go to church with Bella, and who had provided the necessary white dress for Rosie's confirmation. Rosie was obedient to the dictates of her religion and attended church every week, as well as making her confession. Her faith was a simple but strong belief in God, although war and the horrible things it was bringing sometimes tested that faith. However, because her father was of a different religion, Rosie stood slightly outside the traditional observances in the Italian community, where many of the older women went to church every day – sometimes more than once. Rosie did say her prayers every night, though, always asking God to protect those who were in peril, especially her father.

She had almost reached the chippie when three young Italians, still just boys, walked past her going in the opposite direction. Two of them were supporting the third between them, as he struggled to walk. One of the two had obviously received a head wound, and dried blood was visible on the bandage tied around it.

Rosie shivered. What was happening to people? To the city she loved? Those boys had grown up here in Liverpool. Suddenly she longed desperately for her father, with his slow reasoned way of speaking and his gentle strength. He might not be a handsome man like Aldo, nor possess the musical talent and hospitable warmth of Carlo, who drew others towards him so easily, but her father had his own special strength and Rosie loved him with a fiercely protective intensity. She hated it when her mother snapped at him and taunted him because of the limp he had developed as a young boy, when he had fallen downstairs and broken his leg so badly that he was left with it slightly shorter than its fellow, and which made it uncomfortable for him to take her dancing.

'If you're mekin' for Pod's I shouldn't bother, it's closed,' a woman called out to Rosie from the other side of the street, showing her the empty bowl she had obviously intended to have filled with pease pudding.

Thanking her, Rosie regretted her own decision earlier not to stop to get herself something to eat. The larder would almost certainly be bare.

The summer light was beginning to fade from the sky, which was now streaked the colour of blood. Blackout curtains were going up in those windows that hadn't been broken, and outside those that were, small groups of men were gathering to examine the damage and make temporary repairs. At least it was summer and rain was unlikely to hinder their efforts. The look on the victims' faces made Rosie feel shamed of her own nationality. She wanted to go to the Italians and assure them that not everyone felt the same way as those who had rioted against them.

When she got home she found her mother in the parlour, sitting on the sofa with her feet up on a worn leather pouffe, smoking a cigarette, her hair already rolled up in rag curlers, and a scarf tied round them turban style.

'Where's us supper?' Christine demanded irritably. Her lipstick had bled into the lines around her mouth, Rosie noticed absently. And there was a button unfastened on her blouse.

'Pod's was closed.'

'So why the hell didn't you go somewhere else? It's not as though there ain't enough ruddy chippies around here,' Christine complained acidly.

'Yes, and they're all Italian-owned,' Rosie reminded her, ashamed that her mother was only thinking of her stomach at a time like this.

'Aye, well, they've only got themselves to blame,' Christine told her. 'That Sofia thinks she's bin so bloody clever getting her Carlo in with that Fascist lot and her Bella enrolled at one of them language schools what they run, but you mark my words, she'll be regretting it now.'

There had been a lot of talk in the area whilst Rosie was growing up about Mussolini and his effect on Italian politics. Being a passionate race, Liverpool's Italian community talked as intensely and fiercely about 'Fascismo' as they did about everything else. Rosie knew from sitting in the Grenellis' kitchen whilst these often heated discussions were going on that to the older generation of immigrants, Mussolini's desire to treat them as though they were still 'Italians', albeit living away from their homeland, meant so much to them emotionally. They saw what Mussolini was doing as a means of uniting them, of giving them respect and status, and of preserving their Italian heritage. They couldn't see, as their younger British-born children could, the dangers of Fascism.

Hadn't Mussolini shown respect for their patriotism? the older men argued. Hadn't he encouraged 'his' people living outside Italy to set up social clubs where the men could meet to talk about their homeland and to share their sense of what it meant to be Italian? Hadn't their mother country sent delegations to talk to them and, thanks to them, hadn't an Italian school been opened in Liverpool so that their children could learn their true mother tongue? If some of their non-Italian neighbours in their adopted country chose to resent what Mussolini was doing for his people, then that was their problem. For themselves, they were now doubly proud to be Italian and to know that their mother country valued them and recognised them as such.

Stubbornly these often elderly men believed that Fascism was more about an upsurge of patriotism and a love for their homeland, than about politics, which they did not really understand or want to accept.

Many of the younger men, on the other hand, especially those who worked alongside non-Italians, were concerned that in clinging so determinedly to the mother country their fathers and uncles and grandfathers were ignoring the realities of just how antagonistic towards Mussolini the English people and the British Government were, and this led to heated arguments within families when they gathered together. Rosie had seen the way Maria shook her head when they took place in her own kitchen. Sofia was fiercely proud of her Italian heritage, and determined to encourage her husband and her daughter to be equally patriotic, so easy-going Carlo was bullied into joining their local Fasci club, and Bella was sent to the Italian school in the evening for Italian lessons, even though she complained that she already spoke Italian perfectly well.

Rosie had felt slightly left out at first and a little bit hurt when Bella came back talking about the new friends she had made, but Rosie was a gentle-natured girl and she couldn't resent her best friend's obvious enjoyment of the fun the classes provided for too long.

It had been in 1935, after Italy invaded Abyssinia, that people had begun to realise the possible implications of Fascism. About that time Rosie could remember hearing a great deal of talk of some members of the Italian community deciding to naturalise and become British citizens. The Grenelli men hadn't though, mainly because Sofia had been so insistent that to do so would be unpatriotic.

'Sofia and Carlo aren't Fascists, they're just patriotic,' Rosie protested.

'Huh, that's what Sofia might say, but there's folk around here as thinks different.'

Rosie frowned. 'I thought that the Grenellis were our friends, but you're acting as though you don't even like them. Maria's always—'

'Oh, Maria's well enough,' Christine stopped her. 'But ruddy Sofia, she's allus had it in for me. I've warned Aldo many a time not to let Sofia go dragging him into that Fascist lot with her Carlo. Well, I just hope that Aldo's listened to what I've bin saying to him and not got hisself involved, now that there's all this trouble brewing and folk taking against Italians. Did you try the chippie on Christian Street?' Christine finished.

It was typical of her mother that it was her hunger she was thinking about and not the fact that she, Rosie, could have been in danger if there had been another outbreak of violence, Rosie accepted ruefully.

'I'm not going back out again tonight,' she told her firmly. Other girls with stricter mothers might have been wary of being as outspoken as she was. She was a gentle girl, not normally argumentative, but she knew with her mother she had to stick to her guns – or risk being bullied into doing whatever it suited Christine to have her do.

'I'll be glad when Dad gets back,' she added.

Since Rosie had overheard her father discussing his ship's near miss, she had prayed extra hard, not just for her father but for all those men who had to make that perilous journey across the Atlantic to be kept safe. War was such a very dreadful thing but, as her father had told her, they had no option other than to stand up to Hitler and to fight as bravely as they could.

'Well, if I'm not goin' to get me supper I might

as well go to bed. Pity we didn't get a bit of sommat at number 16. We would have done an' all if bloody Sofia hadn't started havin' a go at me like that.'

'I don't think she liked the way you were with Aldo,' Rosie told her mother uncomfortably.

Christine dropped her cigarette, cursing as it burned a hole in the thin carpet. 'What do you mean?'

'You should have let Maria be the one to greet him first. She is his wife, after all.'

Christine gave a dismissive shrug. 'We all know that. Old Giovanni had both Aldo and Carlo shipped over from the old country so as he could have husbands for his daughters. Mind you, it were the only way he *could* get them wed. Maria's that saintly she should have been a ruddy nun, and as for Sofia, she's got that sharp a tongue on her, the Grenellis don't need no knife-grinder comin' round.'

'Mum . . .' Rosie objected. It disturbed her to hear her mother running down the two women who were surely her closest friends, but she knew better than to take Christine to task when she was in this kind of mood.

TWO

Rosie plumped up her pillow and tried to get comfortable. There was silence outside in the street now, but the earlier violence had left her feeling on edge and unable to sleep, even though she was bone tired. Right from being a little girl, Rosie had been afraid of the dark. Then she had been able to creep into her parents' bed when her father was at home, seeking reassurance. She couldn't do that now, of course, but no matter how much she tried to rationalise away her fears, the blackout was something she hated.

Further up the street she heard footsteps and then the sound of a knock on a neighbouring door. Silence followed, suddenly broken by a woman's screams of anguish. Quickly Rosie slipped out of bed and hurried over to the window, easing back the blackout curtain.

Several doors down from them she could see four burly policemen marching seventy-odd-year-old Dom Civeti away from his front door whilst his wife pleaded with them not to take him.

Rosie couldn't believe her eyes. Everyone knew and loved Dom Civeti, who was the kindest and most gentle man you could imagine. He trained the singing birds that so many Italian families liked to keep, and he was also famous throughout Liverpool for his accordion playing. Rosie could remember how Dom had always had barley sugar in his pockets for the street children, and how he would patiently teach the young boys to play the accordion.

As her eyes accustomed themselves to the darkness, she saw that there were other men standing at the end of the street under the guard of the unmistakable bulk of Constable Black, a popular policeman from Rose Street police station. Having escorted Dom to where Constable Black was standing, the other policemen turned back down the street, heading, Rosie recognised with a lurch of her stomach, for the Grenellis'.

She let the blackout drop and raced to pull on her dressing gown as she hurried into her parents' bedroom, switching on the light and demanding urgently, 'Mum, wake up.'

When there was no response from the sleeping figure, Rosie gave her mother a little shake.

'What the . . . Turn that ruddy light off, will you Rosie?' Christine objected grumpily, rubbing her eyes and leaving streaks of mascara on her face. Christine claimed that it was a waste to clean her mascara off every night when she was only going to have to put fresh on in the morning, and she often derided Rosie for her insistence on thoroughly removing nightly what little bit of makeup she did wear.

'It's the Grenellis,' Rosie told her mother. 'I've just seen the police going to their door.'

'What?' Christine was properly awake now, pushing Rosie away and sitting up in bed, the strap of her nightgown slipping off her shoulder. Several of the rags she had tied in her hair had come out whilst she had been asleep, leaving tangled untidy strands hanging round her face. The air in the room smelled strongly of cheap scent and, despite her anxiety for their friends, Rosie was guiltily aware of how much she wished that her mother was different and more like other girls' mothers.

'Are you sure it was the Grenellis' they were going to?' Christine demanded.

'Yes . . .' Rosie tensed as they both heard the sound of angry male voices outside in the street.

'Pass us me clothes then, Rosie. We'd better get dressed and get over there to find out what's going on,' Christine asserted. 'No, not that thing,' she refused when Rosie handed her her siren suit, as the unflattering all-in-one outfit everyone was urged to keep to hand to wear in case of an air raid in the night, was called. 'Over my dead body will I go out in that. You'd better go and get summat on yourself,' she added, when Rosie had handed her the discarded skirt and twinset Christine had been wearing before going to bed and which she had simply left lying on the floor.

Five minutes later they were both dressed and on their way to the Grenellis'.

There was no question in Rosie's mind about any risk to their own safety. The Grenellis were their friends and if they were in trouble then Rosie and Christine should be there to help them if they could, or share it with them if they couldn't.

'What the bleedin' hell . . . ?' Rosie heard her mother suddenly exclaim sharply, both of them coming to an abrupt halt as they saw Constable Black shepherding Giovanni, Carlo and Aldo out through the Grenellis' front door.

Rosie's stomach tightened with shocked disbelief when she saw Giovanni, the once proud head of his household, looking so shrunken and old and, even worse, so very frighteningly vulnerable. As she and her mother hurried up to them Rosie could see the tears on his lined cheeks.

'What's going on?' Christine demanded as she ran forward and grabbed hold of the policeman's uniformed arm.

'You can't do this,' Sofia was protesting angrily as she came out of the house. 'You have no right to come into our house, saying that you're looking for Fascist papers and taking away good innocent men.'

'I'm sorry, Sofia,' Constable Black apologised gruffly, 'but orders is orders and we've bin given ours. There's no need for you to go carryin' on like this. Like as not your dad and the others will be sent home in the morning, once everything's bin sorted out.'

Christine was now deep in conversation with Aldo. La Nonna was standing just inside the open door, still dressed in her nightgown, her long white hair in a plait. Bella was at her grandmother's side, her own thick black hair curling softly onto her shoulders. Where Rosie was fine-boned and slender, with delicate features, Bella was slightly plump, with warm olive skin and large dark brown eyes, that could flash with temper or dance with laughter, depending on her mood. Immediately Rosie rushed over to her friend.

'La Nonna cannot understand what is happening,' Bella whispered tearfully to Rosie, as Rosie reached for la Nonna's thin veined hand to give it a comforting squeeze. It felt so cold, trembling in the comforting grasp of her own.

'They are taking my Giovanni away, Rosie,' she wept, 'but he has done nothing wrong.'

'Hush now, Mamma. It will be all right. You will see.'

Rosie turned with relief to see Maria, neatly dressed as always in her plain black clothes, her hair, like her mother's, confined in a neat long plait, and looking as calm as though it was nothing unusual to be woken in the night and forced to watch the family's menfolk being marched away by the police.

'You're a fool if you think that, Maria,' Sofia cried out bitterly. 'Mamma and Papà should have left this country and gone home to Italia where we would all have been safe. I have told them that so many times.'

'England is our home now, Sofia,' Maria reproved her sister gently, whilst Rosie and Bella stood protectively either side of la Nonna, trying their best to comfort her.

'How can you say that? Look at the way we are treated! See the way our men are dragged from their beds, and our homes are invaded. Is that the way to treat people?'

'Constable Black has explained to us that he is simply carrying out his orders. It is for Papà and the other men's safety that they are being taken to the police station. Especially whilst there is so much rioting going on in the city . . .'

'That's nonsense,' Sofia stopped Maria scornfully. 'Look at Mamma . . . see how distressed she is. This will be the death of her, you do know that, don't you?' Sofia turned to challenge the policeman bitterly. 'Is that what you want? To have the blood of an innocent Italian grandmother on your hands?'

'Sofia, please, you are upsetting Mamma and Papà,' Maria reproved her sister quietly.

'Oh, Maria, why are you such a saint that you cannot see what is beneath your own nose?' Sofia rounded on her angrily.

'What's happening, Constable Black?' Rosie questioned the policeman shakily, as Maria struggled to calm her volatile sister.

'Like I said, it's orders, Rosie,' he answered her

46

reluctantly. 'But there's nothing to worry about, you'll see.'

'It isn't just our family – all our men are being rounded up like animals,' Bella told Rosie fiercely. 'They are to be taken into custody on the government's orders in case they are Fascists. That is what we have heard from the other families.'

'Oh, Bella. How can such a dreadful thing be happening?' Rosie hugged her friend, and they clung together, both in tears.

'Constable Black, I implore you,' Maria protested. 'You know my father. You know he is a good man. My cousin's boys are in the British Army. My father is not a Fascist – none of us are. Please do not take him away. My parents are old and frail. They have never been apart before,' she whispered urgently.

'I'm sorry, Maria, but orders are orders . . .'

'But where are you taking them? How long will they be gone? At least give us time to pack some things for them – clean clothes, food . . .'

'There's no need for that. Like as not you'll have your pa back in the morning. And now if you'll tek my advice you'll all get yourselves back to bed.'

Rosie felt sick with shock and disbelief. She was shivering as though it was the middle of winter, not a warm summer night. She thought of Giovanni and la Nonna as her own grandparents, because that was what they had been to her. She had never known her father's parents, who had died before she was born, and her mother had fallen out with her own family, so she had told Rosie, because she had married outside her religion. How could this be happening – men being taken from their homes in the middle of the night without any warning and marched away as though they were criminals? Carlo looked worried but determined to remain calm, whilst Aldo was protesting noisily. But Giovanni wasn't saying anything. Instead he was simply standing there, an elderly man robbed of his pride and dignity. Rosie's heart ached with love for him. As she had done earlier in the evening but for different reasons, she wished desperately that her father were here.

'Where are you taking them?' she asked Constable Black, who had not answered Maria's question.

'I can't tell you that, Rosie,' he said gravely, 'but I promise you there's nothing to worry about.'

Constable Black was a great favourite in the area, and Rosie's anxiety eased slightly. He was a kind and trustworthy man and if he said there was no reason for concern then surely that was true.

Bella had come to stand beside her so that Rosie was between Maria and her friend. Rosie reached for Bella's hand and squeezed it as tightly as Maria was squeezing hers.

'It's going to be all right,' she told Bella. 'Constable Black says so.'

Bella's mother was still protesting loudly, whilst Rosie saw that her own mother was crying as the men were marched off to join the others. Maria released Rosie's hand to guide la Nonna gently inside and then came back for Sofia. Automatically Rosie went inside with Bella.

La Nonna was seated in her chair, rocking herself to and fro, making a soft keening sound, her apron flung up over her face. As always the kitchen smelled of good food and warmth. From further down the street they could hear the sound of another family being woken up and fresh shocked protests of disbelief and grief.

Rosie could see in Bella's eyes the same dull glazed look of shocked disbelief she knew must be in her own. She went over to her friend and reached for her hand. Wordlessly the two girls clung together. Yesterday they had been giggling about the soulful looks they had received from Dino and one of his cousins as they passed them in the street, and talking excitedly about the new dresses they hoped to buy. Tonight they were wondering if life would ever be the same again.

'You'd better get off home, Rosie,' Sofia told her. 'Your ma's already gone. But then, of course, there's nothing for her to stay here for now.'

Rosie saw the small gentle shake of her head that Maria gave in her sister's direction whilst Sofia's mouth tightened as hard as though she were eating a sour grape. Sometimes Bella's mother could be very sharp, and over the years Rosie had learned not to be hurt by that sharpness.

'You'll tell me as soon as you hear anything, won't you?' Rosie begged Maria.

'Constable Black will have it right, Rosie. Our

men will be back home here in next to no time once the authorities realise that they're good men,' Maria announced firmly.

'Oh, Bella . . .' Rosie hugged her friend tearfully.

'It isn't your fault, Rosie,' Bella told her emotionally, 'even though you are English and it's the British Government that's doing this, and I shall hate them for ever for it.'

'Oh, Bella!' Rosie hugged her even more tightly, not knowing what to say.

They were so close to the longest day that the sky was already beginning to lighten as Rosie walked home. It was three o'clock in the morning and she had to be at work at eight, but she knew already that it would be impossible for her to sleep. The street was empty now and silent. Where had the police taken the men? Rose Street station, the nearest police station, was surely too small. The authorities couldn't intend to keep them for very long, Rosie tried to comfort herself as she let herself into her home, not if they hadn't let them take any clean clothes.

Her mother was seated at the kitchen table, smoking. There were even darker black tracks down her face now where her mascara had run. Her hand trembled as she put out her cigarette. As well as selling ice cream, the Grenellis also sold cigarettes and sweets from their handcart. Rosie suspected that sometimes these cigarettes came from the black market and her heart thudded in sudden anxiety. If that came out, would that mean trouble for the Grenelli men? Not that they were alone in supplying their customers with black-market cigarettes. Indeed, buying goods that 'had fallen off the back of a lorry' coming out of the docks had become part of the city's culture, and often the only way in which poor families could feed and clothe their children.

Christine worked in a hairdressing salon, but right now she did not look like a good advertisement for the business, Rosie reflected sympathetically as she took in her mother's haggard expression. Her hair was now untidier, and without the red lipstick she always wore, her face looked pinched and pale. It touched Rosie's heart to see her mother, who often seemed so hard and unemotional, so distressed on behalf of her friends. Lovingly she reached out for her hand and squeezed it.

'Maria was wonderful the way she took charge, wasn't she? You'd have thought that Sofia would be the one to do that but—'

Almost immediately, her mother dragged her hand free, and snapped, 'Stop going on about it, will you, Rosie? I told Aldo there was goin' to be trouble, but of course he wouldn't listen. Ruddy fool . . . Now look at the mess he's got hisself into. I'm goin' up to me bed. Oh, and when you go to work you can call in at Sarah's and tell her that I won't be in on account of me nerves being bad.' She reached down and scratched her leg and then stood up, lighting up a fresh cigarette as she did so. 'A ruddy slave, that's what she thinks I am, paying me next to nowt and expectin' me to work over when it suits her.'

Rosie sighed. As usual, Christine managed to turn the situation to herself, complaining about the hardships she constantly suffered. Life might hold dramatic changes, as she had witnessed that very evening, but some things would always stay the same.

As she had predicted Rosie hadn't really slept, but at least she now had plenty of time to nip across to the Grenellis' before she needed to leave for work, just in case they had heard anything. Her mother was still in bed, and Rosie made as little noise as she could when she brewed herself a cup of tea, and put up some sandwiches for her dinner.

She was halfway across the road when she saw Bella coming towards her.

'Has there bin any news?' she asked anxiously.

Bella shook her head. 'La Nonna is taking it that badly, Rosie. Cryin' all night, she's bin. Me mam as well, rantin' and ravin' she were, sayin' as how we should all have left and gone back to Italy, and how it's me Uncle Aldo's fault that we didn't. It would be different if all of them had teken out British nationality, but it's too late for that now.' She gave a small shiver. 'Me Auntie Maria were up all night trying to calm them both down.'

'Oh, Bella.'

The two girls looked at one another.

'Mebbe they'll know a bit more at Podestra's. I've told me Auntie Maria that I'll send word if I hear anything and that she's to do the same for me. That's if there's any of our men left to tell us anything,' she added bitterly.

Bella worked in the back of one of the Podestra family's chippies, peeling and chipping potatoes, and it was expected between the two families that eventually Bella would marry the young Podestra cousin who was lodging with the family. Rosie had once asked Bella if she minded her future being decided for her but Bella had simply shrugged and said that it was the custom and their way, that she liked Alberto Podestra well enough and that she would rather marry him than some lads she knew.

'But don't you want to fall in love, Bella?' Rosie had asked her.

Once again Bella had shrugged. 'Marriage isn't about falling in love for us, it's about family,' she had told her.

Rosie had mixed feelings about love and marriage. Her father had fallen passionately in love with her mother but their marriage had not been a happy one, so far as Rosie could see. Sofia, however, married to placid easy-going Carlo, seemed perfectly happy with the man her parents had chosen for her. But there was Maria, who had also had her husband chosen for her and who anyone could see was not treated kindly by Aldo. From what she had seen around her in the marriages of those closest to her, Rosie wasn't sure if falling in love was a good thing. On the other hand, all the girls at work could talk about was falling in love like they saw people doing in films, and living happily ever after. And what she did know was that she certainly did not want her husband chosen for her. In that, if nothing else, close as she and Bella were, they felt very differently, Rosie admitted.

After she had said goodbye to Bella, imploring her not to worry with a strength and cheeriness she really didn't feel inside, Rosie called round at the hairdressing salon where her mother worked to deliver her message, and then headed up into the city, trying not to look too closely at the broken glass and damaged buildings as she did so. People were already outside cleaning up the debris.

Newspaper sellers were out on the street, and Rosie hurried to buy a paper, scanning the headlines quickly, her eyes blurring with tears as she read about the violent rioting of the previous night, which had been caused, according to the papers, by patriotic feelings overwhelming some people on hearing the news of Mussolini's decision. The paper did of course condemn the violence, but although Rosie searched the print several times, she couldn't find anything to tell her what was going to happen to the men who had been taken away, other than that Mr Churchill had acted swiftly to ensure that dangerous Fascists were 'combed out' from Italian communities, and would be interned as Enemy Aliens for the duration of the war. Her heart jumped anxiously inside her chest when she read the words 'Enemy Aliens', but of course they did not apply to men like the Grenellis. And there was some comfort in knowing that it was only those men who were a danger to the country that the government wanted to detain, not men like Giovanni, Carlo and Aldo. She tried to cheer herself up by thinking that by the time she finished work tonight they would be safely back at home, and that Bella's mother would be back to her normal self. No doubt too la Nonna would be spoiling them and cooking up a celebration supper for them. Her own mouth watered at the thought of it. She hadn't eaten since yesterday dinner time, apart from a piece of dry toast without butter before she left the house this morning.

It had been left to Rosie to deal with the complexities of shopping on the ration, Christine having no intention of standing in line for hours for scarce cuts of meat, and learning to experiment with the recipes the Ministry of Food was recommending.

Stopping to talk to Bella meant that Rosie was the last to arrive at the shop, despite her early start. Several of the girls were clustered around Nancy, who was standing in the workroom, with her back towards the door.

'Go on, you're 'aving us on,' Rosie heard Dot, the cleaner, protesting.

'No I'm not. It's as true as I'm standing here,' Nancy retorted. 'Me dad's an ARP warden and he said he'd heard as how the police 'ave arrested every single one of them and that they've bin told not to stand no nonsense from any of them. About time too, that's what I say. We don't want their sort over here. A ruddy danger to all of us, they are, not that some people have got the sense to see that,' Nancy added with a challenging toss of her head, having turned round and seen Rosie standing in the doorway. 'Ruddy Eyeties. Me dad says if he had his way he'd have the whole ruddy lot of 'em sent back to Italy before they start murderin' us in our beds.'

'That's not true.' The hot denial was spoken before Rosie could stop herself. Everyone fell silent and looked at her. She could feel her face burning with a mixture of anger and self-consciousness. She might know her own mind but she wasn't generally one for speaking out and being argumentative. There was no way, though, that she was going to stand here and let Nancy Dale speak like that about her friends.

'Oh, and you know, do you? Well, that's not what Mr Churchill says. P'haps seeing as you think so much of them as is decent people's enemies you ought to have bin teken away by the police along wi' them.'

'I'd rather be with my friends than with someone like you,' Rosie responded. She could feel her eyes starting to burn with angry tears. The arrival of

56

the police in the middle of the night to take away the men, even if they had been led by kindly Constable Black, whom they all knew, had left her feeling frightened and upset. Not that she was going to let Nancy Dale see that, she told herself fiercely, but she was still glad that Mrs Verey's arrival had them all hurrying to their posts, and the argument was brought to an end.

Rosie was supposed to be working on the uniforms belonging to some friends of Mrs Verey who were members of the WVS. With limited 'standard' sizes to choose from, many women were finding that the regulation uniforms they were supplied with simply did not fit, and dress shop owners like Mrs Verey, anxious to find ways to keep their business going at such a difficult time, were now offering alteration services.

Normally Rosie took a pride in turning the not always flattering clothes into neatly tailored outfits that brought grateful smiles from their pleased owners, but today she simply couldn't focus on her work. When yet another accidental needle stab to her already sore fingers brought a small bead of blood, tears filled her eyes and her throat felt choked with misery. What *was* going to happen to Papà Giovanni and the other men? She looked at her watch. It wasn't even eleven yet. She didn't think she could manage to wait until after work to find out if there was any news. If she was quick and she could slip out the minute the dinner bell went, she would have time to run back home.

The workroom door opened and one of the other girls came in carrying two mugs of tea.

'Here, Rosie, I've brought yer a cuppa,' Ruth announced, putting down both mugs and then heaving a sigh as she sank onto one of the room's small hard chairs. 'There's not a soul bin in the showroom, nor likely to be with a war on. I 'ate standing round doin' nuffink; it meks me legs ache far worse than when I'm bein' run off them.' She took a gulp of her tea, and then added, 'Mrs Verey sent me up to tell you that Mrs Latham will be coming in later to collect her suit, and that you're not to take your dinner hour but that you can leave early to make up for it.

'Oh and I need a favour of yer. I've torn me spare work frock. Can you mend it for us, on the quiet, like?'

All the girls who worked for Mrs Verey wore neat plain grey short-sleeved dresses trimmed with removable white collars and cuffs for washing. The dresses were made in the workroom, and the cost of them deducted from the girls' wages so that any damage to them meant they had to be replaced.

'I'll try,' Rosie agreed. 'But I'll have to have a look at the tear first. If it's a bad one . . .'

Ruth grinned and winked before telling her, 'It's one of the buttonholes that's bin torn. My fella got a bit too keen, if you know what I mean. Mind you, since it was his first time home since he joined up last Christmas, and he were at Dunkirk, I suppose there's no point in blamin' him. I'll bring it up later when Mrs V. is chatting with her friend. I've got to run. Me mam's asked me to collect us ration from the butcher's this dinner time and if I don't get there dead on twelve there'll be a queue right down the ruddy street. Ruddy rationing. Me da was saying last night that there'll be clothes rationing next. Mrs V. will certainly have summat to say about it if they try that on.' She stood up, gulped down her tea, and had almost reached the door when she turned round and said, 'There's a few of us goin' dancing at the Grafton this Saturday, Rosie, if you fancy coming wi' us.'

Ruth hadn't mentioned the argument earlier with Nancy but Rosie knew that the invitation was her way of showing Rosie that she had her support, and she was grateful to her for that. Nor was she shocked by Ruth's talk of how her dress had come to be torn. No one could live for very long in the Gerard Street area without becoming aware of what went on between the sexes. Not that Rosie herself was one for letting lads think they could get away with anything. Perhaps because she had spent so much of her time in a traditional Italian house-hold, she had automatically absorbed the Italian attitude towards the difference in the freedoms allowed to young women and young men and the different way in which their transgressions were regarded. No way was Rosie going to have any lad or his family talking about her behind her back as being 'easy'. She didn't hand out her kisses like she had seen other girls do, as they embraced the new freedoms the war had brought, giggling that it was their duty to offer fighting men a little bit of 'home comfort'. Rosie was a sensible girl, though, and she was ready to accept that she could well feel differently if she were to fall in love. Just as she had witnessed the behaviour of those girls who saw the war as something that was providing them with fun, so too she had seen the very real grief and despair it brought to those women who feared for the lives of the men they loved.

She was a long way from being ready to fall in love yet, though, and as she admitted to herself now, she was also secretly relieved that she was not subject to the same rigid traditions that prevented Bella from being able to go out to any social function, never mind dancing at the Grafton unless she was doing so under the watchful eye of an older married female relative.

Once Ruth had gone, Rosie went back to her sewing, trying not to feel too disappointed that she wouldn't be able to nip home. She would eat her sandwiches just as soon as she had finished this seam, she promised herself, even though her appetite had vanished. The anxiety inside her was making both her head and her insides ache. Six o'clock – five o'clock now since Mrs Verey had said she could go home an hour early to make up for working through dinner – seemed like a lifetime away.

THREE

In the end Rosie's need to be with her friends compelled her to take the short cut home, almost running there despite the city's evening heat.

There was no sign of broken glass any more but the boarded-up windows and doors were a chilling reminder of what had happened.

She was halfway down Gerard Street when one of the neighbours called through her open door, 'If you're on your way to the Grenellis', Rosie, there's bin no news yet.'

'But surely the men must be home by now,' Rosie protested, shielding her face from the evening sun as she looked up to the narrow balcony where the young woman was standing, her baby on her hip.

The other woman shook her head. 'I've heard as how they're not letting any of them go until they're sure that they aren't Fascists. Daft, I call it. All the ruddy government needs to do is to come down here and ask around to find out what they want to know, not go locking up decent men. I heard this afternoon as how Bella's ma has teken it real badly, screaming and yelling and sayin' as 'ow she were going to end up wi'out her father and her hubbie, on account of the government as good as murderin' them. Maria were down at the church asking if the priest would come up and see her, so Fran Gonnelli two down from me, were sayin'.'

Like Rosie, Doreen Halliwell was not Italian, and Rosie guessed that she was more interested in gossiping about what had happened than offering any helpful information, so she didn't want to linger in the street. Besides, her comments about Maria going down to Holy Cross church had made Rosie even more anxious to get to the Grenellis' house and find out what was happening.

Fortunately the baby started to cry, giving her the excuse to hurry on her way.

Bella opened the door to her brief knock. Her olive skin had lost its normal warmth, leaving her looking sallow, her brown eyes shimmering with tears as the two girls embraced one another before Bella drew her inside.

'Are they back?' Rosie began, even before she had closed the door, desperate to be reassured that all was well.

But Bella was already shaking her head, telling her brokenly, 'No! There is no news, good or otherwise, Rosie. I wish that there was.' Her eyes, already red-rimmed from crying, swam with fresh tears. 'All we do know is that all the men who were rounded up last night have been taken to the North Western

Hotel on Lime Street for questioning, and that we aren't allowed to see them or speak with them. Aunt Maria has been down to the police station with food for them and clean clothes, but even though the police were sympathetic, they said there was nothing they could do to help, not with Mr Churchill himself having issued a general internment order against all Italian men aged between sixteen and seventy. They were saying at Podestra's that even the Italian Consul in Liverpool has been taken.' Her voice dropped. 'My mother is taking it very badly. You know that she's always wanted the family to go back home.'

Rosie nodded. Over the years there had been many passionate discussions around the Grenelli kitchen table about this subject, with Sofia saying how much she would like to go back to the village she had left as a small baby. Rosie could remember them quite clearly and she could remember too how much they had scared her and how much she had worried about the Grenellis going back to Italy and leaving her behind in Liverpool, pining for them. She had loved the whole family so much she had not been able to bear the thought of them not being there. As she grew older, every time the subject of 'going home' was discussed, Rosie had tried hard not to think selfishly of her own feelings but to recognise instead how hard it must be for the older generation of Italians, who had come to Liverpool genuinely believing that their absence from their homeland would only be temporary, and that once they had made enough money they would be able to return home to retire. Now, in view of what was happening, Rosie could understand why Sofia wished they had left.

'Aunt Maria is worried that she will be reported to the authorities, and she has begged her not to say any more. I hadn't realised myself until now how strong my mother's convictions are, or that she and my father . . .' Bella chewed worriedly on her bottom lip. 'Rosie, you must promise me not to say anything to anyone about what I have just said.'

Was Bella saying that her parents *were* Fascists? Rosie didn't know very much about Italian politics other than what she had heard in the Grenelli kitchen, but she could see how shocked and fearful Bella was and so she nodded vigorously and gave her promise. It was ridiculous that anyone could think that men like Giovanni and Carlo could be mixed up in something dangerous and illegal.

'Father Doyle has been round this afternoon,' Bella added, 'to see la Nonna and my mother . . .'

'Doreen Halliwell was on her balcony as I came down Gerard Street and she told me that Maria had been to fetch him. Did he manage to . . .' The girls were exchanging whispers in the scullery, and Rosie tugged on Bella's sleeve, not wanting to go into the kitchen and join the others until she knew everything there was to know.

Bella shook her head dispiritedly. 'Mamma won't listen to anyone. Like I said, she is taking it very badly, Rosie. I have never seen her like this before. One minute she's furiously angry, and the next she just won't speak at all. Then she says that we will never see our men again and that they are as good as dead, and that without them we might as well all be dead.'

Rosie shivered as she heard the fear in her friend's voice. Somehow she had expected that it would be gentle tender-hearted Maria who would be the one to suffer the most, not her more fiery sister, but as though she sensed what Rosie was thinking, Bella offered sadly, 'My mother has always been devoted to Grandfather Giovanni, and him to her. Aunt Maria says it is because she is so like his own mother. She cannot bear the thought of him suffering in any kind of way, and she is distraught that this has happened to him. Even Father Doyle was unable to comfort her. She has spent all afternoon on her knees praying that they will be set free and allowed to return home, but Father Doyle says that the British Government will not free any of the men until they are sure that they have combed out those amongst them that are true Fascists. He has asked permission to visit them, but he has been told that at the moment that is not possible. But with our consul taken along with the others, there is no one to speak to the authorities on their behalf.'

Bella's revelations left Rosie too shocked to make any response for a few moments. 'But surely the authorities must know which men they truly suspect of working against our country,' she protested when she had recovered herself.

'You would have thought so,' Bella agreed, 'but

according to Father Doyle there is a great deal of confusion caused by so many of our men socialising with one another and being unwittingly drawn into the Fascist organisation, although they are not Fascists in any way. It does not help that so many of the older men do not speak English very well, and have been saying how much they want to return to Italy, like my mother. It is only pride that makes them say such things and our own local police understand that, but Constable Black is concerned that the government may not understand this. And, of course, there are those who resent us and who are glad to see this dreadful thing happen to us,' Bella added. 'Let's go into the parlour. Aunt Maria and la Nonna will be glad to see you.'

Bella did not say that her own mother would be glad to see her, Rosie noted, but she was too fond of her friend to say anything.

The good smell of soup and garlic from the large pan on the stove made Rosie's stomach growl with hunger, but for once there was no familiar call to her to sit herself down at the table whilst la Nonna demanded to be told about her day, and Maria hurried to bring soup and bread, along with a glass of the watered-down wine the whole family drank.

La Nonna was seated in a chair beside the fire, watching Maria's every movement with an anxious gaze, but it was Sofia who caused Rosie to feel the greatest fear. Bella's normally assertive mother was sitting in a chair staring into space without blinking or even turning her head to look at them as they entered the room.

'She has been like this since Father Doyle left,' Bella whispered.

At the sound of her granddaughter's voice la Nonna broke into rapid Italian, speaking too quickly for Rosie to be able to understand.

'La Nonna says that we need an Italian priest to help us speak both to the authorities and to God,' Maria explained with a sad smile.

Italian priests without parishes of their own were permitted to preach within the Italian communities by the Catholic Church, but since they travelled from parish to parish, they were not always on hand.

'Surely there is something that can be done,' Rosie protested, a small frown creasing her forehead as she wondered why her own mother wasn't here with their friends.

'Everything that can be done has been,' Maria assured her gently. 'Those of our leaders who have not been taken have tried to speak to the government, but we have been told that we must wait and that there is nothing to fear for those who are not Fascists.' Her mouth trembled and she blinked away tears.

'But if that is so, then why do they continue to hold our men?' Bella burst out fiercely. 'Especially my grandfather. You know how devoted to one another he and la Nonna are, Rosie,' she appealed to her friend.

Rosie nodded.

'La Nonna cannot understand why they have not let him come home. We have tried to explain to her but she doesn't understand. She is worrying about his chest, and if there is anyone at the police station to give him some cordial when he coughs. She is desperately afraid that the police will come back and take her away next and that she will never see Grandfather or any of us again. And my mother is just as distraught. She says it will kill my grandfather to be treated like this and that we will never see him or my father alive again. Oh, Rosie, I am so scared that she could be right,' Bella admitted.

'Oh, Bella, don't,' Rosie begged her, white-faced. 'You mustn't think like that because it isn't going to happen,' she went on stoutly. 'It's all a terrible mistake, Bella, it has to be. And as soon as the police realise that—'

'But what if they don't, what if—'

'They will. They have to,' Rosie insisted quickly. It was unthinkable that an elderly man like Giovanni should be taken away from his family and not allowed to return. Unthinkable too that kind-hearted Carlo could be mixed up in anything as dangerous as Fascism.

'You can say that, but why are they keeping them for so long? Surely by now they must have realised that they are innocent.'

'These things take time, Bella,' Maria intervened in her calm gentle voice. 'All we can do is pray for patience, put our trust in God and wait. Mr

Churchill knows how many of our boys are fighting for this country. He is a fair and just man and once he has assured himself that there is no danger he will set our men free, just as Father Doyle says.'

'If that is true why aren't they free already?' Bella announced fiercely. 'I am going to go to Lime Street now and demand to see my father and my grandfather.'

'I'll come with you,' Rosie offered immediately.

Maria shook her head and bustled both girls out of the parlour, closing the door behind her as she did so.

'There isn't any point in going to the North Western Hotel.'

'We could take them food and clean clothes . . .'

Lowering her voice, Maria said tiredly, 'You won't be allowed to see them and besides . . . Father Doyle has already been down to Lime Street and been told that they are going to be moved in the morning. I haven't told la Nonna or Sofia yet.'

Both girls looked at her in fresh shock. 'Moved where?' Bella demanded.

'Huyton,' Maria told them quietly.

'The internment camp?' Rosie whispered. She felt as though hard fingers had taken hold of her heart and were squeezing it so tightly she could hardly breathe. Early on in the war, certain streets on the new Huyton housing estate had been converted for use as an internment camp to hold those individuals who were considered a threat in the event of an invasion. Several roads in the estate had been sealed off with an eight-foot fence of barbed wire, and internees were billeted in the cordoned-off houses, where they faced the prospect of being sent to the Isle of Man, or even deported to Canada.

'Yes,' Maria answered. As she spoke Maria's head dropped as though in shame and through her numbness Rosie felt a fierce surge of anger that she should be made to feel like that.

'They can't be going to Huyton.' Bella's voice was more that of a frightened child than a young woman. Rosie could feel her own hope draining out of her, to be replaced by cold disbelief and shock. How could this be happening? 'They might say they are being interned but that's just another word for being imprisoned, isn't it?' Bella whispered, tears filling her eyes. 'Oh, Aunt Maria, what's going to happen to them?'

Maria shook her head. 'I don't know. Father Doyle says he'd heard that all those Italians who had been taken into custody were to be sent to somewhere near Bury – Warth Mills it's called – where they'll be held until the government combs out the Fascists. Then when that's been done . . .' Her voice trailed away, tears brimming in her eyes and rolling down her cheeks. 'Promise me you won't say anything about this to your mother or la Nonna, Bella. There's no point in getting either of them even more upset than they already are.'

Rosie's heart went out to Maria. She guessed that whilst it was concern for her elderly mother's health that made her want to protect *her* from the news, it was the worry about what Sofia might say or do that made her feel her sister couldn't be trusted with the truth.

'You'd better go home now, Rosie,' she added gently. 'Your mam will be waiting for news.'

Rosie hugged her tightly before turning to leave. She could sense that this was a time when the family needed to be alone although it hurt her too to know that she could not be part of the tight-knit circle of grieving, worried women because she did not share their blood, or their nationality.

'At last. Put the kettle on, will yer?' Christine demanded when Rosie opened the back door. 'I'm parched.' Christine was sitting with her feet up on a chair whilst she painted her nails a vivid shade of scarlet. Her hair and makeup looked immaculate and she was wearing one of her best frocks. Tight-fitting and in bright red imitation satin, it was a dress that Rosie knew her mother loved, whilst whenever she saw her in it, all Rosie could think was that she wished her mother wouldn't wear it, and that it looked both cheap and too young for her.

It astonished Rosie to see Christine looking all dressed up and full of herself, when the Grenellis were experiencing so much heartache, but the last thing she wanted to do was provoke a row with her, so instead of saying what she felt she said quietly instead, as she filled the kettle, 'I've just been round at the Grenellis'.' Trying to keep the reproach out of her voice, she continued, 'They've had some news, but it isn't very good. The men are going to be moved to Huyton in the morning.'

'Yes, yes, I know all about that,' Christine interrupted her, looking bored. 'I went down to Rose Street this dinner time and managed to sweet-talk Tom Byers into telling us what was going on. I suppose Sofia's still carryin' on about how she wishes they'd all gone back to Italy, is she? Ruddy fool. She wants to watch her tongue, she does, otherwise it won't just be her Carlo who'll end up being deported as a Fascist.'

Rosie couldn't conceal her shock. 'The Grenellis aren't Fascists, Mum.'

'Well, you could have fooled me the way Sofia's bin carryin' on. I've bin warning Aldo to keep his distance from Carlo – not that Carlo's to blame. It's ruddy Sofia wot's got them all into this mess, if you ask me, allus goin' on about Italy and that Mussolini. Of course, she's allus bin able to twist her dad round her little finger. It should be her wot was taken off, not Aldo. Anyway, Tom Byers has tipped me the wink that them as is found to be Fascists will end up being interned on the Isle of Man, wi' the worst of them shipped off to Canada. I'm going up to Huyton in the morning to see if I can manage to have a word wi' Aldo and warn him to keep his mouth shut when he's questioned at this Warth Mills place they're all going to be sent to.'

Rosie could only stare at her mother. How had she managed to find out so much when poor Maria had been told next to nothing? Rosie winced inwardly as she took in her mother's smug expression and dressed-up appearance.

'I would have thought you'd be straight round to the Grenellis to tell them what you'd heard,' was all she could manage to say.

Christine reached for her cigarettes. 'Wot, and 'ave to listen to Sofia ranting on? No, thanks. Besides, I don't want to get tarred wi' the same brush as them, and if you've any sense in that head of yours, our Rosie, you'll keep a bit o' distance from Bella whilst all this is goin' on. Hurry up with that cuppa, will yer, Rosie?' Christine looked down at her legs and added, 'I hope that yer dad remembers to bring us some stockings back wi' him this time. Honestly, he's that daft at times. Fancy goin' all the way to New York and not thinkin' on to fetch us some stockings.'

'They were almost torpedoed the last time, Mum, and Dad said that they were lucky not to be sunk. I dare say he didn't have time to go looking for stockings with them having to unload and come back so quick so as not to miss the convoy,' Rosie told her.

She was still trying to come to terms with the change in her mother's attitude towards the Grenellis – a change that left her feeling ashamed and determined to make sure that the family knew they could count on *her* loyalty and friendship at least.

*　　*　　*

The week dragged by with no real news about what was going to happen to the men. Rosie had no idea whether or not her mother had visited Huyton as she had said she was going to because Christine had flatly refused to discuss the subject with her, saying that it was her business what she did and no one else's. There were times, Rosie acknowledged, when she found it very hard to understand the way her mother's mind worked. Her mother's behaviour made her feel guilty when Bella told Rosie that she and Maria were going to Huyton with the Podestra family to see if they could somehow or other manage to see their menfolk.

'We're going to take them some food and some clean clothes.'

'I'll come with you,' Rosie volunteered immediately.

Bella shook her head. 'You can't, Rosie. We're goin' in the morning because that's when Louisa Podestra reckons the guards let the men come out for some fresh air. You'll be at work. Louisa has told me I can have the time off. Not that we've got that many coming into the chippie since it all happened, exceptin' to ask if there's bin any fresh news. It seems to me that me mam's in the right of it and it would have bin better for us if we'd gone back to Italy,' Bella added with a new bitterness in her voice.

'Bella, don't say that,' Rosie protested. 'You're as English as I am.'

'No I'm not. I'm Italian, and proud of it even if I were born here.'

'We're at war with Italy now,' Rosie reminded her, trying not to look shocked.

'*I* don't need telling that, do I?' Bella retaliated. 'Not wi' me dad and me granddad in a concentration camp.'

'Huyton isn't a concentration camp.'

'Huh, those who run it may not be callin' it that, but what else can it be when they've got men imprisoned there?'

Rosie said nothing. She was beginning to feel as though she didn't know her friend properly any more. She hadn't missed the bitter looks Sofia gave her whenever she went round to the Grenellis', and now here was Bella treating her more as though they were enemies than friends, and as though England wasn't her home at all. Rosie was confused by her own feelings. She felt hurt by Bella's attitude towards her and, if she was honest, she felt angry as well when Bella complained and said that she wished she were living in Italy. She had understood when Bella had been upset about what had happened to the Italian men, but she couldn't agree with what Bella was saying now.

'I hope you manage to see your dad and granddad,' was all she could manage to say eventually. And for the first time since they had grown up they did not hug one another when they said goodbye.

FOUR

'You're still on for Saturday at the Grafton, aren't you, Rosie?' Ruth asked cheerfully as the girls put on their coats to leave work.

Rosie hesitated before replying. The truth was that the last thing she felt like doing was going out dancing, but she didn't want to let Ruth down by backing out now.

'Of course she is, aren't you, Rosie?' one of the other girls laughed. 'You won't catch me missing out.'

'Meet us outside at half-past seven, Rosie,' Ruth told her, adding with a wink, 'And thanks for sortin' me dress out for me. I'll write and tell my Fred not to be so eager next time.'

As she walked down Springfield Street half an hour later, Rosie wondered whether or not she should call at the Grenellis'. Don't be so soft, she chided herself. There was no call to go getting all upset and taking it to heart because Bella had been a bit funny with her. Chances were that she had only been like that because she was so worried and feared for her dad and granddad. She had probably read too much into Bella's wild talk. Reassured by her own thoughts, Rosie felt her spirits start to lift as she headed for number 16. She had missed Bella even though it had only been a couple of days since she had last seen her.

It was Maria who opened the door to her knock, hugging her briefly, her expression betraying the strain she was under.

'If you've come to see Bella, she's round at Pod's,' Maria told her before Rosie could ask after her friend.

'Who is it? Oh, it's you, is it?' Sofia announced in a hostile tone, answering her own question as she came into the kitchen. 'Where's your mother, or daren't she show her face here after what she's been doing?'

'Sofia . . .' Maria protested.

'What's wrong?' Rosie demanded, indignant at her mother being talked about in such a way even though she had been feeling ashamed of her behaviour herself these last few days. 'What's my mother supposed to have done?'

'There's no *supposed* about it,' Sofia answered bitterly. 'Seen at it, she was. Acting cheap around our men, wi' them wot's guardin' 'em and we all know why. Some of us have allus known what she is, even if others . . .'

Sofia's voice was rising higher with every word she spat out. She was trembling with fury whilst

Rosie had started trembling herself. All her life she had thought of the Grenellis as her family, never imagining that anything could change the deep bond she had believed they shared. That belief had been turned on its head the moment the trouble had started in Liverpool.

'Sofia, please . . .' Maria begged her sister urgently in a low voice.

Rosie heard her but she was too shocked to be able to react. Somewhere in a corner of her mind she had always known that her mother's behaviour wasn't like that of Maria and Sofia, but she had put that difference down to the fact that they were Italian, not because . . . She couldn't stand here and let Sofia call her mother cheap without defending her. She took a deep breath.

'I know my mother went to Huyton Camp but—'

'She had no right to go there,' Sofia shouted her down angrily. 'What's she to us? Nothing! And you can go home and tell her we don't want her coming round here any more. Not that she'll dare to show her face here after what she's done . . .'

Rosie looked helplessly at Maria, not knowing what to say or do and not really able to understand why Sofia was so worked up.

'You'd better go home, I think, Rosie,' Maria advised her, bustling her out of the room. 'I'm sorry that Sofia spoke to you like that. She's not herself at the moment.'

'I know how much you must all be worrying,

Maria,' Rosie agreed, swallowing down the tears that were thickening her voice. 'How is la Nonna? Have you managed to get any word of the men?' The questions she wanted to ask came tumbling out on top of one another as Maria hurried her towards the back door.

'You're a good girl, Rosie. A kind girl,' Maria told her, without answering her. 'But with things the way they are, it's best that you don't come round for a while. Just until things settle down and Sofia's back to her normal self.'

The tears burned in the back of Rosie's eyes. She wanted to throw herself into Maria's arms and be told that everything was all right, just as she had done so many times as a little girl: when she had lost both her first front teeth and had been teased at school; when she had not been chosen for the school pantomime; when the goldfish her father had won for her at the fair had died, to name just a few of the small sadnesses that had coloured her growing up. But this was different. Everything was not all right, and she wasn't a little girl any more. Poor Maria. Rosie could hardly bear to think about what she must be going through.

Squaring her shoulders, she reached out and gave Maria a fierce silent hug, and then hurried away before her emotions got the better of her.

FIVE

Rosie frowned as she studied her appearance in her dressing-table mirror. Having dipped her forefinger into a pot of Vaseline, she then drew the tip of it along the curve of her dark eyebrows to smooth and shape them, a beauty aid that Bella had shown her.

She was wearing a frock she had made herself from a remnant of pretty floral cotton, bright yellow flowers against a white background. She had bought a roll of it at St John's market in the spring. There had been just enough to make herself a halter-necked frock with a neat nipped-in waist and a panelled skirt.

She had made the halter and trimmed the top of the bodice with some white piqué cotton, and then used the offcuts from the floral material to trim the little matching bolero jacket she had made. The result was an outfit that had brought her more than a few admiring comments. The smile that had been curving her mouth at the memory of those comments dimmed when she remembered how many of them had come from the Grenelli family and how Bella had begged her to make a similar frock and jacket for her. Together they had gone to St John's every market day until they had found the perfect fabric for Bella's dark colouring: a deep rich red, patterned with polka dots. They had both worn their new outfits for Bella's birthday early in May. Less than two months ago but it might as well have been a lifetime ago, so much had changed, Rosie admitted sadly. Her mother hadn't said anything about the fact that neither of them was visiting the Grenellis any more and, having heard Sofia's bitter denunciation of Christine, Rosie had felt unable to talk to her about what had happened or why she had stopped visiting their old friends.

'Where are you off to then?' her mother demanded now when she saw Rosie dressed up to go out.

'The Grafton,' Rosie answered. 'I'm meeting up with the other girls from work. It was Ruth's idea. I think she's feeling a bit low with her Fred in the army, and she wanted a bit of cheering up.'

'Huh, well, we'd all like a bit of that, I'm sure,' Christine said sharply. She lit a cigarette and inhaled, then exhaled the smoke, narrowing her eyes. 'I wouldn't mind comin' with yer meself to be honest, Rosie. How do yer fancy havin' yer old mam along? Mind you, I bet I could show you young 'uns a thing or two,' she added, her pursed lips relaxing into a small secretive smile.

Rosie's heart sank. It wasn't that she didn't love her mother – she did – but she didn't feel comfortable about her coming out with them, especially after what Sofia had said.

'There isn't time for you to get ready now. I promised the others I'd meet up with them at half-past seven,' she blurted out.

Her mother's eyes narrowed again but not against the smoke this time. 'I see you don't want me along spoiling your fun.' She gave a small contemptuous shrug. 'Please yourself then. I can soon find meself summat to do. As a matter of fact them from the salon are going to the Gaiety tonight and they've asked me to go along wi' them,' she said, referring to the cinema on Scotland Road.

Rosie felt guilty at how relieved she was to be leaving the house without her mother. It was a pleasant evening, and the city's streets were still busy with people coming and going, making the most of the light evening and the freedom from the blackout that the dark nights brought.

Like everyone else, Rosie was carrying her gas mask on her arm in its protective box. She had hated having to carry it around all the time at first. It had looked so ugly and felt so cumbersome. But soon, along with other girls, Rosie had been finding imaginative ways to dress up the carrying case with a cover made from scraps of fabric, just like the fancy carrying cases she had seen in the magazines. Automatically she stopped to scan the headlines written up on the newspaper sellers' sandwich boards, sucking in her breath, her stomach tensing with anxiety that there was more bad news about the Italian men being held.

'You can allus buy a paper instead of trying to memorise it, love,' the newspaper seller told her drily, causing passers-by to laugh. Rosie blushed but she too laughed and shook her head. However, the three young lads who had stopped to listen to what was going on, and admire her as they did so, bought a paper apiece.

'Here, you can stay if you like,' the seller grinned, winking at her. 'Pretty lass like you is good for business.'

Rosie laughed again. She was going to be late meeting the others if she wasn't careful. The lads who had bought papers watched her from the other side of the road, and whistled at her.

Cheek, Rosie thought to herself, tossing her head slightly to let them know what she thought of their impudence, but still secretly pleased by their harmless admiration.

'There you are. We was just thinking you weren't going to come,' Ruth told Rosie, grabbing hold of her arm. 'Let's get inside and get a table before it gets too packed.'

The Grafton was one of Liverpool's most popular dance halls. It had a wide double stairway that led up to the dance hall itself, and on busy nights the stairs could be packed with people eager to dance, as well as some couples standing there smooching, oblivious to the crowd around them. The Grafton was well known for having the very best dance bands on, led by the likes of Victor Silvester, Oscar Rabin and Ivy Benson. As Ruth had predicted, it was already almost full of young people, all keen to enjoy themselves whilst they still could. Of course, the young men in uniform attracted the most interest from the girls in their dance frocks.

'And remember,' Ruth cautioned the party from Elegant Modes as they wriggled through the crowd just in time to grab the last vacant table close to the edge of the dance floor, 'no one's to go encouraging any RO lads.'

RO lads were the men who were doing very necessary reserved occupation work, but who lacked the glamour of a uniform.

'That dress looks ever so pretty on you, Rosie,' Evie Watts, a window dresser at the shop, commented admiringly. 'I thought so the last time I saw you wearin' it. Mind you, you 'ave got the figure for it.'

Rosie had just started to thank her for her compliment when Nancy butted in nastily, 'For meself, I allus think that shop-bought looks smarter than home-made, especially when you've had the fabric off of the market and half of Liverpool's wearing it.'

'Don't mind Nancy, Rosie,' Ruth whispered. 'She's just jealous of you on account of her thinking she were the bee's knees and the prettiest girl in the shop until you come along.'

The band had already started to play and Ruth

nudged Evie as a group of young men several yards away edged a bit closer to their table.

'I'm dancing wi' the one with the blond hair and blue eyes, in the corporal's uniform,' Ruth announced with a predatory gleam in her eyes. 'He's got his stripes and I like a lad wi' a bit of experience about him.'

'Wot about your Fred?' Evie demanded

'Wot about 'im?' Ruth came back smartly.

When Evie pulled a face behind Ruth's back and whispered to the others, 'I fancied that blond lad meself,' Rosie couldn't help giggling, her spirits starting to lift.

Ruth might be more outspoken than she was herself but she was such good fun that you couldn't help but enjoy being in her company. Ruth was always the one for a bit of quick backchat and never behind the door when it came to putting a cheeky lad in his place if she felt like it. Rosie remembered how much it had made her laugh when Ruth had riposted to one particular lad who had swaggered over to them like he was really something, to ask her to dance, 'Come back in five years when you're old enough – and tall enough.'

Two girls who Rosie didn't recognise made their way over and were introduced by Evie as her cousins Susan and Jane. Drinks were ordered, cigarettes lit, and the girls settled down to the ritual of pretending they were oblivious to the way the boys were eyeing them as they smoothed already straight seams and patted immaculately rolled curls, thus showing off slim ankles and shining hair.

''Ere, that blond lad's on his way over. Remember what I said. Hands off, everyone else,' Ruth warned with a wicked grin.

After a few muttered comments about some girls having the cheek to grab all the best lads before anyone else had a chance to get a good look at them, the girls dutifully clustered together in such a way that the young man was automatically channelled towards Ruth.

'I reckon it were you he really wanted to dance with, Rosie,' said Evie as they watched Ruth dancing past them in the arms of the young soldier, who had introduced himself as Bob. 'There's no Italian lads here tonight by the looks of it. Shame, 'cos they're good dancers, and good-lookin' too.'

Rosie's smile faded. Evie's comment had reminded her of the dreadful things that had been happening to the Grenellis. Because of her family's plans for Bella to marry one of the Podestra boys, Sofia did not allow Bella to go dancing with Rosie, but Bella had always been eager to hear about the fun Rosie had. Dances at the Grafton would be the last thing on Bella's mind now, Rosie thought, her happiness suddenly shadowed by guilt because she was here and enjoying herself. One of the other young men in army uniform who had been watching them came over and asked her to dance. He was blushing slightly, his brown hair slicked back, and his gaze fixed on a point somewhere past her shoulder. Rosie didn't have the heart to turn him down. His hand, when he clasped hers, felt hot and slightly sticky, and she could see how self-conscious he felt. His accent wasn't Liverpudlian, and under her kind questioning he admitted that he had only recently joined up and that he was feeling a bit out of his depth.

'I didn't realise that Liverpool was going to be so big,' he confessed, his honesty and humility making Rosie warm to him.

'So where are you from, then?' Rosie asked him.

'Shropshire,' he told her. 'My dad works on a farm down near Ironbridge. I've never seen so many houses all together before I came to Liverpool. Nor the sea neither.'

He sounded rather forlorn and Rosie felt quite sorry for him.

'You must have made friends with some of the other men who joined up at the same time,' she suggested.

'Oh, aye, I done that all right,' he agreed, looking happier. 'A nicer bunch of blokes you couldn't hope to meet.' He gave Rosie a shy grin. 'After all, it were them as persuaded me to come here tonight. Aye, and it were them an' all that said I should ask you to dance.'

By the time their dance was over and he had returned Rosie to her table it was surrounded by a jolly crowd of mostly uniformed young men.

Ruth was a flirt, there was no doubt about that, but she was also a big-hearted girl, and Rosie saw how she made sure that even the shyest girl on their table was invited to get up and dance.

'Here's Nancy coming over wi' that cousin of hers wot thinks he's God's gift with bells on,' Evie muttered. 'Watch out, girls.'

Rosie turned to look at the man coming towards their table. Nancy was at his side and two other young men who were also obviously part of the small group were walking slightly behind him. He was tall, with broad shoulders, his dark hair brilliantined back, and almost film star good looks, apart from the fact that his eyes were too close set, but Rosie knew immediately why Evie had disparaged him. It was all there in those eyes, everything a person needed to know about him, and it made her recoil from him physically. There was not just a coldness but a brutality in his eyes as his darting gaze moved arrogantly over the girls seated at the table. There had been a boy very similar to him at school, Rosie remembered, a bully and a liar who had terrorised the younger children, stealing from them and physically hurting them, until one day the big brother of the small first year he had pushed to the playground, stamping deliberately on his glasses and leaving him crying, had come down to the school and taught him a much-needed lesson.

'Come on, Lance, you promised you'd dance with me,' Nancy was wheedling, when they reached the table. She was hanging on to his arm, and looking up at him in a way that was more lover-like than cousinly. It was plain, though, that he did not return her interest because he disentangled himself from her quickly and almost brutally. Rosie could feel him watching her, staring at her, she realised indignantly, as he struck a pose and lit up two cigarettes, withdrawing one from his mouth and then trying to hand it over to her. His action was so deliberately intimate that it made her face burn, not with self-conscious female delight but with anger.

'No, thank you,' she told him coolly. 'I don't smoke.'

'But you do dance, right?'

He had put out the cigarettes now, but he hadn't stopped looking at her and he had moved closer to her as well – so close that she instinctively wanted to put some space between them. But that wasn't possible with her still seated.

'What's happened to them Italian Fascist friends of yours?' Nancy cut in, taunting Rosie, unhappy the limelight wasn't shining on her. 'Or need we ask? All bin imprisoned, I expect, and so they ruddy well should be – aye, and all them wot support them as well. You should be reportin' her to the authorities, Lance, not asking her to dance.'

'Supportin' Fascism – that's treason, that is,' Nancy's cousin announced. The way he was looking at her made the fine hairs on Rosie's neck rise in angry dislike.

'Having Italian friends doesn't make anyone a traitor and it doesn't mean that they're Fascists either,' she defended.

'I know a group of handy lads, who have their

own way of deciding how ruddy Fascists need to be treated. Aye, and they've proved it already,' Lance taunted.

The other girls were beginning to look uncertain and uncomfortable now. Was Nancy's cousin saying what Rosie thought he was saying? Was he implying that he was one of those who had been involved in the violent riots?

'Mebbe there are some Italians fighting for Blighty but there's a hell of a lot more fighting our lads, aye, and killin' 'em as well. Why take any chances, that's wot I say. A concentration camp is the best place for the ruddy lot of them,' Lance told her. His voice had risen as he became more animated, so that the rest of the revellers could hear what he was saying and Rosie could see the approving nods that some of the people standing around them were giving. The earlier light-hearted mood had been replaced by a dark undercurrent of anger and hostility that made her feel vulnerable and afraid.

'Well, I reckon it's daft to start thinking that all Italians living here are Fascists because they're not.'

Everyone turned to look at the young man Rosie had been dancing with earlier. He was facing Lance with an expression of dogged determination on his face that said he wasn't going to be bullied into backing down. Rosie felt her heart lift as she smiled at her unlikely champion.

'Alan's right,' another young soldier chipped in. 'We've got several Italian lads in our unit and they're as British as you and me.'

'Come on, Lance, let's go and dance,' Nancy demanded, bored now, grabbing hold of her cousin's hand and tugging him in the direction of the dance floor.

'He gives me the willies, that Lance does – those eyes . . .' Evie shuddered after they had gone. 'You did well standing up to him like that, Rosie.'

'It wasn't me, it was Alan,' Rosie replied, giving him a grateful smile.

Perhaps everything would work out after all, especially if there were more people like Alan around.

It had been an enjoyable evening, all the more so when Nancy and Lance had gone over to another table to join some of Lance's friends, Rosie admitted as she put her key in the back door of number 12. Alan had offered to walk her home but she had walked back as far as Springfield Street with Evie's cousins instead. She had liked Alan but it didn't do to go encouraging lads, not even the shy ones, though she was looking forward to telling Bella all about him . . .

Her smile abruptly disappeared. Ever since Maria had told her that it would be best if she stopped calling round, Rosie had been trying to push her unhappiness about the situation into a corner of her mind where it wouldn't keep bothering her. But of course she couldn't. She and Bella had been friends all their lives. They had been best friends practically in their cradles, playing hopscotch together, learning to skip, riding the tricycle that Maria had bought second-hand for them to share, taking it in turns to pedal whilst the one who wasn't pedalling stood on the back. Then had come their first day at school, when they had stood hand in hand together. If she closed her eyes, even now she could recall the stickiness of their joined hands in their shared nervousness, just as she could recall the loving warmth of Maria's cuddly body next to her own on her other side. Her own mother had been working and so it had been Maria and Sofia who had taken the girls to school.

Then later she and Bella had walked there together, holding hands, and giggling over their shared secrets and jokes. Then had come 'big' school where their friendship had remained as strong as ever. There had hardly ever been a cross word between them. They were as close as sisters – closer. Or rather they had been. Rosie had never imagined that could ever change, but now it had and her heart felt sore and hurt.

She pushed open the door and stepped into the kitchen, quickly closing the door to block out any light that might attract the interest of a watchful ARP patrol.

The first thing she saw was her father's jacket hanging on its peg and the second was her father himself, propped up asleep in one of the kitchen chairs.

'Dad!'

He woke immediately at the sound of her excited voice, a smile splitting his face as he looked at her.

Rosie almost flew across the kitchen, flinging herself into his arms, half laughing and half crying. 'When did you get back?' she demanded breathlessly.

'We docked just turned midnight, and they let us off more or less straight away. The Port Authority don't like us docking until it gets dark just in case the ruddy Luftwaffe teks it into its head to have a go at bombing the docks, so that meant we'd bin waiting out on the other side of Liverpool bar since early this morning. It made me feel right bad being so near but not being able to come and see you straight away. Let's have a look at yer, lass.'

Obediently Rosie let him hold her at arm's length whilst he scrutinised her. They had always been close, and Rosie often felt guilty that her love for her father was stronger and went deeper than the love she had for her mother.

'Summat's botherin' you,' he pronounced shrewdly, his inspection over.

Rosie shook her head in rueful acknowledgement rather than in denial of his judgement.

'What is it?'

'Has Mum told you what's happened to the Grenellis?' she asked.

She could see him start to frown. Her father was not part of the close friendship she and her mother shared with their Italian neighbours. This was, Rosie had always believed, because he was away so much and had therefore not had the chance to get to know them in the same way. But he was also a quiet man who valued his own fireside when he was not at sea. The busyness of the Grenellis' kitchen, with people constantly coming and going and voices raised in lively conversation and sometimes equally lively argument, was not something he would enjoy.

'I haven't seen your mam yet. She's out somewhere,' he muttered.

'I think she's gone to the Gaiety, with the others from the salon,' Rosie told him, 'and then I expect she went back with one of them for a bit of supper. You know what she's like about not wanting to be in on her own.'

'Aye, your mam's never bin one as has enjoyed her own company,' Rosie's father agreed. 'So you've bin worrying that soft heart of yours about the Grenellis, have you? I heard summat down at the docks about the Italian men being taken off.'

'Dad, it was so awful. There were riots, and then the police came and took the men away. La Nonna was dreadfully upset, and Sofia as well.'

'They haven't got anything to worry about if they haven't done anything wrong,' her father said reassuringly.

'Of course they haven't done anything wrong,' Rosie immediately replied.

Her father's expression softened. 'I know it must be hard for the families that have got caught up in this, Rosie, but it won't do them or you any good you worrying yourself about it, lass.'

'I can't help it . . .' She paused and shook her head. 'Giovanni is nearly seventy-six, Dad, and he

94

doesn't always understand English properly even though he's lived here for so long. I can't understand why the government hasn't released men like him already.'

'Governments have their own way of doing things, Rosie, and they don't allus make a lot o' sense to ordinary folk like us. How's your mam taking it?'

'She hasn't said much. She went up to Huyton when they first took the men there, but . . .'

'But what?' her father pressed her gently.

Rosie shook her head. 'I don't know really, Dad, only that Sofia's taken everything really badly and there's been a bit of a falling-out. Mum hasn't been round to see them since the men were taken and Maria's asked me not to go until things are sorted out.' Rosie's voice thickened, her eyes suddenly filling with tears at being separated from close friends. 'It made me feel so bad when she said that. I know we aren't Italian, but we've always been friends, and now it's as though . . .'

'It won't be easy for them, Rosie. Maria's a good woman and she won't have intended to hurt you. But sometimes it's best to stay close to your own when things like this happen. Like to like, kin to kin.' He gave her a warm hug. 'You have a good cry if it will make you feel better.'

Rosie gave him a wobbly smile. 'What a way to welcome you home, Dad – Mum not here and me crying all over you about other people's problems. I'm so glad you're home, though. I think about you all the time and I say a special prayer every night that you'll be kept safe.'

'You've always had a soft heart, you have, our Rosie. Don't ever lose it. I'm going up to Edge Hill tomorrow to see your Auntie Maude,' he told her, changing the subject. 'Why don't you come with me? She'd like to see you.'

Rosie seriously doubted that but tried not to look unenthusiastic. She knew how strongly he believed he owed his sister for looking after him when their parents died in an outbreak of cholera when he was only twelve years old, and she knew too how much discord it caused between her parents when her mother refused to go and see Maude.

'Of course I'll come with you,' she assured him, and was rewarded with a smile and another hug.

'I'm for me bed,' he told her as he released her. 'I only waited up on account of you not being in.'

'Don't you want to stay up for Mum?' Rosie asked him.

'No. If I do that I could end up staying down here all night. I didn't send word to her that we'd docked, and you know your mother . . . if she's had a few drinks like as not she'll stay over with her pals and not come home until morning.'

He said it quite dispassionately but Rosie's tender heart couldn't help but feel sad for him. By rights her mother ought to be here waiting to welcome him home but, as they both knew, Christine just wasn't that sort of woman.

SIX

There was a joke in Liverpool that with each intersection a person crossed as they walked up from Edge Hill through Wavertree, the houses got larger and the accents got 'posher'.

Gerry Price's elder sister might live closer to Edge Hill than the poshest part of Wavertree, with its tennis club and its smart big houses, but she certainly acted as if she was something special, Rosie acknowledged as she got off the bus with her father and crossed the road to turn into Chestnut Avenue.

Since it was a summer Sunday it was no surprise that the avenue's inhabitants, especially its children, should be out enjoying the sunshine. Rosie was grateful for the warm smile one of a trio of young women, their gas masks slung casually from their shoulders, gave her as they walked past. The other two young women were both wearing smocks and were obviously pregnant, one of them holding on to a pretty little girl.

Rosie suppressed the sharp pang of envy she felt

for their friendship. The one who had smiled at her had her arm linked with the one without the little girl and it was obvious how close they all were.

'Come on, June,' Rosie heard her saying. 'We'd better be getting back, otherwise Dad will wonder what's happened to us.'

There had been no word at all from Bella since Rosie had last seen her, although to be fair she had heard that she had been spending most of her time at Podestra's, helping the family keep the chippie open. Rosie had tried to mend the breach between them. She had slipped a note through the Grenellis' front door, asking Bella if they could meet somewhere, and she had told her how much she missed them all and how much she would like to hear any news they had had of the men, especially Giovanni. She had waited eagerly, convinced that Bella would get in touch with her, and then when she hadn't done, Rosie had become very downcast and upset. After that rebuff she had told herself that she had too much pride to go running after a 'friend' who didn't want her friendship any more, but then her pride had crumpled and she had been so desperate to see Bella and have news of the family that she had gone to the chip shop and waited outside, hoping to catch Bella when she left work. However, when Bella had eventually come out, she had been with her intended, and his parents. Rosie had felt so uncomfortable about stepping forward when Bella was surrounded by other people that she had ducked back into the shadows, creeping away once they were safely out of sight.

She told herself that Bella knew where she was if she wanted to see her, but deep down Rosie grieved for the friendship she had lost, and found it hard to understand how Bella could neglect it either. She had tried to put herself in Bella's shoes and to imagine how she might have felt had their circumstances been reversed, but she just couldn't imagine ever not wanting Bella to be her friend.

Maude Leatherhall lived at number 29, one of a row of three red-brick houses that, like the rest of the estate, had been built by a private developer at the beginning of the century.

Heavy lace curtains shielded the interior from the curious stares of passers-by whilst, Rosie suspected, still allowing her aunt to keep a watch on everything that was going on. A privet hedge enclosed the small front garden and its immaculate 'rockery' of a few pieces of soot-lined limestone brightened by pockets of brightly coloured annuals, planted with regimented precision. The window frames and the front door were painted cream and green, and twice a year Maude summoned Rosie's father to come round to clear out her gutters and wash down her paintwork.

As they drew level with the gate, the ARP warden coming towards them slowed down, obviously wondering who they were. Since it was his responsibility to know the occupants of all the houses in his area, Rosie wasn't surprised to hear her father informing him easily, 'We're just visiting m'sister.'

'Thought I hadn't seen you around before,' the other man responded.

The path was so narrow that Rosie had to walk up it behind her father, but the front door opened so quickly after their knock that Rosie knew she had been right in thinking that her aunt kept a beady eye on the goings-on of the avenue from behind her lace curtains.

'Oh, you've brought Rose with you, have you?' Maude sniffed.

'It's a good while since you last saw her, Maudie, and I thought that with it being a Sunday and her being at work during the week, it would be a good opportunity for her to come along with me.'

'You'd better come in then,' was her grudging response as she led the way into the back parlour.

The house smelled of polish and pride. The parlour was cold, as though the sun never warmed it, the back door closed, unlike the door of the adjoining house, which Rosie could see through the window was propped open, as though in invitation to anyone who might want to call.

'I can't offer you a cup of tea, I'm afraid, not with this rationing.'

Rosie saw her father smile and reach into his pocket. 'You get that kettle on, Maudie,' he insisted, giving her a wink. 'I've brought you a bit o' summat you can put in your teapot.'

'I hope this isn't off that black market, Gerry.

You know I don't approve of that kind of thing, not like some I could name,' Maude answered disagreeably. But Rosie saw that she still took the packet of tea and the small bag of sugar her father was handing her.

'It's not black market. I bought the sugar in New York and traded the tea with another sailor.

'So how've you bin keeping, Maude?' he asked when she had filled the kettle and lit the gas.

'Well enough, I suppose, seeing as there's a war on, and I'm living on me own with no one to care what happens to me. A poor frail widow, that's what I am now, without my Henry. It takes all me strength some days just to get meself out of bed and dressed.'

Her aunt certainly didn't look or sound the slightest bit like a frail widow, Rosie reflected. She was a well-built woman, with a slightly florid complexion and a steely expression that made her look rather formidable. When war had first been announced Rosie had heard her mother saying to her father, 'Well, we won't need no tanks to defend Liverpool, not when we've got your Maude, what with her being built like one.' Rosie could see just what she meant.

'It was nice to see the young 'uns out in the street having a bit of fun when we walked up,' Rosie's father commented. 'This war is hard on them.'

'I'll thank you to remember that this is an avenue, not a street, if you please, Gerry, and if you ask me these modern youngsters have far too much fun. They make far too much noise as well. Of course,

I blame the mothers. It's not like it was in our day. I was saying as much to one of me neighbours the other day. Widowed like me, she is. Only she's got a son. Mind you, he's not going to be much comfort to her now he's gone and got himself married. She was telling me about all the trouble she's bin having with her daughter-in-law and now there's a baby coming. No sense of responsibility, some people haven't. You'd think the girl would know that a widow needs her son to look after her, especially now.

'Put me in mind of how Christine persuaded you into getting married before you'd known her five minutes. Which reminds me, there's a house just come up for rent at the other end of the street. You should go and have a word with the landlord, Gerry. It's a pity you didn't move up here years ago like I wanted you to, especially now that there's bin all that trouble with them Italians. Of course, it was bound to happen. Foreigners. Fascists. I've never understood how you could go on living down there instead of wanting to better yourself a bit.'

'Christine likes it . . .'

Rosie saw the way her aunt's whole face tightened, and her own stomach did the same as she anticipated what was going to come next.

'Well, you know my opinion, Gerry. You've let Christine have far too much of her own way. It's the man who earns the wages, and pays the bills, and if Christine hasn't got the sense in her head to know that you'd all be better off living up here, then you should put your foot down and make her see sense.'

'It doesn't seem fair for me to be telling Christine where she should live when I'm away at sea so much. Besides, Gerard Street's handy for the docks.'

'Yes, and it will be handy for Hitler's bombers when they come over as well, but I don't suppose she's thought of that. I don't suppose she thinks of anything other than doing her hair and painting her nails and going out spending your money. When was the last time she had a hot dinner waiting on the table for you when you got back from sea? I'll never know why you married her in the first place.'

Her father was looking red-faced and uncomfortable, and no wonder, Rosie thought angrily. Aunt Maude had no right to speak about her mother like that, but neither could she really blame her father for not trying to defend her. Somehow she didn't think that Aunt Maude would have been convinced. No wonder her mother had likened her to a tank. And no wonder too that she didn't want to come and live up here close to her sister-in-law. Rosie didn't blame her one little bit. Did her aunt ever have a good word to say about anything or anyone? Rosie wondered. She hoped they wouldn't have to stay for very much longer. Already she was longing for the visit to end.

'You didn't have much to say for yourself at your auntie's, Rosie,' her father commented when they were on their way home.

'I'm sorry, Dad, but I was afraid that if I opened my mouth, I'd say the wrong thing. I know she's my auntie and your sister, but it isn't right the way she's always finding fault with others, and especially with Mum.'

Her father sighed. 'No, they've never got on, and your mother doesn't help matters, acting the way she does when she does see her.'

Rosie gave him a swift look. 'Mum's always said that Aunt Maude didn't want you to marry her and that she didn't think she was good enough for you.'

'Aye, well, to be honest they never hit it off right from the start. I suppose with your Aunt Maude looking after me from being a nipper she was more like a mother to me than a sister, and I dare say she wouldn't have thought *any* girl was good enough for me. Of course, your mum doesn't see it that way. She reckons she's the one that could have done better for herself.'

'Well, I certainly don't think she could. No one could be better than you, Dad,' Rosie told him, rubbing her face against his shoulder. 'You're the best dad in the world.'

She could see the fine lines, put there by years of wind and salt spray, crinkling out from the corners of his eyes as he smiled. 'Go on with you, trying to soft-soap me.'

'I'm not. It's the truth. There's no one I would rather have as my dad than you.'

He looked down at her. 'Aye, well, there's no

lass I'd rather have as my daughter than you, Rosie.'

'It's just as well that I am then, isn't it?' she teased him, before raising herself up on her tiptoes to kiss his cheek. 'Come on,' she urged him. 'I'm getting hungry.'

'Well, your auntie was right about one thing: your mother won't have a dinner waiting for us.'

Rosie laughed. 'We can call at the chippie on the way back and get some pie and chips.'

'It's Sunday,' her father reminded her.

'Podestra's will be open. They always open on a Sunday,' Rosie told him, giving him her sunny smile and linking her arm through his.

'Rosie,' he suddenly stopped dead right in the middle of the road, reached out and took hold of her hand, 'if anything was to happen to me, I want you to promise me you'll mek sure you keep in touch with Auntie Maude. For my sake.'

Rosie stared up at him, the horror at what he was saying showing in her face. 'Don't talk like that, Dad,' she begged him fiercely. 'Nothing's going to happen to you. I won't let it . . .'

'Oh, well, if you won't let it then of course it won't,' he laughed, teasing her. 'I'll tell that Father Doyle that you've got the ear of God, shall I?'

'Don't talk daft,' Rosie smiled.

'I meant what I said about your Aunt Maude, though. Promise me, Rosie,' he repeated quietly, seriously.

'She doesn't like me, Dad. She loves you but she

105

doesn't even like me. And as for Mum . . . But all right, I promise, just for you,' she gave in.

'You've only got three days' shore leave, so why you have to go and spend one of them with your ruddy sister, I don't know,' Christine complained angrily before lighting a fresh cigarette and pacing the small parlour. 'All on me own, I've bin, all afternoon.'

'You could have come with us.'

'Huh, if you think I'm going visiting that old battleaxe you've got another think coming. I suppose she was calling me from here to New Brighton, was she, Rosie?'

'She never mentioned you, Mum,' Rosie fibbed.

'So what did she have to say for herself, then?' Christine demanded with narrowed eyes.

'She didn't say much at all, only that she wished we'd move up to Edge Hill.'

'Oh, I might have known. She won't rest until she's got you living up there and back under her thumb, Gerry. If you had anything about you you'd put her in her place good and proper.'

'She's me sister, Christine.'

'And I'm your wife. Wives come before sisters, and it's time you made sure she knows that. 'Cos if you don't, one of these days I will. You're just not man enough to stand up to her, that's your trouble. If you were a proper man you'd tell her that it's not up to her to say where we live.'

There was a bottle of gin on the table, and Rosie felt her heart sink as she listened to her mother's complaints. Christine often talked wildly when she'd had a few drinks.

'We brought you some pie and chips back,' she told her mother. 'It's in the oven, keeping warm.'

Christine had been out when they had got back and so they had eaten their own meal together without waiting for her. However, it seemed there was no pleasing her. Instead of being grateful that they had thought about her she burst out bitterly, 'Pie and bloody chips! If you was any sort of a man, Gerry, you'd make sure we had something a bit better than that on the table.'

'Like what?'

'A decent bit of meat, for a start.'

'There's a war on.'

'Yes, and there's a black market as well. If others can get it then why can't you? Kate Hannigan from five doors down was boasting the other week about how her Kieron works down the docks and brings them all sorts. Oh, there's no point in talking to you. I'm going out.'

'Mum . . .' Rosie protested, but it was too late; her mother was already yanking open the back door.

'Let her go, Rosie,' her father told her quietly.

'But she hasn't had anything to eat, and—'

'Your mother can look after herself.' There was an unfamiliar hard note in her father's voice. 'Come on, lass. I'll give you a hand with the dishes, and then how about we put the wireless on?'

*　*　*

'Look after yourself, Dad.' Rosie gave her father a fierce hug two days later, burying her face against the rough fabric of his jacket to hide her tears as she stood with him in the shadow of the grey-hulled ship towering over them.

Rosie had got permission from Mrs Verey to leave work early so that she could come down to the dock to say goodbye to him. Her mother had said that the salon was too busy for her to get time off and, as she always did when she witnessed the tension between her parents, Rosie wished desperately that things were different between them. It made her miss the warmth and conviviality of the Grenellis even more. Having her father home had eased the pain of that enforced separation. But now he was going again she felt more alone than ever.

'I'll bring you back some stockings, and maybe a bit of perfume,' her father promised.

Rosie shook her head. 'You just bring yourself back safe, Dad, that's all I want.'

She hugged him again one final time and then stood and watched as he joined the other men going on board, their kitbags slung over their shoulders.

A pretty blonde girl standing close to her was drying her tears, a shiny new wedding ring on her finger glinting in the sun. Rosie eyed her sympathetically as she stood watching the ship, sensing that, like her, she wouldn't move until the vessel had not only sailed, but disappeared completely from sight.

SEVEN

'Bella!'

Rosie had seen the other girl turning into Gerard Street ahead of her and she had hurried to catch up, thrilled to have a chance to speak to her at long last.

Bella might have stopped and turned round, but she was not returning her smile, Rosie saw. However, she was so pleased to see her friend that she immediately exclaimed, 'Oh, Bella, I've been thinking about all of you so much! I've been longing to come round and see how you all are. Has there been any news yet?'

'We've heard that Dad and Aldo are to be sent to the Isle of Man and interned there, but at least Granddad is going to be released and allowed to come home. Not that Liverpool feels like home to us any more after what's happened.' There was an unfamiliar stiffness, not just in Bella's voice but also in the way she was standing.

Looking at her, Rosie felt her excitement draining away into worry.

'Bella, please don't say that,' she begged her. 'This *is* your home, of course it is.' Hot tears filled Rosie's eyes as she reached out towards her. 'I miss you so much, I really do. I know we aren't related, but I think of you all as family.'

'But we aren't family, are we? We're Italian and you're English. The police didn't come for your father in the middle of the night and take him away, did they? He isn't being sent to a . . . a concentration camp . . .'

'Bella . . .' Rosie recoiled from her hostility.

'I'm sorry,' Bella told her, not sounding sorry at all, 'but it's the truth.'

What had happened to the soft, kind Bella she had thought she knew? Rosie didn't recognise this new Bella, who was looking at her with such contempt.

'When will your grandfather be home? Do you know?' she asked her eagerly, determined to ignore her hostility.

'No, not yet.' Bella's answer was given reluctantly, as though she would rather not have to talk to Rosie. 'We've heard that some of the men your government have decided are Fascists are going to be deported to Canada.'

Rosie didn't know what to say. There were so many conflicting stories and rumours going round the city, it was hard to know what was or wasn't the truth. She had read the papers avidly, looking for news about the Italians, and she understood why the government had felt it had to take a strong line on the real Fascists who might work against the country from inside it. And, of course, she had heard the nasty comments made by people like Nancy, who claimed that all Italians were tarred with the same brush.

'Well, when it comes to those that really are Fascists,' she offered awkwardly, 'then—'

Anger flashed in Bella's eyes. 'Showing your true colours now, aren't you? You're siding with your own government. What if they aren't? What if they are just innocent men like my dad and my granddad? You say you think of yourself as part of our family, but you don't and you aren't – you never were and never will be! How can you be? It's right what my mum says. You've got to stick with your own kind. How can you even begin to understand what it feels like to be me?'

'Oh, Bella,' Rosie protested, unable to hide her distress, but Bella shook her head and then pushed past her and hurried down the street, leaving Rosie to fight back her tears. She *was* trying to put herself in Bella's shoes, but it was hard when Bella was being so nasty to her, and acting as though they were enemies and not friends. She continued home, feeling more sick at heart than she had ever imagined she could feel, and wondering whether Bella would even speak to her again.

'I saw Bella when I was on my way home,' Rosie told her mother later. 'She told me that Carlo and

Aldo are being sent to the Isle of Man and that Grandfather Giovanni is going to be released.'

'Yes, I know,' Christine agreed carelessly. 'I managed to send word to Aldo when I was up at Huyton the other day, and he sent a message back to me.'

'You never said anything.'

Christine shrugged dismissively. 'So what? Pass us me ciggies, will you, Rosie?'

'So can anyone go up to Huyton and do that then?' Rosie asked her mother curiously. 'Only Bella never said that she'd been in touch with her dad.'

Christine lit her cigarette and blew out a ring of smoke, studying it for several seconds before replying, 'No they can't, and don't you go telling Bella that I've done it neither. It all depends who you know. It just happens that I've got to know one of the chaps up there on guard duty, and he sorted it all out for me.'

There was something that her mother wasn't telling her, Rosie felt sure, something about her story that didn't quite ring true.

'What do you mean, you've got to know one of the chaps?' she asked uncertainly. As a child Rosie had never questioned the fact that it was the men of the Grenelli household with whom Christine spent most of her time when they went there, but now as a young woman she hadn't been able to help noticing that her mother was a woman who seemed to prefer men's company to that of her own sex.

'Oh, for heaven's sake, Rosie, stop questioning me, will you? If you must know I do his wife's hair. Now give it a rest, will you? You're making me head ache.'

'What are we having for tea? There's some of that tinned fish left and we could make a bit of a fish hash pie with it,' Rosie suggested.

Christine shook her head. 'You have some if you want, but I don't want anything. I'm going out to the Gaiety with some of the others from the salon and then we're all going round to Flo's for a bit of supper afterwards. I don't know what time I'll be back. You know what that Flo is like once she's had a couple of drinks. She'll keep us natterin' at her place all night if we let her. I might even end up staying over with her. Are you doing anything?'

Rosie nodded. 'I've promised to meet up with Evie and her cousins and go to the pictures with them.'

'You mean you're going to the Gaiety as well?' Christine demanded sharply.

'No, Evie said to meet her up town outside Lewis's.'

'Well, just you mind what you're doing. Your dad thinks you're the next best thing to a ruddy angel and he won't be too pleased if he comes home to find you've gone and got yourself in trouble with some lad in a uniform who's taken himself off and left you.'

'There's no need to say that,' Rosie assured her

indignantly, her face pink. 'I know better than to let any lad mess around with me.'

'You can say that now, but there's a war on, remember. Maggie Sullivan, her as looks after Father Doyle and Father Morrison, was saying in the salon the other day that people are queuing up to book weddings, and that most of them should be booking the christening at the same time, by the look of them. And that's only them as are with lads who are willing to stand by them and do the decent thing. There's plenty of the other kind around who won't.'

'There's no need to worry on my account.'

'Well, you just make sure it stays that way. I've had enough trouble with your dad's bloomin' sister, without you giving her more ammunition to fire at me.'

'I don't know why you're having a go at me like this,' Rosie objected. 'I haven't done anything wrong.'

'Not yet you haven't. Like I just said, there's a war on,' her mother answered darkly.

Later that evening, queuing for the pictures with Evie and her cousins, Rosie had cause to acknowledge that her mother had a point when she claimed that the war was affecting the way people behaved. There were several couples in the queue who were wrapped in one another's arms and behaving as brazenly as you liked.

'Here, look at them two over there,' Evie urged Rosie, giving her a nudge in the ribs. 'Just look where he's got his hand! You won't catch me letting a fella show me up like that in public.'

Rosie peered over Evie's shoulder, automatically avoiding stepping back on the heavy sandbags, which had been put in place when war had first been announced, to protect buildings from bomb damage, but which were turning green, and leaking trickles of sand.

'No,' Jane giggled. 'Me neither. It's best waiting for the blackout if you want to get up to that kind of how's-your-father.'

It was impossible to pretend to be shocked and Rosie didn't try, joining in with their raucous laughter.

'They were doing this new dance at the Grafton last weekend. It's all the rage in London,' Evie informed the others. 'It's called "the Blackout Stroll". All the lights go off whilst you're dancing and then you change partners in the dark. Last weekend I ended up with this Canadian chap – a pilot he told me he was, and ever so handsome.'

Rosie could well imagine what her Aunt Maude would think of Evie's revelations.

The queue moved forward slowly. There was a big crowd to see the latest newsreels of the war, as well as the main film. Rosie loved the cinema; she had done ever since she was a small girl and her father would take her to see the latest Disney film as a treat when he was on leave. As she grew up, she couldn't wait for the Saturday afternoons of darkness and excitement, of adventure and passion. The women were all so beautiful, the men so brave.

But just because they fell in love and lived happily ever after, it didn't mean that that could happen to real people, Rosie always reminded herself warningly. She would hate to end up in a marriage like her parents', where one partner loved too much and the other not enough.

Now the cinema fulfilled a different function. It was a means of escape, certainly from the devastation and drudgery, but also it was a way of finding out more information on the hostilities, of seeing for oneself the progress of the war.

'Last time I came here they were still showing them newsreels of them taking the men off the beaches at Dunkirk,' Jane told them all, as the queue moved towards the door. 'Sobbed me heart out, I did.'

'Me an' all,' Evie agreed.

Rosie nodded. She couldn't imagine that anyone could not have been affected by the pictures of those brave men waiting patiently to be brought home to safety, knowing that the Germans were advancing on them.

In the clear evening sky the barrage balloons down by the docks were clearly visible, glowing a misty pink in the rays of the setting sun. Rosie couldn't look at them without a small shudder. They were a constant reminder, if one was needed, of the fact that they were at war. She shuffled along again, grateful of the chance to escape into the world of film for an evening.

*　　*　　*

'Well, I say that it's good riddance, and the more of them Eyeties they get on board the ships and get out of our country, the better,' Nancy insisted, taking a bite out of her sandwich and then pulling a face. 'Cheese again. I'm that sick of it.'

'You should think yourself lucky. I've only got a bit of pickle on mine,' Evie told her.

'Swap you one then,' Nancy offered. 'I'm surprised *you* haven't got summat to say about them Eyeties being shipped off, seein' as how you think so much about them,' she challenged Rosie.

They were all in the workroom having their dinner, and the truth was that Rosie was trying valiantly not to get dragged into the conversation Nancy had initiated about a ship – the *Arandora Star* – which had been lying off the Liverpool landing stage and had left in the early hours of the morning, sailing for Canada, carrying on board a large number of Italian and German internees. They were being sent to Canada where it was deemed by the government they would not be able to participate in the war as enemies of Britain.

'It must be very upsetting for Italian families who have lived here for a long time,' was all she allowed herself to say.

'Rosie's right,' Evie supported her. 'I wouldn't like it if it were my dad or hubbie wot was being sent all them miles away from me.'

'It's no different than having your dad or your man away fighting,' another girl chipped in. 'And

117

at least them Italians will be safe. No fighting for them like our lads are having to do.'

'A lot of the families have sons in the Forces,' Rosie felt bound to remind the others.

There'd been stories going round the neighbourhood about men returning from active duty or off their merchant ships to find their fathers and younger brothers missing and their mothers and sisters distraught. Rosie knew too that this was causing a lot of bad feeling amongst Italians who had previously considered themselves to be British, but who now, like Bella, felt alienated and badly done by. There had been talk too of members of those families who had relatives on board the *Arandora Star* going down to the landing stage in an attempt to say a final goodbye to their loved ones, but that armed guards had been posted there to prevent them from doing so. Rosie gave a small shiver. What a dreadful thing it must be to know that someone you loved was being sent so many thousands of miles away. It was different in families like her own, where the breadwinner was in the merchant navy. He might be gone for weeks on end sometimes and there was always the sea itself to fear but you knew that he would be coming back – at least you hoped. Those on board the *Arandora Star* could be separated from their families for years.

Although she had been hungry, suddenly Rosie couldn't stomach her sandwiches.

'Come on, back to work,' Evie called out as the

dinner bell rang, adding, 'A girl I know was telling me that in London the girls are getting dressed up and wearing long frocks now when they go out dancing. Mrs V. was saying as how she'd had one or two ladies in already asking if she can sort them out with evening frocks. I'm going to try and get meself a few yards of chiffon and satin and mek meself up something.'

'Satin and chiffon? Where do you think you'll get that?' Nancy scoffed.

'There's plenty of second-hand stuff around if you know where to look. What about it, Rosie? Why don't you do the same, so that we can go out together in them?'

'Don't you listen to her, Rosie,' another of the girls chipped in. 'You know what she's after, don't you? She can't set a stitch to save her life and she's hoping you'll make hers for her as well as your own.'

There was always some good-natured bantering going on amongst the girls so Rosie laughed and answered pacifyingly, 'Well, I don't mind doing that.'

'You're a real pal, Rosie,' said Evie warmly. 'And as a matter of fact, I do just happen to have seen a *really* nice dark red taffeta frock in a shop up by the Adelphi Hotel. Proper posh-looking it is, and I reckon it must have belonged to someone rich. The colour would suit you a treat. We could go and have a look on Saturday after work if you like.'

Rosie wasn't really sure she needed or even wanted a full-length evening dress but Evie was so enthusiastic she found herself giving in and agreeing. It would be a welcome distraction from her ever-confused thoughts. She did so miss the happy times she and Bella had shared when they had hurried off to St John's market to look for bargains.

'Ta-ra then. See you tomorrow,' Evie sang out when she and Rosie reached Great Crosshall Street where their routes home separated. 'And don't forget about Saturday and us going to look at that frock.'

Rosie still hadn't got used to the unfamiliar silence of the streets of Little Italy. Those Italian families that hadn't already moved to be with their relatives in Manchester or London, where there were larger Italian communities, were keeping themselves inside their houses, with the doors firmly closed against the outside world. Less than a month ago virtually every door would have been open, with women calling out to one another and children playing happily in the street, men pushing home their ice-cream carts and gathering on street corners to talk, whilst the sounds of music from accordions and flutes mingled with the smell of freshly ground coffee and herb-flavoured tomato sauce cooking, but now all that was gone.

Michael Farrell, whose wife, Bridie, did all the local laying-outs, was leaning against a lamppost, obviously the worse for drink.

'Oh, it's yourself, is it, Rosie,' he greeted her. 'And sad day this is and no mistake, all them poor sods drowning.'

As he spoke he was wiping his arm across his eyes to blot away his tears. 'Over a thousand of them, so I've heard. Aye, and the ruddy ship torpedoed by their own side. Complaining they was being sent to Canada, but there's many a family here in Liverpool will be wishing tonight that that's where they are instead of lying drowned at the bottom of the sea.' He swayed and staggered slightly, belching beer-laden stale breath in Rosie's direction but she barely noticed. A horrible cold feeling had seized her.

'What do you mean? What's happened? Tell me please,' she begged the Irishman.

He focused on her and blinked, hiccuping. 'It's that *Arandora Star* what was taking them Italians and Germans to Canada,' he told her. 'Gone and got itself sunk, it has.'

EIGHT

It couldn't be true. Michael Farrell must have got it wrong. But somehow Rosie knew that he hadn't. After she left him she started to walk home as fast as she could and then broke into a run, driven by a sickening sense of dread.

Her mother was in the kitchen. She was standing right beside the wireless, a fixed expression on her face, even though she was listening to someone singing. Rosie knew immediately that she too had heard what had happened.

'You've heard,' she still said.

Her mother nodded. 'Someone came and told us at the salon. There's bin hundreds drowned, so they say.'

'Has the BBC news . . . ?'

'I haven't heard anything official yet. Mind you, I haven't bin in that long.'

'It can't be true,' Rosie whispered, still unwilling to accept that something so terrible could have happened. 'The *Arandora Star* wasn't a warship. It was carrying Germans and Italians.'

Christine gave a small shrug. 'Well, perhaps someone ought to have told ruddy Hitler that.' She reached for her cigarettes, her hands trembling as she lit one. 'Apparently there's a crowd of women down at the docks already, waiting for news, daft sods. More than likely they'll be ruddy lucky to get a body back, never mind news, and it won't be here they'll dock, more likely somewhere up in Scotland.' She spoke with all the authority of a sailor's wife.

'At least the Grenellis weren't on board.' Rosie felt guilty even saying that when so many families would have had men on the ship. 'I'm going to go round and see them,' she announced. 'Why don't you come with me?'

Christine shook her head. 'We won't be welcome there, Rosie,' she warned. 'If I was you I'd stay away.'

'I can't do that. Not now that this has happened. And anyway, I don't understand why they don't want to be friends with us any more.' When her mother made no response she told her fiercely, 'I've got to go round; it wouldn't be right not to.' None of the Grenelli men would have been on board the *Arandora Star* but there were bound to have been men on the ship whom the family knew and Rosie felt she couldn't live with herself if she didn't at least go round and offer her sympathy and her help.

'Why don't you leave it until after your tea?' Christine suggested. 'There might have been something on the wireless by then.'

Rosie shook her head. 'I couldn't eat a thing. Not now . . .' she said, rushing out of the door.

As she slipped down the alleyway that led to the Grenellis' back door, Rosie could see Father Doyle up ahead of her, stepping into the home of one of the Italian families. Seconds later the fine hairs on Rosie's skin lifted at the unnerving sound of a woman's single solitary anguished scream of denial. The grief it held was like a physical blow.

Outside the Grenellis' back door Rosie hesitated. Her palms were sticky with sweat. What was she going to do if Bella's mother answered and slammed the door in her face or, even worse, started to shout at her? She took a deep breath, wiped her hands on her skirt and then knocked on the door before she could lose her nerve.

To her relief it was Bella who opened it, but there was no smile of welcome in her eyes or lifting of her mouth. Instead she looked as blankly at Rosie as though she had been a stranger.

'We've heard the news. I had to come,' Rosie began in a rush. 'I know that Carlo and Aldo and Granddad Giovanni weren't on board, but—'

Bella looked at her and then said bleakly, 'They *were* on board.'

Rosie's heart jerked. 'No,' she protested. 'You said . . . you told me *yourself* that Granddad Giovanni was coming home and that your father and Aldo were going to be interned on the Isle of Man.'

'They were, but some . . . someone my father owed a favour to asked if they would swap places with them.' The words came jerkily as though it hurt her to say them.

'I don't understand . . .'

'Families were being broken up, fathers sent to the Isle of Man, sons sent to Canada, brothers and cousins separated. Our most important men held a meeting at Huyton and it was decided to change around the papers everyone had been given so that families could stay together. There was one family . . . an important family in our community to whom my father owed . . . loyalty who had pieces of paper for the *Arandora Star*.'

'But the *Arandora Star* was sailing for Canada,' Rosie protested. 'And Grandfather Giovanni is so old, surely—'

'It was a matter of duty,' Bella told Rosie fiercely, 'a matter of honour; Grandfather agreed that my father had no choice. That is what my mother said. We only found out last night that they were to sail. There was a message . . .'

'No,' Rosie repeated. A wave of sickening heat surged over her and then retreated, leaving her feeling icy cold and trembling violently. She desperately wanted to sit down. But how could *she* give in to her weakness when Bella was standing there looking so in control of herself? 'Maybe they weren't on the *Arandora Star*? I've heard that there is another ship sailing tomorrow. Maybe—'

'No. We know they sailed on the *Arandora Star*.'

'There will be survivors,' Rosie told her eagerly. 'Maybe—'

'My grandfather can't swim; he is old; they were put in the very bottom of the ship. This is what we know and what we have been told. The German sailors, they will have survived, but not our men.'

'You can't know that,' Rosie protested. 'Bella, you mustn't give up hope. Not yet.'

'Who are you to tell us not to give up hope?' Bella rounded on her bitterly. 'We should not need to have hope. Our men should not have been taken away and imprisoned. They should not have been sent to Canada. I will *never* forget what your country has done to us, Rosie, and I will *never* forgive it. My mother is right – you are all our enemies.'

'Bella, that isn't true.' Rosie was trembling with the force of her emotions.

'Isn't it? Ask your father what he thinks of us, Rosie; ask those men who rioted against us and destroyed our homes. Go and ask them if they are our friends.'

'My father wouldn't have wanted this. He's a sailor. No sailor would ever want something like this to happen.' She knew that that was true, but she also knew that Bella was right and that her father had never really understood her mother's friendship with the Grenellis.

Bella gave a small uncaring shrug. 'It doesn't matter much any more. We are leaving Liverpool as soon as it can be arranged. We have relatives in Manchester who will take us in, for how are we to

126

earn a living now when there is no sugar for us to make ice cream and no men to sell it? You'd better go,' she added coolly. 'My mother will be coming downstairs in a minute and if she knows that you are here she won't be pleased.'

Rosie wasn't quite sure how she managed to get home. She certainly couldn't remember walking there. She stood in the middle of the shabby parlour and told her mother emotionally, 'I've just seen Bella. They *were* on board, all three of them – her father, Grandfather Giovanni and Aldo.' And then her whole body was shaking, racked by the sobs that seemed to be being torn away from her heart itself.

'Stop that.'

The sharp slap her mother gave her shocked her into a stunned silence. Her cheek burned. Slowly she lifted her hand to touch it.

Her mother's eyes were glittering with anger, her own face burning almost as bright a red as Rosie's cheek.

'You must have misunderstood what Bella was saying. Mind you, she's as much of a drama queen as that ruddy mother of hers. Their men couldn't have been on board. I spoke to Aldo meself on Saturday night. He told me then that they was going to the Isle of Man.'

'You *spoke* to Aldo? But that's impossible. You couldn't have done. No one was allowed to talk to the men.'

'Well, I did. And don't go looking at me like that.

It's the truth. Like I've already told you, there's always ways and means, Rosie, if you know how to go about things and you know the right people. Bella's got it wrong. Aldo was full of it, and that relieved . . .'

'Bella said that they'd changed places with someone,' Rosie stopped her mother quietly.

Between one breath and another Rosie saw her mother's expression change, and the colour leave her face, only to rush back into it to burn in two bright spots on her cheeks.

'The stupid bastard,' she breathed. 'The stupid, stupid bastard. I warned him not to . . .' Suddenly it was her mother who was shaking from head to foot. She dropped down into a chair and leaned her elbows on the table, holding her head in her hands.

'Mum . . .' Rosie begged her uncertainly. She was upset – devastated – but her mother was inconsolable.

'It's that ruddy Carlo – he's the one who's responsible for this.' It was as though she was talking to herself. 'He's the one who dragged Aldo into that Fascist lot on account of Sofia nagging at him. She's the one who's to blame for them all being drowned . . . She might as well have murdered them with her bare hands.'

Had the news somehow affected her mother's brain? How was it possible for her to know so much?

'We don't know what . . . what's happened yet, Mum. They might still be alive . . .'

Her mother was giving her the same look that Bella had given her when she had said that to her.

'No, they won't be alive,' she told Rosie bitterly. 'I need a drink.'

'I'll put the kettle on,' Rosie offered.

'Not that kind of drink. A proper drink. There's a bottle of gin in the sideboard – go and get it for us.'

'Mum, I don't think—'

'All right, don't get it, I'll go and get it meself,' she glowered.

'I don't understand,' Rosie protested. 'Why did they change places with these other people, and why did you say it was Sofia's fault? They aren't Fascists.'

'Aldo certainly wasn't. Sofia's had it in for Aldo for a long time – well, I hope she's happy now with what she's gone and done.'

'I don't understand,' Rosie repeated.

'No, you don't understand, Rosie, and that's the ruddy truth.'

It was another week before they knew for sure that the Grenelli men were indeed amongst those missing, presumed drowned. And not once in that week had the Grenellis' door opened to Rosie's knock, even though she had gone round every day hoping to be allowed to share their grief. Rosie went with her mother to the service that was being held at Holy Cross in memory of those who had died, both of them dressed in their most sombre clothes.

The church was packed full, and it was almost

impossible to hear the voice of the priest because of the noise of women crying, Rosie and her mother included. And then during the prayers one woman screamed so loudly in her despair that Rosie thought she herself was going to faint from her pain. The grief they were all feeling couldn't be contained. It spilled over and filled the church as the mourners gave themselves over to it.

All Rosie could think about was how the Grenellis must be feeling and how much she wished she had been allowed to share this dreadful time with them. All week she had hoped that today of all days they would relent and accept that although she and her mother were not Italian, they shared their sense of loss and bewilderment. But the church was so packed that it was impossible to find anyone particular amongst the huge crowd. Many of the widows and children of the men who had lost their lives were given seats at the front of the church, but although Rosie craned her neck to see if the Grenellis were amongst them, she couldn't find their familiar faces.

The grief of the mourners brought home to Rosie not just the cruel tragedy of what had happened but also the reality of what it meant to have a beloved husband or father die in such a dreadful way. It had always been her fear that one day her own father might not return home, and witnessing the anguish here reinforced that fear and added to her grief for all the lost lives.

She and her mother clung to one another for support when they left the church after the service.

Rosie had never seen Christine so emotionally affected by anything. For once her mother was not wearing her trademark mascara and bright red lipstick, and it tore at Rosie's tender heart to see her looking so unexpectedly vulnerable, as some of their Italian neighbours glowered pointedly at them, making it plain that they considered them to be outsiders.

'Did you see the way that Carlo Cossima were looking at us, like we was to blame for what's happened, when it were me wot tried to save Aldo? If there's anyone to blame for them drowning then it's that Sofia and not me,' Christine wept as she clung to Rosie.

Rosie could feel her mother trembling. She squeezed her arm, trying to comfort her, not trusting herself to speak. Her mother seemed fixated on Aldo's fate, whereas Rosie recognised that it was for all of their men that most of the women had come to mourn, and that was why they were looking so bitterly at them – because they were English and it was the British Government they believed had sent their men to their deaths.

Everyone had been saying that the war was going to change people's lives for ever, but Rosie felt sure that nothing else could ever have the impact on hers that the internment and deaths of the Italian men from Liverpool had had. She felt bereft without the closeness and friendship of the Grenellis, but her pain went deeper than that, and she knew that a part of her would never recover from the words

Bella had thrown at her. They had grown up together, both innocent of any differences between them, bonded by a friendship Rosie had believed would last for ever. But now that innocence was gone. Rosie's tender heart ached for all the Italian families who had suffered so much pain and loss, but it ached as well for her own loss.

It ached too for her mother, who had begun to frighten Rosie with the way she was drinking. All week Rosie had lain in bed at night, hearing her mother walking around downstairs, wanting to go down to her to beg her to come up to bed, but knowing that Christine would have had too much to drink to pay any attention to her. It had been the early hours before she had eventually come upstairs and then in the morning she had been sleeping so heavily that Rosie had been unable to wake her up properly so that she could go to work. Rosie was astonished that her mother had actually made it to the service.

She longed for her father to come home, and yet at the same time she felt guilty because he was alive whilst so many other men from the neighbourhood were dead. Over seven hundred had drowned, so it said in the papers, most of them Italian. Amongst them had been the man she had thought of almost as her own grandfather. She and Bella should have been mourning his loss together, supporting one another and comforting one another. How could her friend not understand that she had loved him too?

Everyone else who had been at the service would

be going home with family members with whom they would share their mourning. Only she and her mother had no one else to grieve with, Rosie acknowledged, as she guided her mother back down their street, past the familiar door that was now closed against them.

Surely it wasn't possible to cry any more. She had cried so much that her tears had run dry and her heart had cracked with pain. Across the landing in her own bedroom her mother would be lying motionless in the bed Rosie had managed to help her into last night – when she had gone downstairs, worried by her silence, to find her collapsed across the kitchen table, an empty bottle of gin telling its own story.

Her mother was suffering just as she was herself, Rosie knew. She had never seen her looking so wretched. Surely it would soften Sofia's heart if she could see how much her mother mourned the men they had all lost? Rosie couldn't believe how hard-hearted Sofia was being. She knew that if their circumstances were reversed she could not have denied Sofia or Bella the comfort of sharing her grief.

It was only six o'clock, too early for Rosie to get up for work, but she knew that she wouldn't be able to go back to sleep. Pushing back the bedclothes, she put her feet on the cold lino and then padded into the bathroom.

Half an hour later, when she heard the milk cart being pulled up the road by the patient horse, she opened the front door, only to stand there in shock as she saw that the front door to the Grenellis' house was open and furniture was being carried out and put into a waiting van.

As Rosie watched she saw first Bella, who was dragging a heavy-looking shabby suitcase, and then Sofia and Maria, who were escorting between them the bowed figure of la Nonna emerging from the house.

The sight of la Nonna and Maria galvanised Rosie into action. She rushed out and across the street, coming to a halt in front of Bella.

'Bella, what's going on? What are you doing?' Rosie demanded.

For a moment she thought that Bella wasn't even going to answer her, but then a young man whom Rosie recognised as Bella's intended stepped out of the van to take her suitcase and give Rosie a frowningly critical look.

'If you want me to handle this, Bella . . .' he began.

'No, it's all right, Alberto,' Bella told him, before turning to Rosie and saying coldly, 'What does it look like we're doing?'

'You're moving? Without saying anything. Without . . .'

'Without what? Without our menfolk? Oh, you may well look like that, but it isn't you that's without a father and a grandfather, Rosie, for all that you've bin acting like you are, turning up at our memorial service where you had no right to be, and crying like you had lost someone.'

'You saw me? I looked for you but—'

'Oh, yes, I saw you, and as for you looking for us, well, we was with those of our kind, thank you very much. We don't need any pity from English folk like you.'

'Bella, why are you being like this with me? I loved Giovanni and the others. You know that. Bella, I miss you so much. We've been friends for so long . . .'

'That was then, Rosie; this is now, and you and me aren't friends no more. I don't want you for my friend now. All I want is to be with my own kind. Me and Alberto are going to get married and then we're going to go back to Italy just as soon as we can. That can't happen soon enough for me. No way do I want my children to be born here where my sons could be taken away from me and drowned at sea.'

'But Alberto naturalised and so he's British – that's why he wasn't taken with the others,' Rosie pointed out. 'It was only the men who didn't take up British nationality when they were offered the chance who were rounded up.'

'He might have naturalised but that means nothing to him now, not after what's happened,' Bella told her bitterly.

Whilst they had been talking Alberto had been helping Sofia and Maria get la Nonna into the van. Now, ignoring Rosie completely, he gave Bella a brief nod.

'Bella,' Rosie protested as her friend walked past

135

her to join her mother, but Bella totally ignored her as she and Sofia climbed into the van.

Only Maria was left, having gone back to close and lock the front door.

Sick with misery, Rosie reached pleadingly towards her, begging her tearfully, 'Mamma Maria, please, at least say that you'll write to me. I love you all so much . . .'

Maria's eyes filled with tears. '*Ah, bambina,*' she whispered chokily, responding to Rosie's despair and opening her arms to her.

But before Rosie could go into them, Sofia was there, almost dragging her sister away, hissing at Rosie as she did so. 'Go away, and stop upsetting my poor sister. You are nothing to us – nothing!'

Sofia had bundled Maria into the van and followed her inside it before Rosie could react. She heard the engine being started but was unable to move, tears pouring down her face, watching as it trundled down the road.

It was only when it turned the corner and disappeared from sight that Rosie gave a sharp forlorn cry and started to run after it. But it was already too late. The van was gone, and with it her hopes of a reconciliation with those she loved so very dearly.

PART TWO

October 1940

NINE

'Well, we might 'ave won the Battle of Britain, but it ain't doin' us much good here in Liverpool, is it?' one of the girls complained as they all sat down in the workroom of Elegant Modes to eat their dinner. 'There's bin that many bombs dropped on the docks that my da says we'll be having Hitler and his army marching up Scotland Road by Christmas.'

'We'll have less of that talk, if you please, Marjorie Belham,' Enid, who was now the senior sales assistant, ticked off the new junior sharply. 'Walls have ears, just you remember.'

The new junior blushed fiery red, her small face burning.

Sympathetically Rosie went to sit next to her and gave her a reassuring smile. 'Don't let her upset you,' she whispered. 'Her bark's worse than her bite, and I dare say she meant it for the best.'

''Ere, Rosie, you're still coming down the Grafton wi' us tonight, aren't you?' Sylvia Bennett, another new girl, demanded, planting herself down on the bench next to Rosie.

There had been several changes at the shop over the summer, some girls leaving and others taking their places, and Rosie had been relieved when Nancy had been one of those to leave.

'Yes, but I don't want to stay late because I've got to go to a fire-watch drill on Sunday morning,' she warned.

The government had given instructions that everyone over sixteen who was physically able to do so had to take their turn on fire-watch duty of their local area, and under the guidance of their local ARP officers everyone had to attend regular fire-watch and fire-fighting drills.

During the summer months these drills had been treated with derision and mockery by some people but September's bombing raids on the docks had brought home to the inhabitants of Liverpool just how vigilant they needed to be. The city's Central Station had been hit on the night of 21 September, and some coaching stock had been damaged. Then five nights later there had been heavy bombing over the docks and warehouses, with a huge fire at one dock that was still burning twenty-four hours later. Two theatres, one the world-famous Argyle Theatre in Birkenhead, had been set alight by incendiary bombs, but most telling of all was the fact that the bombing raids had started off what was now a regular late afternoon trek to air-raid shelters by mothers and children who lived down by the docks.

Rosie had seen them on her own way home from work, her heart aching for them and for the city of her birth. Their own street was just about far enough away from the docks to be considered that bit safer, and the houses that had been left empty by the exodus of Italian families moving to Manchester or London were now being taken over by new tenants. The street might be coming to life again, but it was not the same and it never could be.

Rosie would never forget those who had been lost and the friendship that had been destroyed, but she had willed herself not to dwell on what had happened or to think too often or too unhappily about Bella and the rest of the Grenelli family. But sometimes it was hard, and she still missed her friend very much.

'Oh Gawd, I hate them drills,' Sylvia grimaced, joining in the conversation. 'Last time I had to go to one I had to crawl through this smoke tunnel they'd set up, helping to drag this bloomin' stirrup pump, and I thought I were going to choke to death. Wot I want to know is, what 'ave we got a fire service for? It should be them wot's dealing wi' fires, not us.'

Rosie tried to give Sylvia a warning shake of her head but it was too late. Bernadette Chester, whose husband was a full-time fireman working down by the docks, had heard her comment and, putting down her sandwiches, she stood up and put her hands on her hips.

'We have to do our duty and watch out for fires

because our firemen are risking their lives down on the docks tryin' to save the ships and their cargoes that this country needs for the war effort, that's why,' Bernadette told Sylvia angrily. 'Five nights in a row my Jack hasn't made it home this week on account of them being called out to the docks. Nearly got his bloody head blown off last week, he did, when they was ordered to go into one of the warehouses that was on fire. He's already lost two mates, and another one is in Mill Road Hospital and not likely to come out alive, so don't you go talking your selfish talk about not wantin' to do your bit.'

'I'm sorry, Bernadette,' Sylvia apologised immediately, white-faced. 'I wasn't meaning no 'arm. I just meant it as a bit of a joke. I just wasn't thinking, that was all.'

'Aye, well, next time perhaps you just had better think before you go saying summat stupid,' Bernadette told her sharply. But to Rosie's relief Bernadette was looking slightly mollified, and was sitting down again and picking up her sandwiches.

The early September euphoria of the RAF winning the Battle of Britain had caused great jubilation, but that had made the crash back to the harsh reality of the war all the harder to take when the bombs had started falling again on Liverpool's dockland area.

Now Rosie prayed not only that her father would be safe at sea, but that when he did come back it would not be in the middle of one of the bombing raids.

'I'm getting that fed up of working here that I'm thinking of going for a new job at Bear Brand's,' Sylvia whispered to Rosie. 'I've got a cousin who works there and she was saying as how you get given stockings as part of your wages. Aye, and if you play your cards right, there's a foreman there what will see to it that you get more than one pair an' all, if you get on the right side of him, if you know what I mean.'

The saucy wink that accompanied Sylvia's comment made Rosie choke on her sandwich.

Sylvia was a one and no mistake. She had certainly livened up the atmosphere at the shop since she had come to work there in July. She was the youngest of a big family, with older sisters who liked their fun, and so although she was younger in years than Rosie, being only sixteen, in terms of worldly experience and knowledge she was very much Rosie's senior.

Rosie had desperately missed the closeness of her relationship with Bella, and so had welcomed Sylvia's overtures of friendship, even though she knew that no one could ever replace Bella. In the early weeks after Bella had gone, Rosie had hardly been able to bear walking past their empty house. Even going to church had reminded her painfully of all those occasions during their shared growing-up when they had gone there together hand in hand, and walked together in all the special saints' day processions the Italians loved so much. When Bella had ended their friendship she had taken away

143

with her a huge chunk of Rosie's childhood, and Rosie felt that nothing could ever be the same again.

But with a war on, people were having to cope with much worse than losing a best friend. Rosie knew that, and she felt that it was her duty to try to put a brave face on her misery and get on with things as best she could, just like others were having to do. And so when Sylvia had made it plain she wanted them to be pals, Rosie had told herself that she was very lucky to have a new friend in her life.

'We can have much more fun if we pal up together,' had been Sylvia's shrewd comment when she had suggested that she and Rosie started going out to the cinema and the Grafton together. 'We can watch each other's backs and mek sure that we don't get landed with the lads that we don't want.'

'How would we do that?' Rosie had asked her naïvely.

Sylvia had heaved a sigh, rolled her eyes and then informed her firmly, 'You don't know much, do you? We'll have a little sign that we give one another when a chap asks us to dance – you know, like a wink means clear off and leave me wi' him and a frown means you're not interested, that kind of thing.'

A little uncertainly Rosie had agreed, but so far she hadn't seen Sylvia do much frowning.

'I want to go to Houghtons before we go dancing. I need some more leg tan and they mek their own, and our Jean says that it gives a really nice tan colour. Do you fancy coming with us, Rosie?'

Houghtons shop in the Old Swan area was out of Rosie's direct route home but good-naturedly she agreed.

'I just hope that we don't get any bombers coming over tonight,' Evie Watts said tiredly. 'Her next door to us has a new baby and it's bin bawling its head off every night since she brought it home. What wi' it, and having to go down the air-raid shelter, I'd give anything for a decent night's sleep.'

'We haven't bin bothering usin' the shelter this last week,' Sylvia announced. 'Me cousin Frank reckons there isn't any point, and that if a bomb's got your number on it, it will find you anyway.'

'Well, more fool you, that's what I say,' Bernadette told her critically, adding firmly, 'Rules is rules, after all.'

'Oh, trust her to think that. She's a real miss goody-goody,' Sylvia whispered to Rosie.

The buzzer rang, warning the girls that a customer had entered the shop.

'I'll go,' Clarice Baird, one of the other girls, announced, jumping up determinedly.

'It isn't your turn. It's Rosie's,' Sylvia tried to stop her, but Rosie shook her head.

'Why did you let her take your customer, Rosie?' Sylvia demanded indignantly when Clarice had gone. 'If she makes a sale then that's threepence in the pound you've lost. She's allus pushing in and taking customers when it isn't her turn, and it's not as though any of us is paid that much.'

This was true. Rosie earned twelve shillings and sixpence a week, whilst the new girls received only ten shillings, so every penny of commission the girls earned was worth having.

'It doesn't matter, Sylvia,' Rosie told her friend. 'After all, it's not as though we've got that much stock left to sell now, what with Mrs Verey deciding that she's only going to hire out gowns and wedding dresses now until the end of the war.'

The elegant and expensive clothes sold in the shop had come mainly from France, and with the fall of that country Mrs Verey had swiftly recognised that she would not be able to replace her stock. She had been fortunate to have obtained a large delivery of silk underwear, blouses and accessories just prior to Dunkirk, but as she had told the girls, if clothing coupons came in, as she had heard they would, then the shop would not have any customers for these expensive items anyway.

'We're still getting soldiers and the like coming in, though, wanting to buy bits and pieces for their girls, and with the prices Mrs Verey is charging for her stock, even selling a pair of knickers adds to your commission.'

'I know that,' Rosie agreed, 'but Clarice was telling me the other day that they've had a telegram to say that her dad's missing, presumed dead,' she told her friend quietly. 'There's six younger than her at home, and they need every penny she can earn.'

'Aye, well, there's plenty that's in the same boat. By, but you're a real softie, Rosie. Fall for any hard luck tale, you would.'

'Dinner break's over, you two, just in case you hadn't noticed,' Bernadette interrupted them sharply.

'Aw, give us a chance, Bernadette,' Sylvia protested. 'It's not as though there's a shopful waiting to be served, after all.'

'Mebbe not, but there's plenty of stock wants an ironing, and Mrs Verey will be wanting someone to take the money over to the Midland Bank this afternoon.'

Sylvia pulled a face behind Bernadette's departing back. 'I hate doing that bloomin' ironing.'

'Well, mind you don't scorch anything,' Rosie warned her, knowing Sylvia was easily distracted and quite careless. 'Otherwise you won't be getting any wages until you've paid for it.'

'I don't know why I bothered gettin' teken on here. There's better jobs going wi' more pay and more fun, an' all. They're paying five pounds per night for night shift work at the munitions factory, so I've heard.'

'That's dangerous work, though, and the girls end up all yellow,' Rosie pointed out. 'I've heard that there's been a few accidents and that one girl got her fingers blown clean off.'

'Ooooh, don't, Rosie, you're mekin' me feel right sickly. Fancy havin' that happen to you.'

'I don't. That's why I wouldn't go and work

there,' Rosie told her firmly. She had developed an almost elder sisterly protectiveness towards Sylvia, whom she thought was the last girl suited to work with anything as dangerous as munitions. It might seem unkind to tell her something so horrible, but Rosie hoped it would stop Sylvia taking a job where she was all too likely to end up hurting herself. The shop buzzer rang again and Rosie stood up, smoothing down her skirt and checking her hair before hurrying to answer it.

Two women, obviously mother and daughter, were waiting in the shop, the girl's face animated and excited, and the mother's tight with maternal anxiety.

'Miss Price will show you the wedding gowns we have for hire, Mrs Simpson,' Mrs Verey was informing them as Rosie stepped into the room.

The bride-to-be wasn't much older than she was herself, Rosie assessed as she led the way to the salon at the rear of the shop, which was kept especially for the trying-on of bridal and evening gowns.

Rosie realised that it had been a shrewd move on Mrs Verey's part to conserve her stock by hiring out gowns instead of selling them outright, but she could see too that Mrs Simpson was not happy about the idea of her daughter wearing a dress already worn by someone else. They were the kind of customers Rosie had grown used to since coming to work at the shop – well-to-do, with a different way of speaking to her own – posh folk from higher up in Wavertree. But as Rosie listened to the bride-to-be explaining shyly that her fiancé was a pilot in the RAF, and realised that her mother's tight-faced anxiety was caused by her concern both for her young daughter, her fiancé, and her own son whose friend he was, Rosie recognised that whatever their social position, the Simpsons were just as vulnerable to losing their loved ones to the war as everyone else.

It was some time before the bride-to-be and her mother had finally chosen a lovely duchesse satin dress with a fitted bodice and beautifully draped full-length skirt.

The dress had a fifteen-foot-long train in the same heavy satin, and the young bride pulled a face and complained to Rosie, 'I'm sure I shall never be able to keep it straight when I walk down the aisle,' as Rosie kneeled on the floor to pin the hem of the dress, which needed shortening.

'Don't be silly, darling,' her mother chided her. 'Your matron of honour will see to it that the little bridesmaids and pages do that.'

'That's all very well, Mummy, but if I have to have Hugo and Charles, one of them is sure to tread on it. Wretched little beasts.'

'Darling, they are your cousins,' her mother protested, whilst Miss Simpson gave Rosie a meaningful look.

Rosie responded with a sympathetic smile as she marked out the other small alterations that would be needed. Although socially they were poles apart,

Rosie couldn't help but like the girl, and feel sympathetic towards her in her anxiety for her special day to go well. It would certainly be a shame if such a beautiful dress were spoiled by the clumsiness of two little boys.

When Rosie returned with them to the main part of the shop, the girl's fiancé and her brother, who had subsequently arrived, were patiently waiting, both young men looking very handsome in their RAF uniforms.

A small pang clenched Rosie's heart as she watched them leave. The engaged couple were so obviously in love and so happy together. It must be wonderful to feel like that, Rosie decided. Deep down she longed to have a truly happy marriage filled with mutual love. The kind of marriage that so far her experience of life had shown her was more of a dream than reality. But maybe one day she would meet someone special and they would fall deeply in love with one another. It would be wonderful if that were to happen. It was her most secret and special dream and one she had not even shared with Bella, knowing that Bella's views on marriage were far more practical than her own.

Dreamily Rosie imagined how wonderful it would be to have met her special someone and be planning her own wedding. She would have a simple very plain wedding dress, trimmed with lovely French lace, and she would carry a bouquet with white freesias in it. They had always been Maria's favourite flower because of their wonderful scent. Tears blurred

Rosie's eyes. Very fiercely and determinedly she blinked them away.

'I suppose you'll be off down the Grafton tonight, will you?' Rosie's mother asked her. 'Only I'm going out meself tonight, wi' some of the others from the factory.'

Her mother had left the hairdressers and was now working at Littlewoods parachute factory off Hanover Street instead. Although it was further away from their home than the hairdressers she claimed that it was easier to get to since, because it was war work, the company laid on transport to take the women to and from work. The factory also had a canteen, and once a month the management put on a show for the workers with well-known singers like Vera Lynn coming in to sing for them. The pay was better as well, Christine had told Rosie – nearly five pounds a week if you worked evening shifts, which was a huge amount compared to Rosie's own earnings. Money they could do with, Christine had announced, with a war on and having to pay extra for 'under the counter' luxuries, like proper soap, tinned fruit and nylon stockings, if you wanted them, and them with no extra money coming in to pay for things like that with Rosie's father away at sea for weeks on end.

'Yes, I am.'

'You haven't got a spare pair of stockings you could lend me, I don't suppose?'

Rosie shook her head. 'I've got some leg tan, though, from Houghtons. I called there on the way home.'

'Oh, well, I suppose that will have to do, but mind you wash all yours off when you come back. I don't want to be washing sheets all covered in leg tan stains come Monday. I've got better things to do wi' me time than run around all over the place looking after you. You're not a kiddie any more, Rosie, and I've got a right to a bit of life of me own, especially now that there's a war on and none of us know whether or not we'll be here tomorrow.'

Rosie shivered. 'Don't say that, Mum.'

'Why not? It's the truth, after all. And you won't catch me staying at home knitting like some folks seem to think I should, when I could be out dancing and having a good time.'

Rosie didn't say anything. Since she started working at the factory Christine had become worse, acting more as if she was a girl of Rosie's age than a grown woman and a mother. It made Rosie feel both uncomfortable and angry.

'You haven't forgotten that Dad's ship is due in next week, have you, Mum?' she asked her mother now, anxious she should be home to greet him, especially after last time.

'No, I haven't,' she replied, and then started to frown. 'You wouldn't be trying to drop hints about something, would you? 'Cos if you are, like I just said, if I want to go out and have a bit of fun then that's my business and not yours.'

Rosie's face burned. None of the other girls she knew had mothers who went out dancing, or who behaved in the way that her mother did.

'It doesn't seem right that you should be going out when Dad's not here,' she protested awkwardly.

Immediately her mother gave her an angry look and demanded, 'What do you expect me to do? Stay in and be miserable? I've allus said that you tek after your dad more than you do me. A dead ringer for that sister of his, you are. And who are you to tell me what to do? I suppose your dad's bin telling you to spy on me, has he? Well, if he doesn't like it, he knows what he can go and do. There's plenty of men around who appreciate a woman who likes a bit of fun. You should hear the compliments that manager down at the factory gives me, when he sees me. A proper gentleman, he is, and no mistake.' Christine tossed her head vainly. 'I'll bet he knows how to treat a woman.'

Her mother's words were conjuring up a mental picture inside Rosie's head that brought a hard lump of misery to her throat. But she knew better than to tell her mother how she felt. The war seemed to be changing so much and Rosie wasn't sure that she liked some of the changes. The city was full of young men in uniform, some of whom were a bit too free with their attentions. Rosie had been forced tactfully to reject the too flirtatious remarks of a couple of young soldiers only the previous week, when they had stopped her in the street when she was on her way home from work, pretending that they wanted a light for their cigarettes. They had taken her polite rebuff goodnaturedly, fortunately. Many, though, were not as respectful as they might be in the opinions of protective parents of young women. Not that her own mother would care what she got up to so long as it didn't affect her.

The dance halls were full of men from the Forces, standing round the dance floor, eagerly watching the girls and trying to catch their eye. Some girls encouraged them, enjoying flirting with them, but Rosie preferred to keep them at a bit of a distance.

To Rosie's relief her mother had already left the house when she came downstairs. She had deliberately lingered in her room rather than come down and risk provoking another argument.

As she walked through the streets, Rosie looked around her with new, more worldly eyes. The sparkle and magic, the hustle and the bustle of the place had left with the Grenellis. It seemed to Rosie now that without the Grenellis and the other Italians, not only had the heart gone out of the area, but somehow the warmth seemed to have gone out of her mother as well, turning her into a different kind of person.

Rosie often thought about their friends, especially Bella, and hoped that somehow they were managing to survive the war without their men. The dreadful nature of their deaths, so cruel and so unnecessary, had left a permanent shadow on Rosie's own heart. She often visited the small memorial that had been placed in the churchyard to commemorate the deaths of those, like the Grenelli men, whose bodies had not been recovered. Every Sunday when she went to church she said a special prayer for them, and for those who were having to go on living without them. It was hard at times not to let her grief overwhelm her, but Rosie knew that she had to try.

She forced herself to focus on the evening ahead. Sylvia would certainly be eager to have a jolly time and that would help cheer her up as well, Rosie acknowledged.

Sylvia was a true scouser with a true scouser's wry sense of humour and, as shocked as she sometimes was by the things Sylvia came out with and did, Rosie couldn't help but laugh at her cheeky jokes and good humour. Small and on the thin side, Sylvia had a brazen cheekiness about her that half shocked Rosie and yet at the same time lifted her spirits. Sylvia was as different from Bella as it was possible for two girls to be.

Bella . . . She must stop grieving for her lost friendship and accept that Bella and her family had needed to get away from everything and everyone that reminded them of what they had lost. She hoped that they had found some comfort in the large Italian community that lived in Manchester, and that Bella was happy with Alberto. Were they married yet? Had Bella thought of her on their wedding day and how she had always sworn that she would not get married without Rosie being her chief bridesmaid? They had even planned the colour of Rosie's dress – pale pink to match her name – and the flowers Bella had wanted her to carry.

Rosie could feel her throat thickening with tears. The past was over, she reminded herself fiercely. Over . . . like Bella's friendship. She had to concentrate on the present now and her new life without Bella. A life that included new people and friends, like Sylvia.

Rosie could feel her misery lightening as she thought about her giddy new friend. No one could be around Sylvia for very long and remain down in the dumps.

'What do you think of these?' Sylvia greeted Rosie with a grin when they met up outside the Grafton, opening her coat to show off her suspiciously shapely bosom, beneath the low-necked ruched top of the floral cotton dress she was wearing.

Rosie's eyes widened. She knew quite well how much Sylvia deplored her somewhat flat chest.

'What . . . ?' she began uncertainly whilst Sylvia laughed and then explained proudly.

'I borrowed this frock off my sister Bertha, and I've borrowed one of her brassieres an' all, and stuffed it with all sorts. I tried using a bit of leftover blackout material at first, but it itched me that bad, and left me covered in black dye an' all.'

'So what have you used?' Rosie asked uneasily.

'Well, you know them balls of wool we was sent to knit up things for soldiers?'

Rosie gasped reproachfully. 'You've never used that, Sylvia! That would be like stealing.'

'Only them socks I was knitting that didn't turn out right, that's all,' Sylvia assured her, adding gleefully, 'The lads will be swarming all over us tonight, Rosie, you just wait and see. Mind you, I'll have to mek sure that none of them gets up to what they shouldn't and starts trying to put his hands where I don't want them.' She grinned, giving Rosie a naughty wink. 'A bit of a shock they'd get if they did.'

'Sylvia—' Rosie began, but Sylvia shook her head vigorously.

'Oh, don't start going all po-faced on me, Rosie. It's all right for you. You've got a lovely figure and no mistake. That was one of the reasons I wanted you for me friend,' she added forthrightly, adding bluntly when Rosie looked slightly affronted, 'Well, there's no point in getting friendly with a girl that the chaps aren't going to fancy, is there? You and me are a real pair of lookers and that's the truth. It's no wonder that all the lads want to dance wi' us. And now they're going to want to even more.'

Rosie could see that there was no point in trying to argue with Sylvia's logic, and besides, the queue had almost reached the door to the dance hall.

'You'd better cover them up before we go in,' she warned Sylvia drily, 'otherwise we might end up having to pay for an extra ticket for them.'

'Cheek,' Sylvia laughed, unoffended. Linking her arm through Rosie's as they walked up to the cashier to buy their tickets, she added in a whisper, 'Mind you, I dare say our Bertha is going to have summat to say when she can't find her new brassiere. I'll have to tell her that it must have got lost down at the wash house.'

Like the women in a lot of families living in the poorer parts of the city, Sylvia's mother had to do her washing in the public wash house.

As always, the Grafton was seething with young people, all determined to show Hitler what they thought of him by having as good a time as they could despite the blackout and the bombs.

Tonight one of the city's all female bands, led by Ivy Benson, was providing the music, and Rosie was not surprised to see how many young men in uniform were clustered as close to the band as possible, admiring them.

'Come on, there's a table over there,' Sylvia announced, grabbing hold of Rosie's arm and practically dragging her through the crowd.

Rosie didn't see the table until they had reached it and Sylvia was asking the couple already occupying it if they minded if they sat down on the free chairs.

'Sylvia,' Rosie protested in an embarrassed undertone, sensing that the couple would have preferred to remain alone, but Sylvia tossed her head and whispered to Rosie, 'Don't be daft. Besides, there's nowhere else to sit.'

Giving the couple an apologetic look, Rosie sat down, and only then realised that Nancy's unpleasant cousin Lance was seated at the adjoining table with some of his friends.

''Ere, Rosie, tek a look at that tall, good-looking, dark-haired chap on the next table,' Sylvia breathed excitedly. ''E looks just like a film star.'

Rosie's heart sank as she realised that Sylvia was referring to Lance, and it sank even further when she saw that he had seen Sylvia looking and was now smirking knowingly at them. He turned and said something to one of his friends, who laughed, and then to Rosie's dismay the whole table were staring openly at them.

'Sylvia,' Rosie hissed pleadingly to her friend, '*don't* look at them; you'll only encourage them.'

Sylvia, though, wasn't listening. Ignoring Rosie, she preened herself, pushing out her enhanced chest, and then tossed her head, thus ensuring that even more male attention was focused on her body. Not that Sylvia was giving away the fact that she knew that, Rosie acknowledged, as her friend managed to look as though she hadn't noticed the effect she was having.

'Good, isn't it?' she whispered to Rosie, grinning. 'I saw that Rita Hayworth do it in one of her films.'

The female half of the young couple they were seated with moved closer to her boyfriend and Rosie was mortified to see the look of disapproval she was casting in Sylvia's direction, but as she

159

already knew, Sylvia was irrepressible. And it wasn't as though she meant any real harm.

'It's hot in here,' Sylvia complained. 'You haven't got a bit of Ponds or Snowfire in your bag, have you?'

'I have but you can't powder your face here in public,' Rosie reminded her, scandalised. Even her mother wouldn't dream of putting on her 'slap' in a room full of people.

'Well, I'm not getting up and having our seats snapped up by someone else,' Sylvia responded promptly. 'And promise me you won't go telling the other girls about this, will you?' she begged, indicating her enhanced bust.

Rosie shook her head. 'You'll have to be careful when you get up and dance,' she warned, eyeing the protuberance uneasily. 'What do you want to drink? Port and lemon?'

'If you hang on a minute,' Sylvia hissed to her, 'we probably won't have to buy our own drinks.' She opened her handbag and to Rosie's astonishment extracted a packet of cigarettes.

'What are you doing?' Rosie asked her, mystified. 'You don't smoke.'

'They're our Clara's,' Sylvia told her, adding mischievously, 'Watch this.'

To Rosie's discomfort, the moment they saw the cigarette packet, several of the young men at the adjoining table leaped to their feet, pushing one another out of the way in their determination to be the first to offer Sylvia a light. Lance didn't get up, though, Rosie noticed. He stayed where he was, leaning back in his chair and eyeing Sylvia through the smoke from his own cigarette.

Rosie had heard the girls at work talking about how Lance was involved in the kind of 'business' activities that involved obtaining and selling goods from the docks that had 'fallen off the back of a lorry'.

'A real nasty temper he has on him – even Nancy herself used to say as much,' Bernadette had told them.

Other girls might think that Lance was handsome but there was something about him that made Rosie feel inexplicably uncomfortable.

It quickly became obvious, though, that Sylvia didn't share her feelings, and whilst Rosie looked on in dismay, Sylvia put on an act of demure naughtiness that wouldn't have discredited a screen actress, and somehow, despite Rosie's protests, within five minutes of them arriving, they had moved from their own table to share that of Lance and his friends.

'Sylvia, I wish you hadn't done this,' Rosie protested under cover of tucking her handbag beneath her chair. 'I'd have rather we'd stayed where we were.'

'Wot, and give up the chance of talking to a few lads? Don't be daft. This is wartime, Rosie. We've got to enjoy ourselves whilst we can. We could all be dead tomorrow.'

Rosie shivered, her mother's words from earlier

161

ringing in her ears. She just wondered what Christine was up to . . .

Rosie knew it wasn't the 'few lads' Sylvia was interested in – just one of them. And she could see from the way that Lance was watching Sylvia that he knew it as well. Sylvia might think she knew what was what, but Lance was closer to thirty than twenty, and obviously worldly-wise. Rosie wasn't happy about the situation they were in. However, it was impossible for her to tell Sylvia how she felt now that they were actually sitting here, and Rosie's own sense of responsibility wouldn't allow her to leave Sylvia all alone with a man she disliked so much. Still, even if she couldn't leave, she could make her feelings plain, which she did by steadfastly refusing to allow anyone to buy her a port and lemon, insisting that she bought her own drink and that it was just lemonade.

'For heaven's sake, Rosie, why are you drinking lemonade? Do you want them to think that we're just kids?'

'I'd rather have them thinking that than thinking that we're easy,' Rosie retorted sharply. 'A bit of fun's one thing, Sylvia, but a person can take things too far. You know what they say about girls who start making up to every lad they meet.'

Sylvia's face crumpled and she looked so upset that Rosie immediately felt guilty.

'I just thought that we could have a bit of fun, that's all,' Sylvia protested. 'Just a few dances and a bit of a laugh. Where's the harm in that?'

162

Her distress made Rosie feel that she was being unnecessarily prim and critical. And it was true that the other men seemed to be decent enough sorts, even if they were drinking a fair bit. They were certainly full of fun and good humour, exchanging jokes with one another and competing to sit next to Rosie and Sylvia and compliment them, but Rosie was still glad when a discreet look at her watch told her that it was time to leave.

'It's getting on for ten, Sylvia,' she warned her friend, reminding her, 'I've got fire-watch drill in the morning.'

'Fire-watch drill? Ah, come on, you don't go doing that, do you?' Lance jeered. 'You won't catch me getting roped in for anything like that. I can think of better things to do wi' me time of a blackout.' He winked at Sylvia.

'It's the law,' Rosie told him stiffly, and then wished she hadn't brought herself to his attention when he leered at her.

'Well, there's them wot's daft enough to let others tell 'em wot to do and then there's them like me wot does what they want. And when you know the right people like I do, you don't have to bother with that kind of stuff,' he told her.

Rosie's face burned.

'I bet you could get away with anything if you set your mind to it, Lance,' Sylvia told him flirtatiously.

'Pretty much,' he agreed. 'I can certainly see to it that a pretty girl like you gets a good time.'

Sylvia giggled and moved closer to him, ignoring Rosie's hint that it was time for them to leave, but then to Rosie's relief, she saw two of Sylvia's sisters heading towards them.

'Sylvia,' she warned, nodding meaningfully in their direction.

Immediately Sylvia, who had just moved her chair closer to Lance's, stood up, grabbing her coat and her handbag and holding them tightly in front of herself.

'Oh Gawd, quick, Rosie. Come on, I need the cloakroom,' she muttered, hurrying through the crowd, leaving Rosie to follow her.

'There's no point hiding from them in here,' Rosie told her when she finally caught up with her.

'It's not me sisters,' Sylvia wailed, putting down the bag she was clutching to her chest. 'It's this – *look*.'

Rosie stared at the now lopsided curve of Sylvia's chest and started to giggle.

'It's all right for you,' Sylvia groaned. 'But I can't go back in there now . . .'

'Well, that's what you get for flirting like you were doing,' Rosie told her, trying to sound stern but failing miserably.

'I could feel Lance trying to get his hand round me back,' Sylvia admitted. 'It's just as well he couldn't get any further. What would he have thought when he got hold of a handful of unfinished knitting and old socks?'

Rosie couldn't help it. She started to splutter with laughter again and after a few seconds even Sylvia herself joined in.

'Mind you, it's p'raps just as well we're leaving. I don't want our Clara telling me dad on me.' She pulled a small face, but Rosie could understand why Sylvia's elder sisters might be concerned.

'You are only sixteen,' she reminded her.

'I'm seventeen next month. Rosie, it's only ten o'clock and we don't normally leave the Grafton until at least eleven.'

'Like I said I've got fire-watch practice in the morning, and besides . . .' Rosie looked uncertainly at Sylvia, 'I can tell that you like him, Sylvia, but that Lance . . . well, he's a lot older than you and . . . I've heard that . . .'

'I don't care what you've heard about him, Rosie. I mek me own mind up about folk, and if you want the truth, I think you was a little bit put out because he fancied me more than he did you.'

Rosie couldn't believe her ears. 'I wasn't put out at all,' she denied emphatically.

'Well, that's not how it looked to me,' Sylvia retorted huffily as they left the dance hall. 'Anyway, you're out of luck because Lance told me that he wanted to see me again.'

Outside they stood still to get their bearings whilst their eyes adjusted to the darkness of the blackout. It never got any easier.

'If I were you I wouldn't count on seeing him again,' Rosie warned her firmly. 'And I can't see

165

your dad being too pleased if he comes round to your house looking for you.'

Sylvia gave a small shudder, and then admitted reluctantly, 'No, I don't want me dad knowing about him. He's allus yellin' about what he'd do to us if any of us were to get ourselves in the family way unwed. Not that that's goin' to happen to me! Oooh, Rosie, just think what it would be like though, marrying a handsome chap like Lance who knows what's what. And he's not short of a bob or two either, from the way he was talking and the clothes he wears. He was telling me how he'd have had this posh new Morris car but for the war.'

Rosie shook her head. For all that she pretended to be so 'grown up', Sylvia could be so very naïve at times. 'Talk's cheap,' she warned Sylvia firmly.

'And what does that mean exactly when it's at home?' Sylvia challenged her angrily. ''Cos if you're trying to say that Lance was lying—'

'You've only just met Lance, Sylvia, and you and me are supposed to be friends. We were supposed to be out having fun tonight,' Rosie reminded her.

'Mebbe so, but a girl knows when she's met the right one, and I reckon that me and Lance—' Sylvia broke off and sighed. 'I really do fancy him, Rosie. And I don't have to worry about him going round to our house either, because I didn't give him me address. But I did tell him where we work and that we go dancing at the Grafton every Saturday,' she added smugly, linking her arm through Rosie's as she cajoled her. 'You want to loosen up a bit your-self, Rosie, and not be so starchy. Here, put your torch on, will you? The battery's gone in mine.'

Rosie gave a small sigh as she switched on the small torch such as everyone carried round with them to use in the blackout. Her father had brought her it back from New York along with a good supply of batteries, and she didn't really begrudge using it more than her friends used theirs because she knew how hard it was for them to get replace-ment batteries.

'See you at work on Monday,' Sylvia called after her when they parted to go to their respective bus stops.

Rosie waved her off. She couldn't help enjoying Sylvia's good-humoured company, despite the fact that sometimes her behaviour was not how Rosie would have acted herself. Rosie hoped that she wasn't a spoilsport, the kind of girl who didn't like a bit of fun, but Sylvia was very young and Rosie couldn't help worrying about her and wanting to protect her. She and Bella had got on so well, and had under-stood one another so completely that there had been no need for things like this. It was true that at times Rosie had thought that Bella's mother's refusal to let her go dancing or have a bit of fun was mean, but she had still understood that Bella was expected to behave in a certain way because of her Italian upbringing. Sylvia was just the opposite from Bella, and being older than Sylvia, Rosie was more aware of just how easy it was for a girl to get the wrong kind of reputation. She liked Sylvia far too much to want to see something like that happen to her.

Rosie wasn't surprised to find the house in darkness when she unlocked the door and walked into the kitchen. After all, she had known that her mother was going out and she was hardly likely to be back so early. She closed the door and turned on the light.

The kitchen was cold and damp, making her shiver. She was just reaching for the kettle, intending to fill it so that she could make herself a cup of cocoa, when she heard a noise coming from the front room. It gave her such a shock that she almost dropped the kettle.

'Mum,' she called out, nervously, 'is that you?' Putting down the kettle, she went into the hallway and tentatively opened the front room door. The only light in the room was the glow from the small electric fire, but it was enough for Rosie to see its two occupants – her mother, who was struggling to sit up on the sofa, and a man who was hurriedly pulling on his pants.

Rosie was so shocked that she could only stand in the doorway staring at them, unable to move. Her mother had jumped up off the sofa and was saying something to the man, whom Rosie didn't recognise. A cold sweat of revulsion and angry disbelief engulfed her, followed by a sickness that gripped her stomach. Unable to say or do anything, she stumbled back into the kitchen, where she sank down onto one of the hard wooden chairs. Her whole body was overcome with shock, whilst her teeth chattered together and she shivered violently. She heard the front door open and then swiftly close, and then her mother came into the kitchen. Rosie stared numbly at her.

'Why have you come back so early? You told me you were going to the Grafton, and you never get back from there until after eleven,' Christine burst out angrily, as though she were the one at fault. 'You've done it deliberately, haven't you, so that you could catch me out? Someone's told you, haven't they? I bet it was that old gossip Mabel from number 78; she saw me with Dennis last week, and I could see then what she was thinking—'

'No one told me anything,' Rosie stopped her, unable to endure hearing any more. 'How could you?' she demanded, white-faced. She could hardly bring herself to speak, she felt so outraged and in despair. 'How could you do that, Mum? When Dad finds out—'

'Well, he won't find out, will he, unless you go running telling tales to him?'

Rosie looked at her. How could her mother do this to her gentle kind father? How could she betray him and their twenty years of marriage like this?

'Rosie, promise me you won't say anything about this to your dad.' The anger had gone out of her mother's voice now, to be replaced by anxiety and pleading. 'I didn't mean for it to happen.'

'Then why did you let it? Why, Mum, why? How could you do such a thing? Poor Dad . . .'

Christine's face tightened. 'Oh, that's right, you go and take his side. I might have known you would.' Her mother had started to cry now, her voice rising, as she protested accusingly, 'It's all right for you, Rosie. You're young yet and you don't know how cruel life can be, or what it's like being tied to a man who—'

'How can you say that?' Rosie stopped her, shocked. 'Dad loves you.'

'No he doesn't. That bloody sister of his means more to him than I do. If he really cared about me he'd be here with me instead of leaving me to cope with this bloody war on me own without a man to look after me. And I need that, Rosie. I need it badly.'

This was a side to her mother that Rosie hadn't seen before and it shocked her.

'How can you say that? Dad's away in the merchant navy and at sea, working for us, for our country. I don't understand.'

'No you don't understand. No one does. They never have and they never will.' There was a wildness in her mother's voice now that alarmed Rosie. 'Dennis is good to me. He spoils me, and he looks after me; allus giving me stuff and paying me compliments, right from the first day I started at the factory. Came right up to me, he did, and said how pretty I was. I could see then of course that the other women – a load of old trouts they are an' all – were jealous.'

'The manager?'

'Yes. Dennis is the manager of the factory, and a proper gentleman. He's not like your dad. He told me straight out that his wife wasn't treating him right.'

Rosie knew that her parents' marriage wasn't a happy one but she had never imagined that her mother would do anything like this. 'He's married as well!' Rosie couldn't conceal her revulsion. She was still too shocked to accept what she had witnessed. 'You can't do this, Mum. Promise me you'll stop seeing him,' she begged her. 'You've got to. You must see that . . . what you're doing is wrong, and . . .'

Her mother was crying now.

'You've got to, Mum,' Rosie insisted. 'If you don't, Dad is bound to find out and then what's going to happen?'

'All right, but don't you go saying anything about Dennis and me to your dad. Not that he'd care, exceptin' that bloody Maude would kick up a right fuss.'

Rosie couldn't bear to say anything. She knew that she wouldn't tell her father but she also knew that it wouldn't be for her mother's sake that she kept her silence.

TEN

'Right, now what we're going to do is mek a bit of a fire at the far end of this 'ere air-raid shelter, wot will fill it with smoke and then you girls are going to crawl through it to the other end with the stirrup pump, and put out the fire.'

Angela Flynn, who had been paired with Rosie for this exercise, pulled a face and looked disgruntled, whilst the good-looking young fireman who was standing listening whilst the group of girls were given their instructions caught Rosie's eye and winked at her.

Rosie gave him a withering look and turned away. Men were all the same and all after the one thing. What she had witnessed last night had put her off all of them for good. First Sylvia making a fool of herself over Lance, and then her own mother. How could she have betrayed her father like that, and with a married man? Rosie felt sick all over again. She had hardly dared close her eyes last night when she had gone to bed for fear of the unwanted images that would form of her mother with her lover. Rosie knew that she would never ever forget what she had seen. She was still in shock from it.

Three other pairs of girls had to go into the smoke-filled shelter under the careful watch of the ARP warden and the firemen before it was Rosie and Angela's turn.

As they waited, Angela grumbled, 'I don't see what putting out a fire in a blooming air-raid shelter has to do with being on fire-watch duty. Me da says that they shouldn't be askin' girls to go climbing about on roofs watching for fires anyway.'

The young fireman had made his way round the edge of the waiting group and was now standing next to them. Angela's face brightened immediately.

'So what's your name then?' she demanded. 'I'm Angela, I live at number 28, and this here next to me is Rosie from round the back on Gerard Street.'

'I'm Rob Whittaker. My family's from the Wirral but I've been transferred here to Liverpool and I'm boarding down at number 35. Nice to meet you both. As for what's happening here, it's to show you how to deal with the fires that are caused by incendiary bombs,' he explained patiently.

'Bombs? You mean we're going to be expected to mess around with bombs?' Angela shrieked. 'My dad will never agree to that.'

'It isn't the incendiaries themselves, it's the damage the fires they cause can do if they aren't put out straight away,' Rob Whittaker continued calmly. 'There's no danger in putting out these fires if it's done promptly and properly.'

'Come on, Angela, it's our turn next,' Rosie commanded her partner, ignoring their new neighbour's friendly overtures. She had grown up vaguely aware of the fact that some of their neighbours disapproved of her mother, but after what she had seen last night she felt acutely conscious of her own position. If Rob Whittaker thought she was the kind of girl who had no respect for herself then he could think again and find someone else to come over all smiles with. Out of the corner of her eye Rosie could see the way her cold response had made the smile fade from his eyes. She told herself she should be pleased and not feel guilty.

'Right, you two next,' the ARP warden was calling out.

'What's got into you?' Angela demanded crossly. 'Proper rude, you were.'

Had she been? Rosie looked back over her shoulder but Rob Whittaker had his back to her and was deep in conversation with someone else. As though he could feel her looking at him he turned round but there was no smile for her this time.

Mortified, Rosie looked away. Her throat felt raw from the combination of the cold October air and the smell of smoke hanging in a pall over the city from the bomb-damaged docks.

Hitler's attacks on their city had been relentless. There had been twenty air raids in September and already in October they were into double figures. Night after night people's sleep was disturbed by the warning sound of the air-raid siren, bringing those who had not made the decision to head for the shelters 'just in case' tumbling from their beds with fast-beating hearts. But despite all that, somehow they had all got used to living on the knife edge that had become their lives, Rosie recognised. To panic at the sound of the siren, or to act scared was seen as letting the side down, and everyone tried to bolster their own and other people's courage by straightening their shoulders and announcing that Hitler could do his worst, but he wasn't going to beat them.

At first it had been frightening to turn a corner and see a gaping hole in a street where only the previous day there had been buildings, or to look towards the docks and see the glow of flames from something burning, but with the papers full of reassurances that bomb damage to the city and loss of life was minimal, and the docks turning round more ships faster than ever and securing their precious cargoes safely, the people of Liverpool were holding their heads up high, fiercely determined not to let Hitler demoralise them.

The truth was that Rosie was far more worried about her mother's affair than she was about Hitler's bombs. It was occupying her thoughts virtually to the exclusion of everything else.

Perhaps she had been unfair to her mother but she was still finding it difficult to think straight.

The image of her mother and her lover both struggling into their clothes in the dim light of the fire was one that she knew would be burned into her mind for ever. She didn't want to keep on thinking about it but she couldn't stop.

Her mother had still been in bed when Rosie had left this morning and she hadn't been able to bring herself to go in to her. Not that it would have made any difference. Christine would no doubt refuse to talk to her about it.

'Off you go, and remember, keep low under the smoke, and when you get to the fire at the bottom of the shelter, use the stirrup pump to put it out.'

Rosie shuddered as she dropped down on all fours and started to crawl into the thick grey smoke. Even though she knew that they weren't really in any danger, she still felt slightly sick and apprehensive as she followed the instructions. Angela had gone in first but suddenly she started to turn round.

'I've got to get out of here,' she told Rosie frantically. 'I can't breathe. I've got to get out.'

'Angela, it's all right,' Rosie tried to calm her, but Angela was clutching at her throat and trying to stand up – the very thing they had been told not to do.

'Get down,' Rosie begged her, pulling on the straps of her dungarees, but to her shock Angela struck out at her, and then suddenly collapsed, pulling Rosie down with her. Rosie tried to save herself but it was too late. She felt something hit

176

the side of her head, causing pain to explode inside it. She could hear the ARP warden calling their names, her head was throbbing and she badly wanted to be sick. Angela was breathing in a funny way and making a frightening noise, her eyes bulging.

'What's going on in there?' the ARP warden yelled angrily.

Rosie shouted out, 'Angela's not well, Mr Walton. She's breathing funny and she won't move . . .' The smoke had thickened and Rosie could only just about make out the hunched shape of Angela's frighteningly inert body. She tried to drag the other girl towards the exit but she was too heavy for her, and Rosie's chest felt so tight and sore from inhaling smoke that she could hardly breathe herself. And then suddenly she saw Rob Whittaker materialising in front of her out of the smoke, and reaching for her.

Rosie shook her head. 'Take Angela first,' she insisted. She saw the look he gave her before he turned away to help the other girl, and now it wasn't just the smoke that made her eyes sting.

'Come on, Rosie, lassie . . .'

Rosie clung on gratefully to the hand the ARP warden had extended to her, his voice so much warmer and kinder now. In no time at all, or so it seemed to Rosie, she was out of the shelter and coughing the smoke out of her lungs, then breathing in fresh air, whilst two of the men went back in to put out the fire.

'How's Angela?' Rosie asked anxiously as soon as she could speak.

'She's pretty poorly but she's going to be all right,' the ARP warden assured her. 'Daft thing didn't think to tell us that she suffers from a bad chest. Now hold still whilst we have a look at that bump on your head . . .' Rosie winced as she felt the sting of iodine being applied to her wound.

Someone had sent word to Angela's family and her father pushed his way through the small crowd that had gathered. Having assured himself that his daughter was unharmed, although badly shocked, he had come over to thank the ARP warden.

'It's not me you should be thanking but young Rosie,' Mr Walton told him firmly. 'If it hadn't been for her managing to keep calm and acting promptly, your Angela could have been a sight worse off than she is.'

Rosie blushed and protested that she hadn't really done anything, but when Angela's father had left to take Angela home, Mr Walton told Rosie firmly, 'You've got the makings of a good fire-watch guard, Rosie. Your dad would be right proud of you. You've got a nasty bump on your head, though.' He looked up and then called out, 'Rob, will you walk Rosie home for us?'

'Oh, no,' Rosie protested uncomfortably, 'I can walk myself home. Honestly.' But it was too late. Rob Whittaker was already helping her gently to her feet from the upturned bucket where Mr

Walton had made her sit down whilst he looked at her injuries.

'Mr Walton was telling me that your dad's in the merchant navy,' Rob commented after they had walked to the end of the street in silence.

'Yes,' Rosie agreed.

'So's my brother, and I was all set to join him when a pal told me about this job that had come up in the fire service.'

As they turned the corner Rosie suddenly felt dizzy. She put her hand out towards the wall to support herself but immediately Rob Whittaker took hold of her in a firm but gentle grip.

'Take it easy,' he cautioned her. 'You're bound to feel a bit sickly, like. It's the shock.'

'I thought Angela was going to die,' Rosie admitted shakily. 'She was breathing that funny.'

'It's the smoke. It affects some that way.' Something about the way he was looking at her made Rosie feel safe and very comfortable with him. Perhaps she had been wrong to give him the cold shoulder earlier, she admitted. He was every bit as tall and as dark-haired as Nancy's cousin Lance, but where his eyes held an expression that Rosie didn't like, Rob's showed only kindness and warmth.

They had almost reached her front door so she stopped walking.

'I'm all right now,' she told him. 'Thanks for seeing me back safely.'

He didn't try to go any further with her, but

Rosie saw when she reached the door and turned round to look, that he was still standing where she had left him, watching over her.

'So what's bin happening to you then?' Sylvia demanded on Monday morning when she saw the bruise on Rosie's forehead.

'There was a bit of an accident when we were doing our fire-watch practice,' Rosie told her.

It was a relief to come into the shop and get back to normality after the events of the weekend and the atmosphere they had left behind. Rosie and her mother were not on speaking terms and Rosie had hardly slept for worrying about what she had seen. Her mother had gone out on Sunday afternoon and had not returned until late in the evening. Rosie had been unable to help wondering if she had been with her lover, but since her mother was refusing to speak to her she knew there had been no point asking.

They had a busy morning, so Rosie didn't see much of Sylvia, but when the dinner bell rang, instead of going to get her sandwiches and join her, Sylvia hurried to put on her coat, announcing that she was going out.

'It's raining cats and dogs,' Rosie protested.

'It's not that bad, and besides, I want some fresh air,' Sylvia told her.

'It might be summat fresh she's after but it isn't fresh air,' Fanny Williams, one of the older girls, snorted after Sylvia had gone. 'She'll be after meeting up with that cousin of Nancy's wot came into the shop as bold as brass earlier, looking for her. Well, she'd better watch her step, that's all I can say, because it's as plain as the nose on her face what he's after. You could see it in his eyes.'

Enid, the senior assistant, was already compressing her mouth with disapproval. 'She'll be getting a name for herself if she starts going with the likes of him, if what I've heard about him is true. And she's got no business telling him to come to the shop. Mrs Verey would have a fit if she knew.'

Rosie's heart sank. She hadn't thought that Lance was serious enough about Sylvia to come looking for her at work. Rosie might not be very experienced where men were concerned but she instinctively knew a predator when she saw one.

It was well beyond their allotted lunch hour when Sylvia finally returned, pink-cheeked and almost giddy with excitement.

'You'll never guess who I've just seen,' she said to Rosie.

'That's what you think,' Rosie checked her. 'Fanny told us all about Lance coming into the shop asking for you. You'll be in real trouble if Mrs Verey finds out.'

Sylvia pouted and tossed her head. 'Why shouldn't he come in? He's got the money to treat his girl.' Her eyes shone. 'Oh, Rosie, he's just like an actor out of a film. He's ever so handsome. He was asking if you and I would go out on a double date with him and that Johnny on Wednesday.'

Rosie shook her head. 'Dad's ship is due in this week, and I wouldn't go anyway. We don't know them, Sylvia, and if you want my opinion I don't think—'

'Well, I don't. And I'm going even if you aren't.' Sylvia looked close to tears.

'Sylvia, you can't,' Rosie protested. 'Your dad would never allow it.'

'He isn't going to know, is he? Oh, don't be such a spoilsport, Rosie. You only live once, you know.'

Rosie could see that there was no reasoning with her, but that didn't stop her feeling concerned.

It was Fanny's turn to go to the bank with the day's takings and when she came back she burst into the workroom white-faced. Her brother, like Rosie's father, was in the merchant navy and there were tears in her eyes as she told them the news she had just heard.

'It's one of the convoys. It's bin torpedoed really badly, three ships sunk and others damaged. They was only a hundred miles off the Irish coast an' all nearly home. Not that that means much with Hitler bombing the docks like he is. Our Marty was due home this week.'

Rosie felt as though all the blood was draining from her body. Her father's ship was due in any day as well.

'Did you hear which ships it was?' she asked anxiously.

Fanny shook her head.

'Quick, Sylvia, go and put the wireless on,' Enid demanded sharply. 'It will be on the news.'

Rosie's mouth had gone dry and her heart was pounding heavily with sick dread. 'It won't,' she said. 'They don't give out that kind of news – not at first.' She bit her lip and tried to fight back her fear.

The Elegant Modes workers had still not heard any fresh news when it was time for them to go home. Rosie had been unable to concentrate all afternoon.

'Try not to worry, Rosie,' Enid told her in a kinder voice than she normally used to the junior girls. 'I'll have a word with my hubbie for you. With him working down at the docks, they normally get to hear the news before anyone else.'

Rosie gave her a grateful look. She couldn't bear to think of anything happening to her father. It was too atrocious even to contemplate. She cheered herself slightly at that – if she couldn't imagine it, then it couldn't happen, could it?

Normally she and Sylvia left the shop together but today Sylvia had rushed off without a word and although she was so worried about her father, Rosie still felt concerned for her friend.

It was still raining, and Rosie shook the rain-drops off her umbrella as she let herself into the empty house.

She had just got the fire lit and made herself a much-needed cup of tea when she heard someone knocking on the front door. In her haste to answer it she almost knocked over her tea cup. In her mind's eye she could already see the telegram boy waiting outside to hand her the message every household dreaded receiving. But when she opened the door it was Rob Whittaker standing there, his bicycle propped up against the wall. Rosie had never felt so relieved.

Rob was wearing his fireman's uniform and he removed his cap when he saw Rosie, squeezing it in his hands.

'I hope you don't mind me calling like this, but I heard earlier on today that one of our convoys had been badly torpedoed and—'

'Yes, I heard that too,' Rosie sighed. 'My dad is—'

'It's all right, Rosie. Seeing as I'm based down near the docks, I checked up, remembering you'd said he was due back any day. He's on the *Aurora*, and she's part of a different convoy. They should be anchoring up out over the Liverpool bar later on tonight and getting into the dock in the early hours, all being well.'

Rosie couldn't speak at first, she was so delirious with happiness. When she did finally find her voice all she could say was, 'Oh, thank God.' And then her expression changed and her face became shadowed. 'I was dreading hearing bad news. In fact I thought when I heard you knock that it was the telegraph boy, but here's me over the moon because my dad is safe, whilst that boy will be knocking on the doors of some poor families tonight with the news that their men won't be coming home.' She pressed her hand to her mouth in an attempt to stop her lips from trembling. 'I'm really grateful to you for taking the trouble to let me know that he's all right, Rob.' She hesitated and then opened the door a little bit wider, and offered shyly, 'I've just brewed a pot of tea and you're welcome to come in if you want.'

'That's kind of you, Rosie. I'd like to but I'd better not. Mrs Norris, whom I'm lodging with, will have the tea on. Mr Norris always gets in at seven o'clock. Woe betide if I'm a minute after. I tell you, even Hitler would be defeated by Mrs N.'s moaning.'

Rosie could hear in his voice that he would have liked to have accepted her invitation and she gave him a small smile, suggesting, 'Well, perhaps another time – when my dad's here. I'm sure he'd like to meet you and have a chat with you, what with your brother sailing under the Red Duster as well.'

'I'd like that.' He was smiling so much she might have offered him the moon, and despite his dinner waiting, he was still standing on the doorstep as though he couldn't bear to leave.

'Your tea will be getting cold,' she reminded him.

'Rosie . . .'

'Yes?'

'I was wondering if sometime you might fancy going to the cinema with me?'

Rosie's stomach did a little dance. 'I might do,' she told him, 'if there was to be a good film on.' She didn't want him thinking she was too keen. Rob nodded and finally stepped back off the doorstep.

As she closed the door, Rosie told herself severely that if she had had any sense she would have turned him down, but there was a small bubble of happiness inside her that hadn't been there before, and as she went to tend to the sulky small fire with its covering of slack, she was humming happily under her breath, thinking maybe the world wasn't such a bad place after all.

'I'm thinking of changing me job to the night shift.'

Rosie looked at her mother, who had just arrived home. Rosie had told her immediately that her father was safe – the first words they had shared in days. Christine had been typically blasé about the news.

'Why would you want to do that?'

'Well, I've bin talking to one of the other women there and she was saying, like I told you, that you can get five pounds a week if you do nights. With that kind of money we could afford to move out of here and rent somewhere a bit safer. That'll please yer dad. He's never liked living here.'

It sounded a logical reason for her mother's decision to work nights, but Rosie could hear a note of evasion in her voice, so she pressed her uneasily, 'You want to move out? But you've always said that you'd never move from here.' She brought out the fish pie to dish up, which was in reality mostly mashed potatoes with a small helping of the reconstituted dried fish that everyone was being exhorted to eat. No matter its quality, she wanted something proper for her father to eat when he came in later.

'That was before Hitler started bombing the docks,' her mother retorted. 'I can't sleep in me bed at night any more for fear that we're going to be killed, and as for that ruddy air-raid shelter . . . Besides, I thought you'd be pleased, seein' as you was on at me to change me ways,' she told Rosie meaningfully.

'I didn't say that you should work nights, Mum. In fact . . .' Rosie paused. Now that her mother was speaking to her properly again this surely was an ideal opportunity for Rosie to say what was on her mind. '. . . It seems to me that it would be a good idea if you were to leave Littlewoods, and look for a job somewhere else.'

'Oh, it does, does it, and why would that be, I wonder?'

Rosie tensed at the hostility in her mother's voice, but she wasn't going to back down now.

'It would be for the best, Mum; you must know that.'

'Because of Dennis, you mean?'

Rosie had to look away. She couldn't bear hearing the man's name on her mother's lips but she dare not risk antagonising her too much She knew her mother and how she could fly off the handle if she was pushed too hard.

'He's married, Mum, and so are you, and with you both working at the factory . . .' When her mother didn't respond Rosie accused her miserably, 'You're still seeing him, aren't you?'

'What if I am? You think you know everything, Rosie, but you know nothing. Why shouldn't I have a bit of happiness in me life? I've had precious little of it with your dad—'

'Mum, can't you see how much better it would be for everyone if you got another job?' Rosie interrupted her.

'For everyone but me and Dennis, you mean?' Christine challenged her bitterly. 'But of course what we want doesn't matter, I suppose.'

'Mum, you're both married.'

'Look, me and him won't be seeing one another no more, all right, and I don't want you going on about it to me all the time, Rosie, 'cos if you do I'll start wishing that I hadn't stopped seeing him. And as for me job – well, if you think I'm going to turn down the chance to earn a fiver a week then you can think again, miss.'

Rosie pushed her plate away, her appetite gone.

Her mother did the same, standing up and announcing, 'I'm going up to get changed. I'm going down the factory to see about changing over to nights.'

'Dad's ship's due to dock any time,' Rosie reminded her quietly. 'The least you can do is be here to welcome him.'

But her mother wasn't listening. She had already disappeared into the hall.

Rosie sighed. What would happen to them now?

The sound of the air-raid siren brought Rosie out of her sleep. Getting out of bed, she pulled on her candlewick dressing gown, practically bumping into her mother on the landing. In the hallway they pulled on their wellingtons and grabbed their gas masks and the emergency boxes everyone was supposed to keep ready for air raids, with a few basic necessities in them: tea for a hot drink, matches, a torch, toys for children if one had children, along with all their important papers, like their birth certificates, ration books and anything else of value.

As they hurried down the street towards their designated public shelter, overhead they could hear the drone of planes, heading for the docks – and their target. One of them picked out a target by the searchlights from the defence battery, banked and suddenly, up ahead of the people making for the shelter, a shower of incendiary bombs were fizzing from it, to explode in a dazzle of light.

'Watch out, everyone,' someone called.

Instinctively Rosie flung herself to the ground, covering her head protectively with her hands as the incendiaries fell all around them. One rolled so close to her she could feel its heat. Automatically, she kicked it out of the way and then jumped up to help cover the fires all around the street with sand.

'Come on, let's get into the shelter before he comes back with his big brothers,' one of the men called out semi-jokingly, whilst the ARP warden urged them to hurry. The half-kilo incendiary bombs had become so commonplace that they no longer caused Rosie's heart to contract with fear. So long as they didn't have a direct hit and their fires were put out immediately, the damage they caused was limited. Unlike the much bigger parachute bombs the Germans were now dropping, and which were responsible for the ugly gaps that were appearing all over the city where once there had been buildings.

Overhead the bombers droned menacingly, the sound of their engines interspersed by the heart-stopping whistle of the bombs they dropped. Rosie could hear one now, but she refused to give in to her fear and look back over her shoulder. They said anyway that you never heard the one that got you and she could certainly hear this one. She winced as a dull boom echoed from a nearby street, whilst the ARP warden grabbed her arm and half pushed her into the shelter.

'They've had a hit in Bessie Street so them from there have had to come in here,' one of their neighbours informed Rosie as she looked in dismay at the already crowded interior of the shelter. Unfamiliar faces stared back at her, illuminated by the thin blue light from the special-issue lanterns that was all they were allowed inside the shelters. A young woman was trying to quieten her crying children, whilst an old man was complaining that he had come out without his teeth.

Christine had followed Rosie into the shelter and somehow they managed to find a space where they could sit down.

'I hate these ruddy shelters,' her mother complained. 'They stink to high heaven, and I swear summat bit me the last time we was down here.'

A small child screamed as more incendiary bombs exploded somewhere close at hand, whilst a neighbour who was known to be the street's worst gossip, seated opposite Rosie, announced, 'I saw young Rob Whittaker calling round at your house this tea time, Rosie, just before your ma got home.'

Rosie could feel her face growing hot but she ignored the insinuation and answered pleasantly, 'Yes. He was calling to let me know that Dad's ship wasn't one of those in that convoy that was torpedoed.'

'A good lad young Rob is,' Mr Walton, the ARP warden, who had overheard, nodded approvingly. 'Very thoughtful and conscientious.'

'Yes, it was kind of him to come and tell me,' Rosie agreed.

'So what's this, then?' her mother demanded, giving her a nudge in the ribs.

'It's nothing,' Rosie answered her curtly. She didn't want to discuss Rob with her mother. She didn't want her barbed comments sullying their conversation.

'What are you up to?' she asked suspiciously.

'Nothing as bad as you,' Rosie hissed.

'Shush! Mind you remember what you promised me, Rosie, and no telling your dad about me and Dennis,' Christine said under her breath. 'It's bad enough with gossips like her around,' she continued, nodding in the direction of the busybody sitting near them.

'You promised me you wouldn't see him again,' Rosie hissed back angrily.

'I wasn't going to, but he was that upset. See, Dennis's got feelings, not like your dad.'

'Mum, you mustn't do this,' Rosie urged. 'Please don't. Please don't see him any more. It's wrong and . . . it's shameful . . . and – and someone's bound to find out.'

The all clear sounded, making it impossible for them to say any more.

'Bloody Hitler, I'm sick of him getting me out of me bed night after night,' one woman was complaining as they all started to make their way up the steps into the damp night air.

'Aye, well, you'd be a hell of a lot sicker if you was bombed in your bed,' someone else replied grimly.

The smell of smoke, burning wood, soot and old buildings hung heavily on the air. Gerard Street and the streets around it smelled so very different now from how they had done when Rosie was growing up. Those happy days seemed so far away. Her eyes smarted with tears as she remembered the rich aroma of freshly made coffee and the wonderful smells in the local Italian grocer's, with its delicious salamis and cheeses, and its freshly made pasta, and fat juicy tomatoes. In those days, or so it seemed to her looking back, every door in the street had always been welcomingly open so that the air of the street itself had been warmed by the smell of Italian cooking. Just thinking about Maria's special basil-flavoured pasta sauce made Rosie's mouth water.

Maria! Did she and Bella ever think about her and wish, as she did, that things might have been different? Or was their mourning for those they had lost still so intense that they had no thoughts or emotions to spare for her?

Swallowing hard against her pain, Rosie looked towards the docks. As much as she longed for her father's return she was also now dreading it. There was no way her mother could keep this secret for long and it would kill Rosie to try to act normally in front of her father. No good could come from any of this. For the first time ever, Rosie wished that her father wasn't taking shore leave.

ELEVEN

'And Lance was telling me that he could get me anything I want, and that a girl my age shouldn't have to ask her parents' permission to go out on a date, and—'

'Oh, for heaven's sake, Sylvia, if Lance told you the moon was made of blue cheese would you believe that as well?' Rosie snapped.

'There's no call for you to go being like that,' Sylvia complained, looking hurt. 'I was only saying . . .'

'Have you told your parents that you're seeing him yet?' Rosie demanded.

Sylvia gave her a sullen look. 'I would have told them but my dad's got this bee in his bonnet about me goin' out wi' lads. He says I'm too young.'

The workroom buzzer went and Enid called out, 'Rosie, shop – it's your turn.'

It was a pity that Sylvia had ever had to meet Lance, Rosie decided, protective of her friend as she hurried into the shop, and then came to an abrupt halt as Lance himself turned away from the display he had been studying and smiled sneeringly at her.

'Well, well, if it isn't Miss Stuck Up.'

Rosie cast an anxious look over her shoulder to the small office where she knew Mrs Verey would be. One of the rules she made plain to her staff when she took them on was that they were not allowed to have friends or family call on them whilst they were at work. Sylvia was so besotted with Lance that she had probably forgotten to warn him about this, Rosie decided.

'If you've come to see Sylvia—' she hissed, but Lance shook his head.

'Did I say that? As it happens I've come in to buy a bit of summat for someone special. You know the kind of thing I mean, don't you, Rosie? Something in silk with lots of lace . . .'

Rosie swallowed. There was something not just about the way he was looking at her, but also in the way he was speaking that was making her feel very uncomfortable. Now instead of dreading her employer coming into the shop, she almost wished that she would.

'Our stock is rather limited at the moment,' she began formally. That much was true but they did have the kind of things he was referring to and Rosie knew that Mrs Verey wouldn't be pleased if she turned away a sale for something so expensive. 'But of course I will show you what we have. If it's for Sylvia . . .' she began uncertainly.

'That's for me to know, isn't it?' he answered with an unpleasant leer.

'Do you know the size of the lady in question?' Her pride wouldn't let her show him just how much she hated asking him that question and seeing the way he smirked at her in response.

'Well, let me see . . .' The way he was looking at her made Rosie's face burn. He was embarrassing her deliberately and enjoying doing so, she was sure.

'Well, she's about your size, I expect, so if you show me what you've got and hold it up against you then I'll be able to imagine how it's going to look on her, won't I?'

Rosie was glad that she had ducked down beneath the counter to slide out one of the wooden drawers. Her hands were trembling as she carefully removed a pair of delicate cream silk, lace-trimmed French knickers.

'We have these,' she told Lance, making sure she avoided looking directly at him as she placed the knickers on the glass countertop.

'Well, now, I reckon I was thinking of summat a bit more saucy than that, Rosie. You know, a bit more cut away. The kind of thing a lad would like to see his girl almost wearing.' He was smirking at her again.

She hadn't liked him right from the first and now she liked him even less.

'I'm sorry but these are the only style we have in,' she told him truthfully.

'I suppose the brassiere is just as old-fashioned, is it? Go on then, I might as well have it, seeing as it's all you've got. Let's have a look at it.'

Still refusing to let him see how much she was hating serving him, Rosie dutifully unfolded a matching brassiere in a size she knew would fit Sylvia.

Immediately Lance picked it up off the counter top and held it up, frowning as he studied the small cups before dropping it back on the glass, and then cupping his hands and telling her uncouthly, 'She's big enough to fill me hands nicely, not some kid, so get me summat bigger.' There was a gleam in his eyes that turned Rosie's stomach. 'You're a smart girl, Rosie, and a pretty one, and I can tell you now that you're the kind of girl I like, so how about you and me going out together tonight?'

Rosie couldn't believe her ears. How could he ask her out like that, as cool as you please, when he was already seeing Sylvia? Even if she had liked him – which she most certainly did not – the fact that he was seeing her friend would have meant that she would refuse him in a heartbeat.

'No thank you,' she told him shortly. 'I don't go out with men who are seeing other girls.'

'Please yourself, it's your loss. And I was wrong about you 'cos a really smart girl would have known when she was in luck.'

She could see that she had annoyed him, but she didn't care, Rosie told herself. Ten minutes later, when he finally left the shop carrying the knickers and brassiere set he had bought, Rosie was shaking inwardly. How could Sylvia be silly enough to like him? He was arrogant and loathsome. It was almost as though he had wanted her to think he was buying the underwear for someone else and not Sylvia.

'Do you fancy going to the pictures with me after work tonight?' Sylvia asked her when she got back to the workroom.

'I can't. Dad's ship's docked and he'll be coming home.'

Rosie knew she didn't need to make any further explanations. Home leave was so precious that everyone knew and understood that families wanted to spend every minute of it together. Or at least most families did. Her face clouded at the thought of what the evening ahead had in store.

Rosie shivered in the cold wind whipping up Bold Street as she stepped out of the shop. They were almost into November and although only half-past six it was already pitch-black. Several stars shone, throwing out just enough light for her to recognise the man standing waiting for her.

'Dad!'

Rosie threw herself into her father's arms with a small cry of delight. He hugged her close and it was all she could do to stop herself crying.

'I wasn't expecting you to come and meet me from work,' she told him as she tucked her arm through his.

'Well, your mam said that she had to go out to do someone's hair so I thought I might as well come into town and walk back with you as be in on me own.'

Rosie stiffened. Was her mother genuinely out working or had she broken her promise and gone out with her married lover? Even Christine couldn't be so cruel, could she?

'Did she tell you that she's changing her shift to work nights?' she asked her father hesitantly, half afraid to enquire what had been said between them.

'Aye, and she said as how she wants to find somewhere to rent further away from the docks on account of all the bombing. I must say it would be a load off my mind, knowing that the two of you were living somewhere safer.'

Rosie bit her lip. The truth lurked dangerously on her lips. She hated being deceitful but somehow she couldn't bring herself to tell him the truth about her mother. She just couldn't bear to hurt him like that. All she could hope for was that her mother would come to her senses.

'I'm so glad you're home,' she told him instead, squeezing his arm lovingly. 'We had news the other day about one of the convoys being torpedoed. I was so worried about you until Rob Whittaker told me that your ship was safe.'

'Rob Whittaker? And who might he be then?' Her father was trying to sound as though he was joking but Rosie could hear the sharp note of fatherly concern in his voice.

'He's a fireman, lodging with the Norrises. He's working down near the docks. You'll like him, Dad. His brother's in the merchant navy.'

'Oh, I will, will I? Well, we'll have to see about that. Any lad who comes round courting my daughter—'

'Dad, it isn't like that,' Rosie protested indignantly, her face on fire. 'Don't you go letting him think that I've told you that it is. How much leave have you got?' she asked, swiftly changing the subject.

'Only forty-eight hours, lass, and then we won't be back again until Christmas.'

Rosie's excitement faded. Christmas was weeks away.

'But I haven't forgotten that a certain someone will be having a birthday soon,' her father teased. 'I've got a bit of summat in my kitbag for you, Rosie. Brought specially all the way from New York. A few pairs of stockings and some perfume and a couple of lengths of fabric for you and your mum to make yourself a new dress apiece. And mind, no trying to get me to let you unwrap them until your birthday! I'll be at sea then, but I'll be thinking about my girl opening her presents and thinking of her old dad.'

'Oh, Dad . . .' Rosie said emotionally. 'You shouldn't have. It isn't presents I want. It's having you safe.' She hugged him fiercely again, burying her face in the warmth of his reefer jacket.

'Aye, I know that, Rosie lass. You're the best

daughter a man could have, and when I saw all the pretty girls in New York I thought to myself that none of them was half so pretty as you.

'Have you managed to call round and see your Auntie Maude whilst I've been away, Rosie?'

Rosie shook her head guiltily. 'I will try, Dad,' she promised, 'but what with fire-watch duty, and all the other things we have to do, there just doesn't seem to be time.'

'I can't get over how much it's changed round here,' her father commented as they walked past the closed shops that had once been so busy.

'It is different without all the Italian families,' Rosie agreed sadly. 'That was so awful what happened to them, Dad.'

'Bad things happen during wartime, Rosie.'

Rosie felt shamed, knowing that her father must have seen such horrors himself. She determined there and then that she would make his leave, no matter how short, as pleasurable as possible. She just hoped that her mother would come to her senses and realise how lucky she was to be married to a man like her father.

TWELVE

'So where's Sylvia this morning? She's going to be in trouble with Mrs Verey for being late. She's not still seeing that cousin of Nancy's, is she, Rosie?' Enid asked Rosie as they all huddled round the single-bar electric fire in the workroom, trying to warm the damp November chill out of their cold hands prior to starting work.

Rosie hesitated before answering. The truth was that she and Sylvia were no longer friends – Sylvia's decision, not hers – but she was as reluctant to say so as she was to explain why. Not because she felt she was at fault – she didn't unless it was for forgetting just how young Sylvia was – but because she still felt a sense of loyalty towards Sylvia, and a need to protect her.

'She is still seeing him, yes,' she acknowledged reluctantly when it was plain that she was going to have to give some kind of answer.

The quarrel that had brought about the end of their friendship had happened earlier in the month, when Rosie had stuck firmly by her decision not to give in to Sylvia's pleas that she make up a foursome with her and Lance and one of his friends.

'Aw, go on, Rosie,' Sylvia had urged her. 'Lance will get his mate to get you some stockings.'

'No, thanks,' Rosie had refused firmly. 'Dad's told me that he's brought me stockings back as a birthday present and, to be honest, Sylvia, I'd rather not have things that I know others are having to do without. It doesn't seem fair somehow.'

She hadn't wanted to seem to be critical of Sylvia or to offend her but Rosie had seen from the defiant toss of Sylvia's head that her frankness hadn't been well received. But there had been worse to come.

'Huh, as for that, you can't tell me that a few cans of this and that haven't made their way into your larder from the docks, just like they've done into ours.'

'No, I can't,' Rosie had been forced to admit. She certainly suspected that her mother was obtaining her cigarettes from the black market, even though Christine had never come out and said so.

'So what's the difference between that and having a boyfriend like Lance who knows what's what?' Sylvia had demanded.

In truth there wasn't any logical difference that Rosie could explain, other than that somehow she knew it would make her feel uncomfortable to be accepting the largesse of a man like Lance.

In the end she had felt obliged to say quietly, 'Sylvia, I don't mean to interfere, but I think I should warn you that Lance—'

To Rosie's horror Sylvia had stopped her immediately to say scornfully, 'Oh ho, so that's how you're going to do it, is it? Lance warned me as how you'd bin trying to mek up to him so as you could steal him away from me. But me thinking you was my friend, I told him that he must have got it wrong. But it was me that got it wrong, wasn't it, Rosie, 'cos it's as plain as the nose on me face what you're up to. You're trying to put me off Lance, so as you can have him. Well, it won't work. And as for us being friends – you're no friend of mine and I don't want nothing to do with you no more.'

Rosie could only stare at her in shocked disbelief. Surely Sylvia couldn't be serious? Rosie had made her own feelings about Lance abundantly plain. It was laughable that anyone should think she was so much as able to tolerate him, never mind anything else.

When she had got over her astonishment she shook her head and told Sylvia gently, 'Look, Sylvia, I can see that you might not like me being so frank about not thinking that Lance is right for you, but I've only said what I've said for your own good.'

'For *your* own good, more like,' Sylvia came back at her quick as a flash. 'There's no point in you trying to soft-soap me, Rosie, not now that Lance has told me what you've bin up to.'

'I haven't been up to anything,' Rosie protested indignantly. 'I don't know what Lance has told you but—'

'Oh, come off it, you know perfectly well what I'm talking about. I'm talking about how you've bin chasing after my Lance, asking him to meet up with you secretly when he came into the shop asking for me.'

'I did no such thing,' Rosie gasped.

There was a look of fury in Sylvia's eyes. 'I hope you aren't trying to call my Lance a liar! Hah, that would be a fine thing, coming from you. And to think I thought you was my friend.'

'I am your friend,' Rosie insisted. 'And if you had any sense you'd know that.' She recognised her mistake immediately as Sylvia stiffened angrily and stepped back from her.

'It's because I've got some sense that I want nowt to do wi' you any more. Because I've got enough sense to know when a girl is after my chap and enough to know just what to do about it.' Rosie could see that Sylvia was working herself up into an angry frenzy. 'I dunno why I bothered trying to defend you to Lance. You're no friend of mine no more and I'll thank you to remember that.'

Rosie didn't know what to say. She tried to tell herself that Sylvia was very young and very much in love, and that her feelings for Lance were blinding her to the truth of how unfair and unkind she was being. But in her heart Rosie felt not just badly let

205

down but very hurt. This was the second time someone she had thought of as a friend had turned on her and ended that friendship. There was no point in trying to reason with Sylvia. Anything she said now would only lead to a slanging match and Rosie was not one for that kind of thing.

Very much on her dignity, she inclined her head and said quietly, 'I certainly don't want to be friends with someone who doesn't want my friendship, Sylvia, but if you ask me you're a fool for trusting a chap like Lance.'

'You're the one who's the fool – for thinking that Lance wouldn't tell me what you was up to. I've a good mind to tell the other girls, an' all.'

'I wish you would, 'cos if you did they'd soon put you right about a fair few things,' Rosie felt driven to retort.

That had been over two weeks ago now, and Sylvia had only spoken to her when she had had to since then. Rosie had too much pride to let the other girls know that she had been accused of trying to snatch another girl's chap, and so she had done her best to act as though everything was normal and they hadn't fallen out. Luckily, with the war on the other girls had their own worries to think about, and no one had seemed to notice that Sylvia was going out at dinner time leaving Rosie to sit in and eat her sandwiches on her own.

Rosie suspected that part of the reason Sylvia was going out was so that she could see Lance, and despite their falling-out, she was still genuinely concerned for Sylvia and worried that ultimately Lance would let her down and leave her very hurt.

'Well, she's good and late now,' Enid said, 'and Mrs Verey will have summat to say to her when she does come in. There was no air raids last night so it can't be that they've bin bombed out or owt like that.'

'Maybe she isn't feeling very well,' Rosie offered, still not wanting Sylvia to get into trouble, even though she had behaved so unkindly to her.

'Huh, if you ask me she's probably gone and stayed out too late with that Lance and then not wanted to get up for work,' Ruth offered critically. 'Pity she's not here, 'cos that means she won't get a piece of the cake that we'll be having at dinner time on account of it being someone's birthday.'

Enid and Ruth were both smiling meaningfully at her, Rosie realised, her own face brightening with a wide smile as she blushed and shook her head, saying, 'If you mean me then—'

''Course we mean you. Who else would we mean?' Enid demanded, mock derisively. She nudged Ruth and demanded, 'We clocked the date, didn't we, Ruth, when we heard you saying that your dad had brought you back summat from New York but that you wouldn't be going to open it until your birthday. Don't you remember, Rosie, Ruth asked you when your birthday was?'

She did remember now, Rosie acknowledged,

although she hadn't twigged the significance of why she was being asked at the time.

'All the girls put a bit in and Mrs Verey said as how we could have a bit extra for our dinner hour and that she'd see to it that there was a bit of a cake.'

Tears filled Rosie's eyes. After what had happened, first with Bella and now with Sylvia, the kindness of the girls she worked with meant so much to her.

Waking up this morning she hadn't been able to help contrasting this birthday to those she had enjoyed in the past when Bella had never been able to wait for her to call for her on the way to school but had instead come rushing round with a card, whilst Rosie was still having her breakfast.

Then after school they would go back to the Grenellis', where Maria would have made a special birthday tea that would include Rosie's favourite chocolate ice cream. There would be cards from la Nonna and Maria, and always a special present for her from Maria, a pretty dress she had made for her and which she would be dispatched upstairs to Bella's small bedroom to change into. Bella would change too and then they would go downstairs together, all giggly and self-conscious, to be made a fuss of and told how pretty they looked.

Neighbours would come in to wish her a happy birthday and then stay to share in the celebration, which often included someone playing some music and someone else singing. But this year, of course, there had been no Bella to wish her a happy birthday and no Grenellis to make it and her feel special. She had felt so low this morning, especially since her mother was now working nights and Rosie had been in the house alone. And now here out of the blue the girls she worked with had lifted her spirits immeasurably with their kindness. Rosie couldn't begin to tell them how much they had cheered her up.

The birthday she had been dreading because it would be the first she could remember having without her 'second family' to celebrate it with her had not been as bad as she had feared after all, Rosie admitted as she hurried home in the November dusk, carefully carrying what was left of the wartime carrot cake Mrs Verey had got for her.

The house was cold and empty. Her mother had forgotten to stoke up the fire with some of the slack, a mix of coal dust and small pieces of coal, which households used to keep their fires smouldering whilst they were out in the hope of preserving some warmth at the cost of very little coal.

She also seemed to have forgotten her birthday as well, Rosie recognised sadly, as she put her cake down on the kitchen table and took off her coat before switching on the wireless and then going to sort out the fire and relight it.

That done, she filled the kettle and then went

upstairs to bring down the carefully wrapped presents her father had left for her. He had teased her about her not wanting to open them until her actual birthday, but Rosie had remained adamant. She had put the brightly wrapped parcels on the kitchen table and had poured the boiling water over the tea leaves before she remembered to go and check the front door for any post just in case her mother had forgotten to do so.

There was some mail, and Rosie felt both nervous and excited when she picked up one envelope and saw Maria's familiar writing on it.

Desperate to read what Maria had written, she started to open the envelope as she hurried back to the now cheerfully blazing fire and pulled a chair up close to it.

The first thing she noticed was that Maria hadn't put any address on the letter and that made her heart sink a little.

Dear dear Rosie,

I am hoping that this letter will reach you on your very special day and that you will know now that I am thinking of you. How could I not do, Rosie *cara*? You have been as a daughter to me and there isn't a day when I don't think of you and miss you.

It was for the best that we left Liverpool, though. La Nonna is so much happier here amongst the family we have in Manchester. They help to take her mind off the dreadful thing that happened, a little. You will remember how, as a small girl, you used to sit at her feet and listen to her stories of the old country. Now the little ones of my cousins and their sons and daughters do the same and when I look at them I think always of you.

You will want to know I think that Bella is now betrothed to Alberto Podestra, although they cannot be married yet since Alberto, because his family became naturalised some years ago, has now decided that it is best for him to join the Pioneer Corps, since he does not want to find himself fighting against his own countrymen as some of our boys have already had to do.

Oh, Rosie, this is such a sad world we live in. Sofia is still fiercely angry with the British Government, I'm afraid, and like many in our local Italian community she refuses to have anything to do with English people. But today is your birthday and I wish so much I could be there to wish you 'happy birthday' in person.

Thinking of you,
Your loving 'aunt' Maria

Rosie was weeping softly long before she had reached the end of the letter. And then once she had, she had to read it again and then a third and a fourth time before she could bear to put it down.

Darling Maria. Had she known how much it would mean to her to hear from her today? Rosie wondered tenderly. There was no message in her letter from Bella but Rosie refused to feel down about that. She did wish that Maria had written down her address. Reading between the lines, though, she guessed that Maria was trying to let her know that Sofia would be against any contact between them. But at least Maria had cared enough to write to her and that eased her sore heart so much.

The fire was burning up well now, although the tea she had brewed had gone cold. Drinking it anyway, Rosie turned to the presents her father had brought home for her.

She opened the stockings first, recognising which parcel they were from the shape. Six pairs! 'Oh, Dad,' she protested, 'you spoil me.' In the next parcel she found a small bottle of Evening in Paris scent. Very carefully she unstoppered the dark blue bottle and sniffed the lovely fragrance. She would use it very sparingly, she promised herself, to make it last a long time.

The final parcel would she knew contain the fabric her father had bought her. Her mother had already had hers, and it had made Rosie's eyes sting with tears when she had seen that her father had chosen a soft wool in her mother's favourite shade of red.

Inside her own parcel was a generous length of the same soft wool, in the prettiest shade of soft lilac blue Rosie had ever seen. It would be perfect for her colouring. She pressed her face against it, loving its softness and loving even more the knowledge that her dad had touched it too. If she closed her eyes she could almost imagine that he was here with her, ready to give her a birthday hug.

'Sylvia's going to get herself into a lot of trouble, if she doesn't watch out, not coming in to work yesterday and not sending any message to say why not. Mind you, if you want my opinion, she's bin getting a bit above herself since she started seein' that Lance. It's Lance this and Lance that all the ruddy time,' Enid declared sharply, coming into the workroom. 'Mrs Verey's just bin asking where she is and she's said, seeing as how you and Sylvia are friends, Rosie, you can finish a bit early tonight and go round and find out why she hasn't come in to work.' Enid gave a disgruntled sniff. 'If you was to ask me, I'd say that Mrs V. is being too soft, and that if Sylvia wants to go meking a fool of herself over someone like Lance, then she's welcome to do so. I've heard that he allus keeps two or three girls on the go at the same time, boastin' that there's safety in numbers.'

Rosie gave her an uncomfortable look, not wanting to say that Sylvia had fallen out with her. Instead, she nodded in acceptance of this charge, even though she had already planned to go up to Edge Hill after she had had her tea to fulfil her promise to her father that she would call on her aunt and make sure that she was all right. The truth was that she was anxious on Sylvia's behalf and worried about her not coming in to work, despite the fact that they had fallen out.

Knowing her Aunt Maude as she did, Rosie had already taken the precaution of writing to her to make sure that her visit was convenient. Originally she had hoped to call and see her the previous Sunday afternoon but her aunt had told her that she was too busy and demanded instead that Rosie call on a day and time of her own choosing. Rosie knew that if she tried to alter it now there would be a terrible fuss. It was just as well she had only planned to have the last of the vegetable soup she had made from the root vegetables she had been given in return for having done some sewing for a neighbour whose son had an allotment.

'Oh, and she said to tell you that Mrs Simpson has been on to say that her daughter won't be needing that wedding dress now. Her fiancé's plane was shot down over the English Channel last week.'

Rosie's face paled. 'Oh, no! They looked so in love. Oh, that poor girl.'

'Aye, well, she isn't the only one,' Enid reminded her brusquely. 'My cousin's lad was with the BEF and he was her only one, and then Phyllis's brother was killed when that bomb dropped on Central Station in September, never mind all them sailors that's bin lost.'

Rosie gave her an unhappy look. She hated

214

being reminded about how vulnerable her father was to Hitler's torpedoes.

Even though it was only four o'clock, the dank day was already fading into semi darkness as Rosie stepped off the tram and turned into the street where Sylvia lived. Mrs Verey was a kind employer and she had allowed Rosie plenty of time to get round to Sylvia's in work hours to find out why Sylvia hadn't come in to work.

The sight of a queue outside a butchers had tempted Rosie to join the end of it on the off chance that she might be lucky and get something for dinner, but her conscience had refused to let her use her employer's time for her own ends, so instead she had headed for the tram and the dock area.

It was one of Sylvia's sisters who opened the door to Rosie's knock, giving a brief wary look up and down the street before inviting her in.

'It's all right, our dad's gone down the docks to see a mate of his, and he'll probably not be back now until the pubs close, with it being a Saturday, otherwise I'd daresn't let you in, seein' as how our Sylvia's gone and told him it was on account of you that she's bin seein' this Lance.'

'What? But that's not true,' Rosie protested before she could stop herself. 'What I mean is . . .' She stopped uncertainly. She wasn't sure how Sylvia would react to her visit, and whether or not she would welcome her.

'Oh, it's all right. Me and Bertha didn't believe it

anyway. We'd both already warned her about what was going to happen if our dad caught her sneaking out behind his back. Given her a real pasting, he has. Her backside will be black and blue – just like her eye. Daft, she was, to think she could get away with it. She might have known that someone would see her, carrying on like she was. Only went and got herself caught in a doorway three streets away, doin' what she shouldn't, for anyone to see.' Clara snorted in derision, oblivious to Rosie's shock.

'You wait here,' she told Rosie, showing her into a shabby cold front parlour lit by a flickering gas mantle that hissed and smelled.

Her mother might not be much of a housewife, but Rosie had grown up watching Maria and Bella's mother take a pride in keeping their home not just clean and polished but in making it homely with flowers and ornaments, and she had automatically absorbed their homemaking skills so that the little house she and her parents shared shone with love and care, unlike Sylvia's home, which smelled of neglect and dust, Rosie recognised, wrinkling her nose against the odour of the gaslight and averting her gaze from the dust on the linoleum and the mantelpiece.

The apprehension she had sensed in Clara had transferred itself to her and she jumped nervously when the parlour door opened, half expecting to be confronted by Sylvia's irate father but instead it was Sylvia herself who stood there, a large bruise swelling her cheekbone.

'Oh, Sylvia . . .' Rosie whispered sympathetically, whilst Sylvia's eyes filled with tears that spilled
down her face.

'Oh, I'm right glad you're here,' Sylvia sobbed
as she threw herself into Rosie's arms. 'And I'm
sorry for what I said about you and Lance. Oh,
Rosie, I'm that upset. I haven't seen Lance since
me dad caught me with him. But I've written to
him and he'll be round here quick as a flash to
get me, you can be sure of that. 'Cos now that
we've bin together proper like, it means that we're
a couple, and anyway he said the last time I saw
him how much he loves me.'

Rosie's heart sank further with every betraying
word Sylvia recounted. Couldn't Sylvia see what
was happening, and what Lance was?

'When me and Lance are wed, it's me dad who's
going to be sorry because I won't want anything
to do with him. And when we have money, then
he'll be sorry.'

The hysterical outburst continued, Sylvia
pouring out her feelings. But although she was
angry with her father for having told her that she
wasn't to see Lance again, and obviously cowed
by his physical punishment of her, so far as Rosie
could tell Sylvia felt no remorse or discomfort over
the situation she had been caught in.

'Mrs Verey wants to know what's wrong and
when you'll be coming back to work,' Rosie
informed her as soon as she could get a word in.

Sylvia shook her head. 'I won't be coming back

217

to the shop. Me dad has said that I've got to find another job as brings in more money. And besides, he wouldn't let me come back anyway because of you.'

'Clara said something . . .'

'Yes. He thinks it was you as encouraged me to go out with Lance,' Sylvia told her. When she saw Rosie's expression she defended herself, saying quickly, 'Well, I had to tell him summat, didn't I?'

'But I was the one who told you not to get involved with him,' Rosie reminded her.

Sylvia gave a dismissive shrug. 'Me dad's told me that I'm not to see Lance again but I will. And we can be married, and I won't have to bother about what me dad says no more.'

'Sylvia, you're only sixteen; Lance is close to thirty. You're too young to get married.' Rosie didn't want to upset her by suggesting that marriage was probably the last thing on Lance's mind, but at the same time she felt that she had to try to warn her.

However, to her dismay, Sylvia tossed her head and said, 'Well, as to that, Lance has already promised that he will wed me, so there.'

The door opened, causing Sylvia to give Rosie a warning look as Clara came in.

'You'd better go,' she told Rosie, 'just in case our dad does come back, otherwise we'll be for it – me included for letting you see our Sylvia. Has she told you that he's said that she's not to go back to the shop?' she asked as she left Sylvia in the parlour and escorted Rosie to the front door.

Rosie nodded. 'I'll tell Mrs Verey.'

As shocked as she was by Sylvia's father's violence towards his daughter, she was equally shocked by what Sylvia had done. What was it about women like Sylvia and her mother that led them down the path towards the wrong men? Sylvia was young and naïve enough to believe that Lance really would marry her, but her mother already had a husband and from all accounts had been around the block . . .

An hour later, when she let herself into the cold kitchen of her own home, her mother's behaviour was on Rosie's mind again. On the cold air of the empty room she could smell quite plainly the strong smell of the Brylcreem used by her mother's lover – she had smelled it that night she had discovered them.

How could her mother continue to behave so badly? Rosie wondered miserably. She hardly saw her now that Christine was working nights, and Rosie couldn't banish the suspicion that her mother had chosen to work those hours not so much for the money as the opportunity it could give her to have the house to herself whilst Rosie was at work.

'I'm lonely, Rosie,' she had defended her actions when Rosie had challenged her. 'And Dennis is good company. He makes me laugh and I have fun with him.'

Fun! How could her mother even think about

having fun when brave men like her father were losing their lives every day, fighting to protect their country and those they loved?

Tears stung Rosie's eyes as she heated up what was left of the soup.

Rosie had just got off the bus on Wavertree Road, when she heard the warning wail of the air-raid siren. Automatically she looked up towards the sky, crisscrossed now with the dazzling bright glare of the searchlights. She was close enough to her aunt's to feel it would be safer to hurry there and join her in the small shelter she shared with her neighbours, installed at the bottom of their garden. Breaking into a run, Rosie prayed not to see the dreaded shape of the green parachutes attached to the deadly bombs the Germans had started to drop on the city at the beginning of the month.

When she reached her aunt's house she was surprised to be told that her father's sister had no intention of going to any air-raid shelter.

'Unhygienic, that's what they are,' she sniffed as she let Rosie in and instructed her to take off her shoes so that she didn't tread any dirt onto her pristine floors.

'But, Aunt Maude, it isn't safe for you to stay here when there's a bombing raid on,' Rosie protested, mindful of how concerned her father would be if he knew the risk his sister was taking.

'I've got me cupboard under the stairs. That's plenty safe enough for me. Besides, the Germans won't drop any bombs here in Wavertree. It's the docks they're after,' she told Rosie almost complacently, as if the Germans wouldn't dare bomb somewhere she lived.

'I wasn't sure you'd be coming so I hope you've already had your tea, because I've nothing to spare. You'd better come into the kitchen.'

It was just as well she was used to her aunt's peremptory manner and hadn't been expecting a warm welcome, Rosie acknowledged ruefully.

'So what's this I've been hearing about that mother of yours?' her aunt demanded as soon as Rosie was sitting down – in the chair furthest from the fire that heated the back boiler, Rosie noticed, as she tried not to shiver as her aunt blocked the heat from her.

Rosie tensed, her heart sinking. Surely it wasn't possible for Aunt Maude to have discovered what her mother was doing.

'A fine thing, her taking on night work. It isn't respectable! Not for a married woman. What's going to happen when my poor brother comes home on leave and needs looking after if she's out all night at some parachute factory?'

So it was her mother working nights that Aunt Maude was objecting to. Rosie felt shaky with relief.

'Mum is just doing her bit for the war effort, Aunt Maude,' she shouted out to her aunt above the noise from the bombers overhead and the fire from the ack-ack guns protecting the city. 'Our men need the parachutes the factory is making.' Another time Rosie admitted that it would have amused her to see the way her aunt was struggling to find some way of criticising her mother whilst refraining from denying that parachutes were badly needed. But she wasn't convinced her mother was doing it for the best motives herself.

'I really think we ought to be in a proper shelter,' Rosie told her aunt. 'I'm surprised your air-raid warden hasn't been round to tell you that.'

Every air-raid warden had a list of all those living in his area and was responsible for making sure they reported to their shelters.

'Mr Dawson knows better than to try to tell me what to do,' Aunt Maude responded sharply. 'There's no telling what a person might catch in one of those places.'

'But you've got a shelter next door that you only share with your neighbours,' Rosie pointed out.

'I did have, but they have her cousin and her children billeted on them,' her aunt sniffed disparagingly. 'And they aren't the Wavertree sort at all.'

Rosie gasped as several planes roared so low overhead that she actually ducked her head and then tensed as several seconds later they heard a tremendous explosion, which caused the china on her aunt's kitchen dresser to rattle.

'It will be the docks,' her aunt declared, but Rosie wasn't convinced. 'It sounded much closer than that, Auntie.'

It was gone ten o'clock before the sound of the

planes died away and Rosie finally felt it was safe enough for her to make her way home. Her aunt didn't press her to stay, but, if she was honest with herself, Rosie decided she would feel safer taking refuge in one of the public shelters than staying with Aunt Maude.

Ten minutes later, as she reached Edge Hill and saw the extent of the damage caused by the bombs that had been dropped – not as her aunt had insisted on the docks but on the suburbs of the city – Rosie shivered in shocked disbelief at the carnage. Rescue workers of every kind, fire engines and ambulances clustered around what had once been whole streets and buildings, whilst overhead the searchlights probed the sky.

'Here you, miss . . . there's a shelter over there. Get yourself into it,' an ARP warden called out sternly to Rosie when he saw her staring in shock at the heap of rubble from which several bodies had just been removed. Half blinded by a mixture of soot, dust and tears, Rosie followed his instructions, and made her way to the already full basement shelter beneath the Junior Technical College on Durning Road.

'Just about room for one more little 'un in this section here,' someone called out cheerily as Rosie gave an apologetic look in the direction of the female ARP warden taking people's names.

'There's a chair here, love,' she told Rosie, when Rosie had given her name and explained where she had been.

'I don't want to take it if someone else needs it,' Rosie told her.

'That's all right,' the other woman said. 'It's not normally like this here but some of the other shelters in the area caught it in the bombing raid so them as should have been there have been sent here, and we've had two tramloads drop on us as well. I'm Mrs Taft, by the way.'

'Is there anything I can do to help?' Rosie asked her.

Mrs Taft smiled at her. 'Thanks, love. If you could keep an eye on some of the little 'uns and their mums, I'd be grateful. Get them having a singsong or something. It's hard for mothers, having to keep getting their kiddies out of bed, and once one of them sets off crying all the others seem to start.'

Obediently Rosie did what she could to coax half a dozen crying youngsters to stop and 'help' her to sing a Christmas carol instead. Within a few minutes other children and some of the adults had joined in. When a man produced an accordion and started to play it, Mrs Taft gave Rosie a relieved look.

'I knew you were the right sort,' she told Rosie with a smile. 'I'll have a cuppa for you if you can just hang on for a while.'

Sharing the companionship of the public shelter was more comfortable than being at her aunt's, Rosie acknowledged, and the time flew by as she made herself useful and discovered that somehow or other she seemed to have become Mrs Taft's assistant.

'Sounds like they're back,' Mrs Taft murmured to Rosie at one point as they both stopped what they were doing to listen to the throbbing sound of the engines of returning bombers. Silence fell as one by one others in the shelter tensed to listen with them. And then a baby cried and an elderly woman muttered a prayer and tugged on her rosary beads, and slowly the shelter began to hum with noise again.

'It's nearly bloody two o'clock,' someone protested. 'When are we going . . .' The rest of his words were drowned out as an explosion ripped violently through the shelter, filling the air with choking dust and darkness.

As Rosie struggled to get to her feet she could hear people screaming and moaning.

'The roof's fallen in and we're trapped!' someone called out.

In the panic as people tried to find an exit, Rosie almost lost her balance when she bent down to pick up the child she could feel clinging to her legs. There was something soft and wet on the floor beside her and her stomach turned over as she realised that it was someone who had been badly injured. The child's mother? Another child? It was too dark for her to see.

She turned to Mrs Taft, who was standing next to her. 'There's someone . . .' she began, but the ARP warden shook her head.

'Dead I'm afraid,' she told her quietly. 'I've just checked. You're a sensible girl. I'm going to have to rely on you to keep calm and to help the mothers look after the little ones whilst I try to find a way out.' Raising her voice, she called out, 'Everyone, please keep calm.'

'How can we when we're going to drown?' someone howled in fear. 'I can feel water creeping up me legs . . .'

'Those with small children, please pick them up to keep them above the level of the water.'

A young mother standing next to Rosie sobbed frantically, 'I can only find one of my two. Where's my Jenny . . . ?'

'The exits are all blocked,' a man called out in panic.

It was almost impossible to move and the shelter lights had fused, but everyone was struggling to follow Mrs Taft's example as she said steadily, 'Let's keep calm and try the emergency exits.'

'We'll never get out,' someone cried, whilst Rosie's heart contracted at the sounds of the wounded and dying they could hear from the other side of the wall dividing them from the main shelter.

'Yes we will,' Mrs Taft called back firmly. 'They'll get us out safe and sound.'

'Oh Gawd, look, there's a fire there in the main part of the shelter.'

Rosie froze as she looked towards the wall that divided the part of the shelter they were in from the main part, and sure enough she could just see the flames on the other side of it.

'That's where the school furnaces are,' a man close at hand groaned. 'If they've bin hit then we're goners.'

The smell of the acrid smoke starting to pour into their part of the shelter reminded Rosie of her fire-watch practice, but it wasn't possible for them to drop down to the floor beneath the smoke as she had been taught because of the water slowly filling the shelter and rising coldly up her legs. Everyone was pressing towards the emergency exits.

'The emergency exits are jammed.' The words were passed from one to another in an anguished whisper as people instinctively sought to keep calm whilst their hopes died.

Rosie hugged the small child she was holding. They would die together in here, strangers united by their inescapable fate. Then miraculously she heard Mrs Taft calling out, 'I can see a light,' and even more miraculously Rosie realised that the warden had found a window leading out of the shelter, which somehow had not been totally blocked by the falling debris that surrounded it.

Four men struggled through the press of people. One of them had a torch, which he flashed by the window until the rescue workers outside saw it.

Within an unbelievably short space of time, or so it seemed to Rosie, she was helping the children to climb to safety over the debris and out into the waiting arms of their rescuers. It was only when one of them cried out to Mrs Taft, 'Nana,' that she realised that the ARP warden's daughter and grandchild were amongst those who had been trapped. At last it was Rosie's own turn to be helped out into the freedom of the smoke-laden night air.

As she was led gently to where a group of WVS women were handing out blankets and tea, Rosie saw the pitiful sight of the small bodies being laid gently on the ground as they were removed from the main part of the building. Tears filled her eyes and splashed down her face.

'That's right, love,' someone told her gently. 'You 'ave a good cry.'

Although she insisted that she was all right, somehow or other Rosie ended up being taken to Mill Road Hospital to have what the WVS lady had described as 'a nasty cut' cleaned and dressed. She had no recollection of receiving the wound, which had sliced open the upper part of her arm, ruining her clothes, but thankfully it was not deep enough to require stitching.

Daylight was just beginning to lighten the sky when Rosie, feeling faint and queasy, bumped into someone on her way back to the hospital reception. Firm hands took hold of her shoulders and a familiar voice exclaimed worriedly, 'Rosie!'

Numbly she looked up and saw Rob Whittaker gazing back at her.

'What's happened to you?' he demanded anxiously.

'She's one of them they brought in from the Junior Technical College that was bombed on Durning Road,' the nurse who had dressed her wound answered for her. 'She's had a nasty cut on her arm but she'll be all right. Not like some poor buggers. Over three hundred dead, so I've heard – kiddies and all.'

Rosie's stomach heaved as she remembered the sounds she had tried to blot out.

'Come on, let's get you home,' Rob told her gently.

'You can't. You're on duty,' Rosie protested.

'I finished my shift an hour ago. I was just helping out.'

Rosie didn't have the energy to object, and besides, she wasn't sure if she could manage to get home without his help. Her whole body seemed to have gone strangely weak and her arm was now throbbing agonisingly.

'There was something. Someone on the floor at my feet,' Rosie whispered, shivering as Rob guided her out into the pre-dawn cold. 'Mrs Taft said that they were dead . . . They must have been standing right next to me . . .'

'That's how it happens sometimes, Rosie. If it's got your number on it then it just has.'

Somewhere in the city she could hear the sound of a church bell. 'It's Sunday morning.'

'Yes,' Rob confirmed

'Sunday morning and all those people dead,' Rosie told him, and promptly burst into tears.

Very gently Rob took her in his arms, holding her carefully. Her hair and her clothes were covered in dust from the explosion, and the tip of her nose was pink with cold, but as he looked down at her, Rob Whittaker thought that he had never seen a more beautiful girl.

'So what's up with Sylvia then, Rosie?' Enid asked briskly. It was Monday morning, and although it was only a few hours since her ordeal, Rosie had still gone in to work, the bandage on her arm concealed by the sleeve of her sweater. She didn't want to have to talk about the events of the day before and relive the trauma of what she had seen.

'Her dad found out about her seeing Lance, and since she told him that I was the one to encourage her to date him, he's told her she's got to find another job and that she can't come back here,' Rosie answered.

'She blamed you? Cheeky young madam. Well, I'd better go and tell Mrs Verey that she isn't going to be coming back. Not that she'll be missed that much. Workshy she was, and no mistake.'

Rosie watched her leave the workroom. The pain in her arm had eased off slightly, but she still blushed when she thought about the fool she had made of herself, crying all over Rob Whittaker like that. But Rob had been kind and understanding, and somehow or other Rosie had let him persuade her to go to the cinema with him on Wednesday night.

The shop was quiet with it being a Monday,

but by dinner time Rosie's head had begun to ache unpleasantly.

'That were awful about the Technical College, weren't it?' she heard one of the girls commenting as she unwrapped her sandwiches, carefully so that the paper could be reused. Everyone was getting used now to having to 'make do and mend', as the government slogan exhorted them to do. 'My sister's boyfriend's uncle was one of them helping to get them out. He . . .'

Inside her head Rosie could see the images she had been trying to blot out. People so dreadfully injured, just standing there in silence, covered in their own blood, one little girl who had lost her arm, other children, their little bodies lifeless, their mothers crouching over them, holding them, a woman sitting there nursing her dead baby, her eyes wide and blank, two young children miraculously unharmed sitting either side of their obviously dead mother. And then all the bodies, on the ground after they had been recovered. Bodies everywhere, or so it had seemed to Rosie.

She jumped up in agitation begging, 'Please don't talk about it . . .'

When the other girls looked at her curiously she admitted shakily, 'I was there in the shelter . . . I saw . . .' Her head was swimming and suddenly she started to sway on her feet. She felt quite dreadfully faint she thought dizzily as it started to go dark . . .

* * *

What on earth was she doing lying on the work-room floor? Rosie struggled to sit up and was stopped by the kind pressure of Mrs Verey's hand and her voice insisting firmly, 'Lie still, Rosie.'

'Oh, I'm ever so sorry, Mrs Verey.' Rosie was mortified by the realisation that she must have fainted.

'That's all right, dear.' Mrs Verey leaned closer to her. 'Enid tells me that you were involved in that terrible tragedy at the Technical College on Saturday night.'

'Yes,' Rosie whispered. 'I'd been to see my Auntie Maude and I was on my way back . . .' She bit her lip. 'It was so dreadful. All those poor people . . . So many children.' It gave her an un-expected feeling of relief to talk about what she had experienced, even though she felt guilty at burdening others with her own distress. Tears filled her eyes and spilled over onto her cheeks as she relived seeing the small bodies. 'I'm sorry, Mrs Verey.'

'You've nothing to be sorry for, Rosie. I'm going to send you home for the rest of the day.'

'Oh, but I'm all right, really I am,' Rosie tried to protest, but her employer was shaking her head firmly.

'I can see that you've hurt your arm, Rosie, and I can imagine what a terrible ordeal you must have had. I hope that I'm not such an unfeeling person that I expect my staff to carry on working after that kind of experience.'

Rosie wanted to protest that somehow she felt better coming to work than being at home alone, reliving what had happened, but she felt that it would be rude to throw Mrs Verey's generosity back in her face, so she thanked her and allowed Enid to help her to her feet.

'Why on earth didn't you tell us?' Enid scolded her half an hour later as she walked Rosie to the tram. 'Marjorie said she feels ever so awful now for going on the way she did and making you faint.'

'I just didn't want to talk about it at first,' Rosie admitted. 'I saw the children, Enid, the ones they'd brought out. Their little bodies . . .' Rosie put her hand to her mouth and fought her emotions.

The tram was virtually empty, and Rosie tried to avoid looking at the new gaping holes and craters caused by Saturday night's bombing. She got off the tram at the top of the road and walked reluctantly down it. Her mother would be in bed, of course, since she was working nights. Rosie hadn't even told her about what had happened yet – not that she'd care, she decided bitterly.

When she stepped into the kitchen she saw the cup and plate her mother must have used when she had come in from the factory still on the table, unlike her own breakfast things, which she had washed and left neatly stacked on the draining board before she left. Her head was throbbing sickeningly now and so was her arm. She opened the door into the narrow hallway and then stopped, staring in disbelief at the stairs as she heard the sound of rhythmic squeaking bed springs coming from her parents' room.

Rosie might not be as worldly as some of the girls she worked with but she wasn't so completely naïve that she didn't know what the sounds she could hear meant. Nausea gripped her stomach and filled her throat as she recognised just what was going on upstairs in her parents' bedroom. With a small choked cry, she ran back into the kitchen and out of the house, angry tears burning her eyes.

'Here, Rosie, what are you doing home at this time of the day?' she heard one of their neighbours call out to her, but she didn't stop to answer her. She couldn't. Her head down, she kept on walking, ignoring the cold wind and the curious looks she was attracting as the tears ran down her face unchecked.

Rosie walked until her feet ached, locked in her own thoughts of grief and despair, oblivious to everything but her own inner turmoil.

She hadn't even realised that she had walked down to the docks until she dragged herself out of her misery and looked up and recognised her surroundings. She couldn't bear to go back home. She couldn't endure the thought of seeing her mother, knowing what she had been doing. She shivered violently, her teeth chattering with a mixture of shock and cold.

It was growing dark and she couldn't stay out much longer. She could only hope that by the time she got back her mother would have left for work, because she didn't trust herself to be able to see her without telling her what she thought of her. She was no better than Sylvia. In fact she was worse. Sylvia at least was free to cheapen herself and carry on with Lance.

It had started to rain by the time Rosie got back home, the fine drizzle causing her hair to curl wildly. She had managed to repair her damaged coat but the damp was bringing out the smell of the shelter and evoked everything that had happened in it, curdling Rosie's stomach and plucking at her fraught nerves.

'Rosie, is that you?'

She froze as she heard her mother's voice coming from the hallway when she stepped into the kitchen.

'What's all this I've bin hearing about you being caught in that Technical College bombing?' her mother demanded. 'Is it true?'

'He's gone then, has he?' Rosie demanded, flatly ignoring her mother's questions.

Christine's face paled. 'What do you mean? What are you talking about?'

'You know perfectly well what I mean. He – your – *him*.' Rosie's voice betrayed her misery as she emphasised the word. 'He's been coming round here whilst I've been at work, hasn't he? Don't bother denying it, Mum. I heard the two of you –

upstairs.' Her control broke. 'How could you?' she cried. 'How could you do that?'

'Rosie, keep your voice down. Do you want the whole street to hear you?' her mother demanded.

'Why not? They've probably heard the pair of you – I certainly could,' Rosie told her brutally.

She could see the shock and fear in her mother's eyes but they no longer had the power to touch her. She felt as though her mother had become a stranger to her; worse than a stranger because she actually felt as though she neither cared about her nor even liked her any more. All she knew was that she felt desperately alone and equally desperately angry with and disgusted by her mother's behaviour.

'What are you going to do?' Christine was asking her in a high panicky voice. 'You can't tell your father; you mustn't. You'll upset him terribly if you do, Rosie.'

'I'll upset him terribly?' Rosie laughed mirthlessly. 'That's so typical of you, Mother, blaming someone else for your own sins. And as for me telling Dad – I won't need to. You can bet that someone else will and before he's so much as got his foot inside the door.'

Christine's face blanched but the protective pity Rosie would once have felt for her had been deep frozen by her own trauma.

'What am I going to do?' Christine whispered helplessly. 'Your dad's a good man, Rosie, I know that, but I've been so lonely. I love Dennis and he loves me.'

She looked and sounded like a child caught out in some misdemeanour and afraid of the consequences of her own actions. Rosie's anger softened as other emotions were stirred up inside her by the sight of her mother's fear.

'Mum, he's married and so are you. You've got to give him up,' she told her mother tiredly. 'There's no other way. And you'll just have to hope that no one says anything to Dad in the meantime.'

'I've really enjoyed tonight, Rosie.' Rob squeezed Rosie's hand meaningfully as they left the cinema, and then determinedly kept hold of it. 'Will you let me take you to the Grafton on Saturday?'

Rosie hesitated, and then nodded her acceptance. She liked Rob and she had enjoyed their evening out together. She liked the way he treated her with courtesy and respect, and she liked as well the safe comfortable feeling he gave her of knowing that he wasn't the kind to try things on. Other girls she knew might laugh at her for those feelings and swear that she was missing out by not wanting the excitement of falling passionately in love, and all the special intimacies that went with that. All the girls at work were talking about how the war had changed everything and now it was a girl's duty to see her lad off to war happy, knowing that she had committed herself to him, even if they hadn't had time to legalise things by getting married.

'There's no point in telling your lad "no" and

hanging on to it when he might not be coming home,' Phyllis Brookes, one of the seamstresses, had said bluntly when they had been talking about such things. 'Me, I'd rather know I'd given my chap summat to remember me by if he shouldn't make it and come back. And I do not care what anyone else says. After all, it's not as if I'm one of that sort that is cheapening themselves with every lad that looks at them. No, what me and my Percy have is summat that's only for him.'

Phyllis had spoken with the kind of passion Rosie had yet to experience, a passion she didn't think she felt for Rob. She wanted to feel safe and to be able to hold up her head in public and, above all, not be like her mother.

'You'd better let go of my hand,' she warned him, 'otherwise people might see and get the wrong impression.'

'And what impression might that be?' Rob teased her.

Rosie gave him a reproving look. 'You know perfectly well what I mean, Rob Whittaker. You and me aren't a couple.'

'Not yet, but I don't mind admitting that I'd like us to be, Rosie. There's no one I'd sooner have as my girl than you.'

Rosie could feel herself blushing, Rob was making her feel so confused. Of course it was lovely to be courted, and by such a decent lad, but Rosie was wary of what was happening. Wary and worried that she didn't have the kind of feelings for Rob that she had heard other girls describing with such breathless delight. She liked him, but liking wasn't love. Maybe she just wasn't the sort of girl who would fall recklessly in love? She wished helplessly that there was someone close to her who she could talk to about her confusion and her uncertainty. But there wasn't.

'It's too soon for that kind of talk,' she told him quietly. 'I'm happy to go out with you as a friend, but that's all.'

'Saving yourself for someone special, are you then, Rosie?' he challenged her jealously. 'Someone with plenty of money in his pocket perhaps, like your m—'

Immediately Rosie swung round to confront him. 'No I'm not and I won't listen to any of that kind of talk,' she told him fiercely.

'I'm sorry. I shouldn't have said that.'

'No you shouldn't,' Rosie agreed. Her heart was thumping with anxiety and she wasn't really comforted by the regret she could hear in his voice. She hated knowing about the talk about her mother that must be going on behind the blackout curtains in the other houses in their street. It made her determined to make sure that she didn't give anyone any cause to talk about her like that. It would be so awful for her dad if he were to hear that both his wife and his daughter were gossiped about as having loose morals. She intended to make sure that he would be able to be proud of her and hold his head up high, instead of being shamed by her behaviour. It was as though she felt she had to do everything she could to counter the damage her mother was doing to their family name. It made Rosie shudder with revulsion to think about people describing her as 'her mother's daughter' in that knowing way that gossips had.

'You'll still let me take you to the Grafton, won't you?' Rob begged her, worriedly.

'I've said I'll go and I don't go back on my word.' Rosie had pulled her hand free of his now and she pushed it into her pocket, refusing to let him take hold of it again. Knowing what her mother had done was ruining everything.

THIRTEEN

It was the Saturday before Christmas and the shop had been busy all day, mostly with lads in uniform coming in, hoping to buy something for their 'girls' although, to Rosie's relief, Lance hadn't been one of them.

'You going down the Grafton dancing tonight, Rosie?' Fanny asked.

'No I can't. I'm on fire-watch duty tonight.'

'Pity, it's Mrs Wilf Hamer as will be conducting tonight and she's allus good.'

'I dare say Rosie won't be too disappointed; not if that handsome fireman wot's bin meeting her from work is going to be helping her with her fire-watch duty,' Ruth teased whilst Rosie's face went as pink as her name.

'Are you and him sweethearts, then, Rosie?' Fanny asked.

'He's just a friend, that's all,' Rosie answered her quickly.

'Oh ho, and since when did friends grab hold

of your hand and hang on to it like they was never going to let it go, like he was doing when the two of you was at the Grafton the other week? He was dancing with you like he was more than just a friend from what I could see.'

'Give over teasing her, Fanny,' Enid remonstrated. 'Rosie's got more sense than to go flinging herself at a lad, not like some as I could name. Have you heard about that Sylvia, Rosie?'

'No,' Rosie answered her truthfully. She missed Sylvia and her fun-loving ways, and she felt very sorry for her. Lance had taken advantage of her and Sylvia had been too young and naïve to see the truth about him. Now she was the one left having to pay the price for that. Rosie wished that there was something she could do to help Sylvia, but she knew that there wasn't.

'I saw her sister Bertha the other week and she was saying as how there's bin a real to-do. Seemingly the daft thing thought that Lance meant it when he said he would marry her, and she's bin letting him carry on wi' her like they was already wed. Then she found out he's bin seeing another girls as well, and she carried on like you wouldn't believe. Her Bertha said she was so upset that they've had to pack her off to live with some cousins in Wales.'

'Oh, poor Sylvia,' Rosie sympathised, and wondered if she would be getting Sylvia into more trouble if she tried to make contact.

'Well, I wouldn't be surprised if there was a bit

more to it than Bertha was saying, and the reason they've packed her off is because she's got herself in the family way and with no ring on her finger or proper marriage lines,' Enid said disapprovingly. 'It's girls like her behaving like that – and not just *girls* neither – wot give the rest of us a bad name.'

Was she being oversensitive in thinking that a couple of the girls were looking embarrassed and uncomfortable and they made a point of not looking in her direction, Rosie wondered miserably, or could they have heard about her mother?

'Well, I hope Hitler gives us a rest tonight and we do not get no more of his ruddy bombers coming over,' Evie grumbled, thankfully changing the subject. 'The air-raid warning went off at half-past six yesterday tea time and it was gone four o'clock this morning before the all clear finally came. The little 'uns next door have been crying their eyes out in case Hitler drops a bomb on their presents, bless 'em, not that they'll be getting much this year.'

'I heard that the Adelphi Hotel got badly hit, along with the town hall and the landing stage.'

'Aye, and what about what happened in Bentinck Street? Took a direct hit, them railway arches down there did, and I've heard as how they can't get the blocks of concrete off as is under them no matter how they try. Lucky it hasn't disrupted the train services too much.'

Rosie turned away, not wanting to be reminded

of her own recent ordeal. Being trapped like she had had left her with a fear of enclosed spaces and sometimes she even woke up in the night, terrified of the darkness surrounding her until she was awake enough to know that she was safe in her own bed, and not trapped beneath the ground.

Once she was outside the shop on Bold Street, she gulped in a breath of cold air, as Rob materialised at her side out of the darkness.

'Rob,' she protested, 'you didn't have to come and meet me. You're on duty tonight.' She felt both pleased to see him and yet anxious because she still didn't feel that her feelings for him were as strong as they ought to be. Could liking and love be the same thing? Maybe she just wasn't the kind of girl to get all excited about a lad. Even when Rob held her hand, although it felt nice, it didn't make her go all daft like she had heard other girls describe. 'I've got to walk back by St John's fish market to collect the turkey we've ordered for Christmas Day.'

'You're still hoping that your dad will make it back in time for his Christmas dinner then?'

'Yes. He said that he would before he sailed. What about you? Have you changed your mind about staying in Liverpool and not going to the Wirral to be with your family?'

'There wouldn't be time. I've volunteered for duty over Christmas. For one thing, it gives the men who've got families a chance to be with then and for another . . . well, Christmas is about being with the person you love, isn't it, Rosie? And since you're going to be here in Liverpool . . .'

'Rob, you promised me you wouldn't say any more about that,' Rosie reminded him uncomfortably. 'It's like I said: you and I get on well and I like you a lot, but I don't want to go rushing into something we might both regret just because there's a war on.'

The closer they got to the market, the busier the Saturday evening city streets became, as housewives hurried towards the poultry-crammed stalls, eager to enjoy the treat of a traditional Christmas dinner after the privation of living on the ration. Rosie was forced so close to Rob by the press of people that she could feel the warmth of his body next to her own. It wasn't an unpleasant sensation, she had to admit.

'I wouldn't regret it, Rosie. I know how me feelings are, and . . .'

The sharp warning wail of the air-raid siren cut across whatever he had been about to say. They looked at one another in alarm. There was a flurry of activity in the street as people hurried to find what shelter they could as the glare from the searchlights started to crisscross the night sky and the ack-ack guns swung into action, the staccato rattle of their gunfire mingling with the deadly throb of the incoming bombers' engines.

'There's a shelter at the other end of the street,' Rob began, but Rosie shrank back as he tried to grab hold of her hand and hurry her to safety.

'Rob, I can't,' she told him. 'Not after . . .'

The rattle and whine of the bombs being dropped on the docks made it impossible for them to speak, so instead, Rob hurried her into the nearest doorway. A warehouse, receiving a direct hit, went up in flames, followed by another, and then shockingly up ahead of them the market itself suddenly took the full force of an exploding bomb. Rosie cried out, covering her mouth with her hand, her whole body trembling whilst, through the screams and shouts and the smoke, the smell of roasting poultry and duck filled the evening air.

'Bloody hell, there won't be no Christmas dinner for us now,' a woman standing in the next doorway to them grumbled.

'Come on,' Rob urged, and somehow or other, against the backdrop of the noise from the bombers overhead, the ack-ack guns valiantly defending the city and the dull deadly thump of the exploding bombs, they managed to make their way back to their own local air-raid shelter.

'Get inside, quickly,' Rob begged, but Rosie shook her head.

'I can't. I'm on fire-watch duty tonight. Don't worry about me, though; I'll be fine . . .' She could see the anxiety in his eyes. 'Go,' she repeated. 'You're on duty, remember . . .'

Rob nodded, and then before she could stop him, he leaned forward and pressed a clumsy kiss on her lips.

He had gone before she could remonstrate with him, leaving her to take up her position on the flat roof of a nearby building along with her co-fire watcher, an elderly neighbour, Mick O'Brien, who had served in the First World War. He rarely spoke about what had happened to him then, but Rosie had heard her father say that those who had gone through the First World War had had a much worse time of it than they were doing now.

'Jerry's got it in for us tonight,' he told Rosie grimly as they both kept watch on the streets below them, ready to call out a warning to those waiting below should they spot any incendiaries.

Rosie gasped as a bomb hit the chemical factory on Hanover Street, resulting in an explosion so loud that it numbed her ears and left her unable to hear anything for several seconds.

'Ruddy hell,' Mick swore. 'That felt like they'd blown the heart right out of the city.'

In the distance a shower of falling incendiary bombs caught St George's Hall but none of the bombs was landing close to their own area until suddenly they both heard the low thrum of a plane and then saw the incendiaries falling from it.

'They've got the church,' Mick called out. 'They've got Holy Cross . . . I've seen it all now. Come on.'

Rosie needed no second bidding to scramble down after him and hurry towards the church, along with others who had seen the bombs falling.

It only took them a matter of minutes to reach

Great Crosshall Street but by the time they got there the church was already well alight.

'Holy Mother of God,' Rosie heard someone breathe close to her as they all stood and stared in shocked disbelief at the old church. Then John Kinsella from Standish Street yelled out, 'Come on, don't just stand there!' And everyone rushed forward to do what they could, whilst Father Doyle and Father Morrison stood there, tears running down their faces as the flames ravaged their beloved church.

They seemed to have been battling the heat and speed of the fires for ever before a fire crew finally arrived. Rosie turned round half expecting to see Rob come striding towards her whilst the man next to her said bitterly, 'At bloody last.'

'Haven't you heard the news?' the fireman nearest to them demanded tersely. 'We've lost an engine and its crew on Roe Street. Hit a bomb crater in the road – eight men dead.'

Rosie trembled and almost lost her footing, someone calling out to her, 'Watch out . . .' Numbly she bent to take the bucket of water being passed to her along the human chain, endeavouring to save the church whilst she prayed that Rob hadn't been part of the lost fire crew. Her heart felt like a dead weight inside her chest whilst a sense of doom tightened her skull until her head was pounding with a dull remorseless ache of fore-boding. She couldn't leave her post, though, not even though fresh bombs were falling and exploding all around them, not even when after what felt like hours of battling against the fires, the roof timbers finally gave way.

'Get back. Get back, everyone,' one of the fire team warned. 'It's too dangerous.'

John Kinsella, his face streaked with soot and tears, called out above the roar of the fires, 'We've got to save the vestments and the sacrament whilst we can,' before plunging into the church.

Rosie's arms ached from passing the heavy buckets of water.

Another fire engine arrived and, unbelievably, through the smoke she saw Rob walking towards her.

'Rob . . .' Half running and half stumbling she hurried towards him, not resisting when he caught her in his arms, as she sobbed, 'You're alive. Thank God . . . oh thank God.'

He held her tightly, rocking her in his arms whilst she laughed and cried, light-headed with exhaustion and relief.

'We couldn't save the church,' she told him. 'We tried but we couldn't . . .' She was crying more than laughing now.

'No, I know.'

Something in the sombre starkness of Rob's voice made her push back to look up at him.

'Something's happened,' she guessed. 'What is it? Tell me . . .'

'Rosie . . .'

'What is it? Tell me.'

'The street's caught it,' Rob told her gruffly. 'A parachute mine.'

'The street? *Our* street, you mean . . . ?'

There was something in the way he was looking at her, a mixture of pain and pity, that caught at her heart and stopped its beat, and immediately she knew.

'The house,' she whispered. 'It's hit our house.' She whirled away from him, catching him off guard, and started to run whilst he ran after her, calling her name. The cobbles were slippery with a mixture of water, smoke and soot, and several times she nearly lost her balance but finally she rounded the familiar corner and then skidded to a halt. In the light from the torches of the heavy-duty damage team she could see the empty space where her home had once been. The crater made by the bomb had spewed out bricks and roof timbers into the street, the force of the blast tearing the roof off two other houses, shattering windows, to leave the street full of broken glass and the side of another house without an entire wall so that the rooms gaped open.

'Rosie, don't go any closer,' Rob shouted behind her, catching her up and reaching out to pull her away. But it was too late. Rosie had already seen what the men were removing from the wreckage.

'No! No!' she screamed as she pushed Rob out of the way and, ignoring everyone, ran to where the men had placed the lifeless bundle of what looked like rags on the ground. Only it wasn't a bundle of rags, Rosie recognised, it was her mother. Her mother!

Rosie kneeled down in the street next to her. Her mother was covered in soot but there wasn't a single mark to be seen on her face once Rosie had gently cleaned it with her handkerchief. Her eyes were open wide and staring into nothing. Rosie's hand trembled as she closed them, and tried to ignore the jagged wound she could see on the side of her head.

'Rosie . . . don't . . .' Rob begged her, but Rosie ignored him.

'She wouldn't have felt anything,' one of the rescue workers tried to comfort her. Rosie couldn't say anything. Her throat had closed up too tightly around her pain. Several yards away in the rubble where the men were still working she could see something that looked like a male hand and an arm, a wedding ring gleaming on one finger. She stood up and started to walk towards it, only Rob wouldn't let her, and started dragging her away.

'That was him, wasn't it?' she demanded tonelessly. 'He was with her. She died with him . . .'

'Rosie. I'm sorry . . .'

Her mother had died with her lover. If it hadn't been for her affair with him she would probably still be alive. Pain and anger tore at Rosie.

A knot of women and children were already gathering in the street and Rob guided her towards them. A woman in a WVS uniform came up to them and started telling them that they would be able to get a cup of tea and somewhere to sleep for the night at the local school where the WVS had set up a temporary shelter for those made homeless by the bombs.

'I can't go,' Rosie told her politely. 'I need to stay here with my mother. My father's away at sea, you see, and I'm all she's got.'

'That's all right, dear. You do not need to worry about all that now. You go with Gracie here,' the WVS woman told her in a kind but no-nonsense voice.

'I've got to go back on duty,' Rob told her. 'But I could try and come back?'

Rosie shook her head. 'You go. I'll be all right . . .'

Words. Just words . . . She was saying them but they meant nothing. All she could think about was her mother. All she could see inside her head was her mother's lifeless body and that hand and arm betraying them both.

'Right, dear, name and address, please?'

Rosie tried to focus on what she was being asked by the uniformed WVS woman, smiling patiently at her, but the noise from the press of people filling the church hall, combined with her own shock, made it almost impossible for her to answer.

'It's Rosie,' she managed eventually. 'Rosie Price.'

'And your address?'

'It's number 12 . . .' Rosie couldn't speak for

the salt taste of her tears burning the back of her throat as she tried to swallow them back.

'She's from Gerard Street,' the WVS helper who had brought her to the shelter supplied. 'Parachute bomb . . .' she leaned closer to the desk and murmured something so quietly that the only word Rosie caught was 'fatality . . .'

'Betty here will take you to get a cup of tea. Have you got someone you can go to tonight?'

Rosie closed her eyes and squeezed back her tears. Once she would have been able to answer immediately that she had close friends to turn to, knowing that the Grenellis would have taken her in and cared for her; helped her, comforted her and loved her – once – in what seemed to be a different lifetime now. She shook her head.

'I should have left a message at the house for my dad,' she burst out anxiously. 'He won't know. He might think I have been killed . . .' What a dreadful place this was, she couldn't help thinking, packed tightly with people, some of them wearing bomb-damaged clothes, others clutching unwieldy pillowcases and even sacks full of what Rosie assumed must be their personal possessions, all of them looking grey-faced and in despair. They were, she recognised, the new homeless of Liverpool, and now she too was one of them.

'The authorities will deal with that entirely, dear. You can stay here tonight. Betty will find you a blanket. If your papers were in the house . . .'

Automatically Rosie reached for the bag she was wearing over her fire-watch siren suit.

'They're in there, are they? That's good.'

Numbly Rosie allowed herself to be led away by the shy-looking young woman who had come over to her, suddenly aware for the first time of the reality of her own situation. Her papers and her ration book were in her bag, but the only clothes she had left in the world were those she was wearing.

She was taken to a large store at the back of the hall where more WVS women were handing out blankets and other necessities to the line of people waiting patiently to be attended to.

'You wait here, and I'll go and get you a cup of tea,' Betty promised her, disappearing and returning within several minutes with a mug of tea, a couple of plain digestives and a fig roll.

Rosie hadn't realised how cold and thirsty she was until she held the mug between her icy hands. A young woman behind her in the queue was trying to calm her crying children, and as soon as she had drunk her tea Rosie turned round to her and asked if there was anything she could do to help. She needed to do something – anything – to take her mind off the pain.

The young mother gave her a grateful smile and introduced herself as Daisy Oakes.

'This is the second time we've been bombed out in as many weeks,' she told Rosie in a tired voice. 'The kids should have been evacuated and me wi' 'em but my husband wanted us to stay 'ere. I'm not staying for Hitler to have a third go at us, though.' She shivered. 'First thing Monday morning I'm off to me mum's in Cheshire.

'Have they asked you if you've got your ration book with you yet?' Daisy asked her. 'Because if they haven't, if you tell them no you'll get two weeks' worth of coupons. My, you have got a good touch with the little 'uns,' she admired, when the two older children stopped crying to listen to the little story Rosie was making up for them.

Rosie was only too glad to have something to distract her from the terrible events of the evening.

Eventually they reached the head of the queue and were given clean blankets and told that they must return them when they left the shelter.

'If I was you, as soon as it comes light, I'd go and mek sure that if there's anything to be salvaged from your home, you're the one who gets it,' Daisy warned Rosie. 'I wished I'd done that meself, when I saw one of me old neighbours wearing me best coat, I can tell you, and her kiddies decked out in my little 'uns' stuff. You can put your trust in no one these days. Mind you, if you can't salvage nothing then the WVS will do what they can to help you. They kitted me and the girls out a treat.'

Rosie gave her new friend a wan smile as they made their way past all those who had already secured their blankets and their spot for what was left of the night, until they could find a bit of free floor space.

'If you haven't got anywhere to go, then they'll try and billet you with someone, but from what I've heard it can take for ever to get a place on account of them in war effort work taking priority.'

The all clear had finally gone but Rosie knew that she wouldn't be able to sleep. All she could think about was her mother. Sitting with her knees drawn up under her chin, and her blanket wrapped around her, fighting back the burn of her tears, she whispered her mother's name, wishing she had told her she loved her one last time.

FOURTEEN

The last thing Rosie really wanted to do was to go back to the street that had once been home, but she knew that she had to do so, so after a breakfast of tea and a bacon sandwich provided by the WVS, which she somehow managed to eat, she handed back her blanket and steeled herself to make her way home.

A pall of smoke and dust hung over the city, and here and there a thicker, more acrid smoke was still rising from bombed-out buildings. Averting her gaze from where the heavy rescue teams were still working to remove debris, Rosie was suddenly confronted by the sight of the church they had all worked so hard to try to save. Its roof gone and its Gothic beauty destroyed, there was still something about its defiant stance even in its destruction that brought the sharp sting of tears to Rosie's eyes. She found herself joining the quiet throng of worshippers making their way into the burned-out church where its priests were preparing to hold Mass and hear the confessions of their congregation. Once the Italian families from the area would have been here to share everyone's grief at the destruction of their church. Rosie thought sadly of the many processions she and Bella had walked in together, which had brought them to this church. Now the church, like her friendship with Bella, had been damaged beyond repair.

Keeping to the back of the church, Rosie made her own prayers. Despite the dreadful things that had happened during the bombing raid, there was somehow a sense of calm and peace here this morning, and a sense of unity too amongst those who had come, many of them the same people who had striven so unceasingly, risking their own safety, to save the building.

When the service was over it was hard for her to drag herself away from the church and its atmosphere of faith and strength and make her way back towards what had been her home.

The street was busy with inhabitants whose houses were still standing but who had had their windows blown out by the blast, and who were still trying to clean up the broken glass. Several of them stopped what they were doing to offer Rosie their sympathy.

''Ere, Rosie, come inside, love. I've got summat for you,' Mrs Harris from three doors down called out to Rosie, ushering her into her own pin-neat home whilst cautioning her to 'mind all the broken glass'. 'I was right sorry to hear about your ma, Rosie. I know there was them round here that didn't hold with what was going on.' Rosie winced. 'But your ma was allus a good neighbour to me. I saw her goin' in with that chap of hers many a time.'

Anger joined the desolation Rosie was already feeling.

'I went out this morning and I found this lot,' her neighbour continued, producing two pillowcases filled to the brim with clothes. 'There's not much. Them lads from the council said that everything will have been blown to bits, and what I did manage to find will need a good wash on account of it being covered in soot and dust.'

Rosie thanked her, blinking away her tears as she stared at the pillowcases. She could see the familiar sleeve of her mother's dressing gown dangling from one of the cases. An acrid smell of soot and dust and burned cloth emerged from the bundle.

'You'll have your work cut out, after what's happened, 'cos there'll be the funeral to sort out and all that. If you need a hand with anything you just let me know. I've buried me husband as well as me own mam and dad, so I know what it's all about.'

Rosie remembered that the WVS had said something to her about helping her to deal with the formalities of her mother's death.

'You'll be moving in with your auntie now,

I suppose. Young Rob Whittaker is going to miss you.'

Rosie stood stock-still. After the shock of last night, she'd given no thought to where she would go, where she would live. There was no way in the world she wanted to live with her aunt – and no way her aunt would want her.

Rosie thanked Mrs Harris for what she had done and gathered up the pillowcases.

The gaping crater left by the bomb looked somehow worse this morning than it had done last night. Rosie's gaze was drawn inexorably to the spot where she had last seen her mother's body. There was nothing there now, of course, but she still walked over to where Christine had lain. If her mother hadn't been involved in an affair she would still be alive now. Rosie felt as though a part of her almost hated her for what she had done, even whilst at the same time she would have done anything if only she might still be alive.

Here and there in the tangle of roof beams, bricks and plaster she could see the charred and twisted remnants of pieces of furniture. Putting the pillowcases to one side, she started to search carefully through the rubble.

An hour later she was forced to admit that there was nothing to be retrieved, no keepsake or memento of her mother that she could find to bring her comfort, nothing for her to hold in her hand, just as she would never again be able to hold her mother's hand either. All she would have to hold on to now would be her memories. Her memories – Rosie desperately did not want to have her last memories of seeing her mother alive. How she wished she had not heard what she had heard; not known what she had known. How she wished she could go back to the innocence of her childhood, when she had loved her mother unquestioningly, loving it when she acted daft with her and played with her. Those had been good times, happy times, the times with her mother that she would cherish in her heart, Rosie promised herself.

Picking up her pillowcases, she made her way back down the street to the house where Rob lodged. He had told her last night when he had walked her back to her devastated home that he would ask his landlady if she would rent out her other spare room to her. Rosie hadn't paid much attention to what he had been saying then. She had been too distraught. But now she hoped desperately that he had done as he had said he would. She hated not having her own room and a decent bed to sleep in. It seemed too much to bear on top of everything else.

Rosie knocked on the Norrises' door. Mrs Norris opened it almost straight away.

'I don't know if Rob has said anything to you . . .' Rosie began uncertainly.

'He has, but like I've already told him, I do not hold with a young couple who aren't married living under the same roof,' Mrs Norris said briskly, her expression softening slightly as she saw Rosie's disappointment. 'I've nothing against you, Rosie. You're a decent sort of girl, even if your mother . . .' Her mouth tightened. 'You can see how it is, I'm sure. I've got my reputation to think of and I don't want anyone saying that I'm encouraging the wrong kind of goings-on under me roof. Besides, your dad will be home soon and he'll sort summat out for the two of you.'

She was closing the door already, before Rosie could say anything further, leaving her standing on the doorstep. How many more of their neighbours had been aware of her mother's affair and would judge her because of it? Rosie wondered miserably. And more importantly, what was going to happen when her dad got back? Would they tell him? It was bad enough that he had to return to find his wife dead, without having to learn that she had been unfaithful to him as well.

Rosie straightened her shoulders. There were things that had to be done: formalities to be dealt with and arrangements to be made for her mother's funeral. She needed to pull herself together, to be strong. It looked as if she would be spending another night sleeping in the church hall, since there was nowhere else for her to go. It was hard to accept that in another few days it would be Christmas. Rosie thought of the small Christmas presents she had laboured to make for her friends, the pretty lace-trimmed slip she had saved so hard from her wages to buy for her mother and the warm woolly socks she had knitted for her father.

She spent the rest of the day at the nearest WVS shelter, grateful for the help she was given by the women on duty there, especially the one who offered to take her pillowcases to her own home for her and wash what clothes could be salvaged. She also introduced Rosie to an undertaker and went through with her the necessary arrangements.

It was late in the afternoon as Rosie was helping to entertain a small group of children, like her made homeless by the bombings, when she looked up and saw her father standing watching her.

Clumsily she got to her feet, hesitating instead of running to him as she wanted to do as she wondered how much he knew.

'Have you heard – about the bomb and Mum?' she asked him, eyes brimming.

He nodded, and opened his arms, and Rosie stumbled into them.

'How did you find me?' she sniffed. 'Have you been home . . . ?'

'Not yet. Young Rob Whittaker had left a message down at the docks for me, saying what had happened and where you were. So I came straight here. I've bin given compassionate leave whilst everything gets sorted out.'

'They said that Mum wouldn't have known anything. She wasn't . . . she just looked like she was asleep . . .'

She saw the look of anger that crossed her father's face and asked him, 'Dad, what is it? I did not mean—'

'It isn't you, lass. You shouldn't have had to deal wi' summat like this. I should have bin here with you. Aye, and happen if I had your mother might still be alive. She was allus on at me to give up the navy . . . Where's your things?'

Rosie explained about the pillowcases and the kindness of the WVS woman.

If anything, her father looked even more savagely angry. 'You mean you've got nothing? No clothes, no roof over your head? You've had to sleep here?'

'Everyone's in the same boat, Dad. Or at least those who've been bombed are. I was talking to a young woman last night and she's been homeless for six weeks.'

'Mebbe so, but that's not going to happen to you. Come on.'

'Where are we going?'

'To your Auntie Maude's, of course.'

Rosie hung back, remembering how unwelcome her aunt had made her feel the evening she had gone to visit her, and knowing she couldn't cope if she bad-mouthed her mother even now, but her father had enough to deal with, without her complaining to him about his sister.

An hour later her father was knocking on his sister's door. Rosie watched as her face lit up when she saw him, only to frown again when she realised that Rosie was with him.

'We've come to throw ourselves on your charity,

Maude,' Rosie's father announced. 'A bomb hit the house last night.' He paused and then finished quietly, 'Christine was killed in the blast.'

There was not a word of shock or sympathy over her mother's death, Rosie noted, as her aunt instructed them to come in.

'It's a mercy it was bombed before you got home, Gerry. What time did it happen, only I should have thought that Christine would have been at that job of hers at the factory, seeing as the siren didn't go off until after tea.'

'Mum hadn't been feeling very well.' Rosie felt obliged to protect her mother's honour even if she was well aware herself that it was a sham. 'I was on fire-watch duty, otherwise I would have been with her.'

'Don't go asking the lass any questions now, Maude. The poor girl's had it all to bear and no one to help her.'

'Well, she could have come here if she'd wanted to, I'm sure.'

'We'd been trying to save Holy Cross church so I didn't find out until late on about . . . about everything . . . It was Rob who told the WVS woman and somehow or other I ended up at the shelter. They were very kind there – helped with . . . with everything . . . and then when I went back this morning Mrs Harris from three down had been out and salvaged what she could for me. Not that there was much, and what there was was covered in soot and dirt.'

'I'll get the kettle on. You'll be ready for a cup of tea, our Gerry. Rosie, don't you go sitting down on one of my clean chairs in that dirty fire-watch suit. I must say I don't approve of the way you young women are wearing such clothes in public.'

There could not have been a more marked difference between the affectionate way her aunt spoke to her father and the harsh rejection with which she addressed her, Rosie recognised, as she exchanged looks with her father.

'Have a heart, Maude. The poor kid hasn't got anything else,' he defended her immediately. 'I reckon she'll feel much brighter once she's had a bath and got some clean clothes on. Lucky I brought you a few things home with me from New York, Rosie.'

'A bath, is it?' Rosie heard her aunt sniff disdainfully. 'And where does she think the hot water's going to come from for that, may I ask? A stand-up wash is what she'll have to make do with.'

'She needs a bath, Maude. If heating the boiler's the problems then I reckon I can get you a bit of extra coal. There's a few chaps down at the docks owe me a favour or two. You go up, Rosie, and take your time, lass.'

Rosie could hear her aunt's sharp voice protesting to her father as she took advantage of his ability to win over his sister, and hurried up the stairs. Normally her pride wouldn't have let her accept the cold charity her aunt obviously did not want to give, but right now she couldn't afford to listen to her pride.

Her aunt's bathroom was Spartan and cold, just like she was, but Rosie was too appreciative of the opportunity to wash off the accumulated dirt of her night fire fighting to care.

Standing in the bath, she flannelled off the worst of the dirt before running what little hot water she dared into it to enable her to soak for long enough to get her cold body warm as well as clean.

She had just stepped out of the bath and wrapped herself in a towel when she heard a knock on the door and her father's voice calling out, 'Rosie, I've left you some things outside the door. They were meant to be for Christmas but I reckon you need them now.'

When she opened the door there were two large, beautifully wrapped parcels outside it. Picking one up, she started to unwrap it. Inside she found some underwear in silk and satin, and as she smoothed her fingertips over it, Rosie knew immediately that this had been a gift her father had intended for her mother. She hesitated, remembering how the undertaker had asked her about clothes for her mother to wear and how she hadn't known what to say or do, but then the practical side of her nature, hardened by the experience of war and shortages, reasserted itself and she reminded herself that currently she was without so much as a change of knickers. Also inside the parcel were stockings, scent and a lipstick, and finally a twinset in her mother's favourite shade of red.

Tears pricked her eyes again. She wondered if

the lovingly selected gifts had been meant as a peace offering, as a sign that he wanted to start over.

In the other parcel Rosie found what she guessed had been her father's Christmas present for her: stockings, a lovely soft tweed skirt and a bright red sweater, along with some scent and a pair of lovely soft kid gloves.

Once she was dressed, Rosie went back downstairs, feeling a bit self-conscious in her new clothes, especially her new underwear.

Ignoring the disapproving look her aunt was giving her, she went over to her father and kissed the top of his head.

'Thanks, Dad,' she said softly.

'I hope that you've left my bathroom properly clean,' her aunt demanded.

'Of course she has, haven't you, Rosie?' her father answered for her. 'She's a good girl, is my Rosie, and the two of you are going to get on a treat. Why, I reckon the next time I come home on leave you'll be telling me, Maudie, that you can't imagine life without my girl.'

'We'll have to see about that. Christine was never much of a housewife – or any kind of wife at all so far as I could see – and I doubt that she's taught Rosie the way I'd have taught a daughter of me own how to go about things.'

'That's enough of that, Maude.' Rosie was surprised at how very stern her father suddenly sounded. 'I'll not have you speaking ill of the dead.

My Christine's gone now, God rest her.' Rosie's own eyes filled with tears when her father stopped to withdraw his handkerchief from his pocket and blow his nose fiercely. 'Christine did her best and I don't want to hear another bad word about her.'

Rosie could see her aunt wasn't very pleased.

'Well, you've always bin a loyal husband to her, Gerry. But there's something else I am going to have to say,' she continued defiantly. 'We have standards up here in Wavertree so there'll be none of that getting overfamiliar with young men I've heard goes on in some places these days.'

'Rosie's young man is a very good sort, Maude. You'll like young Rob.'

'He isn't my young man, Dad,' Rosie protested, red-faced. 'He's just a friend, that's all.'

'Well, whatever he is, if he comes calling round here you'll only see him under my supervision. Now what arrangements have been made about the funeral? It's going to be very difficult to do things properly with it being Christmas.'

Rosie had to fight hard to hang on to her temper and to keep the hot words she longed to utter to herself for her father's sake.

'The undertaker told me that they were busy, on account of the number of deaths caused by the bombs,' she told her aunt expressionlessly. She turned to her father. 'I didn't know what you'd want, Dad, so I've asked if Mum could be buried at the church where I was christened, seeing as you and Mum married in Manchester.'

'Aye, lass, that's a good idea.'

Rosie could hear the emotion thickening her father's voice. As bad as this was for her, it must be so much worse for him. She reached out and took hold of his hand, ignoring her aunt's disapproving glare, glad that she had done so when he returned her gentle touch with a warm squeeze of his hand.

'They . . . they asked me about clothes . . . but . . . I'm to go tomorrow to the shelter and the WVS woman said she'd bring our things back then, washed. She did say that they have some second-hand clothes but—'

'Don't you worry about it, Rosie. I'll make sure it's sorted out and that your mum has something pretty.'

Rosie gave her father a grateful look.

'I'll put you in the front bedroom, Gerry. Rosie, you'll have to sleep in the boxroom.'

'Maude, why don't you give Rosie the front bedroom? I'm only here for a few days. I can manage in the boxroom; it will be bigger than I'm used to on the ship.'

Rosie could see that her aunt wanted to argue but before she could say anything they heard knocking on the door.

Her aunt got up to answer it and when she came back she had Rob Whittaker with her.

'I've just explained to your friend, Rosie, that I would have preferred it if he had called first during the daytime.'

'I'm sorry,' Rob said, red-faced, his embarrassment making Rosie feel angry with her aunt and protective towards him. The sight of his familiar face was such a welcome relief after the turmoil of the last twenty-four hours that she reacted far more emotionally to seeing him than she was used to. Now she could really see how much she cared for him, how kind and compassionate he was. But could she love him? That was a different matter.

'There's no need to be sorry, lad,' Rosie heard her father reassuring Rob. 'I'd have thought the worse of you if you hadn't come round just as soon as you could to see how Rosie is. I wanted to thank you as well for making sure they knew what had happened down at the shipping office.'

'I'm sorry I couldn't do more, but I was on duty. How are you, Rosie? Mrs Norris said you'd been round. I'm sorry about . . . about the room and everything . . .'

'That's all right, Rob. I quite understood.'

'What's all this about then?' Rosie's father demanded warily.

'Rob suggested that I might be able to lodge with his landlady, but she wasn't able to help. There's so many people homeless now,' Rosie answered him vaguely and, she hoped, diplomatically. But she could see that her father was frowning and looking upset.

'Why would you go asking strangers to take you in, Rosie, when you've got family nearby?'

Rosie avoided looking at her aunt as she said

quietly, 'I thought it best not to bother Auntie Maude, Dad, and . . . and . . . well, at least with Mrs Norris I'd have been nearer to home and to . . . to Mum.'

'Aw, lass, I'll never forgive meself for not being there with you,' her father told her emotionally.

'It's not your fault, Dad.'

Father and daughter looked tenderly at one another and then fell silent.

'How is everything . . . the arrangements and that? I mean, if there's anything I can do . . .' Rob broke the sad silence awkwardly.

'A funeral is a family affair, young man, and I'm sure that my brother doesn't need any help from outsiders to do what's proper.'

'Now then, our Maude, there's no call for you to go speaking to the lad like that. I appreciate your offer, young Rob, and I'd appreciate it too if you wouldn't mind doing what you can to help Rosie when I have to go back to sea.'

'You don't have to ask, Mr Price,' Rob answered immediately. 'There isn't anything I wouldn't do for Rosie.'

'Rob . . .' Rosie protested, but she could see that her father was relieved.

Typically, her aunt didn't invite Rob to sit down or offer him a cup of tea, and when Rosie got up, intending to see Rob to the front door, she stood between them in a very pointed manner until Rosie's father shook his head and said gently, 'Let them have a few minutes on their own, Maude. Rosie's a good girl.'

'Well, if that's true it will be a wonder with that mother of hers as an example,' Rosie heard her aunt mutter as she escaped from the parlour with Rob and went with him to the front door.

'I'm right sorry about Mrs Norris refusing to take you, Rosie,' he whispered fiercely when Rosie opened the front door. 'She didn't mean anything personal by it.'

'But now that Dad's home he'd have wanted me to come here to my auntie's anyway.'

'Have they set a date for the funeral yet?'

'It's to be in a week.' Rosie bit her lip. 'Dad doesn't know yet about . . . about everything and I don't want him to find out just yet unless he has to. He's got enough to cope with . . .'

She could see Rob's Adam's apple moving in his throat as he battled with his emotions.

'Well, it won't be me that tells him, Rosie, but there has been talk.'

'What about . . . what about *him*?' Rosie asked in a low voice. 'Only even though I didn't want her seeing him, I wouldn't want to think that . . . and then there's his wife . . .'

Rob reached for her hand. 'Don't worry, Rosie, she's to be told that he had gone round to see your mum because she'd gone home from work sick. You don't need to worry yourself about it, although it's typical of your sweet nature that you should care.'

Rob had been gone less than half an hour when the air-raid siren broke into her aunt's monologue

273

about the unfairness of the rationing system when it came to single people.

Rosie's father promptly stood up and refused to pay any heed at all to his sister's insistence that she wasn't going to go into a public shelter, somehow managing to usher both Rosie and her aunt out into the street and then down it to the shelter close to the allotments shared by some of the residents.

Rosie, who had grown up hearing her aunt boasting about the exclusivity of where she lived, was pleasantly surprised by how warmly she and her father were welcomed by her aunt's neighbours, especially the pretty young woman who smiled at her and introduced herself as Molly Dearden.

'We live over the road and down a bit,' she explained to Rosie, having made room for her to sit beside her. 'Me sister would be here but she's away on her honeymoon at the minute. Oh, hello, Sally,' she smiled, welcoming another young woman who hurried in carrying a baby. 'Sally lives further down a bit. Sally, this is Rosie.

'You're Mrs Sefton's niece, aren't you?' Molly continued cheerfully, 'only I've seen you calling there. My sister's mother-in-law lives opposite her.'

'Yes,' Rosie acknowledged.

'Staying over for Christmas, are you?' Sally asked conversationally as she quietened her baby.

'Yes.' Rosie bit her lip, realising that she had sounded unfriendly. 'We . . . I . . . we were bombed out last night,' she explained in a low voice. 'My mother was in the house at the time and I was on fire-watch duty. They said that she wouldn't have known anything about it, that it would have been so quick.'

As Rosie swallowed back her misery, Molly reached out and took her hand tightly.

'We lost our mother when I was little. Have you got any brothers or sisters?'

'No, there's just me and Dad.'

Everyone ducked instinctively as they heard the sound of a bomber low overhead, but within seconds it was gone, and one of the men stood up and called out, 'Come on, everyone. Let's get singing like the government have told us to do.'

'That's my uncle,' Molly explained to Rosie. 'He'll get everyone going, just you wait and see. He's a real card and no mistake.'

Rosie soon discovered that her new friend was right, and even her aunt thawed enough to join in the rousing Christmas carols Molly's uncle was exhorting them to sing, although Rosie noticed that her mouth pursed up primly when someone suggested they open a bottle of beer and pass it round.

Her father had joined the other men and she could hear him singing.

'My mother would have loved this,' she began to tell Molly, and then stopped.

'You talk about her if you want to, love,' a kind-faced older woman, seated close to Molly, encouraged her.

'That's our neighbour Elsie,' Molly informed Rosie. 'She's been like a mother to me and my sister. You need people like her in times like this. I hope you have an "Elsie".'

By the time the all clear came, Rosie had begun to feel better about moving in with her aunt than she would have believed possible. Far from being the snobbish types she had expected, her aunt's neighbours were friendly and kind-hearted.

Rosie couldn't ever remember feeling so tired, she decided a couple of hours later, lying in the icy cold sheets of her aunt's boxroom bed. Her aunt had got her own way, and in the end her father had given in and allowed his sister to put him in the larger room, leaving Rosie with the small boxroom. Not that she minded. Just having a room to herself with a bed in it was wonderful after last night, and after thinking that she'd be spending another night homeless.

FIFTEEN

'Will you be all right then, Rosie?'

Rosie could hear the awkwardness as well as the kindness in Enid's voice. 'Yes. I'll be fine,' she assured her.

'Because if you're wanting me to stay with you for a bit . . .'

'No, honestly, I'll be fine,' Rosie repeated. The truth was that she actually wanted to be on her own.

It wasn't that the girls she worked with, and Mrs Verey herself, hadn't been kind and understanding – they had, fussing over her the minute they had learned what had happened and Mrs Verey giving her as much time off as she needed to get herself ready for tomorrow. It was just that right now she welcomed the solitude of the workroom and the chance to give in to her emotions instead of having to put on a brave face.

Christmas had come and gone, and although Rosie had longed to have her father to herself, she hadn't complained about the way her aunt had monopolised him, not even when she had insisted on taking his arm on Christmas morning when they had gone to her church when Rosie had wanted so much for just the two of them to go to the place where her mother was to be buried so that they could mourn their loss alone together.

It was Rosie's opinion that her aunt was a mean woman in a variety of different ways: mean in her kindness to others, mean with her affection and her money, mean with her food, and Rosie had endured every one of those meannesses over the last few days. It had been a relief to her to go back to work after the Christmas break. She felt starved of food and warmth and love, all the things she had taken for granted in the chaotic comfort of the house she had shared with her mother, and which were so very lacking in her aunt's. Her mother had her faults, Rosie didn't deny that, but she had had a warmth that Rosie now missed desperately. But the trouble was that her mother had not been able to keep that warmth just for those she should have done. She had shared it around where she shouldn't have done, and the knowing looks Rosie had seen being exchanged after her mother's death had made her even more determined that she wasn't going to follow her mother's example.

Her mother! A part of her still couldn't believe that she was dead. But the mourning clothes she had had to buy when she had gone out to replace her bomb-damaged wardrobe were real enough.

It had been Enid who had told her hesitantly about the second-hand clothes exchange run by the WVS.

'You'll be wanting something for the funeral, Rosie. It's only right that you'll want to show respect. I'll go with you, if you like.'

Rosie had nodded her head and the two of them had spent their dinner hour going through the neatly organised racks of clothes until Rosie had found a black skirt that fitted her and a black coat to go over it.

It was Mrs Verey who had offered the little hat with its black spotted veil, saying quietly, 'I had it for my own mother's funeral, Rosie.' And Rosie had decided that her own grey sweater, salvaged from the rubble and washed, would have to do on top of the skirt.

Her father would wear a dress uniform he had managed to borrow from another seaman, and because there was a war on, the hearse was going to be drawn by traditionally plumed black horses instead of a car. The funeral procession would start from outside the old house and the mourners, led by Rosie's father, would walk behind the hearse to the church. Much to her aunt's disapproval, Rosie had insisted that there was to be a proper wake afterwards.

'Well, I'm not having it here,' Aunt Maude had refused angrily. 'I do not hold with that kind of thing.'

'I wouldn't want you to,' Rosie had told her

fiercely. 'I've already arranged with Father Doyle for us to use the church hall at St Joseph's.' With the Holy Cross church being bombed Father Doyle had suggested to Rosie that her mother be buried at St Joseph's which was the nearest Catholic church to Holy Cross. 'The neighbours are going to provide the food, Dad. It won't be much, but I know it's what Mum would want.'

'Aye, your mother always liked a bit of a party, Rosie,' her father had agreed heavily.

'Perhaps we shouldn't be having the wake,' she had worried to Rob the night before, when he had met her after work. 'It might come out about Mum and *him*.' Rosie just couldn't bring herself to use his name.

'No one will say anything about that to your dad, Rosie,' Rob had reassured her. 'Not at your mum's funeral.'

Mercifully Hitler's bombers were leaving them in peace, giving everyone some much-needed relief.

Rob had asked Rosie to go with him to the New Year's Eve dance at the Grafton, and at her father's insistence Rosie had agreed.

'It won't be respectful for me to be going out dancing with Mum only just buried,' she had protested.

But her father had told her firmly, 'Sitting in moping won't bring your mother back, Rosie, and no one doubts how much you loved her.'

Except herself, Rosie thought. If only she'd been more understanding of her mother's loneliness, talked to her instead of judging and admonishing her, perhaps she'd still be here.

Unlike the other girls at the shop, though, Rosie could not get excited about the dance and what she would be wearing.

Mrs Verey had given her leave to go home early on account of the funeral, and although she hadn't expected him to be there, when she left the shop she found that Rob was waiting for her.

'I came by on the off chance,' he told her.

'You don't have to fuss around me so much, Rob.'

'Happen I want to do it.' He reached for her hand and reluctantly Rosie let him draw her arm through his.

There were so many servicemen home on leave that the city seemed full of men in uniform and she saw the way Rob looked at them.

'You're doing every bit as much for the country as they are,' she insisted, reading his thoughts.

'Mebbe, but don't tell me that you wouldn't rather be going out with a chap in a uniform than a fireman, Rosie.'

She stopped walking and turned to him. 'That's not true.'

'No? Then why are you always so cold towards me? I'm sorry,' he apologised gruffly immediately. 'It's just that when I see other chaps cuddling up to their girls I want to do the same with you.'

'I've told you before that I'm not that sort,' Rosie reminded him sharply. 'I'm a respectable girl,

Rob Whittaker, and that's how I intend to stay. Just because my mother—'

'Oh, don't talk so daft, Rosie. No one who knows you would ever think of you as being like your ma, but there's nothing wrong with a couple enjoying a bit of a kiss and a cuddle, especially now.'

'It's all right for you to say that. That's what all the men say to their girls, but that doesn't make it right.'

'So when am I going to get a kiss from you, Rosie?'

'When I say and not before,' Rosie told him sternly.

'I don't know about you worrying about folk thinking you're like your mam; it seems to me that you tek more after that auntie of yours,' Rob grumbled as he walked her home.

'No I don't. She can't cook, and I can,' Rosie told him, tongue in cheek, peeping up at him and smiling when she saw that her comment had made his own mouth curl in amusement.

'Well, one day, when you're Mrs Whittaker, I'll put that to the test,' he told her meaningfully.

Although he had made it plain that he wanted them to be serious, this was the first time he had gone so far as to mention marriage. But even though marriage would confer respectability on her and on their relationship, Rosie didn't feel the enthusiasm and excitement she knew she should. It was probably all this worry about her mother and Dennis that was making it hard for her to think about her and Rob sharing the same kind of intimacy she knew they had done. It just didn't seem right, somehow.

'There's no need to come any further with me,' Rosie told Rob once they had reached Edge Hill Road. 'I know you're on duty tonight.'

Once she had left Rob, Rosie started to walk more slowly, reluctant to return to the cold hostility of her aunt's house. Her father had been given compassionate leave until his ship returned to Liverpool, well after the funeral, but he had taken to going round to one of his sister's neighbours, an old Red Duster man himself, now retired, who lived on his own. Rosie guessed that they played cards and enjoyed exchanging yarns over a bit of a drink, and she certainly couldn't blame her father if he found his new friend's company more congenial than that of his sister.

As she turned into her aunt's road she saw Sally Walker coming the other way with her baby. Rosie smiled at her and they stopped to exchange pleasantries.

'I hope it all goes well tomorrow. Are you bearing up all right?'

'I'm fine. The girls at work have been really kind and Mrs Verey, who owns the shop where I work, has even lent me her own hat.'

'I'd come and walk with the procession but for baby here,' Sally told her. 'You know you can always come round for a bit of a chat if you want to, do you not? It can't be much fun for you living with your auntie. June says that she's even more of a dragon than her husband's mother. Whoops. I hope I haven't spoken out of turn.'

Rosie shook her head. 'Her and me have never really got on. She doesn't . . . *didn't* like my mother and she didn't want Dad to marry her. You and Molly and June have been ever so kind to me since I came to live up here, Sally. I'm really grateful to you all.'

'Aw, Rosie, there's no need to thank us. You're a smashing lass, and with June and Molly having lost their own mum as girls, they understand how you'll be feeling right now.'

The funeral was at one o'clock so that everything would be done before the blackout and the possibility of an air raid. Rosie hadn't been able to sleep and now, at just gone six o'clock in the morning, she was sitting in her aunt's kitchen, white-faced and sick to her stomach with dread over what was to come. She heard the tread of feet on the stairs and swung round to face the door as her father opened it.

'I guessed it would be you,' he told her.

'I'm sorry if I woke you, Dad.'

He shook his head. 'I couldn't sleep neither. Is that pot still hot?' he asked, nodding in the direction of the teapot.

Rosie touched it with her hand. 'No. I'll make a fresh brew.'

'Me and your mother would have been married twenty years come this next June,' he commented whilst Rosie filled the kettle and struck a match to light the gas. 'I thought I was the luckiest lad alive when she agreed to have me. Nagged her for weeks, I did, until she gave in. She was that pretty and lively that she had lads buzzing round her like bees round a honey pot. Allus laughing and singing, she was in them days, Rosie. Of course, I didn't realise then . . .' He broke off and shook his head, as though shaking away something he didn't want to see, whilst Rosie's stomach muscles cramped. What had he been going to say? That he hadn't realised then that her mother wasn't the sort of girl a sensible man married?

The kettle was boiling so she went over to the stove to pour the water onto the carefully measured-out tea leaves. Her aunt didn't do with waste. 'I'll just leave it to brew,' she told her father.

'I never thought it would end like this,' he said gruffly. 'I thought that I'd be the first to go, not her. She was allus that full of life, allus wanting to go out and have fun. It just doesn't seem right.'

Rosie shivered as she poured his tea. Her father must never know about the kind of 'fun' her mother had been having whilst he was away. Somehow she felt as though she was not just the guardian of her mother's public respectability but also the one who was responsible for her betrayal of her marriage vows. She hoped that when they laid her mother to rest, the past could be buried as well.

'I still can't believe she's gone,' her father was saying in a heavy dull voice. 'Not Christine. It just doesn't seem possible.'

Rosie saw the tears trickling down his face. Quickly she went over to him and hugged him tightly.

'There, lass. I'm sorry, upsetting you like this. You've had a lot to bear, I know. But you've got a fine lad in young Rob – make sure you grab the chance of happiness with him with both hands. He'll look after you. Thinks the world of you, he does.'

'Oh, Dad . . .' Rosie protested, about to tell him her confusion about Rob, and then stopped as she heard her aunt coming downstairs. She couldn't tell her father how she really felt, not with her aunt there.

Rosie and her father went alone to the funeral parlour. The coffin was closed now, but Rosie knew that her mother was wearing the pretty red twinset her father had bought her, along with a white-patterned skirt she and her father had chosen from the second-hand clothes that were available. Rosie had washed and ironed it herself, unable to comprehend the thought of her mother's cold, stiff body wearing it as the iron travelled over the pleats.

The horses drawing the hearse had black silky coats and cockades of black mourning feathers. The funeral director and his assistants dressed in their mourning clothes, with their top hats and gloves, were ready to walk sombrely behind the hearse as it made its way to the street where Christine had died.

'All right, lass?' Rosie heard her father asking her as they took their places behind the cortège.

Rosie nodded. Her second-hand coat was a bit too big, and it had the greenish tinge of something that had not been well dyed, but Mrs Verey's hat added a touch of elegance and glamour to her appearance that she knew her mother would have loved.

As they made their sombre way to their old home, people stood in respectful silence to see them on their way, heads bowed in recognition of their loss. It was cold and damp, with a rawness to the air that stung Rosie's face and throat.

Their neighbours were there to greet them as the cortège turned into the street. The first person Rosie saw was Rob, wearing a black suit he must have borrowed from somewhere. He fell into step behind them, followed by others who had known Christine. Someone – Rosie suspected it must have been Rob – had placed flowers outside what had been their house at the exact spot where her mother had lain. Others were joining them now: the hairdresser for whom her mother had worked, and some other women Rosie vaguely recognised as pals of her mother, the small procession swelling as they made their sad way towards the church.

Rosie's aunt had refused to walk behind the hearse, saying she would go straight to the church instead. When they walked past what was left of

Holy Cross, Rosie ducked her head, unable to bear looking at the ruined church where she had been when their house had been bombed and her mother killed.

Rosie knew from the funeral parlour that her mother's wasn't the only funeral taking place that day and that all over Liverpool people were mourning those they had lost to Hitler's bombs in the dreadful pre-Christmas raid.

They had almost reached the church now; Rosie made herself focus on the solitary figure of Father Doyle up ahead of her. Her father was walking immediately behind him, his shoulders bowed. What must it feel like to have loved someone and then watch that love turn to the bitterness and resentment she had seen her mother exhibit so often? Rob wanted to marry her but what if their marriage ended up like that of her parents?

Rosie pushed aside those thoughts as the church doors opened and they entered to the dark dread sound of the organ.

The service was over but the worst ordeal was still ahead of them, Rosie acknowledged, as she stood with her father beside the newly dug grave – one of so very many in this small graveyard, trying to push out of her head the knowledge that it was her mother who was lying in the wooden coffin that was now being lowered into the ground.

Someone – one of their neighbours, Rosie guessed – sobbed aloud.

Her father's voice shook as he burst out, 'She allus hated the dark.'

'Don't, Dad,' Rosie begged him tearfully.

He was crying himself, silent tears running down his face as he let the dark soil fall from his hand and onto the coffin.

Silently Rosie did the same. She couldn't believe that this was really happening. Rob had come to stand at the graveside with them, the strong bulk of his body protecting her from the icy-cold wind.

And then it was over, the final goodbyes said and the mourners moving slowly away. Rob had positioned himself protectively between her and her father, offering them each the strength of his arm to lean on as he supported them back out onto the street.

Mrs Harris came up, tear tracks plainly visible through her powder.

'You need to get everyone down to the church hall, Rosie, before they freeze.'

Rosie looked at her blankly.

'The wake, lass, remember?'

Numbly Rosie nodded and allowed Mrs Harris to lead her down to the church hall where their neighbours and the other mourners were already gathering, the dreadful mood of the graveside giving way to the discreet and respectful hum of conversation, interspersed here and there by the laughter of children.

Like a sleepwalker, Rosie moved amongst the mourners, she and Rob shepherding between them her father with his bowed shoulders and grief-stricken face, whilst her aunt, suddenly in her element, held court in one corner of the room, dabbing non-existent tears from her eyes with a lace-edged handkerchief.

Most of the mourners had already left when the event Rosie had been dreading happened.

She was standing with her father, Rob and her aunt when one of her mother's friends from the hair-dressing salon came over to say goodbye. Marion, a thin woman with peroxide hair and a giggly, girlish manner, which Rosie had always found embarrassing in a woman well into her forties, was both crying and hiccuping, the latter, Rosie suspected, caused by her having had rather too much to drink.

'I still can't believe she's gone,' she sobbed noisily. 'She were my best friend, you know – at least we was afore she took up wi' that—'

Rosie froze, knowing sickeningly what Marion was about to reveal and yet unable to say or do anything to stop her.

'Yes, you must have missed her when she went to work at the munitions factory. She often said what good friends you had all been, didn't she, Rosie?'

Rob's voice, his words calm and friendly and so totally believable, brought Rosie out of her temporary paralysis. Giving him a grateful look she took hold of Marion's hand.

'Yes, she did, Marion. Thank you so much for coming. I know Mum would have appreciated it.' As she was speaking, Rosie started to lead Marion towards the door, whilst Rob walked at her other side.

Once she was through it and walking down the street, Rosie turned to Rob and hugged him tightly, unable to find any other way of expressing her relief and gratitude. 'Oh, Rob, thank you for that. If you hadn't stepped in so quickly then she would have let it slip about him, I know she would.'

She was trembling from head to foot, and when Rob's arms tightened round her, for once she didn't try to pull away – not even when he bent his head and kissed her passionately full on the mouth in the protective shadows of the doorway. How could she deny him after what he had just done for her? A surge of emotion flooded through her as she returned his kiss.

'There!' Rob exclaimed triumphantly when he finally released her. 'That's it, Rosie. You're my girl properly now. We should get engaged!'

Rosie didn't argue with him. All she could think about was her relief that the terrible day was finally over, her mother had been laid to rest and her shameful secret with her. Her father would never have to know what she had done.

PART THREE

February 1941

SIXTEEN

Rosie winced as the ice-cold wind hit her the moment she left the shop. They were having what was one of the coldest winters on record, with weather so bad that Hitler's bombers had not been able to fly. After the December bombings the un-expected respite had come as a relief to everyone, even if they were shivering with cold, and hungry all the time, thanks to rationing.

Rosie had one reason at least, though, to smile as she made her way home. Because of the number of cargo ships damaged in the Christmas bombing raid, her father's period of compassionate leave had been extended and he was still at home. Not that she could really think of her aunt's house as 'home'. Rosie would have liked to be able to talk her father into renting somewhere for just the two of them but with so many people homeless she felt it was selfish of her to want to do that, even if it had been possible.

Since Rob was on duty he was not there to walk

her home. Not that she minded, she admitted guiltily. Since he had kissed her the day of her mother's funeral Rob seemed to have taken it for granted that their relationship had become much more serious, and Rosie didn't have the heart to protest that she wasn't sure that was what she wanted. She envied the three other young women in the street who had befriended her, Sally, and the two sisters, June and Molly, who all seemed to be so happily in love with their sweethearts. Didn't they worry, as she would have done in their position, about finding out that they had made a mistake? But then they had probably not witnessed the kind of unhappiness within a marriage that she had seen in her own parents' union. June and Molly had only their father, and Sally and her husband lived far away from her family. But every young woman had to get married otherwise she would end up as a spinster, and that was not to be thought of. All around her Rosie could see young women and their sweethearts rushing to the altar, afraid of being torn apart by the war, and snatching at what happiness together they could. And then there were the other kind, the girls whose behaviour everyone talked about in low whispers, the kind of behaviour exhibited by her own mother. But these girls weren't married. They wanted to have fun, they defended themselves, and if they wanted to dance and sing and flirt and yes, make love too, then that was their affair and no one else's. But with Liverpool bursting at the seams with sailors from the convoys, Commonwealth troops, and army and navy personnel stationed locally to protect the docks, a certain section of the city's young women were beginning to attract a lot of notoriety.

Everyone was talking about it, mostly like Enid, earlier on in the day, with pursed lips and disapproval. Parents were saying that they preferred to see their daughters going steady with a decent young man they knew than going out mixing with those they did not.

The evening skies might be starting to lighten just a touch but the weather was bleak indeed. Rosie had been glad of her father's old darned seaman's socks to wear inside her boots on her walks to and from the bus stop on Wavertree Road where she caught the bus down into the city and the shop.

In some ways, and if it hadn't been for her aunt's continued coldness towards her, she would have enjoyed living in her new surroundings. Her father too seemed to have settled in well, going down to the docks during the day to help out where he was needed and then spending his free time at the allotments with the male residents who gathered there in one of the huts to talk politics and play cards.

With her father's contacts and their shared rations, and Rosie's keen eye for a bargain, they were eating as well as anyone could, given the rationing situation. Rosie had discreetly and tactfully persuaded her aunt to let her take over the cooking. Whilst her mother had simply not been interested in domesticity, her aunt, though obsessive about the cleanliness of her home, was no cook.

Rosie, having virtually grown up in Maria's kitchen, had absorbed the Italian ethos of making even the simplest meal a feast. Even her 'blitz broth', as the soup recipe recommended by the government had been named, was somehow tasty as well as warming, even though it contained little more than cabbage, carrots, sprouts, swedes and turnips added to a stock made from boiling up a few bones or a chicken carcass, to which Rosie added a bit of Bovril and some herbs.

Rosie enjoyed seeing the pleasure on her father's face when he tucked into the food she had cooked for them, even if her aunt's face grew sourer than ever with resentment.

Her father was already in the kitchen when Rosie – let in at the front door by her aunt, who had flatly refused to give her a key – made her way into its grudging warmth. His face broke into a warm smile when he saw her.

'By, but that's a fine pink nose you've got, our Rosie,' he teased her as she shed her coat. 'Come and get a bit closer to the warm, lass.'

'There's no need for you to go mollycoddling her,' Aunt Maude protested sharply.

'I thought you'd be down the allotments,' Rosie said to her father, ignoring her aunt's unkindness, 'not that any of you would be doing much digging with this snow and ice.'

'Aye, well, I would have bin, only when I went

down to the docks earlier, I called at the shipping office and they've offered me a place on a cargo ship going west, day after tomorrow.'

Rosie tried to conceal her sadness as she heard the happiness lifting her father's voice. Seamen might complain about life on board ship but they had salt water in their blood, so it was said, and fretted if they were away from the sea for too long. So she asked him matter-of-factly instead, 'Where will you be going – New York again?'

Her father laughed. 'Wanting more stockings, are you? I'm sorry, Rosie, but this time the convoy will be making for Canada. As luck would have it, when I was down there I bumped into a couple of old mates and seemingly they've signed up for the same ship. Good lads they are, an' all.' He rubbed his hands together, visibly heartened by the news. 'How about summat to eat?'

'It will have to be snoek pie,' Rosie warned him, referring to the reconstituted dried fish that everyone loathed.

Later on, when they were alone, her aunt having gone out to see her only close friend – a fellow widow whom she had known for some years and who, from what Rosie had heard her aunt say about her, was as much of a battleaxe as her aunt – whilst her father dried the dishes she had washed, Rosie told him uncertainly, 'I'm not sure that Auntie Maude will want me staying on here after you've gone, Dad.'

'Don't be daft. Of course she'll want you to stay. Where else would you go?' Rosie didn't say anything but she knew her expression had given her away when her father said firmly, 'Don't you go worrying about it, Rosie. I'll have a word wi' her meself. I suppose you'll be off later, dancing with that young man of yours, seeing as it's Saturday night?'

Rosie nodded. 'But I can stay here with you if you want me to, Dad.'

'You're a good girl, Rosie, but there's no need for you to give up your fun to keep your old dad company. Besides, I sort of promised those mates I met up wi' that I'd see them down the pub a bit later, provided Hitler doesn't send his ruddy bombers over, and we end up having to spend the night in the air-raid shelter.'

'Everyone's saying that it's too cold for them to fly,' Rosie answered, glad that her father had the prospect of some fun that evening too.

'What's this then?' Maude demanded suspiciously on Sunday morning when Rosie and her father appeared downstairs after breakfast, dressed in their mourning clothes.

'Me and Dad thought we'd go to the grave and see Mum, seeing as Dad joins his ship tomorrow,' Rosie answered bravely for both of them. 'You're welcome to come with us if you want to,' she added politely, knowing full well that her aunt would refuse.

'Visit your mother's grave!' Maude's well-corseted bosom heaved, her double chin wobbling with the same fury that was staining her face an unflattering shade of red. 'It's more than a decent person can bear, just knowing that a woman like that is lying buried amongst decent honest folk, never mind me going to visit it,' she announced.

'I won't hear that kind of talk about Christine, Maude,' Rosie's father objected sternly. 'There's no call to go speaking ill of the dead.'

'Mebbe not, but there was plenty of folk speaking ill of her whilst she was alive, so I've heard, and with good reason, it seems.'

Rosie tensed as her aunt shot her a baleful look of angry triumph.

'It's come to my ears that there were things going on that no decent woman should have been involved in.'

Rosie's father was frowning now. 'I know that you and Christine didn't allus see eye to eye, Maude, but she's gone now and can't answer for herself.'

'Mebbe not, but her daughter's here to answer for her, and from what I've bin told she knew what was going on, even if she hasn't had the decency to tell you about it. Yes, she knows exactly what that mother of hers was getting up to – just look at her face.'

Rosie could feel the scarlet flag of guilt burning her face as her father turned to look at her. He looked so uncomprehending and worried that her heart ached with misery.

'What's all this about, Rosie, lass?' he asked her quietly.

'Oh, she won't tell you the truth,' her aunt cut in nastily. 'She'd do anything to protect that mother of hers; just like she turned a blind eye to what was going on whilst you were away at sea and she was . . .' Maude's thin lips folded into a tight line as she shook her head. 'I don't know if I can bring myself to soil my lips by speaking of what went on.' Antagonism beamed from her eyes as she glared at Rosie.

'Perhaps you'd like to tell my brother what your mother was up to when she was supposed to be working at that parachute factory. Working for the war effort, she said she was. Well, we all know now what she meant by that, and it wasn't standing on a production line making parachutes, was it?'

'Rosie, what is all this? If there's something I should know then—'

'Of course you should know. After all, from what my friend Lily was telling me last night, the whole of your old neighbourhood does. She said she'd heard about it from a cousin of hers who lives down there. She said the whole street knew what was going on, and that your Christine was as bold as brass carrying on with some chap she had coming round calling on her. Seen walking arm in arm, they were, and him acting with her like he was her husband – and him a married man an' all – whilst she . . .'

Rosie watched in dismay as the dark red colour rose from her father's collar up over his face. Although he was a kindly man, on the rare occasions when he was roused to anger his temper sometimes ran away with him. Rosie could remember how frightened she had been as a child when he had smashed his fist down so hard on their kitchen table that the pots had bounced right off it and broken on the floor. Not that she had blamed him for his anger, knowing the way her mother had been in the habit of deliberately provoking it. On that particular occasion, her mother had left Rosie at home by herself, even though she had only been six years old, whilst she went to the cinema with a friend. When her father had returned home from sea unexpectedly early he had found Rosie crouched in the hallway on the floor in the darkness, crying and alone. Of course, afterwards, typically, her mother had blamed Rosie for being the cause of the row.

'Is this true, Rosie?' he demanded fiercely now. 'Was your mother carrying on with someone?'

Rosie wished passionately that if he had had to find out it might have been any way but this, with her aunt delivering the blow and standing by in triumph.

'Mum did . . . she was . . . I told her it was wrong and I begged her not to do it, Dad. She promised me she'd stop and that she'd give him up. But . . . she said she was lonely and that she missed you, and I think that the war made her feel afraid. She was going to give him up, she had said so . . .' Rosie hung her head, feeling as though she was the one who was at fault and had been found out.

'Give him up? That's not what I heard, and you haven't heard the worst of it yet. She made a proper laughing stock out of you, I can tell you. You walking behind her cortège like any proper grieving husband should, mourning her, whilst the whole of your street knew that the reason she'd been killed was because she'd been with him when the air-raid siren sounded and that the two of them had stayed there. Fornicating . . .'

'Dad . . .' Rosie pleaded as her father didn't answer her. Instead he stood staring at them both, his face betraying his emotions.

'Now see what you've done,' her aunt told her angrily. 'You and that mother of yours. Cut from the same cloth, the pair of you and no mistake . . .'

Rosie wasn't listening. 'Dad,' she implored. 'Mum didn't mean to hurt you. I know she didn't. What she did was wrong, but—'

'I told you right from the start not to marry her, Gerry,' Rosie's aunt cut in sharply. 'It was plain to me the first time I saw her what she was. I told you then what would happen the minute you turned your back, and I was right.'

'That's not fair,' Rosie burst out angrily.

'Isn't it? Much you know, miss, an' all.' She nodded in Rosie's father's direction. 'He knows as well as I do that this isn't the first time she's made a laughing stock out of him. I told him then what she was, but he wouldn't have it. Carrying on with that Italian under his own wife's nose as well as her husband's, and thinking she could get away

304

with it when everyone could see what she was up to.'

Rosie's eyes widened in shocked rejection of her aunt's sharp words. 'Dad,' she begged her father, 'that's not true . . . it can't be. Maria was Mum's friend. She was always sticking up for her and looking out for her, and for me. You know that. Mum would never have done anything to hurt her.' Rosie couldn't believe what her aunt was saying. She knew that her mother had betrayed her father, but she couldn't believe that she would have done something so low and despicable as her aunt was claiming. But her father wasn't answering her, and the way he was hanging his head made a horrid sick fear crawl through Rosie's stomach.

'Much you know,' her aunt told her triumphantly. 'Friend or not, your mother was after that Italian from the moment she set eyes on him, and her not a year wed to my brother.'

'Dad . . .' Rosie begged frantically, when her father remained silent and refused to look at her.

'No shame in her at all, she hadn't,' Aunt Maude was continuing. 'Neither of them had. How that poor wife of his put up with it I don't know. Even had the priest round, the family did, to give him a talking-to, but your mother talked him round, tempting him like the wicked hussy she was.'

'Dad, Dad . . .' Rosie appealed, taking hold of her father's hand and giving it a pleading shake. 'That's not true, please tell me it isn't,' she implored.

She could feel the deep breath he took as he raised his head and looked at her with a tortured expression that told its own story.

'Rosie, lass, I never wanted you to have to know about any of this.'

'You mean it is true?' Rosie started to tremble violently. 'No,' she denied, unable to accept what she was hearing, but knowing already in her heart that what her aunt had just told her was the truth. Now, just as though someone had lifted a blind that had obscured a view, she could see the past and her mother's friendship with Maria in its true colours. Small incidents, odd memories that had somehow stuck inside her head like leftover pieces that wouldn't fit into a familiar jigsaw suddenly fell into place. Poor Maria. How could her mother have acted out such a terrible betrayal of both her husband and her friend? Gentle loving Maria, who had never ever hurt anyone . . .

'How long was it . . . did she . . . ?' she whispered.

'That's what we'd all like to know,' her aunt told her grimly. 'If you ask me, there's a sight more of that Italian family about your looks, Rosie, than there is of ours.'

'That's enough of that kind of talk, Maude,' her father objected fiercely, suddenly rousing himself. 'Rosie's my lass and there's no one will ever say she isn't.'

Rosie wasn't listening to him. Her face had gone white as awareness dawned on her. Other memories were crowding into her head now: Maria's sad face when she looked at her; the way she had loved and petted her, sometimes calling her 'my little Rosie'; the way people had often mistaken her for a member of the family; the way her mother had always tried to encourage her to be more friendly to Aldo.

'Is it true?' she shakily asked the man she had always thought of as her father, the only man she wanted to be her father, in a hoarse whisper. 'It is, isn't it?' she answered for him when he didn't respond. 'It is.'

'No, Rosie, it isn't,' he told her determinedly. 'I promise you it isn't.'

But it was too late. Rosie ran to the door, yanking it open, ignoring the fact that she wasn't even wearing her coat as she ran out into the icy cold, huge raw sobs of fear and horror wrenching at her chest.

SEVENTEEN

'Rosie?'

She gasped and struggled to escape when familiar hands clamped down on her shoulders, whilst her grief filled her body and tore at her lungs.

'Aw, Rosie, Rosie . . . do not, lass, please. I'm that sorry you had to learn about your mam and everything like this . . .'

Rosie gulped. 'I'm not your daughter, am I? I'm Aldo's.'

'You're *my* girl, Rosie,' came the sturdy answer. 'You allus have been and you allus will be. You're my girl, and I'm your dad, and don't you ever go thinking otherwise. I loved you from the moment the nurse put you into my arms. The bonniest little thing I'd ever seen, you were, with your brown eyes and your curly hair. Here, put this on.' He was holding out her coat to her. Obediently, Rosie slipped her arms into it and then let him fasten it for her as he had done when she had been a little girl. His little girl; safe then in her belief that she was his. Not like now.

'How can you know?' she wept. 'How can you?'

'It's me that's raised you, Rosie. Me that sat up wi' you when you was teething; me you call "Dad" – me not anyone else. And that's all I need to know. It's what's in here,' he thumped his chest, 'that makes me your dad, eighteen years of loving you and wanting the best for you. And your mam never said owt about you not being mine, which, knowing her, she would have done in one of her tempers if you weren't.'

Rosie couldn't feel reassured. 'But if Mum—'

He tucked her arm through his, and started to walk towards Edge Hill Road so that Rosie had to fall into step beside him. 'I don't want you to go thinking badly of your mother, Rosie. It wasn't all her fault, no matter what your aunt says. You see, your mam never really wanted to marry me. It was me who wanted that. I loved her that much that I thought that I'd be able to make her love me back. But love doesn't work like that, Rosie. You remember that and don't you go making the same mistakes I've made. You mek sure when you get married that you both love each other the same. I've thought many a time over the years that I did wrong by your mam by persuading her to wed me, but it was done then, and we had to make the best of it.'

'But Mum didn't make the best of it, did she?' Rosie questioned him bitterly. 'She started messin' around with Aldo.'

Her father sighed. 'Aye, well, he was a handsome chap, and no mistake, and we could all see that he looked a bit disappointed when he realised that it was Maria he was expected to wed. Not that she wasn't a good-hearted girl,' he added hastily when he saw Rosie's expression. 'But she wasn't pretty, not like your mother. Of course, your mam being the girl she was, she tried her best for Maria, going round and helping her with her makeup and her hair, like. If you ask me, it were him that was to blame. Turned your mother's head, he did, with his compliments and his fancy foreign ways.' Rosie felt as though she were a child again, listening to her parents quarrelling, hearing her father telling her mother that he didn't want her spending so much time with her friends. Now though, when she heard the anger and the bitterness in her father's voice, she understood what had caused it.

'You're mine, Rosie,' he said fiercely, 'my lass, and no one and nothing will ever change that, so don't you forget it. I'd never have let that ruddy Aldo take you from me the way he did your mother, even though Maria and them was allus trying to mek out that you belonged wi' them, teaching you to speak their lingo and having you calling them auntie this and uncle that, like you was blood-related to them. Well, you wasn't. You're mine.'

She could hear so much in her father's voice that had previously been hidden from her. He loved her so much, and she loved him too. She wanted to be his daughter more than she had ever wanted anything, Rosie admitted. It scared her – no, more than that, it sickened her – to think that there was any possibility that Aldo could be her father. She wanted to push the thought from her and lock it away where she would never have to think of it again.

'Huh, that Aldo might have liked to think that you was his, giving me that look and swaggering about like he was summat better than me, but he couldn't get his own wife pregnant so what made him think he had done wi' mine? Aye, and I told him so, an' all. Told him what I thought of him and what I'd do to him if I ever caught him trying to steal you away from me the way he had done your mam. Told him that I'd got friends who knew what to do to men who behaved the way he had.'

Rosie shuddered. This was a side to her father she had never seen before, a violent, unforgiving, vengeful side that left her shocked but unable to blame him for what he was saying.

'Why did you stay with her?' she asked, but she thought she already knew the answer.

'I knew if I threw her out like I should have done she'd have taken you with her and gone to him. Aye, and that daft Maria was that soft she'd have let him have your mother living there with them, and you, an' all. Especially you. I could see in her eyes how much she wanted you, Rosie, wi' her not having any kiddies of her own. Of course, that sister of hers was a different kettle of fish entirely. Hated your mam, she did, and she let her know it too. She even came round to see me once and told me that I should make your mam stay at home. Said that in the old country she'd have been locked away by her family for what she'd done.'

'But . . .' But what if I am his child? Rosie wanted to ask, but she knew that she couldn't. She didn't want to be Aldo's and she didn't think she could bear it if she were ever to find out that she was. But that was impossible now with her mother and Aldo both dead.

As she looked at her father, Rosie made a vow that she would do and be everything she could to show both him and the world that she was his daughter. She wanted to be alone to come to terms with her own thoughts and feelings, but at the same time she also wanted desperately to be with him and to be close to him.

'I can't go to the grave now,' she whispered.

'I'm sorry you had to find out about this, Rosie. I'd have given anything to keep it from you. I made your mother swear she would never say a word.'

He might have been able to silence her mother but not even her father had the power to silence her aunt, with her jealousy and her bitterness, Rosie realised. In *her* eyes she would never be forgiven for being her mother's daughter, nor ever allowed to forget what she might also be.

EIGHTEEN

It was almost the end of the evening. The band were playing a slow smoochy number and on the dance floor couples were taking advantage of the opportunity to move closer together.

'Rosie, what is it? What's wrong with you?' There was exasperation as well as hurt male pride in Rob's voice as he tried to draw Rosie closer to him and she pulled back.

'Don't go on, Rob.' Rosie fought back her own misery. 'I just don't like being mauled about, that's all.'

'Huh, seems to me there isn't much that you do like any more. You haven't bin the same since—' He broke off, scarlet-faced and mumbled, 'Sorry, Rosie. I was forgetting for the moment about your mum.'

His apology filled Rosie with remorse. It wasn't after all his fault she felt the way she did. She was lucky to have such a decent lad – very lucky, given her own background. So why did she feel like this?

Why couldn't she be the loving happy girl Rob wanted her to be? Why couldn't she be like the other girls she could see all around her, who were only too happy to kiss and cuddle with their partners? Rosie knew the answer, of course.

'It's not your fault,' she told Rob warmly. 'I'm just worrying about Dad, what with all the bad news about the convoys being torpedoed.' She gave a small shiver. She had heard only that morning that Molly Dearden's young man had lost his life when his ship had been torpedoed.

But her fear for her father now that he was back at sea wasn't the real reason she felt so unwilling to let Rob hold her tight or touch her in any kind of intimate way.

It was over a week since she had learned about her mother and Aldo, but she still hadn't come to terms with what she had been told. Every night her dreams were filled with images and memories from the past: memories of her mother, of Aldo, of Maria and the others. She had even dreamed vividly that she was with Aldo and that he was trying to steal her away, telling her that he was her real father. That dream had been so real and so upsetting that when she had woken from it she had refused to let herself go back to sleep in case it reclaimed her. Outwardly, she was the same person she had always been, yet deep down inside she was afraid that she was not, that she was in reality someone different, someone with a shameful secret that had to be kept hidden. Despite everything the man she would always think of as her dad, and love as such, had told her, the thought that she might actually be Aldo's child wouldn't go away, no matter how much she wanted it to. She had never liked Aldo, always feeling uncomfortable in his presence, and now she hated him and felt bitterly resentful of her mother for making it possible for her to have this fear. Those feelings, however, quickly gave way to guilt. She shouldn't think ill of her mother, should she, not now? But how could she do such a thing?

When she was on her own she searched her reflection in the small mirror in her bedroom, looking for any telltale signs that would confirm her secret dread. She longed now, as she had never done before, for fair hair and not the striking dark prettiness that so often in the past had caused Maria to say fondly that she could almost be Italian.

Before he had gone back to sea, her father had taken her in his arms and told her how much he loved her and how much he would always love her.

'Promise me you'll stay here with your Aunt Maude, Rosie, until I come back?'

She gave him the promise he wanted, but her aunt made it plain that very day how little she wanted her there.

'You've got that Italian's fathering all over you,' she had told Rosie bitterly, earlier in the week, 'even if my poor brother refuses to see it. It's in your blood and your bones, what you really are.'

Rosie had no defences against her bitterness, but her words made her more determined not to be Italian.

She was longing for the evening to be over so that she could be on her own. All around them on the dance floor, other couples were cuddling up to one another but the thought of doing the same filled her mind with images of her mother and Aldo and made her feel sick with bitterness and anger. Sometimes her own feelings confused her so much that she longed to be able to talk to someone about them, but who was there to talk to? Not her aunt; not her father because he wasn't here, and not Rob himself because she didn't want to see the look in his eyes when she told him that she didn't know the identity of her father. No, the shame that was her mother's legacy to her was something she had to lock away inside herself.

'We're in March now. Easter's coming up soon,' Rob continued. 'Did your dad say when he was likely to be back? There's summat I want to discuss with him – man to man, like,' he added meaningfully, reaching for her hand and squeezing it tightly. 'We've bin seeing one another for a fair while now, Rosie, and I'd like to make it official, like, get engaged and—'

'Oh, Rob, please don't. It's too soon . . . I mean,' Rosie amended hastily, not wanting to hurt or offend him, 'I like you, I really do, but I'm only eighteen and with this war . . .'

'It's because of the war that I want us to be wed, Rosie,' Rob told her, ploughing on determinedly. 'You were saying only the other day that you think your aunt wants shot of you. Well, if you and me was to get married . . .'

She could hear the hope and the eagerness in his voice and her chest tightened with a mixture of panic and pain. She hated the thought of hurting Rob, but she couldn't forget what her father had said about her mother not loving him as much as he had done her, or what had happened to their marriage. She didn't want to do anything that might set her off down the same shameful path as her mother.

'Let's wait a while, Rob,' she begged him lamely. 'There's many a couple so I've heard who have rushed into marriage and now wish that they hadn't.'

'I don't understand you, Rosie. If you were the kind of girl who wanted to go out dancing all the time, flirting with other lads and putting herself about a bit looking for a good time, it would be different, but you're not. I love you, Rosie.'

'I know that you think that you do, Rob,' Rosie acknowledged in a low voice. 'But you don't know me properly, and I can't help thinking about what would happen if we got wed and you changed your mind.'

'Don't be daft. Why would I go doing that? Folk get married and then they make the best of things,' Rob told her firmly.

Rosie's heart had sunk lower with every word he had said. She knew now from her parents' marriage the unhappiness that 'making the best of things' could bring. It might be different if she was crazily in love with Rob, in the way she had heard the girls at work talking, but Rosie didn't think she wanted to feel like that. It sounded far too dangerous. She only had to remember the way Sylvia had acted over Lance to convince herself that being crazily in love was not something she wanted to happen to her.

'I'd still rather wait,' she told Rob quietly, 'until we're sure.' So much that she had taken for granted had changed for her with the discovery of her mother's infidelity with Aldo. She now felt that not only could she not believe in her past, she felt she could not trust in her future either.

The silence with which Rob received her comment made her feel dreadful. And so once they got to a quiet street, when he pulled her into the shadows and kissed her, Rosie didn't try to stop him.

'Be quiet all of you! I've got summat to tell you,' Enid called out importantly, raising her voice to make herself heard above the chatter in the dinner hour busyness of the workroom.

'Go on then, tell us,' one of the girls called out cheekily.

Enid gave her a firm look. 'That's enough of your cheek, Marjorie Belham. Mrs Verey has told me to tell you that there's to be a meeting here tomorrow morning at half-past eight so you've all got to mek sure you're here.'

'A meeting? What kind of meeting? What for?'

'Why can't she tell us now?'

'What's it all about anyway?'

Everyone seemed to be asking questions at the same time so that the clamour filled the room.

'I can't tell you nothing more because I don't know nothing more,' Enid told them sharply. 'Just mek sure that you're all here.'

'What do you think Mrs Verey wants to say to us?' Ruth later asked Rosie worriedly. 'Only I hope she isn't going to be laying some of us off. I like working here. I know the money's not as good as at some places, but it's good for getting to the shops and getting in the queues, not like some places where everything's gone by the time you get to hear about it. Has Enid said anything to you on the QT, like? After all, she's allus a bit more friendly towards you than the rest of us.'

Rosie shook her head. She was as much in the dark as the other girls.

The evenings had started to lighten and Rosie could see the men working on their allotments as she walked down her aunt's road, her feet dragging the closer she got to the house. Her father had slipped her his key before he had left, so at least now she didn't have to knock on the door and wait for her aunt to let her in or, even worse, be left standing there if her aunt happened to be out.

Rosie hung up her coat and then headed for the kitchen, where she put just enough water in the kettle to make herself a cup of tea. Mr Churchill and his government were stressing to the people at every turn how important it was to be as frugal as possible with resources. It was, after all, men like her father who risked their lives in the convoys that brought into England the much-needed supplies.

Whilst she waited for the kettle to boil, Rosie went into the larder and removed the mashed potato left over from the previous day. Mixed with winter cabbage and fried up it would make a tasty supper.

Her aunt came in whilst she was halfway through cooking it. She sniffed the air and snapped, 'I thought I told you not to go putting any of that foreign muck on good plain English food.'

'I haven't put anything in it, Aunt. It's just cabbage and mash.'

'Don't you go lying to me. That mother of yours might have got away with lying to my brother, but I'm not as soft as he is. I'm telling you now, I won't have you bringing your dirty foreign ways into my house.'

Rosie could feel the anger expanding inside her chest from a tight hard ball to a burst of fury. Turning the gas off under the frying pan, she turned round to confront her tormentor.

'I am not a liar.'

'Don't give me that. Of course you are. How could you not be with the parents you've had? That mother of yours, little better than a whore, and that Italian she let have his way with her.'

'Aldo was not my father,' Rosie protested.

'Come here.'

Before Rosie could stop her, her aunt had taken hold of her and dragged her across the kitchen to the small mirror in the hall.

'Take a good look at yourself, miss, and then tell me that I'm wrong.'

'You are wrong. I know you are.'

Her aunt had let go of her and was walking away, ignoring her. Rosie's heart was thumping heavily and painfully inside her chest. The humiliation of what she had just endured was burning her face bright red and making her throat ache as she fought back her tears.

She would not let herself be Aldo's daughter, she vowed fiercely. She would not!

She couldn't eat her supper. Her aunt had pointedly made herself a sandwich and gone into the front room to eat it. She was treating her as though she was something vile and unclean, doing everything she could to make Rosie feel bad about herself.

Rosie couldn't wait for her father to get back. Being here without him was unendurable. And if it hadn't been for the promise she had given him that she would be here when he returned, she would have left. Yes, even if that meant that she had to join one of the growing bands of trekkers who trudged about the city every night, carrying their belongings with them to sleep in whatever temporary accommodation they could find, because they had no permanent roof over their heads. Rosie had never felt more alone. There was no one for her to turn to, no one to whom she could explain what was happening. How could she tell them about her mother and risk them turning against her as her aunt had done?

It was almost dawn before she finally fell asleep, with the result that she slept through her alarm and only just managed to reach the shop in time for Mrs Verey's talk.

The other girls were already putting forward their own theories as to what Mrs Verey wanted to say. Rosie took off her coat and hurried to join them.

'You've cut it a bit fine,' Enid remarked. 'That's not like you, Rosie. There's some here as I could name that are allus on the late side but you've allus been one who has come in to work well before time.'

'I'm sorry, Enid. I didn't hear the alarm,' Rosie apologised meekly as she squeezed into the line of girls between Evie and Mary.

Mrs Verey didn't keep them waiting very long, coming into the workroom dead on the stroke of eight thirty. Naturally pale-skinned, with blonde hair that she always wore drawn back off her face in a chignon, today she looked positively washed out, Rosie thought sympathetically. She had always liked her employer and that liking had grown when Mrs Verey had loaned her her own hat for the funeral.

'Thank you for coming in early,' Mrs Verey began. 'I wouldn't have asked it of you if it hadn't been necessary. I'm afraid the news I have for you is bad. This is a very sad day for me, but my husband has put his foot down and I'm afraid that I am going to have to close the shop.'

A shocked murmur filled the room as the girls turned to one another in dismay.

Mrs Verey looked as upset as they were themselves, and Rosie's heart went out to her. She had heard Enid say more than once that Mrs Verey's mother had originally owned the shop and that Mrs Verey had taken it over when her mother's health had forced her to retire. The Vereys lived at the top end of Wavertree, close to the tennis club in one of the leafy avenues of large detached houses. Mr Verey had been a doctor until his own ill health had forced him to retire. The couple did not have any children and Rosie knew that Mr Verey was older than his wife. The shop was her lifeblood.

'My husband feels that he must do his bit for the war effort and so he has accepted the position of general practitioner to a village in Cheshire so that their own doctor can be released to join our troops. Naturally, I must put my duties as a wife first. In addition, you all know, I am sure, of the problems we have been having in obtaining stock, and these problems can only become worse.'

'But what about the wedding dresses that are hired out?' Evie asked. 'That's a good bit of business.'

'Yes indeed, Evie, it is, and that business will continue although not with me in charge, or from this shop any more, I'm afraid. I have made arrangements that Lady Anne's Gowns will take over our existing stock, and I am assured that there will be positions for some of you at least with that emporium, if you wish to apply for them. Of course I am aware that those of you who are still under twenty will, as you reach that birthday, be required to sign up for war work yourselves. I really wish things could be different but alas they cannot. My final words to you all are those of thanks for your hard work here in this shop.'

It was obvious from the strained note in Mrs Verey's voice and the look in her eyes that she was distressed, and Rosie wasn't surprised when she left the workroom immediately after she had given them the news.

'Well, it's all right for her with her husband going to work as a doctor again and getting paid by the government. But what about us? How are we supposed to manage?' Bernadette demanded almost aggressively.

'You can't blame Mrs Verey, Bernie,' Rosie protested. 'She looked properly upset about it all, and like she said, we all know how short of stock we've been, especially since Christmas.'

'Yes, Rosie's right, Bernie,' Enid agreed. 'And

as for us managing – well, like Mrs Verey said, there's plenty of war work going.'

'Sign on at one of them munitions factories, you mean? My Tom won't ever agree to me doing that,' one of the older women spoke up, shaking her head. ''E says that it's downright wicked giving men's jobs to women and that he doesn't hold with it.'

'Well, Mr Churchill will have summat to say to him and no mistake, 'cos he says us women are needed in the factories to mek the munitions and that for our men,' Phyllis said.

'Yes,' Enid agreed. 'Your Tom hasn't worked a day since he claimed he hurt his back down on the docks five years ago, so much he knows, anyway.'

'My mam has bin working at that wot used to be the sweet factory. Bottling fruit, they are now and she's bin on at me since Christmas to go there with her,' said Marjorie.

'You get better pay at the munitions factories, Marj.'

'Mebbe so, but 'oo wants to tek munitions home wi' 'em?' Marjorie winked meaningfully.

'What about you, Rosie, what will you do?' Enid asked her.

'I don't know,' Rosie admitted.

'My cousin – she's your age – she was round our house last weekend and she says she's going to sign up for the Women's Land Army. She says she reckons a bit of fresh air and being away from

Liverpool and the bombs will do her very nicely. Of course, she isn't like you. She hasn't got herself a young man yet. Have you and Rob Whittaker settled anything formal between you yet?'

'Rob has talked about speaking to my dad on his next leave,' Rosie admitted reluctantly.

'Well, you see you don't lose him, Rosie. There aren't many lads like him about. Right, you lot,' Enid announced in a louder voice, 'we've all got to go down to the showroom and start packing everything up ready to take round to Lady Anne's. Mrs Verey wants everything done and dusted pronto.'

It was well past Rosie's normal leaving time when she finally stepped wearily out into Bold Street. As well as packing up the delicate evening and bridal dresses, the girls had also had to carry them round to the new shop, which was situated close to Lewis's.

When Marjorie and Fanny didn't return from their first trip, a grim-faced Enid had tracked them down to Lewis's, guessing they had sneaked into the store, thinking their absence wouldn't be noticed.

'As bold as brass, sitting there in the restaurant, they were,' Enid fumed to Rosie when she had brought them back.

There was no sign of Rob waiting outside for her when she left the shop. Rosie hadn't expected him to be there because they hadn't made any arrangement to meet, but she would have preferred to have gone straight to the cinema with him instead of having to go back to her aunt's. She was half tempted to go and see the newsreels by herself and then treat herself to a fish-and-chip supper. Her mouth watered at the thought, even though she knew that there was very little chance that there would actually be any fish.

It was nearly ten weeks now since the Christmas bombings, and after the initial relief at their absence, people were beginning to get edgy and apprehensive, staring up at the night sky as Rosie herself was doing now, dreading hearing and seeing Hitler's bombers and yet feeling that they were sure to return.

As she walked home, Rosie tried to comfort herself by working out how long it would be before her father was back, but she knew that he wouldn't even have reached Canada yet, and that it could be three weeks or more before he returned. How was she going to manage to cope with three whole weeks of her aunt's antagonism and hostility?

By taking herself out and finding a new job, that was how, she told herself staunchly. Her aunt had made it plain right from the start that she expected Rosie to contribute from her wages to the upkeep of the house, and she certainly wouldn't be prepared to keep her for free. Not that Rosie wanted her to. Her pride wouldn't let her depend on her aunt any more than she had to.

It was already dark when she let herself into the house, its windows blacked out just like all the others in the street. In the dim light inside the hallway – typically her aunt was using the excuse of the blackout and rationing not to light any of the rooms unless she was using them – Rosie stumbled against something lying on the floor. Her initial reaction was to stiffen her whole body, the sensation of something soft and warm lying against her legs taking her back to the night she had been trapped in the bombed air-raid shelter. A shudder went through her and she had to remind herself that she was in her aunt's hallway and not trapped underground, and so she kneeled down to ascertain what she had bumped into.

The door from the kitchen opened, allowing a thin shaft of light to illuminate the hallway so that Rosie could just make out a pile of washing gathered up in an old pillowcase. The same pillowcase surely that she had brought her things here in after they had been bombed out at home.

Her aunt was now standing in the doorway, watching her, a look on her face that Rosie couldn't interpret.

'Everything that's yours is there. I want you out of here tonight and, I warn you, anything you leave behind I'll burn.'

There were tear tracks on her aunt's cheeks and an emotion in her voice that Rosie had never heard before. Grief: Rosie knew enough about it herself to recognise it in others.

'What do you mean? What's going on? You can't just throw me out like this. My dad—'

'Your dad. Your dad was a bloody Eyetie who

fathered you on that whore of a mother of yours. Now he's dead. And so is my poor brother.'

'What are you saying?' Rosie demanded.

'I'm saying that Gerry is dead. Now get your things and get out of here. I can't stand the sight of you, reminding me . . .'

She was already turning away but Rosie didn't let her. She ran to her, taking hold of her arm as she stepped into the kitchen, almost shaking it in her agitation.

'I want to know what's going on. You can't just say something like that . . .' And then she saw the telegram on the table. Releasing her aunt, she walked over to it.

'That's nothing to do with you!' her aunt screeched. 'He was my brother . . .'

'It's addressed to me. You opened it and it's addressed to me. How dare you?' Rosie hadn't known she was capable of such ferocity.

She looked at the telegram, the words blurring as she tried to read them.

'We regret to inform you that Able Seaman Gerald Price has been reported as missing in action, presumed dead.'

NINETEEN

'Are you all right, love?'

Rosie stared at the man who had just spoken to her. Whilst the rest of the city might be quiet, down here at the docks, men were working quickly and noisily to unload the great grey ships drawn up at the dockside. She could hear the concern in his voice.

'Bombed out, are you?' he asked her, nodding in the direction of her bundle of belongings.

'We were,' Rosie acknowledged.

'There's one of them shelters not far away from here. I'm walking that way meself. If you was my daughter I wouldn't want to think you was on your own down here.'

Daughter. Rosie's eyes swam at the word. She nodded her agreement and let him help her with her bundles. She had no idea what time it was or how long she had been down here at the docks. She had no recollection either of having walked here.

The seaman – George, he told her his name was – was chatting easily to her as he guided her out of the dock area and through the maze of narrow streets to a school hall that had been taken over by the WVS to provide overnight accommodation for people.

'Found her down by the docks,' Rosie heard him explaining to the woman at the desk by the door. 'Poor lass was just standing there all on her own and she doesn't look the type what would . . .'

Rosie was distantly aware of the embarrassed note in his voice, and of the WVS woman frowning in concern as she looked at her.

'Bombed out, were you, dearie?' she asked brightly. 'It's a bit late to find you a bed now but we'll see what we can do.'

'It's my dad,' Rosie heard herself telling her. 'There was a telegram . . .'

The WVS woman got up from behind her desk and came towards her, took her bundles from her and then held both Rosie's hands firmly in her own. 'Let's get you a cup of tea, shall we, and then you can tell me all about it.'

Rosie looked at the sharp bright morning sky and shivered. She hadn't been able to eat the breakfast the shelter had offered her; she had barely been able to drink her tea. All around her people were gathering their things together, making ready to face the day, but all she could think about was her father.

Thanks to Mrs Gibson, the WVS worker, she now knew that her father's ship had been torpedoed and sunk on its way to Canada and that many lives had been lost. Rosie knew from growing up listening to her father's tales that the waters where they had been attacked were icy and that a man could not survive in them for very long. A tremor shook her. She couldn't bear to think of her father dying in that cold dark sea. She couldn't bear to think of what he might have suffered. She prayed that he might have died very quickly, and not been alone there, waiting for death, knowing that it was inevitable.

She was completely alone now with no one of her own. No one at all. Had her father really believed that she was his child or had he just told her that to comfort her? She wanted so desperately to be his. She would be his. She would never ever let anything into her life that could make her not be. She would dedicate her life to making him proud.

It was time for her to leave the shelter, but she had nowhere to go, no home and no job either after the end of this week. She wanted to be anywhere but here. And then she remembered Enid talking about her cousin joining the Land Army because she wanted to get away from Liverpool. Just like she did. She hated the thought of being so close to the sea now.

She found the office easily enough and stood outside along with several other girls, waiting for it to open.

'Bombed out?' one of them asked sympathetically.

It was a question that Rosie was getting accustomed to hearing. 'Yes.'

'Us, an' all,' another girl in the queue piped up. 'Me mam said I might as well come down here and sign up because at least that way I'd have a roof over me head.'

Rosie was the first in the queue and the recruitment officer was brisk and efficient. By the end of the morning Rosie had filled in the necessary forms, undergone a brief medical and been enrolled in the Women's Land Army.

'You'll be sent for training first. Come back tomorrow morning and we'll have your instructions ready for you. Here's an address where you can get a billet for tonight. You can go round there now and leave your stuff, if you like. Mrs Fraser puts up a lot of our girls for us, she's a good sort,' she told Rosie. 'When you come back in the morning you'll get your uniform,' she added with a smile.

Rosie couldn't believe it was so easy. A whole new life beckoned, a life where she could forget – or at least block out – her pain.

The girls at the shop had been tiptoeing around her all day since they had heard what had happened, and now Rosie was glad to be escaping from their pity into the sharpness of the early evening air. She had been forced to tell Enid what she had done because she had been so late for work, and then when Mrs Verey had congratulated her so warmly in front of the others on her patriotism she had burst into tears. She had then felt obliged to tell them about her father.

Now it was only just beginning to sink in that she would not be coming back to the Bold Street shop. In addition to her grief she was now experiencing a stomach-churning mixture of apprehension and disbelief at her impulsive actions.

'Rosie.'

Her eyes widened with shocked guilt. Rob! She had almost forgotten about him. What on earth was she going to say?

'Do you fancy the pictures tonight? I'm on duty later but if we go now—'

'I'm sorry, Rob, I can't.' She was growing more sick with nervous misery by the second. There was nothing else for it; she would just have to tell him the truth. The words came tumbling out in a guilty rush. 'There's been a telegram . . . It's Dad,' she told him starkly. 'Missing, believed dead.'

'Aw, Rosie . . .' He made to take her in his arms, his compassion increasing her feelings of guilt.

Quickly she stepped back from him, knowing that she had to tell him what she had done, but still trying to put off doing so. 'The telegram came yesterday. Dad's sister opened it even though it was addressed to me. When I got in she'd got all my stuff packed up. She told me she wanted me to leave. She never wanted me anyway; she only let me stay because of Dad.' The staccato sentences were all she was capable of saying; her tight self-control her only way of dealing with her feelings. She could see the shocked sympathy in Rob's eyes, and for a moment she nearly wavered and let the pain take her into his arms. But she knew that once she did that she would have to stay there, and she couldn't do that. Not now.

'Don't you worry, Rosie,' Rob tried to comfort her. 'I'll look after you. I'll find somewhere for us and we can be married quick, like. It would be what your dad would have wanted.'

This was dreadful, even worse than she had anticipated. 'No . . . we can't.'

'Why not? If you're thinking it's disrespectful then—'

'No, it isn't that.'

'Then what?'

'I've signed up for the Land Army.'

She could almost feel Rob's shock filling the air between them. His mouth opened as though he was going to say something, then closed again. He shook his head, obviously unable to take in what she had said, and then demanded in a thickened raw voice, 'Why?'

'I don't know,' she admitted. She was feeling more guilty and upset by the minute, unable to explain to Rob about the previous night or how she had felt. 'I just know that I've got to get away from here, Rob.' To somewhere where no one knew her, somewhere where she could be the person she wanted to be; somewhere where she had no past with Aldo in it and no one to remind her about him. She couldn't tell Rob any of that, though. She could barely understand or accept it herself.

'At least in the Land Army I'll be doing my bit.'

'You could have done that here.'

'I need to get away,' she burst out, unable to hold the words back any longer.

'From me?'

The pain in his voice wrenched at her tender heart. She hated hurting him like this.

'It isn't you. You're the kindest person, Rob, and I . . . I think ever such a lot of you.'

'But not enough to marry me.' His voice was flat and tight now with disillusionment and pain.

'I never said that I would,' Rosie struggled to defend herself. 'You'll find someone else, Rob, another girl who will make you happier than I can.'

Rob lunged towards her, taking her in his arms and kissing her with a fierce, angry passion she wasn't used to, prising apart her lips with his tongue. Rosie could feel the cold rough scrape of his unshaven jaw and smell the hot male scent of his skin. A wave of emotion she didn't understand surged through her, making her eyes sting with held-back tears of regret. Everything would be so much easier if she could be the girl he wanted her to be; but she wasn't. Her guilt made her endure the unwanted passion of his kiss until he let her go. He was breathing heavily, his face red.

'I thought you were different,' he told her bitterly, 'but you aren't, are you? You're just like her, that mother of yours.'

Rosie recoiled as though he'd hit her. Hot words of denial trembled on the tip of her tongue, but she held them back, knowing with instinctive female wisdom that it was kinder to leave him with the heat of his anger to cling to than the dull pain of a love she could never return.

'You think you'll find someone else better than me, but you won't, and just you think on that and me when you're cleaning out pigsties,' he told her bitterly.

He had gone before she could say anything, turning on his heel and leaving her standing alone. She knew it was her own fault that this had happened but that still didn't stop her from feeling the sharp pain of it. She stood watching him until he disappeared from sight, tempted to run after him and call him back but knowing that she must not.

'Right, Price. Bennett here will take you down to the stores and help you sort out your uniform, and then you will be given a travel warrant. Jolly good.'

A sharp nudge in Rosie's ribs from the elbow of the young woman standing at her side warned her that her brisk interview with the recruitment officer was over. Dutifully Rosie followed 'Bennett', the uniformed redhead, down a corridor and some stairs and then through a maze of small interconnecting cellars until eventually they reached the storeroom.

She was hurrying along at such a pace that Rosie could barely keep up with her. She came to a halt so abruptly that Rosie nearly cannoned into her.

'In here.' As she pushed open a heavy door she called out dourly, 'Here's another one for you to kit, our Parker. Pity you're a bit on the skinny side,' she told Rosie. 'The kit has come up a bit big, sort of one size fits all only they don't so you'll have to mek sure you've got a decent belt to hold everything up or in; that is, unless you're handy with a needle.'

The first thing that struck Rosie as she stepped into the long narrow cellar wasn't so much the solitary light bulb, which threw more shadows in the cavernous space than it did light, as the smell of cloth and dye, so strong that she nearly recoiled from it.

'Parker here will sort you out. When you're ready, come back upstairs. You'll find me in the third office on the left off the main corridor. I'll have your travel warrant waiting for you and your other papers.'

Rosie watched her go, wondering in some alarm how on earth she was going to be able to manage to find her way back.

'Right then, let's get started. Here's a list of the full uniform.'

Rosie took the piece of paper she was handed, and read it slowly.

'Have they told you where they'll be sending you yet?' Parker asked Rosie.

Rosie shook her head.

'Mmm. Well, let's see, the last lot were sent down to Norfolk so my guess is you won't be going there.' The older woman kept on talking as she sized Rosie up and then disappeared, returning with her arms full of a variety of garments.

'If it is Reaseheath you're going to, then they'll expect you to have the full kit. Do things proper there, they do.'

Rosie was glad that the landlady she had been billeted with the previous night had offered to let her leave her pillowcases there this morning. She wouldn't have liked to have turned up here dragging all her belongings around with her and looking very shabby, she thought, as Parker put the pile of clothes down on the nearby table and started to tick them off on her fingers.

'Right, that's the breeches,' she announced, indicating the corduroy pants that seemed like the ones the recruitment officer had been wearing – baggy at the hip and narrowing just below the knee. 'And here's the mackintosh and the jacket.' She put a coat and a fitted tweed jacket on top of the breeches. 'And the hat.' She added a brown felt hat to the pile. 'And here's the rest.'

'The rest' consisted of a khaki overall coat, two fawn shirts with turn-down collars, two pairs of dungarees, three pairs of fawn stockings, a pair of heavy brown shoes, a pair of rubber gumboots, a green armlet with a red royal crown on it, and a green V-necked jumper. Rosie just knew from looking at it that the jumper would itch.

'Oh, and you'll be given a bicycle as well.'

'Ought I to try them on?' Rosie asked uncertainly.

'There isn't any point,' Parker told her drily. 'They come in three sizes, small, medium and large. I reckon you'll be small. Oh, and you'll need a kitbag. Here . . . Now you'd better get yourself back upstairs. Find your way all right, can you?' She had disappeared into the darkness of the storeroom before Rosie could answer, leaving her to gather up her new uniform and put it carefully into her kitbag.

Fifteen minutes later, having taken only two wrong turnings, she was standing with several other girls who looked as uncertain and apprehensive as she felt, waiting to be given her instructions and her travel warrant.

The three girls in front of Rosie were all told they were being sent to Norfolk, but when it came to Rosie's turn she was told to report to the station for five o'clock that evening to wait for a train to take her to Crewe.

'You'll be met there by someone from Reaseheath College. That's where you'll get your four-week training before you're sent to work on a farm. When you're working you'll be paid twenty-four shillings per week, and out of that you'll be expected to pay for your billet. Every six months you'll be given a travel warrant to go home and see your family. If you end up on a milking team you'll only get half a day off every week, otherwise you'll get a day and a half. If you're put on a gang that goes from farm to farm then it's up to whoever's in charge of the gang to sort out your off-duty time,' Bennett explained briskly before demanding, 'Any questions?'

Rosie shook her head. If she had had any she didn't think she would have dared to ask them.

'Very well, then. Good luck, Price. And remember your country is depending on you.'

Rosie looked uncertainly at the details of how she could be contacted, which she had written down on the piece of paper. She owed her aunt nothing – less than nothing she decided fiercely. And she certainly didn't want her to think that she actually wanted to keep in touch with her. But she couldn't help thinking about her dad and what he would have wanted. Which was why she was here, standing outside her aunt's house.

Rosie lifted the knocker. She didn't have to let her know what she was doing, she certainly didn't want to have to speak to her. She let the knocker fall back gently and turned to leave. She had got as far as the gate when, on some impulse she didn't understand, she turned back and ran up to the door, slipping the note with her details and a forwarding address on it through the letter box.

This time as she opened the gate she felt as though her dad was smiling down on her approvingly.

* * *

She had been right. The green pullover did itch, Rosie acknowledged stoically, as she looked surreptitiously around the station, hoping to see someone else wearing the same uniform. She felt conspicuous in it, and very conscious of the looks she was attracting, especially from the RAF group standing a few yards away.

It was only now beginning to dawn on her what she had done: what she had committed herself to, and what she would be losing. She shivered and fought down the uneasy feeling growing in her stomach. She could have let Rob take care of her instead of doing this. He had wanted to. But what if she had and then one day out of the blue she had done something he didn't like and he had accused her of being like her mother?

'Hello, there. Are you bound for Reaseheath College as well, by any chance?' The cheery female voice with its unfamiliar accent had Rosie turning round in relief, at being distracted from her own uncomfortable thoughts.

'Yes I am,' she confirmed, smiling at the tall brown-haired girl who was standing in front of her.

'I'm Mary. Mary Dugdill from Birmingham,' the other girl introduced herself, extending her hand for Rosie to shake.

'There's another eight of us, but the others are looking for somewhere to get a bit of summat to eat.'

'The buffet's over that way,' Rosie told her,

nodding her head in the direction of the station's buffet bar. 'But I don't think they'll find much.'

'Not to worry. They're bound to feed us when we get there. We're lucky, aren't we, being billeted to Reaseheath for our training?'

'Are we?' Rosie asked.

'Oh, yes. It's a real agricultural training college where we'll have proper training. Oh, here come the others now. Are you on your own?'

'Yes,' Rosie confirmed.

'This is Sheila, Jean, Peggy, Brenda, Audrey, Stella, Joy and Pam,' Mary introduced the others. 'And you're . . . ?'

'Rosie.'

'Are you from round here then?'

'Yes.'

'I'm that hungry me stomach thinks that me throat's bin cut,' the girl Mary had introduced as Sheila announced. 'I told yer we should have brought a jam jar of tea and some sarnies with us, Mary. Nine o'clock this morning we left Birmingham. Got held up behind some goods train that had priority, and then they said they was rerouting us through Liverpool, instead of sending us direct to Crewe. Ruddy war. Here, Pam, get a load of them RAF lads over there. I fancy that handsome one with the dark hair. How far from here is this Reaseheath, Rosie? Do you know?'

'Not really.'

'Pity. I was hoping we might meet up with someone with a bit more info on the place, like how far it is from the nearest military base. We want to be near some chaps, after all, otherwise we might just as well have stayed at home.'

Rosie could feel herself tensing.

'Oh, give over, do, Sheila,' Pam cut in firmly. 'You'll be giving us all a bad name if you keep going on like that about the bloomin' military. Just because that Canadian flyboy gave you the eye at the Palais the other week and said as how he could get you some stockings don't mean you have to go acting like you've never seen a lad before. You'd fancy anything wi' trousers on, you would!'

'Not anything, I wouldn't,' Sheila protested vigorously. 'He'd have to be handsome and have a bit about him. I'm not throwing meself away on just any lad.'

'Oh, no, I shouldn't if I were you neither, Sheila,' one of the other girls laughed. 'I mean, any chap would be unlucky to get one of us as a date, smelling of cow muck like we'll be and wearing them wellies we've bin given. The lads will run a mile when they see us coming.'

'We won't let them get away, though,' the pretty blonde-haired girl called Stella chirped up, joining in the fun, 'and we'll be able to go after them on our bicycles.'

'Oh, give over, do, you're making my belly ache I'm laughing that much,' Mary protested. 'Anyway, never mind the cow muck, we'll still scrub up well. And at least with a bit of luck we'll be away from them ruddy air-raid sirens.'

A sudden silence seized the small group.

'I need a wee,' Sheila announced.

Peggy, who seemed shyer than the others, nudged Mary and whispered something to her once Sheila was out of earshot.

'You might as well know, Rosie, since it looks like we'll be training up together, I don't hold with talking about a person behind their back but, like Peggy here says, it's best if you do know just in case you was to say something by accident, like. Sheila's mam and dad, along with her nan and her brother and his girl, were all killed in a direct hit by one of them parachute bombs just before Christmas. Sheila was trapped with them until they managed to get her out. She's me second cousin, Sheila is, and it affected her bad, so when me and Peggy and the others decided to join the Land Army we persuaded Sheila to come along with us. She don't like to talk about what happened but it explains her behaviour sometimes.'

Rosie could see that Peggy was giving her an apprehensive look as though afraid that she might have done the wrong thing. Rosie gave her a reassuring smile and cleared her throat.

'I . . . I've had something similar myself. My . . . my mother . . . the house was bombed whilst I was on fire watch, and then my dad . . . he's – he was – in the merchant navy . . . there was a telegram . . .'

Suddenly she was surrounded by the other girls, each of them reaching out to put a supportive arm around her, offering her the comfort of sympathetic words and a small hug. Their kindness brought back to her how much she missed the friendship she had shared with Sylvia and especially with Bella. But she mustn't think about Bella now, not any more, she warned herself fiercely. Bella belonged to a part of her life on which she wanted to close the door for ever. Even so, the other girls, by their friendliness, lifted her spirits in a way she had thought they could never be lifted again.

'You stick with us, Rosie,' Mary told her. 'We'll all look out for one another and be good pals.'

For the first time in weeks, Rosie gave a genuine smile.

'Come on, this is it, Crewe.'

It was gone ten o'clock and if she felt tired and hungry she could only imagine how the other girls must feel, Rosie reflected sympathetically as they struggled off the packed train carrying their kitbags.

They had been told that transport to Reaseheath would be waiting for them outside the station and when they eventually managed to fight their way through the crowded station and into the cold night air, Rosie knew that hers wouldn't be the only heart to sink at the sight of an open lorry.

They weren't the only group making for the lorry. In all, Rosie reckoned there must be going on for forty young women all lined up to have their names ticked off a list by an older woman in Land Army uniform.

Eventually everyone's name had been called and the girls were instructed to get into the waiting lorry.

It was gone midnight when they finally arrived at their billet, freezing cold and cramped, to be given Spam sandwiches and a welcome mug of hot cocoa.

'Breakfast is seven sharp,' they were warned before finally making their way to the beds they had been given.

'I'm that tired I could sleep on a washing line,' Stella groaned.

'Me an' all,' Sheila agreed. 'How about you, Rosie?'

'Me too,' Rosie answered her. She could feel the small tendrils of a warm sensation beginning to melt the icy despair that had been gripping her. And when she finally closed her eyes, alongside her aching grief for her father and the frightening emptiness his death had left, was the awareness of how pleased she was that she had met the Birmingham girls. They couldn't take her father's place – no one could – but somehow she didn't feel quite so alone as she had done.

TWENTY

'I can't believe that we've been here for four weeks and that this is our last day,' Stella puffed to Rosie as the two of them finished swilling out the cowshed after milking. 'I 'ope when they tell us where we're being sent after we get our final talking-to this afternoon that we'll all be going there together, don't you, Rosie?'

Rosie nodded but didn't speak. It was hard work pushing the heavy broom she was using to clean the cowshed floor. But then, as they had all discovered over the last month, everything connected with working on the land involved hard work.

In four short weeks they had learned how to stook corn, what to do with a 'potato pie', how to hedge and ditch, how to cook up scraps for pigs, how to milk a cow – which was not by pumping its tail up and down, as some of the town-bred girls had initially thought, causing much hilarity – and a dozen more essential farming jobs. In addition to the practical hands-on instruction they had received,

348

the girls had also had proper lessons as well. Those who could not already do so had even had to learn how to ride a bike, because, once they were allocated to the work areas, bikes might be their main form of transport.

The Land Army divided its recruits into three different groups: forestry; gangers, in which the girls would move *en masse* from farm to farm, doing seasonal work; and dairy, where the girls would, for the most part, be billeted at a specific farm.

'That ruddy Daisy nearly managed to kick over the bucket after I'd milked her this morning. Taken a real dislike to me, she has,' Jean grumbled, 'and I feel the same about her.'

'Perhaps it's because of the way you yanked on her tail the first morning we tried to milk the cows,' Rosie teased her, stopping what she was doing to lean on her brush and survey the glistening milking shed floor with satisfaction.

She hadn't expected the sense of camaraderie and belonging that had developed between her and the girls from Birmingham, and at first she had tried to keep herself apart from them, not sure in her still shocked and grief-stricken state that she really wanted to make close friends. But Mary had refused to let her shut herself off from them and had persisted in making her part of their group and now Rosie felt as close as though she had grown up with them, because they had talked so easily and openly to her about their lives. She hadn't been able to be as open with them, though, but they had seemed to understand and accept that, knowing that she had lost her parents so recently. She had been wary about getting too involved with them for other reasons as well. After all, she had already been let down twice by girls she had thought of as good friends. But when she had tried to retreat into herself, politely excusing herself after their evening meal, for instance, Mary had determinedly insisted that she stay, asking her half jokingly, 'What's wrong, don't you like us, Rosie?'

Of course Rosie had had to deny any such thing, and then somehow or other she had found herself joining in with their conversation and their laughter, so that now she felt completely at home with them.

'At least they feed us proper here,' Peggy acknowledged, 'even if we do have to wait for our breakfast until after milking. Not that I can eat much some days, I get that scared thinking about the war and everything.'

Peggy had a sweet nature but she was inclined to be very fearful, Rosie had noticed.

The girls' day started at six, when they were woken up to tumble tiredly out of their dormitories and gulp down mugs of hot tea, before making their way to their designated duties.

Rosie had discovered that she didn't dislike and fear the cows as much as some of the other girls and she had blushed fierily the morning the herdsman had praised what he called 'her natural rhythm' when it came to the task of milking.

For a decision taken out of necessity and in her darkest hours, her new life in the Land Army was working out far better than she had ever anticipated. Sometimes, tired out after her day's work in the fresh air, lying in her bed on the edge of sleep, Rosie allowed herself the comfort of the thought that somehow her father had guided her footsteps and her decision at that dreadful time when she had first learned of his death. She thought about him every day – every hour, if she was honest – but could even talk about him now sometimes as well. She welcomed the change in her circumstances that had enabled her to put the unwanted discoveries of the last year behind her and to go back to being the girl she had been before them. No one here knew about her parents' marriage or her own birth. They did not know either about her mother's affair, or her aunt's hatred of her, and so Rosie was able to pretend to herself that she didn't know about them either. She felt safe and as happy as it was possible for her to feel here with the other girls, and she had no wish to return to Liverpool – ever. Her only regret was the pain she had caused Rob but she knew that she could not have married him and it was for his own good in the long run.

'Right, that's done,' Peggy announced, giving a heartfelt sigh of relief. 'I don't know about you, but I'm ready for me dinner and then I suppose we'd better go and get our best bibs and tuckers on ready for our Pass Out. We won't want to be late,' she added anxiously.

Their tutors at the college took their responsibilities towards the countryside on which they were about to inflict their pupils very seriously indeed, and the girls had been taught and drilled as thoroughly as though they were indeed part of a fighting unit.

It hadn't all been hard work, though, Rosie reflected, in the bustle of the shower block a couple of hours later as the girls showered and joked, calling out to one another, their spirits high.

'Remember when we was sent to work on that potato pie,' Stella giggled, 'and Sheila said as how she didn't understand why we had to have our dinner in the middle of a muddy field.'

Laughter echoed round the showers.

'Well, I wasn't the only one who didn't know what it was,' Sheila defended herself good-naturedly.

'We all certainly know now. Me back was aching for days afterwards, with all that hoeing and bending down,' another girl grumbled.

Rosie joined in with the general laughter. She hadn't realised either what the 'potato pie' was until one of their teachers had explained that it referred to the farming practice of raking up all the potatoes left from the harvest into a large circular mass that the girls then had to go through, picking out the potatoes that weren't fit to be eaten and bagging up the others.

'And so, girls, it only remains for me to say good luck and to caution you, first of all, to remember not to shirk or complain, no matter how hard the task may seem, for the work you are being asked to do will be making an important contribution to the war effort. And secondly I would ask you all to remember in the days ahead, should you come into contact with one of the working parties of prisoners of war the government has allowed to work on the land, that you are at all times and no matter what, representatives of our country and our fighting men.'

Rosie, tired after her early start, had been about to suppress a yawn when the senior instructor had mentioned the prisoners of war and she felt a prickle of unease run up her spine.

'Just as we trust that those of our men who are being held prisoner are treated as they should be, so it is imperative that we ourselves behave with courtesy and respect at all times,' Mrs Eames continued sternly. 'This is an instruction that has come down from Mr Churchill himself and I trust you will abide by it.'

'Huh, prisoners of war, is it?' Sheila announced sharply in the general mêlée after the girls had been formally dismissed. 'Well, you won't catch me having owt to do with the likes of them. Not after what Hitler's bombs did to my family.'

'We have to think, though, Sheila, of our own boys,' Peggy, who rarely said anything forceful, spoke up unexpectedly fiercely. 'I mean, how you would like it if some German girl spoke like that about one of our prisoners of war?' she demanded, her face going bright red with self-consciousness.

'Peggy's right,' another girl chipped in.

'We don't even know that we're going to be working with any POWs yet,' Mary reminded them all sensibly. 'We don't even know where we're going to be sent and we won't find out unless we look sharp and get down to the main office and get our orders.'

'From what I've heard, some of the places you get sent can be really grim – not like it is here with proper dormitories and shower blocks,' said one girl. 'I was speaking to one of the other girls and she said a friend of hers got sent down to Cornwall and that she ended up coming home on account of how bad they treated her.'

'Honestly, that Janet – she's allus trying to spread bad news.' Mary shook her head as she and Rosie watched the other girl go to join her own group. 'If you ask me, how we get on will be up to us. Mind you, I'm not saying that I wouldn't prefer to be billeted somewhere decent, but given the chance I'd rather that all of us are able to stick together than have to be separated, even if that would mean a better billet.'

'Me too,' Rosie agreed, horrified at the thought of being separated from her new friends.

'You're one of us now, Rosie,' Mary told her, giving her a big grin. 'You see, we'll even have you talking like us by the time we're finished.'

Both girls automatically stiffened as they walked outside and heard the sound of a plane's engine.

'Don't panic, it's one of ours,' Mary announced

happily, raising her hand to wave to the pilot of the small plane and laughing when he wiggled his wings in response. 'Come on, we'd better go and find out where we're going to be sent.'

'Appleyard, Benson, Dugdill, Ferris, Holmes, Johnson, Long, Nicholls . . .'

Rosie held her breath as the names of her new friends were called out in alphabetical order, and only released it on a shaky gust of relief when the officer continued firmly '. . . Price and Smith. You are all to report to the warden in charge of the gangers based at Astleigh in Cheshire. Here are your instructions and your travel warrants.'

'Cheshire. I thought we'd be going a bit further away. We won't get much of a chance to rest like 'em as are having to go to Norfolk and Cambridgeshire. It would be just our luck that we'll have to be up for work tomorrow morning.'

'At least we're all going to be staying together,' Mary beamed. 'Come on; this calls for a celebration.'

'What on, and don't you dare say milk?' Sheila objected feelingly, whilst everyone laughed.

'I must say I'd rather we hadn't been assigned to be gangers,' Rosie confided to Mary later when they were packing their kit ready to be transported to their new billet.

'Yes. I'd have preferred to be posted full time to one farm as well, but we'll just have to make the best of it.'

'I've heard that the gangers get all the rotten jobs,' Sheila put in.

'Oh, you and what you've heard,' Mary stopped her. 'I've heard that them as is allus listening in on other people's conversations never hear owt good.'

'Well, I just hope we're going somewhere decent where there's a bit of life going on. Somewhere near one of the military bases,' Sheila grinned, instantly brightening up at the thought.

'Here you are, girls.'

They had left Reaseheath after breakfast, and had been driven to their new billet in a Land Army truck.

'Heard about the bombing raid on Liverpool last night, have you?' the driver asked as they jumped out. 'It was pretty bad, by all accounts. Looks like Hitler is warming up for a real blitz this time.' Rosie shuddered, partly because she was cold and her body was stiff after sitting crushed up with the other girls in the back of the lorry for four hours, but mostly because of what she was remembering. Here in the depths of the country, where the only planes they heard were their own, it should have been hard to imagine the devastation of a major bomb attack, but Rosie found it all too easy and for a moment she was swept back.

'Come on, Rosie . . .'

Sheila's voice broke into the bleakness of her memories. Reaching for her kitbag, Rosie joined the others, already lining up outside the hostel whilst the warden took their names.

The hostel was a large concrete building, big enough, as they later discovered, to house a hundred girls split into teams of ten.

'It was a lucky day for us, Rosie, when we met you, with there being nine of us and just the one of you,' Mary commented.

'It was lucky for me as well,' Rosie assured her. She felt as comfortable with her new friends now as she had done with the girls at the shop – more so in some ways. There was no one like Nancy, making digs about her friends or questioning her parentage because none of her new friends knew anything about Liverpool or her past. And where once Rosie would have been proud to claim friendship with her parents' Italian neighbours, now, because of her mother and Aldo, she wanted to distance herself from everything Italian, especially its people.

Her father had been British through and through and as his daughter so was she, and she *was* his daughter. No one commented on her thick lustrous dark hair other than to say how lucky she was to have such lovely curls. No one ever looked at her and said that she had a look of 'them Eyeties', causing her stomach to cramp and unwanted images of Aldo to form inside her head.

In fact, if it wasn't for the loss of her father, Rosie knew that she would have been as happy as it was possible for a person to be when their country was at war, and besieged on all sides by its enemy.

By the time the girls had settled into their new quarters – a long dormitory, but thankfully the hostel had proper showers and toilet facilities and a large rectangular recreation room, complete with a table tennis table and a gramophone player – the teams were coming back from their day's work, some on their bikes, others arriving in lorries.

'What with being paid only twenty-four shillings and having to hand over eighteen shillings for our bed and board, we won't have much left if we get caught smoking in the dormitory and the warden fines us for it,' Mary warned when Sheila cadged a cigarette off her, saying she was going to save it to smoke later.

'What's the food like here?' she asked one of the girls who had just come in with her tea.

'It's OK if you like soup,' she replied and then laughed. 'No, it really is OK. You get a proper breakfast, and a decent supper, and some sand-wiches for dinner.' She pulled a face. 'They're pretty awful, but the farmers' wives sometimes give you a bit extra. If they've got POWs working on the farm then you're in luck because the farmers' wives are good at making the rations the government has to give them go round everyone, but if they haven't then you'll have to make do with sand-wiches. The work's not too bad up here,' she added informatively, 'not like down Norfolk way where

358

I was before. It's mostly dairy up here and not crops, although they do grow potatoes. And then there's some arable, as well. If you're really lucky and get put to work on the duke's land then you'll be in clover. Oh, and we have a bit of a collection you have to put into for the gramophone and the records. And the warden's a good sort – she organises tea parties with the locals and a dance every now and again.'

'That'd be all right providing there's someone to dance with,' Sheila joined in.

'There's an RAF camp a few miles away on the other side of the village,' their informant grinned, seeing Sheila's huge smile.

Rosie grimaced at her wellingtons, which were a size too large but she knew that she was lucky to have them. Only dairy workers were guaranteed their wellington boots because of the rubber shortage, and last night over supper some of the girls who had been working in other parts of the country had had horror stories to tell of having to borrow boots from the old farm hands they were working with.

'I tell you, talk about waiting for dead men's shoes,' one girl, Nelly, a Londoner with a sharp cockney accent, had grimaced.

Right now, though, struggling to walk through mud so thick her boots were nearly sucked off her feet with every step she took, as she staggered behind a herd of cows she was supposed to be helping the ancient cowman deliver to the milking sheds, Rosie didn't feel particularly fortunate. The vicious slicing rain had already soaked through the waterproof cape she had been given to wear, and the mud had slurped up over the tops of her wellingtons, where her leggings were now so wet that they felt as though they were rubbing her skin raw. Every time she lifted her gaze from the backsides of the cows in front of her, all she could see was an endless panorama of grey-green emptiness. Somewhere ahead, one of the cows had stopped, causing the others to follow suit. Rosie, engrossed in simply trying to put one foot in front of the other, bumped into the nearest cow and almost lost her balance, her feet squelching in the mud.

'Your legs are younger than mine; get yourself up there and get that cow moving,' the cowman yelled in Rosie's ear.

They had been warned not to provoke the hostility of the elderly farm hands they would be working with, whom they had been told would be set in their ways and unused to working with young women, so Rosie dutifully made her way along the line of cows until she reached the gate, which instead of being open to let the cows through into the yard, was still closed.

With the cows pressing against her, Rosie had to struggle to unlatch the gate and then lift it so that the bottom bar could swing free of the mud so that she could open it.

As she did so, the cows, no doubt sensing the

warmth of the milking shed, pushed so eagerly through the narrow opening of the gate that Rosie was afraid she would be knocked off her feet and crushed. The only way she had of getting clear of them was to scramble up the gate as she swung it open, but in order to do so she had to leave her wellingtons firmly entrenched in the mud, much to the amusement of the cowman and the other farm hands, who had mysteriously appeared in the yard to watch the show.

'Old Harry played exactly the same trick on me,' one of the other girls comforted Rosie half an hour later as they sat side by side on their milking stools, milking the hosed-down and cleaned cows.

'It's a pity someone doesn't give him a taste of his own medicine and plays a joke on him,' Mary spoke up determinedly.

Rosie sighed and shook her head, making herself focus on the comforting rhythm of milking and the satisfying squirt of the fresh warm milk into the pail.

She had had to wait until all the cows were through the gate before she could retrieve her boots and then she had had to wash them out under the pump in the yard, standing there in her wet stockings, her feet so cold she could quite easily have cried. Now her feet were still cold and both the insides of her wellies and her stockings were soaking wet.

'You mind you wash and dry them feet of yours

properly first chance you get,' the farmer warned Rosie when they had finished milking, 'otherwise you'll be getting bad feet.'

Trudging back down the lane, returning the herd to the field, was even more wet and unpleasant than bringing them in, but not as unpleasant as cleaning out the pigsties, Rosie decided. Despite the clothes peg she had put on her nose, her eyes were streaming from the stink, and the back of her throat felt raw from breathing through her mouth.

'You'll get used to it,' the farmer told the girls not unkindly when he came to check up on them, and saw their clothes-pegged noses. 'There's nothing like a bit of pig muck for good manure, as you'll find out if you're here long enough. Frost's broken up the ground now, so I reckon you'll be able to go out and spread this onto the fields next week. Missus wants you to go and collect the eggs now, and think on, you'll need to get down under the henhouses on account of some of them buggers going there to lay. Daft they are, when the ruddy foxes go under there as well.'

The girls ate their sandwiches in one of the hay barns, taking advantage of the protective warmth of the hay to shelter them from the draught as they munched hungrily on their food and drank the hot tea the farmer's wife had provided.

'I'm that tired I can't even be bothered to think of a way to get back at old Harry,' Mary complained at six o'clock that evening when the girls hauled themselves gratefully into the lorry that had come to take them back to the hostel.

There couldn't be anything better than this, Rosie decided, as she soaped her exhausted and filthy body and then rinsed herself off under the thin trickle of a welcome hot shower, unless it was already being tucked up in bed. She smothered a yawn, and then yelped as the hot water stopped flowing and she was doused in icy cold.

'Sorry, we should have warned you about that,' a girl from one of the other gangs yelled out from the other side of the partition. 'The rule is two minutes of hot water and no more.'

They were lucky in their warden, Mrs Johnson, who was a kindly motherly woman. She clucked sympathetically when Rosie nearly fell asleep whilst she was eating the hearty soup that was their supper.

'You'll get used to it, lass,' she offered comfortingly.

'Maybe, but will her wellies?' someone joked, causing everyone, even Rosie, to laugh.

Their first day set the pattern for the next two weeks, with early mornings so that they could be at the farm for milking and early nights when the girls were so exhausted they were glad to get to bed at ten.

When they woke up at the beginning of their third week, it was to discover that the rain had stopped and the sun was actually shining.

'You won't be so pleased when you realise what

sunshine means to farming folk,' they were warned by the more experienced girls. 'You wait, a week of this and you'll be out planting potatoes. Back-breaking, it is.'

'Hey, Rosie,' Alice, a girl from one of the other groups called out, 'I forgot to tell you last night but we think we've found a way you can teach old Harry a bit of a lesson. Seems that him and one of the cows don't get on. Took a dislike to Harry, she did, and she lets him know about it. She might not have any horns but apparently she gave him a kick in the you-know-wots last year that sent him flying across the milking shed, and the milk bucket with him. Since then he's kept out of her way and won't go near her. It's me that milks her – and I reckon I could persuade her easily enough to swap places with one of the other cows. Old Harry's that cocky he won't think nothing of it if I call out to him, all frightened, like, that summat's gone wrong and he's bound to come to see what it is. I can't wait to see his face when he realises that I'm milking Ruby.' She laughed. 'I owe him one for the way he tricked me like he did you when I first arrived, only I wasn't quick enough to make the gate like you was, Rosie, and I ended up flat on me arse in cow muck. We're all moving on come the end of this week and I reckon if we give him a big enough fright and warn him that we'll be telling all the new girls about him, that should put an end to his tricks. So how about it? Will you swap places with me at milking time in the morning?'

'Go on, Rosie,' Sheila urged her.

Rosie agreed. She had grown quite fond of the cows, who were in the main easy-going beasts, and she had seen how old Harry tried to skimp their care when he thought he could get away with it. It wouldn't do any harm to give him a reason to treat his charges, both human and animal, with a bit more respect, Rosie quietened her overactive conscience.

Mrs Johnson, the warden, innocently put the girls' high spirits at breakfast down to the fact that it was another sunny day, smiling approvingly on them all as they hurried through their breakfast and rushed out to the waiting lorry with unusual speed.

Even the smell of the pig muck they had been spreading on the fields no longer seemed as unpleasant as it had done at first, Rosie decided, as one of the girls burst into song and the others enthusiastically joined in.

'Give over, will you, girls?' the driver shouted back to them. 'You'll turn the milk with that cater-wauling!'

There was no mud in the lane now – the sunshine had dried it up – and the cows were now so familiar to Rosie that she knew them all individually. Clicking her tongue, she urged them down the track, humming under her breath as she did so, and then laughing as one of them – Buttercup, with her big brown eyes and determination to slow things down whilst she enjoyed another mouthful of grass – turned to look at her.

'Up, up,' Rosie encouraged them. Old Harry used a nasty thin whippy stick on them but Rosie and the other girls preferred to coax them rather than bully them.

The new grass meant that their milk yield was up and that milking took longer.

Rosie could see Harry standing in the yard, chewing on a piece of grass and looking sour.

'Come on, get them beasts in and stop dawdling,' he yelled bad-temperedly.

Deftly Rosie persuaded her part of the herd to move away from him so that the stick he had raised to thwack them missed its target.

When they got into the milking shed, Alice was already there; she winked at Rosie and whispered to her, 'Down there, third from the bottom.'

Nodding, Rosie guided Buttercup towards the waiting space. Of course the cow, well aware that this wasn't her normal milking station, wanted to object but Rosie stood firm and coaxed her, and eventually Buttercup moved down the line, allowing Alice and Ruby to take their places.

Rosie had just got herself settled on her stool, her head leaning against Buttercup's warm flank as she worked, when she heard Alice scream – loudly. She had to scream a second time though, before old Harry appeared in the doorway, by which time Alice, whom Rosie reckoned must have missed her calling as an actress, was standing up on her stool yelling, 'A rat! I've just seen a rat! It was in me milk bucket . . .'

The big grin on old Harry's face changed to a look of anger at the mention of the milk bucket. A soft townie girl screaming because she had seen a rat was one thing; risking the wrath of the farmer because the milk was contaminated was another.

'Get down off there and stop yer bawling,' he yelled, running towards them.

Alice waited until he was right up alongside Ruby before reaching out to grab hold of his arm and say tearfully, 'Oh, I was that scared and it's set poor Ruby here all of a twitch. Nearly kicked me, she did . . .'

The entire milking shed had gone quiet now. Even the cows seemed to be watching and listening, Rosie thought. Ruby was certainly aware that the enemy was at hand because she let out a bellow and dropped her head, charging old Harry and nearly pinning him against the wall. As he wriggled out and fled, running out of the milking shed as fast as he could, the whole place erupted into laughter.

'That'll teach him,' Alice declared with satisfaction later. 'I reckon we weren't the only ones who had a laugh neither. The other men saw him.'

'I think the cows enjoyed it too.'

'Rosie Price, you're a right soft one, that you are,' Alice teased her.

Instead of just working on one farm, they would now be moving around working on several farms in the area, all owned by the Duke of Aston, they were informed by the warden.

'Ooh, I've never met a real live duke,' Sheila giggled.

'Well, you won't be meeting this one either,' the warden told her firmly. 'His Grace is in the RAF and his squadron is on active duty at the minute.'

It was left to the other girls at the hostel who had been there for some time to give them the lowdown on what they could expect.

One of them, a Manchester girl named Pauline, told them warningly, 'Mostly it's not too bad just so long as you don't fall foul of George Duncan. He's one of the foremen wot manage the farm hands for His Grace, and a right nasty old piece of work he is, and no mistake. If 'e starts picking on yer then you have to stand up to him and give it him back, otherwise he'll mek your life a real misery. We haven't seen that wife of his wi'out a black eye yet.'

Rosie and the others exchanged anxious looks.

'Oh ho, he's that kind, is he?' said Mary. 'Well, we won't stand no nonsense from him.'

'Don't let him get too close, if you know what I mean. Mind you, it's them poor POWs and internees that gets the worst of it from him. Treats them something shocking, he does. Them as knows him say that he's got a real mean streak.'

Rosie stiffened at the mention of POWs and internees, remembering how the Italian men from her old neighbourhood had been interned at Huyton and put into a camp originally planned to hold

POWs. She had such mixed feelings now about the old days and the people who had shared them with her. Originally she had felt so very protective and angry on behalf of Liverpool's Italians, but now her fear that she might after all be Aldo's child had made her want to distance herself from Italians in every way that she could. Her hand had started to tremble slightly, and so she put down her mug of tea in case anyone else noticed. The last thing she wanted was to have to work with Italian internees and POWs. It would make her think too much about things she would prefer to forget. She had never particularly liked Aldo, and now she felt that she hated him. Somehow it was easier to blame him for her mother's dreadful betrayal of her husband and her best friend than it was to blame her mother. Rosie's feelings were so difficult to bear at times and she was afraid that working with Italians would make that even harder. But, of course, she couldn't say anything of this to her new friends, not if she wanted them to go on thinking of her as a respectable girl who had come from a decent family.

'So we'll be working with some chaps at last, will we?' Sheila asked, unabashed by the reproving look Mary gave her. 'What are they like then, these POWs?'

'They're a decent bunch – but the POWs can't speak any English. They haven't bin here that long. The internees are better; you can have a bit of a laugh wi' them,' Pauline told them.

'Yes,' another girl chipped in. 'I feel sorry for

them, I do. But if it's chaps you want then there's an RAF squadron based a few miles away at Hack Green.'

'Typical,' Sheila grumbled on their first morning when they woke up to rain, but worse was to come when they discovered that they would not be working with the cows, as they had expected, but instead were going to be put to planting potato fields.

'That's gangers' work,' Sheila complained. 'We're milkers.'

'Try telling that to 'im,' Brenda muttered, giving a small nod in the direction of the sour-faced man watching them clamber out of the lorry. 'Trust us to get the very foreman we've bin warned against, on our first day.'

George Duncan looked like a bull, Rosie admitted. He might only be of average height but he was a big heavily built man with small mean eyes and the kind of high colour that warned of a bad temper. Rosie had smelled the stale beer on his breath when they had to march past him.

Planting potatoes was back-breaking work, which left them with soil-blackened hands and nails.

'I'll never eat another tattie after this,' one of the girls moaned, straightening her back to wipe the rain out of her eyes and leaving a smear of mud on her cheek.

'You'd never catch me saying no to a nice two pennyworth of chips,' another girl told her.

'Who's talking about chips?' the first girl scoffed. 'These are tatties.'

'And where do you think chips come from, you daft thing?'

The good-natured banter the girls exchanged lightened the hours of hard physical work. Liverpool and the life Rosie had lived seemed a lifetime ago now, she admitted, as she tried not to think about how much she was longing for a hot bath and some hot food. Not that she didn't have her low moments. There was hardly a night went by without her dreaming about her mother or her father and sometimes both of them, arguing and falling out with one another, whilst she cried out to them in her dream not to hurt one another with their cruel words. She dreamed about the Grenellis too, her sleep tormented by her images of Maria, sobbing and accusing her mother of stealing her husband. But during the daytime at least she could keep her mind locked against such images, even if she couldn't close her heart to her pain. She could pretend that she was in the same boat as Sheila, and that all she needed to grieve for was her dead parents and not her own identity as well. Not that she *didn't* grieve for her mother and her father. She missed them desperately, even her mother, for all her bad ways. Rosie would find that her memories of Christine would creep up on her and catch her unawares, so that it almost felt as though she could turn her head and her mother would be standing there, coaxing her into lending her her last pair of stockings, or putting on her favourite bright red lipstick.

And as for her father, she would never cease mourning him, Rosie knew. She couldn't have stayed in Liverpool, with the docks and their seafaring men always there reminding her that he wouldn't be coming back.

She paused in her work now, lifting her face towards the rain so that it would disguise the tears filling her eyes. 'Oh Dad, Dad,' she whispered brokenly. 'Why did you have to be taken from me? I miss you so much.'

It finally stopped raining just before they were told to pack up for the day.

'Ooooh, me back. I don't think I'll ever be able to walk straight again,' Sheila complained, but typically, by the time they got back to the farmyard, she had recovered enough to nudge Rosie and say eagerly, 'Look over there, at that lot. They must be them POWs. That one in the middle's a real good-looker, an' all.'

Rosie had looked over in the direction of the group of men standing on the opposite side of the yard, under the eagle eye of an armed soldier, to get into the waiting army lorry before she could stop herself. The man Sheila had referred to was the next in line to get into the lorry. Tall, and so broad-shouldered that he was straining the seams of the regulation army shirt he was wearing with its telltale insignia on the back to indicate his status, he had the warm-toned skin and thick dark hair Rosie immediately recognised as Italian.

As though he sensed her watching him, he

suddenly turned his head and looked directly at her. An unfamiliar feeling seized her heart, squeezing it tightly. She felt out of breath and light-headed, she felt . . .

Somehow she managed to wrench her gaze away. She was trembling from head to foot – because she was cold and wet and because seeing him had brought back all the painful memories she wanted so much to forget, Rosie reassured herself.

The girls' transport had arrived, and she was only too thankful to clamber into it. When the lorry containing the POWs rattled out of the yard she didn't turn her head to look at it.

Sheila did, though, nudging Rosie to say in a loud whisper, 'Rosie, that good-looking one is watching you. I think you've struck lucky there.'

The first thing Rosie looked for over the next few mornings, when they reached the farmyard, was the POWs – not because she wanted to see them, she assured herself, but quite the opposite. And it was a relief when she was able to reassure herself that they weren't there.

By Thursday it had stopped raining and the sun had come out to greet the first day of May. Rosie noticed as they trudged down the lane to the potato fields that the fat green buds on the blackthorn hedges were ready to burst into leaf, and surely there was a warmth to the air that had not been there before.

'Come on, you lot. You're here to work, not gossip.'

'I knew it was too good to last,' Mary murmured to Rosie as George Duncan strode grimly up and down the line of assembled girls.

'Bloody waste of time, the lot of you,' he told them. 'Farmin's men's work, not wimen's, or bloody useless Eyeties'. You're enough to turn the ruddy milk sour, you lot are. Now get to it. I want to see this field planted by dinner otherwise you'll not be getting none.'

'That's not fair. You can't do that,' Jean protested indignantly.

Immediately he turned on her, his face dark purple with temper. 'Who says I can't, missie? I can do anything I like around here and you had better just remember that or it will be the worse for you.'

'At least it's not raining,' Rosie tried to cheer Jean up when George Duncan had gone.

'He's got no right speaking to us like that,' one of the other girls said angrily. 'Someone should report him.'

'Mebbe so but 'oo are we going to report him to, seeing as he's the foreman, in charge of the job?' Audrey asked drily. 'Unless of course you was thinking of hitching a lift to the front in one of them RAF planes, and complaining to His Grace?'

'Hitch a lift in one? I'd ruddy fly it meself if I had to if it meant getting the best of the likes of him,' someone else offered.

Unlike the milking sheds, where the girls had

often sung to the cows as they milked them, here in the field the only sounds they had the energy to make were those of complaint for their aching muscles.

'Only another day and then we only have to work a half-day,' Mary tried to cheer them all up. 'There's a pub down the village. How about we go down there Saturday afternoon to see what it's like?'

'One of them girls we was talking to the other night said that the vicar had said summat about having a bit of a dance down at the vicarage once the weather warms up a bit,' said Sheila.

Working in the fields was so exhausting that the girls were glad to get to bed at ten after an evening at the hostel spent playing cards, listening to the radio and, when they had the energy, putting on the gramophone and dancing. The dancing in particular was always good fun, especially when they improvised new steps for the popular dance tunes. Rosie had always loved dancing and was very light on her feet, with a natural sense of rhythm that always made her popular as a partner. Because there were no men available, some of the taller girls had to dance the man's part, and one night when Sheila was dancing with a particularly buxom girl who was taking the part of her 'partner', she complained loudly.

'Oi, Felicity, mind out what yer doing with that chest of yours, will yer? You nearly put me eye out.'

Sheila was a real case, and loved the limelight, acting daft when she had everyone's attention and making out that she was dancing like the star of some film, all dressed up in silks and diamonds, even when she was wearing a pair of dungarees. She was a good mimic too and soon got them all laughing by taking off the warden.

Rosie was fast sleep when the German planes flew in low over Liverpool and the air-raid sirens screamed their warning. It was the sound of the defensive planes taking off from the nearby RAF airfield that woke her and the other girls.

'What's that?' one of them demanded fearfully, as the first of the bombs exploded.

'Bombs,' Rosie told her, shivering. 'The Germans are blitzing Liverpool. They'll be aiming for the docks.'

None of the other girls in her dormitory was from Liverpool but she could sense in the darkness of the room their silent sympathy.

It was gone two in the morning when the bombing ceased, and later still when they heard the RAF planes returning to their base.

'They're all back,' Peggy told them shakily. 'I counted them going out.'

Over breakfast Rosie was still subdued, her thoughts on the previous Christmas and her mother. Whilst she could never condone what her mother had done, neither could she deny that she wished that her mother was still alive. Only now was it actually coming home to her slowly and painfully how bleak and empty her future was going to be without her parents. One day the war would be over and other girls would go out to celebrate with their families. Other girls would go out shopping again with their mothers, and share new happy times with them, but she would never be able to do that now. If she were ever to marry – not that she expected or wanted to, not now, what with all she would feel too ashamed to tell a lad and his family about herself – her mother wouldn't be there to see her wed, or to see her children. No, she would never marry. Just thinking about the questions she could be asked by any potential in-laws made her feel sick inside. And yet at the same time Rosie felt so dreadfully alone, and the future, when she did allow herself to think about it, looked miserably bleak. Having the war to concentrate on was a blessing in disguise really. It kept her from thinking about other unhappy things. Most of the time anyway.

Given the mood she was in, the last thing she wanted to be confronted with when they reached the potato fields was the sight of a group of POWs and internees being marched into an adjacent field.

'Your admirer's with them, Rosie,' Sheila whispered excitedly to her. 'He was looking over here, an' all. Why don't you give him a bit of a smile?'

'They are prisoners of war, Sheila; enemies to this country,' Rosie reinforced so sharply that not only Sheila but several of the other girls who heard her also looked slightly taken aback. Rosie was normally so kind and good-natured.

'There was a fair few Italian families living round us at home and they was saying that they'd heard as how a lot of men back in Italy didn't want to go fighting our boys,' another girl commented determinedly.

Rosie flushed guiltily, remembering the Grenellis, but stood her ground. 'You can think what you like. But I don't want anything to do with them,' she told the other girls fiercely. Her heart felt as if it was jumping around inside her chest on a piece of elastic, but she wasn't going to let on to the others about how she felt every time she thought of the tall handsome Italian looking out for her. She didn't even want to admit those feelings to herself. She was glad that the hard work of planting the potatoes meant that it was impossible for them to talk and even more glad that the Italians were set to work several fields away and out of sight. Not that she would have been tempted to look across to see if he was looking back at her if they had been working closer. Not for one minute.

TWENTY-ONE

'I couldn't sleep for them bombs last night. Scared me half to death, they did. They reminded me of what happened to me family, an' all.' Sheila shuddered, and wiped the tears from her eyes as the ten girls, scrubbed and spruced up in their civvies, walked slowly down the lane that led to the small village.

Rosie reached for Sheila's hand and gave it a comforting squeeze.

'Still, at least I'm still alive and I reckon I have to do their living for them now as well as me own for meself. 'Ere, Pam, are you sure you painted them seams straight on me legs?' she demanded, craning her neck to look at the backs of her legs.

'Of course I did. Although just 'oo you're expecting to meet who's going to notice if I hadn't, out here in the middle of nowhere, I don't know.'

Pam had barely finished speaking when a truck came racing round the bend towards them, before skidding to a halt.

'Wow, real live girls. Hello there, girls. Please stop and talk to us poor lonely airmen.'

The truck had been stopped strategically so that it almost blocked the width of the lane, leaving the girls no option but to halt. That this was a tactic the truck's driver had used to good effect before wasn't lost on the girls, especially Mary, who fixed the driver with a scornful look.

However, before she could say anything the RAF-uniformed boys in the back of the truck, who had been calling out to them, jumped out and came over.

'Sorry about our driver. He hasn't seen a girl in so long he's forgotten his manners,' one of them, tall, brown-haired and with a soft voice and a warm smile, apologised. 'I'm Ian Wilton, by the way, and these other chaps are Tom Walker, Charlie Soames, Dick Renfrew, Pete Sayers and Neil Kearns.'

A sharp nudge from Sheila pushed Mary into reluctantly responding with their own names.

'So what are a stunning-looking bunch of beauties like you doing out here?' Neil, the driver of the truck, teased them.

'We're in the Land Army,' Sheila answered him, giving him a bold look. 'And since it's Saturday afternoon we thought we'd walk down to the village to see what's going on.'

'Well, there's nothing. So why don't you climb aboard and we'll all go and look for some fun together?' Neil suggested promptly.

'We aren't that sort, thank you very much,' Mary answered him sternly. 'You'll be based at Hack Green, I suppose.'

'Yes. That's right.'

This time it was the quiet one – Ian Wilton – who answered her and who, Rosie noticed, had moved considerably closer to Mary.

'Luftwaffe's having a go at Liverpool and it's our job to see him off,' Ian told them.

'We've heard the planes going out these last two nights,' Peggy was informing a shy-looking young man who Rosie remembered had been introduced as Charlie. 'I counted them going out and coming back in again.'

Charlie blushed and told her fervently, 'That's the spirit. I'll think about you counting us now every time I fly out on a mission.'

'You were gone a lot longer last night than you were the night before.'

'Jerry sent over a hell of a lot more bombers last night,' Ian told them. 'A hell of a lot more. At one stage it looked as though the whole ruddy city was burning. We did our best but . . .'

Rosie wanted to know more too but was afraid to ask. In her mind's eye she could see the city, with its docks and narrow dock-side streets packed tight with homes – homes like her own. She knew what it felt like to see those homes flattened and to know that loved ones had been lost.

'Well, girls, seein' as you won't jump in and let us take you somewhere exciting like Nantwich, how about we all go into the village and have a drink at the pub?'

Mary looked at the other girls and then nodded. 'But we'll walk there, thank you very much,' she told them firmly.

Rosie doubted the village pub, with its thatched roof and low beams, had ever had so many people in it at one time. The shepherd standing at the bar with his dog at his feet eyed them all suspiciously, muttering under his breath as the landlord served them.

'I don't think they're used to girls going into pubs round here,' Mary laughed, when Ian and the other boys had insisted that they wanted to pay for their drinks.

'I don't think they're used to girls, full stop,' Ian responded.

They were a cheerful bunch, laughing and joking amongst themselves and making light of the danger of what they were doing, and Rosie could see how taken Mary was with Ian. By the end of the afternoon the two of them were sitting together deep in conversation whilst Peggy and Charlie were openly gazing at one another with stars in their eyes.

When it was time for them to leave, there was no hesitation at all from Mary about accepting a lift for them all in the lorry back to their hostel.

That evening when they heard the planes going overhead, Rosie suspected that Peggy wasn't alone in counting them.

Later on, lying in bed, Rosie couldn't stop thinking about Liverpool and those she knew who lived there. The look on Ian's face when he had mentioned the Luftwaffe's attack on her home city had told her far more than any words or protective assurances could have done about the severity of the situation. She might have parted with her aunt on bad terms, but Rosie still couldn't help thinking how her dad would have wanted to know if his sister was all right. She was guiltily aware that although she had left her aunt the details of how she could get in touch with her, she hadn't written to her. Perhaps now she ought to do so, if only because she knew it would be what her father would want her to do.

And then there was Rob. She might not have loved him enough to want to marry him but she had cared about him, and naturally now she was anxious about him, wondering if he was safe, especially knowing that as a fireman he would be exposed to a great deal of danger during the bombing raids. She couldn't ask for time off to go home to Liverpool, and she certainly hadn't got enough money to afford her train fare there and back, but she would write to her aunt and to Rob. It wouldn't do any harm to get in touch with them to ask how they were, Rosie admitted.

On Sunday morning the girls, dressed in their 'formal' uniform, marched down to the village church to attend the service.

The vicar greeted them, whilst his parishioners

eyed them uncertainly. During their training they had been warned that farming communities were cautious about accepting strangers, especially when those 'strangers' were young women. Rosie's eyes stung with tears when the vicar prayed especially for the city of Liverpool and all those in it.

After church they were invited back to the vicarage, where the vicar's wife welcomed them with home-made carrot cake and very weak tea.

Most of the girls who had been at the hostel when they arrived had gone home on Saturday, as they were allowed to, if they could afford to do so, so that Rosie and the others virtually had the hostel to themselves.

The warden served them a roast dinner, laughing when she heard one of the girls exclaiming, 'Potatoes. Boy, am I going to enjoy them after this last week.'

'If you think working potato fields is bad, just wait until you've spent a week in winter hedging and ditching,' she warned them.

Nudging Peggy, Mary took advantage of the warden's good humour to ask her if it would be all right for them to invite some RAF 'friends' round one weekend.

'If you're talking about boyfriends . . .' the warden began disapprovingly.

'It's just a group of young RAF lads we met up with in the village,' Mary told her hastily. 'They said as how they missed having a bit of female company, being so far away from home and their mums and sisters, like, that we thought . . .'

The warden gave her a beady-eyed look. 'Well, just so long as there's no funny business I suppose it will be all right. But that means no going into any dormitories, and you all staying down in the recreation room where I can keep an eye on you. I've heard of these hostels that have got a bad name for themselves with the girls getting up to all sorts, and I can tell you that this hostel is not going to become one of them. His Grace wouldn't approve of that at all.'

'And nor would we,' Mary told her promptly, causing Sheila to stifle a giggle, which earned her a killing look from Mary once the warden had gone.

'Trust you to nearly go and spoil everything,' Mary complained.

'Well, seeing as His Grace has five kiddies he must have got up to a bit of you-know-what in the bedroom himself,' Sheila defended herself airily.

'You can't go saying things like that,' Mary protested, scandalised. 'He's a married man!'

On Monday morning Rosie was delighted to discover that her group of land girls were being taken off working in the potato fields and sent to another farm to do the milking, even though that meant an earlier start and no proper breakfast until after the milking was done.

She hadn't been sleeping anyway, what with

worrying about Liverpool being bombed and trying not to think about the handsome young Italian POW. It made her feel both afraid and angry with herself that she should have let him creep into her thoughts the moment she left them unguarded. She didn't know why she had done, either. He was Italian, after all, and if that hadn't been enough to put her off him, the fact that he was too good-looking for his own good should surely have done. Aldo had been good-looking, or so people had said – she had never seen the appeal. She had to get Italian men right out of her head – all of them – but especially that young man she had seen working in the field, she warned herself fiercely. There was no place for them in her life – or in her heart – and that was the way things were going to stay.

And then just when she'd thought she put every-thing to do with Italians right to the back of her mind, Peggy went and got her worrying all over again when she commented innocently, 'You know, Rosie, you have a bit of a look of them Italians,' after Sheila had complained that they were working with only a couple of elderly cowmen for male company whilst the POWs were working on another farm.

'No I haven't,' Rosie retorted so angrily that she could see that she had startled Peggy. 'I'm as British as anyone else here.'

'Well, of course you are, Rosie,' said Mary soothingly. 'And no one's saying any different.'

'I didn't mean to cause any offence, Rosie, I'm sure,' Peggy offered a bit stiffly, looking hurt. 'I only meant that you are so lucky to have such pretty dark curly hair, just like them Italian lads.' She sighed enviously. 'Mine's that thin and it won't curl no matter what I do to it.'

'Me dad's hair was curly,' Rosie told her truthfully. 'Mine's nothing special, not really.' She felt guilty now for having been so sharp with Peggy, who was always so sweet-natured.

At the first opportunity she got, which was when they all left the milking shed to go for their dinner, she caught up with Peggy and slipped her arm through hers, saying quietly, 'I'm really sorry, Peggy, about how I was earlier. I hope I didn't upset you. I didn't mean to snap at you like that.'

'It's all right, Rosie. You don't have to explain,' Peggy told her generously. 'I should have thought before I spoke, knowing what you must be feeling, what with your mum and dad and all the trouble you've had.'

Rosie stood as still and stiff as though she had become rooted to the milking shed floor. How could Peggy possibly know about her parents' marriage? She hadn't told a soul about her background since leaving Liverpool. She felt cold and sick with shock.

'Rosie, are you all right?' Peggy asked her timidly. 'Only you've gone ever such a funny colour. Mind you, I've bin lying awake meself at night worrying about them lads having to fly into Liverpool so I can understand how you must feel, you being from there, and having lost your mam and dad on account of Hitler.'

The release from her dreadful fear felt like blood returning to ice-cold limbs, bringing with its release an aching physical pain, Rosie recognised as the tension left her body. She realised that Peggy hadn't been talking about her parents' marriage or her own birth after all, but simply about Liverpool being bombed and her mother and father's deaths. Now Rosie felt doubly guilty. She reached out and squeezed the other girl's hand.

'I have been worrying,' she admitted. 'It's horrible, Peggy, seeing houses and buildings and even whole streets ending up just a pile of rubble, or sometimes gone altogether. There's craters in the roads you could lose a bus in, and people with no homes to go to any more. When your house has been bombed you just can't take it in, somehow; you just stand there, thinking that it's like something on the newsreels, that it isn't real and that if you close your eyes and then open them again your house will be standing there, just like it should be.'

'Oh, Rosie, you are brave. I don't know as how I'd go on if that happened to me,' Peggy shivered. 'I feel that scared just listening to you talking about it.'

'Well I won't do then,' Rosie told her firmly, forcing a reassuring smile, as she added, 'There's no need to, after all, because we needn't worry about being bombed out here. The country is the safest place to be.'

Peggy's anxious look gave way to relief. 'Yes, it is, isn't it?' she agreed. 'And I'm going to stay here until the war's over, Rosie, and never go back to live anywhere where there's going to be bombs. It makes me feel sick wi' nerves just thinking about what it must be like being in one of them buildings when a bomb gets dropped on them.'

Rosie didn't say anything. She didn't want to upset Peggy by talking about her own ordeal trapped in the bombed-out Technical College. She would never forget it, though; sometimes she dreamed about it and about her mother being trapped and her trying to reach her, but these were things she could never tell anyone else. And after all, Rosie reminded herself stoically, a lot of people went through worse. There had been those in Liverpool who had been bombed out more than once and who still gamely got on with their lives as best they could. Everyone was different, though. There were some folk like that and some like Peggy. She thought she came somewhere in between. She didn't think of herself as being brave in any way but neither did her fears torment her in the way that Peggy's seemed to do.

To Rosie's disappointment they were only at the dairy farm for two days, whilst they filled in for another gang, and on the Wednesday morning they discovered that they were being sent to a different farm, to do some weeding.

To make matters even worse, when they arrived at the farm they discovered that George Duncan was in even more of a foul temper than usual. When one of the girls from another gang asked to be excused because she wasn't feeling well, he stepped up to her and yelled at her in such a loud voice that everyone including the lorryload of POWs that had just arrived, could hear. 'No you can't. Bloody women and their ruddy women's problems.'

The poor girl looked close to tears and Rosie really felt for her. She gave the foreman an indignant look on the poor girl's behalf as he strode past them on his way back across the yard towards the lorry, and then had to hold her breath as he saw her and stopped to glare at her.

'That was brave of you, Rosie,' Peggy breathed admiringly. 'The way he looked at you just then would have scared me to death.'

'You'll have to watch your step now, Rosie,' Mary cautioned her. 'He's a bully and no mistake, and if you want my advice you don't want to be falling foul of him.'

Rosie knew that she was right, but it was too late to regret what she had done now. The arrival of the POWs had caught her off guard after so many days of not seeing them. They looked so dejected, with their bowed shoulders and general air of defeat, that she felt a sudden twinge of sympathy for them.

Immediately she tried to distance herself from her feelings and to focus on something that would stiffen her spine. Like *him*, for instance. He certainly had had a bit of an air about him that said he thought a lot of himself. Not that she had noticed him that much, of course, but you could tell when a lad was a bit on the arrogant side with just one look. And she certainly wasn't going to look across at the men again just to check to see if he was there with them, and she hadn't noticed.

But thanks to Sheila she discovered that she didn't have to, because the other girl had obviously already had a good look at the men, and was able to tell her teasingly, 'That good-looking lad as fancies you isn't here, Rosie. Shame.'

'Will you stop going on about him?' Rosie hissed back to her. 'He doesn't fancy me, and even if he did, I don't fancy him.'

'Can I have him then? He's a smashing-looking lad, with a lovely smile, and them big brown eyes of his! Oooh, it makes me insides go all funny just thinking about them,' Sheila giggled.

Rosie certainly wasn't going to respond to Sheila's silliness. Why, she hadn't even been close enough to him to see if his eyes were brown! They probably would be, though – that warm gorgeous brown that could melt your heart with a single glance. And Italian men learned young how to give that adoring amorous look that turned girls' heads. They were nothing more than flirts, the lot of them, and she would certainly never be taken in by one of them. Sheila was welcome to him.

It was a long walk to the field they had to work, carrying their hoes and the buckets for the weeds that had to be buried deep in a trench at the bottom of the field the foreman had set the POWs to dig.

'I'm going to go over and have a chat with them lads,' Sheila announced as soon as the foreman had disappeared.

'Sheila, you can't,' Rosie protested. 'We're not supposed to have anything to do with them, and if the foreman catches you—'

'He won't! Anyway, what's wrong? Don't you want to know where your chap is?'

'No I do not,' Rosie replied fiercely, 'and he is not my chap.'

But it was too late. Sheila was already taking advantage of the foreman's absence and edging her way round to where the men were working.

Rosie refused to watch her, concentrating instead on her weeding. Sheila was going to get them all into serious trouble if the foreman came back, and Rosie didn't want to be dragged into her mischief any more than she had to be. Angrily, Rosie jabbed her hoe at the weeds, slicing them off and throwing them into the bucket.

When Sheila finally came back, Rosie pretended not to have noticed, but Sheila wasn't the kind to keep quiet.

She gave a gusty sigh and announced with obvious disappointment, 'Well, that were a waste of time. There's not one of them can speak a word of English. It turned out that they're not the same lot that were around the other day.'

Rosie couldn't avoid the Italians completely,

even though she would have preferred to do so, because the girls had to take their buckets of weeds over to the trench the men were digging to throw them in.

The foreman was back now and bullying them dreadfully, and the POWs had a crushed, exhausted look about them. Brief snatches of their conversation reached Rosie and a wave of nostalgia swept over her, as those fragments of the familiar language of her old friends took her back to her childhood. Just hearing Italian being spoken overwhelmed her with sadness, leaving her feeling miserable and forlorn.

'It's no wonder them poor lads look the way they do with that foreman treating them like that,' Mary said sympathetically when she came back from getting rid of her own weeds. 'There's one down there that doesn't look much older than me own kid brother, poor little thing.'

Rosie had seen the young boy she meant, but whilst the other girls were expressing their sympathy, instead of joining in, Rosie shook her head and said fiercely, 'Well, I don't feel sorry for them. They're the enemy, after all, and if it wasn't for the likes of them then there wouldn't be a war.'

She could see from their faces that she had shocked the other girls.

'That's a bit hard, isn't it, Rosie?' Jean protested. 'I've heard as how that Mussolini was forcing men to fight by threatening their families. There's a lot of Italians who don't agree with that Fascism stuff.

And as for them lads down there, that poor kid looks half scared to death of the foreman already and he's got a bruise the size of an egg on his forehead. If you ask me we should show them a bit of sympathy, just like we were told at Reaseheath.'

'You can if you like, but I'm not going to,' Rosie answered doggedly, but she knew that her face was burning bright red with a mixture of chagrin and defiance.

'Fine. Well, you go and have your dinner with the foreman then, 'cos the rest of us are going to have ours with the POWs,' Jean told her smartly.

Rosie watched them as they walked away. She felt as though a huge uncomfortable lump of misery had taken root inside her chest. But she wasn't going to swallow her pride and run after the other girls. She wasn't going to have anything to do with any Italians, no matter what anyone else said. Italians had brought her nothing but heartbreak and misery. First Bella turning against her, and then Maria and la Nonna abandoning her, and finally the news that Aldo had been her mother's lover. And if her supposed new friends preferred their company to hers, well then, that was their loss, wasn't it? Her throat prickled and her eyes were smarting but Rosie wasn't going to let herself admit that it was her own fault that she felt hurt and left out. It was the Italians that were to blame, just as an Italian had been to blame for causing her father so much pain. Just look at the trouble her mother had brought on their small family, thanks to getting herself involved with one of them. Rosie didn't want to be tarred with the same brush as her mother but, more importantly, she didn't want to betray her father's memory by being friendly to members of a nationality that had caused him so much distress. The other girls could do what they liked. She wasn't going to be budged.

Even so, as the afternoon wore on Rosie was miserably conscious of the way she was being excluded from her friends' chatter. Once again she was all alone.

It was growing dusk before the foreman returned to tell them they could finish work.

''E certainly gets his ruddy pound of flesh,' the girl hoeing next to Rosie grumbled. 'I can hardly see me ruddy hoe, never mind the weeds. And to think they're only paying us twenty-four shillings a week, and we have to pay for our own board out of that. I'm beginning to wish I'd stayed put and got meself a factory job. That foreman's made us work all this time but his breath stank of beer and you can bet he knocked off ages ago and went off to the pub whilst we were still having to graft.'

Rosie didn't say anything but she too had smelled the beer on the foreman's breath.

As the girls were lining up to leave the field for the long walk back to the farm, the POWs were standing beside the trench, but the next moment, the foreman, who had been yelling at them to get in line, grabbed hold of the young lad the girls had felt so sorry for earlier and gave him such a shaking that he dropped his spade. The foreman swore at him and let go of him, bending to pick up the spade, which he then drove down hard into the ground at the boy's feet.

They all heard the boy cry out when he didn't jump back swiftly enough, and they saw the way the sharp spade sliced open the flesh on his leg as he fell over.

Rosie had to smother a horrified cry of her own whilst the other girls protested loudly against the foreman's bullyboy behaviour.

'Poor little sod. That must really have hurt him,' Mary said angrily as the young man struggled to his feet, helped by his friends.

Several of the girls hurried forward, ignoring the foreman, to see if the boy was all right but he was so obviously embarrassed by their concern that they fell back again.

'It doesn't seem too bad,' Audrey reported to Mary. 'He wasn't bleeding very much and he can walk.'

'It was still a rotten thing to do,' Jean objected.

'The man's a proper bully,' Mary agreed as they all started to trudge wearily back to the farm. 'I can't bear that kind of behaviour.'

It was almost dark when they finally got back to the hostel.

'You should have seen my bathwater,' Mary grimaced later on in the evening when they were all in the common room. 'You could grow pot-atoes in it, it was that thick with mud.'

'Just as well George Duncan can't hear you saying that, otherwise he'll have us tekin' it back to the field,' Sheila groaned.

'Shush!' Mary demanded all of a sudden. 'Listen.'

All the girls went quiet as they heard the now familiar sound of planes overhead.

'That's what you should be thinking about when you're saying how sorry you are for the POWs,' Rosie said bitterly once the planes had gone.

'Italians aren't the same as Germans, Rosie,' Mary insisted firmly. 'And I have to say that I was surprised at you for the way you acted today. I thought better of you than that. I really did.'

Red-faced, Rosie bent her head, her eyes burning with tears.

Half an hour later, after Rosie had gone up to the dormitory, feeling that her company wasn't welcome in the common room, the door opened and Mary came in.

'I'm sorry I was a bit sharp with you earlier, Rosie,' she said quietly, 'only I can't help thinking about how it's been on the newsreels – about the way some of Hitler's men have been treating them as they've taken prisoner, and I wouldn't want to think we was like that, in this country. I'd like to think we had some decency – war can't strip you of that unless you let it.'

'I don't mean the Italians any harm,' Rosie told

her, relieved that she was being offered an olive branch. 'I just don't want to get too friendly with them, that's all. And the way Sheila was going on about . . . well, I didn't like it.'

Mary shook her head. 'Well, I don't know, Rosie; they seem a decent enough lot of lads to me. And the girls felt you was being a bit unkind.'

'I have my reasons for what I've said,' Rosie told her, 'but . . . but I can't talk about them.'

'I can't say that I understand, because I don't, but you're a good sort, Rosie, and I don't want us to be bad friends. Why don't you come down and get your supper before Jean eats it for you?'

Mary was smiling encouragingly at her and holding open the door. Jean was always hungry, so Rosie returned her smile and got up.

No one was smiling later on that night, though. They had all heard the noise of the bombing of Liverpool, and then had all listened to it dying away, and now, although none of them had said anything, Rosie knew that, like her, the others were straining their ears for the first sound of the planes returning to Hack Green.

'Here they come,' Peggy squeaked, her voice high with relief.

Everyone was counting silently and as they got to ten, the tension in the dormitory mounted. Everyone knew that two fewer planes had come back than had flown out, but no one dared say so. Rosie was holding her own breath along with everyone else, willing the engine noise of the two final planes to break the tension. The seconds became minutes, and still no one spoke. And then in the darkness someone gave a small muffled anguished sob. Rosie knew immediately that it would be Peggy. Pushing back her bedding, she slid her feet onto the cold lino and pattered quietly over to her bed, only to discover that most of the other girls had had the same thought.

They were all still clustered round Peggy's bed when, just as they had given up hope, they heard the rackety wheezy sound of a damaged plane accompanied by the stronger sound of another.

For once no one cared about breaking the blackout. The girls all rushed to the nearest window, pulled back the blind and looked up into the night sky.

There, coming towards them from the west, they could see two planes flying virtually wing to wing as the stronger one escorted the weaker.

'Oh, thank God, thank God . . .' Peggy breathed.

Rosie knew she wasn't the only one with tears in her eyes as they finally heard the welcome sound of the planes banking for their descent to Hack Green.

Of course, none of them was fit for anything in the morning when the alarm went.

They had been put back on dairy work at yet another farm because, as they found out from another gang who had also been drafted in, there'd been a tuberculosis scare with some new cows that had arrived at the farm, with one of the cows already having to be put down and the rest quarantined. The girls who had been working with them had been sent for tests, and Rosie and the others were given the job of scrubbing down the milking shed with a disinfectant so strong it threatened to take the skin off their hands, and the smell brought tears to their eyes.

After three back-breaking days of scrubbing and re-scrubbing the whole shed, they were told on the Saturday morning that it had been a false alarm and that both the cows and the girls who had milked them were fine.

'They'd tell us owt to keep us working,' one of the girls said gloomily. 'Thank Gawd it's Saturday and we're off for the next day and a half.'

Some of the girls were going home but Mary and Peggy had agreed to meet up with their RAF admirers, and Rosie could see how excited they both were as she watched them get ready.

'You can come with us, Rosie, if you're all on your own,' Mary offered generously. 'I'm sure the boys won't mind.'

Rosie laughed. 'No, not much. I'll bet they've been waiting all week to get you to themselves,' she teased. 'It's kind of you to say, Mary, but I'm quite happy to stay here. I've got a bit of washing and mending I want to get done. The warden said that we could sit outside if we want, so I might do that if it stays fine, and then I can always walk down to the village later for a break.'

'Pity that POW camp isn't nearer. Then you might be able to see that admirer of yours,' Sheila told her mischievously. 'I reckon he'd be pretty keen to get to know you, Rosie, if you was to give him a bit of a look.'

'I'm doing no such thing,' Rosie told her stiffly. 'And I wish you'd stop going on about him and making up daft stuff. I've only seen him a couple of times.'

'It only takes one look,' Sheila laughed. 'Ask Mary and Peggy. And you can say what you want, but I saw the way you coloured up when he looked at you like he did . . . Just like summat out of a film, it was.'

Rosie wasn't going to listen to any more of Sheila's nonsense. But Sheila's words had caused a picture of the Italian to form in her mind. She shook her head to rid herself of the image. Sheila's dramatic ramblings were starting to have an effect on her.

It was almost midnight when Mary and Peggy got back. Rosie could hear them giggling and whispering together as they tiptoed into the dormitory, and a small stab of envy made her heart lurch against her ribs. What was she upset about? Not for a handsome Italian whose name she didn't even know, surely? Just because two girls she'd gone and got a bit friendly with had got themselves boyfriends, that didn't mean she had to go feeling all sorry for herself, did it? After all, if she'd wanted she could have had Rob, couldn't she? He'd been keen enough to put his ring on her finger, after all. Thinking about Rob and the reasons why she hadn't wanted to marry him were enough to have her recognising that it was far better to feel a bit lonely now and again than to be married to a man she didn't truly love.

'. . . And Ian was saying how he thought they was never going to get back, and that he signalled to John to fly home without them just in case they both got shot down, but that John pretended not to see his message.'

Mary was telling for the fifth time the story of how Ian's plane had been helped back to safety by the brave action of one of his comrades, who had flown beneath his damaged wing to help support him, but neither Rosie nor anyone else at the Sunday morning breakfast table cared. They were enthralled and eager to hear everything all over again.

'Ian reckons that John will be decorated for what he did, and he said that when His Grace comes back on leave from Malta, he's going to make sure he knows all about it.'

The Duke of Aston, who was second in command of the squadron of 'our boys', as the girls now referred to Ian and his friends, had been seconded to work with those crews who had been shipped out to Malta along with their planes.

'I'm going to say a special prayer for them in

church today,' Peggy told them tearfully. Her boy was the rear gunner on the plane that had supported Ian's on its return journey, and she was pink with pride over the whole achievement.

Everyone knew that the war meant that relationships were formed quickly and deeply, and no one questioned the speed with which Mary and Peggy were falling in love, eager to grab every moment they could with their men, least of all the two girls themselves.

'I've told Ian about the warden saying that they could come here. He's talking about getting up a party of us so that we can go dancing next Saturday, if they're off duty. Will you come along, Rosie?'

'Oh, yes.' Rosie was prepared to welcome any distraction.

'Ian said to tell you that they reckon that Hitler has given up trying to blitz Liverpool,' Mary told her quietly. 'Not that the ruddy Luftwaffe haven't made a real old mess of it, seemingly. You're lucky to be out of it, Rosie.'

'Yes,' Rosie agreed. She knew that was true and yet a part of her felt guilty because she wasn't there to share the ordeal with her friends. She was safe from harm, deep in the Cheshire countryside, while everyone she had once known – those who had survived and hadn't fled – were facing danger daily. Not for the first time Rosie wondered if she was doing the right thing.

TWENTY-TWO

She never ever wanted to see another potato plant as long as she lived, nor another weed either, Rosie decided tiredly as she worked her hoe in between the straight lines of the planted crop, slicing and digging as she separated the weeds from the roots in a rhythm that had become almost second nature, whilst she tried to ignore the ache in her back and her shoulder.

Behind her another girl was picking up the severed weeds, whilst in front of them the POWs were digging yet another trench. Rosie lifted her head to ease the ache from her back and then frowned as she watched George Duncan heckling and bullying the young Italian who was limping badly as he tried to move out of his way.

Rosie's frown deepened when she realised that the boy – he was little more than that – was protesting that he couldn't work any harder because his leg was hurting so badly. Some of the men were also trying to speak up for their comrade, but since they couldn't speak English and the foreman did not understand Italian, all that was happening was that the foreman was getting more and more angry. She could have gone over and translated for the Italians and her conscience was in fact insisting that she did so, but she was refusing to listen to it, stubbornly telling herself that what was happening was none of her business.

But by dinner time the boy, whom Rosie had been deliberately keeping an eye on, could hardly walk, and Rosie found that she was asking herself if her father would really have wanted her not to try to help.

When the foreman had gone to have his dinner, Rosie took her chance and made her way over to where the Italians were crowded together, eating their rations.

She went up to the boy, who stared at her in mute desperation. His face was hotly flushed and Rosie could see how much pain he was in. She spoke to him slowly, searching for the right words, for although she could comprehend Italian when she heard it spoken, she wasn't sure she could speak it well enough to make herself understood, but to her relief the boy seemed to grasp what she was trying to say and after some coaxing reluctantly rolled up the hem of his trousers so that she could see his leg.

When Rosie saw the swollen and inflamed flesh around the site of the cut she knew immediately the danger he was in. She had been fourteen when

Connor O'Reilly, a neighbour from a couple of streets away, who had worked on the docks, had had to have his leg amputated after a similar kind of injury. The whole area had been talking about it at the time, and automatically Rosie looked for the telltale red line coming away from the injury. She remembered her father talking about going to visit his sick friend and telling her how Connor O'Reilly's wife had told him how a red line coming out from an infected wound was a sure sign that a person's life was in danger. Now she looked anxiously at the young Italian's wound, trying not to let him see her anxiety and praying that she wouldn't find one. But to her horror there was one and she could see it quite plainly. Her heart started to beat uncomfortably heavily, and a sick feeling of panic filled her. What should she do now? She knew that the boy needed medical attention. She had received some very basic first-aid training when she had undergone her fire-watch training, but it was nothing like enough to equip her to deal with something like this. She also knew that the foreman was unlikely to accept her word for the severity of the situation, especially when he was the one who had inflicted the wound on the Italian in the first place. But something had to be done – and fast.

Quickly, Rosie ran back to Mary and told her what was happening.

'I never knew you could speak Italian, you dark horse. Fancy not letting on,' she complained.

'There's no time for talking about that now, Mary,' Rosie said urgently. 'He needs to see a doctor but I don't think that George Duncan is going to be happy about that. Not when he's the one who hurt him in the first place.'

'How bad is the lad?' Mary asked her.

'Very bad,' Rosie admitted. 'I truly think if something isn't done that he could die. He didn't say anything at the POW camp because he was afraid that he would be separated from his friends. If we could get him back to the farm without George Duncan knowing, then we could tell the farmer but I don't think he could walk that far. He really is poorly, Mary.'

'Right,' Mary said purposefully. 'Sheila,' she summoned her cousin. 'You fancy yourself with the chaps, we all know that, so you can run back to the farm as quick as you like and make sure that George Duncan doesn't see you. Tell the farmer that one of the prisoners has hurt himself bad and that he needs a doctor.'

Several of the girls had gathered around Rosie and Mary now, all looking shocked and concerned as Rosie told them about the boy's injury.

'He could end up with lockjaw, an' all,' one of them pronounced. 'You should never let muck get into an open wound – that's what I've heard, any road.'

'Don't just stand there, Sheila, get a move on,' Mary instructed her cousin. 'Rosie, you had better go back and sit with the lad and keep an eye on him, seeing as you're the only one who can speak Italian. Fancy not saying so before,' she repeated, shaking her head.

'What if the foreman comes back and sees that Rosie's stopped working?' Peggy asked timidly. 'He won't like that.'

'No, and he'll find out pretty sharpish that *we* don't like what he's done to that poor young lad. He doesn't have no rights over us, for all that he likes to think he does. It's not him that pays our wages, and it would serve him right if he got reported for what he's done. He jolly well deserves to be.'

By the time Rosie had rejoined the young POW the other men had obviously heard about her ability to speak their language because they all crowded around her, talking at such speed and with such unfamiliar accents that she could only make out the occasional word. They bombarded her with questions and complaints. However, that was enough for her to feel the fierce intensity of their grievances against the foreman.

Slowly and carefully Rosie explained to them that someone had gone to get help for their friend, and urged them to go back to work.

'I will stay here with him until help comes,' she assured them, and then blushed a fiery red as one of them flung himself down on his knees and praised her as a 'true Madonna'.

The boy looked horribly pale, with sweat beading his face and his calf so swollen that Rosie could see where the fabric of his trousers pulled tight against it.

The sudden angry muttering of the men working behind her warned her that the foreman had returned to the field. As she had known he would, he came charging over at a lumbering run to where she was sitting by the hedge with her 'patient'.

'What the ruddy hell do you mean by this, missie?' he bawled out to her. 'Get back to your hoeing. You can do your whoring in your own private time.'

Rosie stiffened at the insult but instead of obeying him she moved closer to the boy, instinctively wanting to protect and to shield him from the foreman's anger.

'This man is injured,' she told him, speaking up clearly and firmly. 'He needs medical attention.'

'What? You stupid girl. Are you really that daft that you can't see that he's pulling the wool over your eyes? Get out of my way.'

To Rosie's horror he thrust her out of the way and took hold of the boy, obviously intending to pull him to his feet. Rosie could hear the sharp cry of pain and fear the boy gave.

'Right, that's it. Not another stroke of work do we do until you leave that lad alone and he's been seen by a doctor.'

Rosie exhaled shakily in relief as she heard Mary's voice and realised that she and the others had come running over to help.

'Get back to your work,' the foreman snarled,

releasing the boy and turning to the girls. 'By God, but you lot will pay for this. You'll wish that you'd never bin born by the time I've finished wi' you.'

The viciousness of his words and the way he was looking at them made Rosie recoil, but Mary stood her ground.

'There are rules that say how POWs have to be treated, and land girls as well,' she spoke up bravely, but the foreman shook his head like an angry bull and advanced on her. Rosie overcame her fear to rush to her friend's side. She didn't know what would have happened if the foreman hadn't swung round at the sound of running feet.

Sheila, accompanied not by the farmer but by an armed soldier, was hurrying towards them. Quick as a flash Mary ran to meet them and by the time the trio had joined them she had already explained to the guard what was happening.

'Let's have a look at this wound of his then, girls,' the soldier told them affably, but Rosie noticed that he winked at the foreman as though expressing male solidarity with him. However, when he saw the young man's leg his expression changed to one of serious concern. 'You're right,' he announced curtly. 'The lad needs a doctor and fast.'

Turning away from the young Italian, he muttered brusquely, 'I've seen a mate die from a wound like that. Swelled up like a rotten piece of fruit, he did. Is there a doctor in the village?' he asked the foreman. 'Only it will take a good few hours to get him back to camp.'

'There's Dr Flint,' the foreman told him truculently, 'but you won't get him coming out to a ruddy field for some bloody POW.'

'Watch your mouth, mate,' the soldier warned him. 'We've got our own lads taken as POWs overseas and I wouldn't want to think they was being treated bad. How far is the village from here?'

'Just over a mile across the field,' the foreman told him.

The soldier looked round the field and then beckoned to two of the strongest-looking Italians.

'Is it true that one of you can speak Italian?' he asked the girls.

Mary pushed Rosie forward.

'Right, I want you to tell these lads that they're going to have to make a chair with their hands and carry the boy to the doctor's. One thing I do know about this kind of wound is that he shouldn't move about too much – spreads the poison, see. You'll have to come with us, miss, so that you can translate for the lad, and tell him what the doctor says.'

George Duncan was blustering and huffing, complaining that he couldn't have the work interrupted like this just because of a bit of a cut, but it made no difference. The soldier was adamant. The young POW needed to see a doctor and double quick.

They must have made a rare spectacle to anyone watching as they crossed the field at an unsteady and laborious pace, the able-bodied POWs joining hands the way the soldier showed them so that they could carry their young comrade carefully along the narrow field path that led to the village. Rosie walked beside Paolo, as she now knew the boy to be called, giving his hand the occasional small comforting squeeze and trying to keep up his spirits by chatting to him. It was obvious that he was in a great deal of pain, and it tore at Rosie's heart to see him trying so valiantly to be polite and answer the questions she was asking him as she tried to distract him. He was so very young and so very poorly that it was impossible for her to hold on to her defensive hostility towards him.

'Which part of Italy are you from?' she asked him, listening attentively when he told her that he came from the countryside some little way from Rome. Until the war had come he had lived at home with his mamma, his sisters and his young brother, he explained. Rosie's heart ached for him when she saw the tears filling his brown eyes at the thought of his family. His papa, he added, had died from a fever whilst working away from home. His family, like all the other families in his village, were very poor and so he had joined the army, hoping that he would have money to send home to his mamma and the little ones, but now he was a prisoner of war, here in this cold country where there was no sunshine. Was he going to die? he asked Rosie anxiously.

'No, of course not,' she reassured him with more confidence than she felt. 'You will get better, Paolo. But first the doctor will have to look at your leg.'

To her relief he seemed to accept what she was saying, although he looked in so much agony that Rosie didn't know whether or not he had understood her properly.

'If you happen to know any good marching songs in their lingo, miss, you might try singing one,' the soldier, who had now introduced himself to her as Greg, suggested. 'Only it might help these lads to give him a less bumpy ride if they had summat to march to and it could take the poor kid's mind off what's happening to him.'

It had been plain to Rosie from the expression on Greg's face, and from what he had not said rather than what he had, just how serious Paolo's condition was.

'I don't know any marching songs, but I do know this,' Rosie offered uncertainly, starting to sing a cheerful song la Nonna had taught her and Bella as young girls, singing it to them whilst they sat on the floor beside her chair.

'That's the ticket,' Greg approved when the men joined in what was obviously a familiar song. Like the Italians from the old neighbourhood, these men too had good voices and Rosie thought that anyone hearing them without knowing the real situation would think they were a happy bunch indeed.

The doctor's house was at the far end of the village and they attracted a good deal of attention as they made their way down the narrow street to the large rambling house set back from the road.

The doctor's housekeeper opened the door to their

knock, standing guard over the hallway behind her whilst she told them that the doctor was resting and did not see patients in the afternoon. To Rosie's relief Greg stepped forward and immediately persuaded the housekeeper of the urgency of the situation.

Within a minute of her disappearing down the hallway, the doctor himself appeared, pulling on his jacket and smoothing the thin wisps of his white hair as he hurried towards his visitors.

After Greg had explained the situation, the doctor said calmly, 'Very well, in that case I had better see the young man. You, young lady, please stay with him as you can speak Italian and I can't. Mrs Beddows, please show them into the surgery.'

'I'll take the men back to the field and then come for the lad with the lorry,' Greg told Rosie. 'It will be knocking-off time for the POWs soon enough anyway.'

When Dr Flint reappeared he smiled in a kind way at Paolo, who had been placed on the narrow hospital bed in the surgery by his friends.

'Now, let's have a look at that leg, young man.'

Swiftly Rosie translated what he had said for Paolo, who was looking very apprehensive.

She stood back whilst the doctor lifted back the leg of Paolo's trousers and looked at his wound.

'Mmm . . . perhaps you would be kind enough to come and stand beside our patient, my dear, and face me,' the doctor told Rosie in a calm voice.

When Rosie had done so, he told her quietly, 'This is a very serious wound indeed. He will be

414

lucky if the leg does not become gangrenous. By rights he should be taken to hospital to have it attended to, but you see this red line?' He indicated the line Rosie had already noted. 'If that were to reach his groin I doubt that anything could save him, not even this new wonder drug, penicillin, I have been reading about that we are told will combat all manner of infections. It is my belief that we cannot risk the delay involved in transferring him to a hospital. The wound needs to be lanced and as much of the poison removed as possible. Have you done any nursing, by chance?'

Rosie shook her head, her stomach tensing.

'Never mind. You are a stout-hearted, sensible girl, I am sure. Mrs Beddows,' he called, raising his voice.

When the housekeeper appeared Dr Flint instructed her to bring boiling water and clean cloths.

'I would like you to tell our patient that I must lance his wound. It will be painful for him but there is no help for that, I am afraid.'

By the time the housekeeper had returned, the doctor had put on a white coat and scrubbed his hands with carbolic. The smell of it stung Rosie's nostrils. She tried not to betray what she was feeling when she saw the sharp little knife the doctor had removed from a locked case and cleaned with some liquid that also smelled very strong.

'Now, first you must come over here and scrub your hands as I have done.'

When Rosie had obeyed his instructions to his satisfaction, the doctor told her, 'Right, now I want you to hold the lad's hand and keep him as calm and still as you can, please.'

Rosie did as she had been told, fixing her gaze on Paolo's face rather than on what the doctor was doing, although she knew the moment that he lanced the wound, not just from the sharp cry of pain Paolo gave just before he passed out, but also from the stench.

'Now quickly, Rosie, go and scrub your hands again and then come and help me here. Watch what Mrs Beddows is doing and copy her,' the doctor instructed.

The housekeeper, her own hands scrubbed, was laying piping-hot cloths on Paolo's leg whilst the doctor stroked firmly down it so that a thick yellow pus spurted from the wound.

Rosie felt light-headed with nausea but she fought it back, working as swiftly as she could to keep up the supply of fresh hot cloths.

Paolo had come round and was moaning and crying out for his mother.

'I will give him a draught of something to ease the pain once I have done what I can to clean his wound. He will have to be hospitalised, of course.'

'Will he be all right?' Rose asked anxiously.

'It is too soon to say. The infection is very bad and has been neglected for too long. Had the cut been properly cleaned at the time he received it, but even then . . . His leg was cut by a spade you said?'

'Yes,' Rosie confirmed.

'I intend to telephone the commander in charge of the POW camp and request that an ambulance is sent to take this young man to hospital. He is very fortunate that you had the gumption to act on his behalf,' the doctor told her approvingly.

Rosie smiled with relief. She was glad she had taken action but should she have done something sooner, she worried. Should she have let on that she could understand Italian beforehand? She would never forgive herself if Paolo didn't make it because of her reluctance to help an Italian. Paolo was just a sick boy, and helping him to get better was what mattered, not what nationality he was, Rosie decided, discounting any thought of disloyalty to her father.

It was late when Rosie eventually returned to the hostel, having waited with Paolo for the ambulance that took him to the nearest military hospital. Rosie had been relieved to see how carefully and competently the stretcher bearers had dealt with their patient and, having assured herself that she had done all she could, she had thanked the doctor and his housekeeper for the tea and toast she had been given and made her way through the village back to the hostel.

Of course, she had to relate to everyone everything that that happened, and then she had been summoned to see the warden, who wanted to hear the whole thing too.

'I am afraid that the foreman at the farm was rather cross with me,' Rosie told Mrs Johnson carefully. She did not want to be accused of snitching on George Duncan, but she wanted the warden on her side in case there was any further trouble.

'There is no reason why he should be, my dear. You acted very properly and promptly. Just as I would expect my girls to do. That poor young man was very lucky.'

Rosie felt warmed by Mrs Johnson's praise. It reminded her of how she had felt as a little girl when her father had praised her for what he had called 'doing right by others'. Her father had held strong views about 'doing unto others as you would be done by'. He had taught her always to recognise a kindness others had done to her and to 'pass it on' by doing a kindness to others herself. Rosie remembered how he would smile at her when, as a young girl, she had told him earnestly that she had run down to the shop for an elderly neighbour, or helped carry their washing down to the local wash house for them, and how he would tell her that he was proud of her for thinking of others.

As she grew older there had been no need for him to repeat the little homilies of her childhood because she was already acting on them and understanding them properly. It had lifted her heart so much and made her feel so proud to know that her father was such a kind and good man, and it still did. She wanted so much to prove herself worthy of being his daughter and to make sure that everything she did underlined and reinforced her pride in that. It was as though somewhere deep inside herself she had wanted to prove to him that whilst her mother had put her relationship with an Italian before her relationship with him, she would never ever do so.

But suddenly she was seeing her behaviour in a different and confusing light. Would her father really praise her for turning against all Italians? She knew how he had always shaken his head when anyone had started talking nastily about 'foreigners'; saying peaceably that there were good and bad people in every country. What would he think of her behaviour if he could see into her heart now? Rosie asked herself uncertainly. Would he be proud of her for trying her best to 'dislike' and distance herself from everything and everyone Italian, or would he say quietly, 'Do as you would be done by, Rosie lass, allus remember that'?

Rosie knew the answer. 'But I've been doing it for you, Dad,' she whispered sadly. 'Because I want to be your daughter, not Aldo's, and because I want you to know how proud I am of you being my dad.' Her thoughts were so painful and confused that Rosie wished she could run away from them. She had been guilty of behaving in a way her father wouldn't have liked, she could see that now. She felt that she had let her father down, not just once but twice over. She missed him so much. Just thinking about him made her heart ache. If only he was still here for her to turn to with her troubled thoughts. But the war had taken him from her just like it could have taken poor Paolo from his family. A family who loved him just as she loved her father. War was a dreadfully cruel thing, but that did not mean that she should let it make *her* cruel, Rosie recognised soberly.

TWENTY-THREE

'Well, I don't care who he is, one more word from him about "ruddy land girls" and I'm not doing no more work until he apologises.'

'It's all my fault,' Rosie said uncomfortably, as she listened to Audrey's determined statement. 'If I hadn't helped Paolo, then George Duncan would never have picked on us and made us do this.'

The girls were standing at the edge of one of the farm tracks where, for the fourth morning that week, they had been sent to repair its potholes using the store of cinders and stones kept for that purpose. It was heavy, dirty work, with the girls having to load and push heavy barrows of cinders and then clean out the potholes before repacking them with the cinders and making them flat. None of them was in any doubt that this was the foreman's revenge for the manner in which they had defied him over Paolo.

'He ought to be grateful to us, not acting like this,' Peggy said fiercely. 'Because if it hadn't been for Rosie that poor lad would be dead and Mr Foreman Duncan would be having to explain to someone in authority how he came to have the injury wot killed him.'

'He'd have lied about that to save his own neck, just like he lies about everything,' Sheila joined in, stamping viciously on the cinders. 'Pig!'

'Well, he won't be bossing us around for much longer,' Mary announced smugly, 'because last night I had a word with my chap and told him what was going on, and since he's off duty today he's going to come by later and have a word with Mr Bullyboy Duncan.'

Everyone turned to look at Mary.

She and Peggy had been seeing their RAF boyfriends just as often as they could, and Mary had already given everyone to understand that she and Ian were now courting seriously.

'That's all very well, Mary, but why should someone like George Duncan pay any attention to your Ian?' Audrey demanded.

'Because my Ian's squadron leader is the duke, that's why, and our foreman is employed by him. Ian's going to have a strong word with him about mistreating POWs and bullying poor sweet land girls, not to mention giving his own wife a black eye.'

'Well, if that's the case, I just wish that your Ian had come and had a word wi' him on Monday instead of waiting until Thursday,' Jean grumbled. 'One of the girls that's bin here a while was telling me that this is the worst job on the farm and that everyone hates it. Mind you, she says that when it comes to haymaking we'll know all about it. She reckons we'll be working sun up until sun down to get the hay in.'

'If I could have me choice I'd prefer to work with the chickens,' another girl piped up. 'Easy they are. All you have to do is just chuck a bit of mash down in the troughs and give them a bit of grain and then collect the eggs.'

'Oh, yes? What about when you have to wring their necks and pluck their feathers? And cleaning out the boxes is disgusting.'

'Pooh, you think that's bad? The last place I was, I ended up having to help to ring one of the young bulls,' a girl from one of the other gangs told them, grinning when she saw the look on their faces. 'Yes, and check to see when the bull had been with the cows as well. Of course, it was lovely when the calves were born. Suck on your fingers that strong, they do . . . I'd have bin there on that farm yet but for my mate,' she added regretfully.

'Why, what happened?' Sheila asked.

'After we'd done the milking we had to load the milk churns onto these floats pulled by a carthorse, and take them to where the Milk Marketing Board would collect them. One day two of the other girls bet my pal to a race to see who could get to the drop-off point first. Word got round and someone set up a book, running bets, you know, and we were the favourites on account of my pal knowing a thing or two. Anyway, when the day came we set off and we were out in front and would have won if this ruddy dog hadn't come from out of nowhere and run barking at old Billy, the carthorse. Didn't like dogs, Billy didn't, not one little bit. So he set off down the hill like he was running the Grand National, me and my pal pulling on the reins and yelling at him to slow down. Then he saw the fence at the bottom of the hill and turned off so as not to run into it, that sharp, like, that me and my pal and the milk churns were thrown off the float. Fined over a month's wages apiece, we were, and put on other duties,' she concluded with a heavy sigh just audible over the noise of everyone's laughter.

At dinner time, just as Mary had predicted, George Duncan arrived, glowering at them as they sat on the bank in front of the hedge eating their beetroot and cheese sandwiches.

'You should be doing better than this,' he snarled at them. 'Lazy buggers, especially you,' he told Rosie, kicking out with his heavy studded boot at her legs.

She had just managed to move them out of the way when they all heard the sound of a lorry chugging up the road. It stopped and Ian, Mary's chap, got out and came strolling over, looking very handsome and stern in his RAF uniform. Rosie could see the suspicion darkening the foreman's face.

'Is this the chap, Mary?' Ian asked.

Mary nodded.

'Here, what's all this?' George Duncan demanded. 'What's going on?'

'I'll tell you what's going on, mate,' Ian spoke up briskly. 'My girl here has been telling me that you've been picking on her and her friends, and it's got to stop, do you hear? And another thing. We do not treat POWs badly in this country, and anyone that does is going to get himself into serious trouble.'

It was plain to Rosie that the foreman wasn't used to being told what to do. His face was burning dark red with temper; his anger glittered dangerously in his eyes. Although he hadn't raised them, his hands were bunched menacingly into fists.

'Says you, mate,' he challenged Ian. 'What do you think you're going to do about it?' he demanded threateningly.

It was plain, though, that Ian was ready for him, and Rosie could only admire the way he said firmly, 'I've heard that you're pretty handy with your fists – when you're using them on women. There are a couple of chaps in the squadron who box and they would be very happy to show you just how good they are with theirs. Besides,' Ian warned him, 'I dare say that His Grace won't be too happy to hear that one of his employees has been mistreating POWs and nearly killing them.'

The foreman's face suddenly lost all its colour. 'You won't be going saying nothing to His Grace,' he blustered. 'You're all talk. The duke will be going back overseas any day, so I've heard.'

'He'll be home on leave at the end of the month and, being the decent sort he is, he'll be making it his business to come into the mess and have a word with the chaps. So remember, you leave these girls alone and pick on someone your own size in future.'

Ian stayed with the girls until the foreman had lumbered away, laughing when they all crowded round him to thank him for what he had done.

'Bossy Boots Duncan won't dare try it on with us now,' Mary boasted, unable to keep her pride in 'her' Ian out of her voice.

'I hope not,' Rosie agreed, but she wasn't convinced.

'There, that's them done,' Rosie said feelingly as she finished darning the lisle stockings that were part of the girls' uniform.

'Thank heavens that it's warm enough now to go bare-legged,' Mitzi Fellowes, one of the girls from another gang, said happily. 'I hate them lisles; they itch me to death.'

'Well, you'll get scratched to death if you go bare-legged once we start harvesting,' another girl told her warningly.

'Not if I get to drive the tractor,' Mitzi replied smugly.

Rosie and the others had spent the week on dairy work, much to their delight. Rosie enjoyed milking and it surprised her just how much she liked living in the country. She had told herself that it was probably because Liverpool held such unhappy memories for her. If there had not been a war she would have continued to live happily in her home city, and perhaps once the war was over she would want to return there.

Once the war was over . . . That seemed so hard to imagine. When she thought of Liverpool now she thought of the warning wail of air-raid sirens, of searchlights crisscrossing the night sky, of the heavy bomb-filled drone of German aeroplanes, of the sickening few seconds' silence between the whine of a bomb dropping and the terrible noise of it exploding. But more than the danger she thought too of all those who had been lost, not just her own father and mother, but everyone: those children in the shelter with her, who would never now grow up; the men who flew the planes; the firefighters like Rob; and the ordinary men and women of the city for whom each night might be their last. The city she had left behind wasn't the city of her childhood any more, but nor had she deserted it as some might think. She wanted to do her bit for the war, but she wanted to help people to live. Working on the land did that. Every bit of food she helped to grow was contributing to keeping the country and its people going, just as her father had helped when he had stuck it out at sea. He would be proud of her for what she was doing here in the country, Rosie knew, and he would be pleased too that she was finding a new sort of happiness and peace here, away from her sadness.

'I suppose Mary and Peggy are out with their chaps tonight, are they?' Audrey asked. 'Only they're cutting it a bit fine. It's ten now.'

The girls were supposed to get in for ten o'clock unless it was the weekend and they had been given special permission to stay out later.

'Mary said that she'd throw a bit of gravel up at the window when they got back so that one of us could go and let them in,' Rosie answered.

'Mrs Johnson won't be pleased if she catches you. She's nice enough, generally speaking, but she's a bit of a stickler over timekeeping,' Audrey warned, adding, 'Has anyone got a ciggie, only I'm desperate?'

Rosie shook her head, but Sheila, although she grumbled about it, produced one for her. Although they were allowed to smoke in the common room, smoking in the dormitories was strictly banned.

'I wouldn't mind finding a nice handsome chap meself,' Sheila sighed.

'Why don't you get Mary to ask Ian if he's got a friend you could make up a foursome with?' Rosie suggested.

'Wot, and have our Mary looking over me shoulder all the time to mek sure I was behavin' meself? That's the last thing I'd want to do if I was with a good-looking lad,' Sheila told her with a wink.

Rosie couldn't help but laugh. There was something about Sheila's frankness that made it hard not to do so.

'So what would you be wanting to do with him then?' Audrey challenged her. 'Just in case I get one meself and need a few tips, like.'

The next morning the girls were driven out to a farm to start helping with the haymaking and when they got there the Italians were already jumping down from their army transport.

'There's your admirer, Rosie,' Mary laughed, digging her in the ribs.

Rosie pursed her mouth and shook off her friend's hand.

'What's up with you?' Mary asked.

'There's nothing up with me,' Rosie answered her shortly. 'It's him that there's something up with.'

'What do you mean?'

'I mean that he's a prisoner of war, an enemy, that's what, and I don't want anything to do with him,' Rosie told her flatly. She was nearly beside herself with anxiety and misery, her angry words tumbling over themselves in her haste to distance herself from the Italian. 'And I'll thank you and the the girls not to go making out that he's interested in me or that I want him to be. Because I don't.'

Mary was looking at her in astonishment. 'Well, what side of the bed did you get out of this morning? I don't know what's got into you, Rosie. I'm sure there are innocent lads of ours in camps all over Europe. Doesn't bear thinking about.'

But Rosie wasn't going to take back what she had said. Keeping her head held high, she marched into the field, ignoring the perplexed and slightly disapproving looks Mary was giving her.

A steam-driven machine was used to cut the hay and the girls and the Italians had to follow behind it, lifting the cut hay into stooks. There was an art to making the stooks properly and at first Rosie struggled with hers, but by the end of the morning she was beginning to get the hang of it.

It was hot, dusty, hard work, but no matter how hard Rosie concentrated on what she was doing, she was still sharply conscious of the handsome Italian watching her, and trying to attract her attention.

'*Bella, bella*,' another young Italian close to her teased her admiringly. 'Ricardo thinks you are much *bella*, pretty girl,' he added, gesturing towards the tall, broad-shouldered figure who worked several yards away. Like the other men he had removed his shirt and was working in boots and a pair of army trousers, his olive skin warmly tanned. Rosie hadn't intended to look at him, but now that she was doing so, somehow she couldn't drag her gaze away and even worse, there was a funny aching feeling in her tummy that was both pleasurable and a bit frightening.

'Ricardo, he wants to talk with you,' the other man told her. 'You speak with him when we have our dinner, yes?'

'No,' Rosie refused fiercely. She felt all quivery

inside and her heart was jolting about inside her chest so much she could hardly breathe.

'Come on, Rosie, you're falling behind,' the girl she was working with called out warningly.

It was just the strength of the sun that was making her feel so peculiar, Rosie told herself, as she turned her back resolutely on the Italians and got on with her work.

'Watch out for us, will you, Rosie? I'm just going to nip behind the hedge.'

Tiredly, Rosie agreed. Trying to find somewhere private to relieve themselves was just one of the many hazards of being a land girl, and the girls all rallied round one another to keep cave at such times.

She swatted at the flies buzzing irritatingly in the heat, and closed her eyes.

'Hey, Rosie, your admirer is on his way over.'

Jean's words brought her to her feet in a speedy if ungainly movement as she looked round warily to see the handsome Italian picking his way through the newly stacked stooks of hay towards her.

'Rosie . . . wait up . . .' Jean called as Rosie made a dash towards the hedge.

'I can't. I'm desperate,' Rosie told her.

Desperate she most certainly was, but not to answer a call of nature so much as to escape from Ricardo.

Why was he pursuing her like this? He must surely be able to see that she wasn't interested.

And that was what she wanted, was it? For him to see that she wasn't interested and keep away from her? Yes, of course it was. How could she possibly want anything else? She might be able to accept that her father would not have wanted her to be actively unkind to anyone, but Rosie felt sure he would not have been happy to see her encouraging the attentions of a big handsome Italian. Not after what he had said to her about Aldo and her mother. And she certainly wasn't going to follow in her mother's footsteps.

'What's up with you?' Mary asked exasperatedly and, Rosie sensed, a bit irritably, later in the day when Rosie had made yet another excuse to avoid Ricardo's attempts to talk to her.

'I've already told you, I don't want to get involved with them,' Rosie defended herself.

'Well, I call that downright mean, Rosie. They might be POWs but they still seem nice chaps. The other girls certainly seem to think so.'

'That's up to them,' Rosie told her uncomfortably. How could she possibly explain to Mary that it wasn't their POW status that was making her want to keep them – or rather, one of them – at a distance, but far more private reasons? 'But like I said, I don't want anything to do with them.'

But despite the fact that she did everything she could to avoid him, in the end Ricardo outmanoeuvred her, trapping her between himself and the gate from the field.

'I have been trying to talk to you all day,' he began, speaking, Rosie noted, in confusion with a distinct note of impatience in his voice. She was also astonished that his English was as good as her own.

'I'm here to work, not waste time talking to internees,' Rosie retorted.

The look that darkened his eyes and made them flash with pride as well as anger would normally have made her feel very guilty about her rudeness.

'If I hadn't given in to my grandfather's urging and agreed to visit our family in Italy in the months prior to war being declared, to report back to him on his land there, I dare say I would have enlisted with my cousins in the British Forces. I am an internee because I made the mistake of believing that I could be both Italian and British. My grandparents came to this country, to Manchester, shortly after their marriage. My parents were both born here. Until war broke out I considered myself to be both Italian and English. The British Government, though, decided that not only could I only be Italian, but that I must also be a Fascist.'

Rosie realised that she could hear not bitterness in his voice or resentment but sadness. It touched something within her, a chord of feeling that made her want to reach out and touch his hand in understanding. She started to panic. She should not be feeling like this.

'I wanted to thank you for what you did for Paolo,' Ricardo was saying. 'I hadn't realised he was so badly hurt. I blame myself for not realising . . .' Ricardo was speaking coolly and formally now, leaving Rosie to digest the fact that he had not been pursuing her because he wanted to flirt with her but because he wanted to thank her. She felt every kind of fool and prayed inwardly that he had not realised what she had thought. But to her dismay he continued quietly, 'I realise that I must have given you the wrong impression, when I heard your friends talking about your disgust at the thought of being admired by an Italian – an enemy of your country.' Now his voice had become clipped and so sharp that she felt as though each word he spoke was cutting into the tenderness of her conscience and her heart. 'I apologise for distressing you in such a way.'

Rosie's face was so red she was desperately glad of the dusk to hide her embarrassment.

'Rosie, come on . . .' Sheila called out.

'Rosie . . . It is a pretty name. You are from Liverpool, I would guess from your accent.'

'How would you know anything about a Liverpool accent?' Rosie felt obliged to challenge him. 'You said you lived in Manchester.'

'Yes I do,' he agreed. 'But like all Italian families, mine is extensive, with branches not just in Manchester, but in London and in Liverpool as well. What part of the city are you from?'

She didn't have to tell him, Rosie assured herself, but it wasn't in her nature not to give a truthful answer to a question and so reluctantly she told him, with a small dismissive shrug, 'We lived off Scotland Road.'

'Liverpool's Italian community live in that area.'

'Yes, down around Gerard Street,' Rosie told him promptly.

She realised that she had given too much away when he queried, 'You lived close to Gerard Street? That's where my relatives lived. Cesare Volante, my grandmother's cousin.'

Rosie knew the Volante family, who had been very good friends of the Grenellis. She and Bella had attended several Volante family parties as they grew up.

Hearing him say such a familiar name, Rosie couldn't control her betraying reaction.

'You know them?' Ricardo guessed immediately.

Rosie wasn't a liar. 'Yes,' she agreed reluctantly. 'Look, I must go . . .'

'No, wait.' He had reached out to stop her from leaving, taking hold of her bare arm. The effect of his touch shocked the breath out of her. It was as though some kind of powerful current had run right through her, taking control of her, depriving her of the ability to speak and yet at the same time jerking her body into taking a step towards him. As he had done towards her. They were standing almost body to body, so close that they were virtually touching. She could smell the warm scent of his skin, and the fingers curled round her arm were moving against her flesh in a soft caress.

'So, it *is* possible that we have met before. I thought so the first time I saw you. There was something about you that I recognised, although logically it seemed impossible that we should have done so. But of course now that I know you were living close to Gerard Street, and my grandmother's relations, I can see that it is entirely possible that we did indeed meet.' He was looking triumphant now, and pleased with himself for having, as he believed, had his recognition of her confirmed. And, for all she knew, he could be right. Rosie knew that the extended family in Italian terms was both large and rambling, and that if he had come to Liverpool with his family it was entirely possible that they could have attended the same family function.

'It is possible,' she agreed, 'but . . .'

Ricardo shook his head and snapped his fingers. 'Yes. I have it now. There was a wedding. You were there, a pretty little thing, who refused to speak to me, although you did allow me to give you my ice cream. I remember being told that you were not Italian.'

Rosie thought back. There had been so many celebrations, so many weddings, but gradually she remembered the right one. Some important members of the Volante family had come from Manchester. There had been children with them, older girls and boys, who in the main had ignored her, and yet one boy in particular had been kind to her, offering her his ice cream when she had dropped her own.

Rosie couldn't speak; she could hardly breathe. Along with her shock she could feel pain and something else, something that tugged at her heart and made it ache with a feeling of loss. She stepped back from him, her face showing her feelings. It made her shiver to think that somehow fate had stepped into her life like this, bringing them together a second time, as though . . . As though what?

'Rosie, come on,' Mary shouted.

Ricardo released her arm. She wanted to touch her skin where he had touched it, to cover the flesh that now felt the loss of his warmth.

Half running, half stumbling, Rosie hurried past him, unable to say anything, her thoughts in frightened turmoil.

TWENTY-FOUR

Rosie glanced anxiously over to where Paolo was slumped against the hedge, his shoulders bowed. He had returned to work with the other POWs at the beginning of the week, but despite the welcome sunshine, which had encouraged the more daring of the girls to cut the legs off their dungarees to turn them into shorts, as they worked under the hot sun stooking the newly cut corn sheaves to allow them to dry, Paolo looked sick and unhappy. He had become so thin that his clothes hung off his body, and Rosie felt almost anxiously maternal about him, although she refused to let anyone else see that.

Anyone else at all, but especially Ricardo. She risked a look across the field from under the brim of her hat. Yes, he was still there, snatching up the corn as it was cut and tied, and throwing the sheaves clear of the machinery. Like most of the other men, he had taken off his shirt. Against the blue of the sky and the dull gold of the newly cut corn, his torso

438

was the colour of liquid honey, sleek with the sweat of working so hard. One of the girls from another gang working close to him said something to him and as Rosie watched he turned to her, giving her a smile, and lifting the sheaf she was struggling to balance as easily as though it weighed nothing.

Rosie didn't want to think about why just watching him talking to another girl should make her feel the way she did, or why she should lie awake in bed at night, unable to sleep as she battled against what was happening to her. Why, why, should she be having these unwanted feelings for Ricardo when she hadn't been able to have them for Rob, who would have made her such a good husband and whom her father would have been happy to see her marry?

Was it because, despite everything, she wanted to believe her aunt had been right and Aldo was her father? Was it the Italian blood in her that was doing this to her? Like to like?

No, she wasn't going to let herself think that. She dragged her gaze away from Ricardo. She *wasn't* Aldo's daughter.

As they worked on through the long hot afternoon and into the evening, Rosie saw how Paolo seemed to grow more and more frail. She had seen too how Ricardo had gone to him, offering him water, giving him some food, and talking with him.

'That young lad doesn't look well at all,' Mary commented, coming over to Rosie whilst she was watching him.

'He's been very poorly,' Rosie reminded her.

When Mary had gone Rosie kept on watching Paolo, and then when they were allowed to break for a rest, she took a deep breath and went over to him. It was just common charity to ask if the lad was all right, she told herself; her dad would have understood that.

Close up, Paolo looked even more poorly than he did from a distance. His skin was drawn tight across the bones of his face, and was tinged almost yellow instead of being warmly olive. The light had gone out of his eyes, and when he looked at Rosie, and she saw the hopelessness in them, her heart ached for him.

'I do not want to die here,' he told her brokenly. 'I want to go home and die in my own country. It is so cold here. Your sun does not warm me.' He shifted his weight from one foot to the other and Rosie saw how he winced when he moved.

'You mustn't talk like that,' she told him fiercely. 'You are feeling low at the moment because you have been poorly, but you will get better.'

'No,' Paolo told her sombrely, 'I shall never be better whilst I have to be here.'

Rosie didn't know what she could say that would comfort him so she patted him awkwardly on the arm and left, sensing that her company was a burden he didn't want to have to bear.

She was halfway across the field on her way back to join the others in her group when she saw the long shadow Ricardo was casting over her as he came towards her. Automatically she started to walk faster, but he caught up with her.

'I saw you talking with Paolo,' he told her.

His hand was on her shoulder and she jerked away from beneath his touch. Her face felt as though it had been scorched, it was burning so hotly. 'Is there any law that says I can't?' she challenged him rudely.

'I was going to thank you and ask you if you share my concern for him.'

Shame filled her. 'It's as though he doesn't want to get properly better.'

'He misses his home and he has convinced himself that he will never see it again. He is young and unable to believe that one day the war will be over and he will be free to return. He doesn't have the patience for that and so instead he is willing himself to escape in the only way he can.'

Rosie shivered despite the sticky heat of the late afternoon. 'You mean he's willing himself to die?' She had turned to look at Ricardo as she spoke and now, with her gaze trapped in the dark intensity of his, it was too late for her to urge herself to caution.

Although he hadn't moved or tried to touch her, there was a look in his eyes that said what he felt. She had seen it before as she was growing up in the eyes of other Italian men when they looked at their women, a look of pride and possession and emotional intensity that locked a band around her, as real as any wedding ring. It was a look that said, 'You are mine and you always will be mine' and Rosie could feel herself responding to it and moving closer to him, leaning into him almost as though in acceptance of her fate.

'You mustn't let him die.' Her words seemed to come from somewhere far away, her voice thick and soft with the weight of her awareness of him.

'I shall do my best.'

She felt as though she was two different people. One of them was angry and fearful, wanting to turn and run from what was happening, whilst the other was filled with the most extraordinary sensation of wanting to go to him and let him take her hand, let him take all of her, Rosie recognised on a swift shiver of sensual awareness.

'Hey you, back to work.'

The foreman's command pushed between them so that they stepped back from one another.

Nothing had happened, nothing had been said or done, and yet Rosie knew that within the silence that had followed the look he had given her a promise had been asked for and given.

An hour later, all that remained of those opposing feelings was the anger and fear. As she worked on, ignoring the ache of her tired body and the irritating whine and bite of the midges that had arrived with the dusk, Rosie felt her anger against the man responsible for her misery rising to the point of explosion. The land girls were working strung out in a line beneath the trees that bordered the edge of the field, the leaves somehow encouraging the midges to swarm, whilst another group of girls were working in the open on the far side of the field, with the Italians working between them. At least soon it would be too dark for them to work any longer, Rosie decided with relief.

The sound of a plane flying in low over the fields towards them had Rosie and the other girls straightening up out of the shadows of the trees to turn, to laugh and wave.

'I expect it will be your Ian, Mary,' Sheila teased her cousin.

Out of the corner of her eye, Rosie saw Ricardo throw down his hoe and start to run towards them, warning, 'Down . . . get down. Santa Maria . . . get down . . .'

What on earth was he doing? And what right did he have to tell her what to do, or to stop her waving at an English plane? She looked across the field and saw him running fast towards her whilst the plane came lower.

'Cheek . . .' she began, and then froze as, not more than fifty yards away from her, where the other gang of girls were clustered laughing and waving to the incoming plane, the evening air was suddenly filled with the staccato rattle of machine-gun fire, and the screams of the young women who had only seconds before been laughing, but who were now the plane's targets. Rosie could see it all: the hail of bullets, the terror on the girls' faces as they tried to escape, and then the look of disbelief in their eyes when the bullets ripped into them, leaving them to fall to the ground.

'No!' Automatically Rosie started to run towards them, wanting to help, but it was too late. Ricardo had reached her and was grabbing hold of her, rolling her beneath him as he flung them both to the ground, making it impossible for Rosie to be aware of anything other than the protective presence of his body pressing hers into the ground. She could feel the heavy thud of his heartbeat, and smell the sun-warmed heat of his skin. She wanted to stay like this for ever, held safe against everything by him and with him. She wanted . . .

She lifted her head and looked up into the evening sky. The German plane was retreating, pursued now through the dusk by a pair of RAF fighters. In the soft darkness of the summer night she could see some of the other girls getting to their feet. Some, but not all.

Ricardo had lifted his body away from hers, but he didn't make any attempt to move away from her.

'You are all right?' he asked her.

She managed to choke out the word, 'Yes.' Her throat felt dry and her face had been scratched by the stubble of the newly cut cornfield.

'I thank the Madonna for it.'

She could hear the emotion in his voice. And then suddenly he leaned forward and kissed her hard and full, right on her mouth. She knew she should not be letting him do this, but instead of stopping him she was kissing him back just as passionately.

'Rosie . . . Rosie . . . are you all right?' It was Mary who was asking her this time.

Ricardo released her and she slipped from his arms to stand up, deliberately turning her back on him and almost running to join Sheila and Mary, who were standing together, tearfully hugging each other.

She couldn't bear to be the person she had just been, the Rosie who had kissed an Italian; the girl who had been her mother's daughter and not the daughter she wanted to be to the father she wanted to have. Her emotions in turmoil, Rosie glanced to where, several yards away, a group of people were standing around looking down at the ground. Their shocked stillness told her what had happened.

'They've been hit? I . . .' She couldn't speak; her throat felt too raw with pain.

'The bastards shot them down without giving them a chance,' Mary choked angrily. 'Two of them are dead, and another one that badly hit they don't think she'll survive.'

'I saw them trying to run. I wanted to help, but Ricardo stopped me,' Rosie began.

'It's lucky that he did,' Jean said quietly, coming up to join them, 'otherwise like as not you'd be lying there dead too.'

Rosie made to go towards them, but Jean

stopped her. 'No, there's nothing you can do. They were hit pretty bad. The other girls from their gang are with them. It's best that we let them do their grieving on their own for now, Rosie, just like we'd want if it was some of our own.'

'Bloody Luftwaffe,' Mary burst out.

'It isn't just the Luftwaffe, is it?' Rosie said wildly. 'It's them as well.' She gestured in the direction of the Italians. 'They're as much to blame as the Luftwaffe.'

'Stop it, Rosie. This isn't the time.' Mary's voice sounded so harsh and sharp that it sliced through her pain and silenced her.

The doctor had been sent for, the Italians had been lined up and were marching back to the farm, but the girls stood huddled together, looking fearfully towards the two crumpled bodies lying on the field.

'I was really surprised by the way you carried on earlier, Rosie.'

Rosie had been sitting on her bed, avoiding the others, sensing that they were taking their lead from Mary and echoing her disapproval of Rosie's outburst in the field. Now though, Mary was seeking her out and there was nowhere for Rosie to go to avoid her. Rosie stood up. Somehow she felt better doing that than letting Mary stand over her looking so cross.

'You do realise, I hope, that if Ricardo hadn't pulled you down like he did you could have been killed like those other poor girls?' Mary shuddered. 'I shall never forget what happened to them. Seeing them shot down like that, like they was nothing. And that could have been you, Rosie, if Ricardo hadn't acted as prompt as he did. As it is, he got shot in the leg. And then you go speaking about him and the other Italians like that. Really shocked me, you have.'

Ricardo had been shot! How badly? Rosie was filled with panic and fear. She swayed, and had to reach out to steady herself, her expression betraying her real feelings, before she could hide them.

Immediately Mary's face softened. 'It's all right, Rosie. There's no need for you to look like that. It was just a flesh wound and he'll be fine. I knew you liked him really,' she added smugly, whilst Rosie fought to get a grip on her treacherous emotions. 'So, seein' as the thought of him being shot had you acting like you was about to drop down dead yourself, why are you acting so mean to him?' Mary demanded. 'If it's to make him want you then let me tell you that all of us can see that he does. He's bin behaving like a proper gentleman towards you, and all.'

'Stop it, Mary, please stop it,' Rosie begged her friend. She was in tears now, torn between her own feelings and what she believed to be her duty towards her father's memory. 'I can't bear it, I really can't.'

'What is it? What's wrong? You aren't already married or summat, are you?'

'No, it isn't that.'

'Then what is it?' Mary demanded.

'Promise me you won't tell anyone else if I tell you? Not even Ian?' Mary agreed.

'. . . And so you see, Mary, I couldn't possibly, you know, get involved with an Italian. Not with what my mother did . . . and everything . . .'

She had been talking what felt like for ever, the words pouring out of her, tumbling over one another in her relief at being able to talk about what she had locked away inside herself.

'You do understand, don't you?' she begged her friend.

Mary leaned across and hugged her fiercely. 'Oh, you poor kid. Fancy not saying a word about all of this before now. And there was me thinking . . . Oh, Rosie! Your dad sounds a lovely man and I can understand how you feel, I really can, but I'm sure that he would want you to be happy.'

'I don't need Ricardo to make me happy,' Rosie told her defiantly.

'Don't tell me that! I've seen the way the two of you keep on looking at one another. He's nuts about you, Rosie, and I reckon you're pretty much the same way about him. Ready to die to protect you, he was today. How do you think you'd be feeling right now if he had been killed?'

Rosie's white face told its own story.

'Why don't you tell him what you've just told me? About your mam and your dad and all.'

'No! No, I can't . . . And you mustn't either. You promised you wouldn't say a word to anyone, Mary,' Rosie reminded her fiercely.

The next day the girls went to work in silence, avoiding looking at the rust-coloured patches in the field where their comrades had died. The gang of workers to which they had belonged had been dispersed, so they had heard on the grapevine, and the girls who had survived sent home to their families before going to join new gangs in other parts of the country, in an attempt to help them to make a fresh start. It didn't do to dwell on things, they all knew that. There was a war on and it was their duty to make the best of things and to keep on working for the good of the country and its fighting men. But even so, the horror of what had happened had touched them all. It seemed so incongruous that anyone should be machine-gunned by an enemy plane here in the country. But as Mary had told Rosie and the others, Ian had explained to her that the German plane had been part of a group flying in to attack the docks, and had somehow lost its way, so its pilot had looked for what targets he could find. It was a tragedy that the girls had been working in the field when he flew over it – and a miracle that more of them hadn't been killed. The tall row of trees had helped to save them, had been Ian's opinion, because it had caused the pilot to veer off or risk crashing into them. Rosie, however, was in no doubt as to what – or rather *who* – had saved her, and in doing so sustained an injury himself. And whilst she naturally grieved for the girls who had lost their lives, and for their families – after all, she knew herself what it was like to lose a loved one, as indeed they all did – her sharpest anxiety and concern was for Ricardo, about whom she had not been able to discover anything, despite all her own and Mary's best attempts to do so.

The sunshine had given way to a sullen pewter sky with thunder grumbling in the distance, and an electricity in the air that mirrored the girls' nervy tension. None of them mentioned the deaths of the girls who had been shot down, but they all knew that each and every one of them was thinking about them, and feeling torn between their grief for their loss and their guilty relief that they had been spared their fate. A heavy sombre silence had taken the place of their normal chatter and happy singing. The slightest sound had them stopping work to look upwards.

A week went by with no relaxation of the girls' shared mood of grief. For Rosie it was an especially long week of sadness for the lost lives, and anxiety for Ricardo. Unusually, there had been no sign of the Italians all week, and Rosie could only assume that they must have been sent to work on another farm. Even though Mary assured her that Ian had checked and could confirm that Ricardo had suffered only a flesh wound, Rosie knew she wouldn't be able to believe that fully until she had seen him for herself.

They were halfway through the following week before Rosie saw Ricardo again, and despite the fact that they were in the middle of a thunderstorm, the sight of him jumping awkwardly out of the army lorry made her feel as though the sun had come out and was shining brilliantly on her.

Ignoring the rules, she ran across to him, and then stopped, feeling acutely self-conscious and uncertain.

He didn't seem to have any such inhibitions, though. He came towards her. 'I . . . I heard that you'd been hurt . . . when . . . when you saved me,' she began awkwardly. 'I wanted to thank you . . .'

'You being alive is all the thanks I need,' he responded, looking at her in such a way that her heart thudded into her chest wall.

'Is your leg . . . ?' Rosie looked down at his body and then flushed brilliantly, looking quickly away.

'The bullet just grazed the skin, that's all.'

'I'm glad . . . I mean, I'm glad that that's all it did, but I wish that you hadn't been hurt at all,' Rosie told him almost incoherently.

'I'm sorry about those other girls.' He sounded as awkward now as she felt, Rosie recognised.

'Yes. It was awful,' she agreed and then shuddered. 'Their poor families.'

'Rosie . . .' He had reached for her hand and had taken hold of it before she could stop him. It felt so small and safe in his. The feel of his calloused palm against her skin made her tremble with unfamiliar excitement edged with another emotion. Rosie tried to pull her hand free but he refused to let her go.

'I've bin wanting to get you all to myself so that I could talk to you proper, like, for weeks,' he told her softly.

'I don't know why you should be wanting to do that,' Rosie felt obliged to say.

'Don't you?'

Her whole body was trembling now, not just her hand.

'You're a very special girl, Rosie, and I . . . I want you to know that I think I'm falling in love with you,' he told her rawly.

'You mustn't say that. You hardly know me,' Rosie protested, but her heart was leaping with a wild joy she couldn't control.

'I can't help how I feel, and as for knowing you, I know what you do to me, Rosie.' His frankness was making her colour up hotly. 'Is there any hope for me, Rosie?' he demanded huskily.

'I . . .' What could she say? He might have died saving her. She might have lost him for ever. Perhaps they were rushing things but everyone knew that that's the way it was in wartime. She knew you had to snatch your happiness whilst you could in case it was taken from you. 'I . . .'

'There's going to be a dance in Nantwich on Saturday. We've been told we can go. Will you dance with me there, Rosie?'

Unable to speak, Rosie nodded. A feeling she could only associate with those times as a child when her father had returned home from sea, picking her up so that she felt so giddy with excitement and anticipation that she thought she could fly was billowing through her. She wanted to both laugh and cry; to turn somersaults and to reach out and embrace the whole of the world. Her happiness was so bright and shiny, so intense and new, that she was afraid that if she blinked it might disappear.

So this was love and the freedom to feel that love.

I love you, Dad, she offered in silent tribute, the words an exchange for her freedom to move on from their shared past to her own new future.

'Quick, Rosie, the foreman's on his way,' Mary hissed warningly.

'You're afraid of him?' Ricardo asked protectively. 'You need not be. I will not allow him to hurt you, my Rosie.'

His words brought a loving smile to Rosie's lips but she shook her head, urging him to leave. 'There's no point in us courting trouble,' she told him, a smile curving her mouth as she added with deliberate emphasis, 'especially now that we're courting one another.'

'I knew all along you were sweet on Ricardo,' Mary announced with open satisfaction when Ricardo had gone back to join the other men and she and Rosie were back at work. 'Didn't we, girls?' she demanded, seeking the support of the others.

'Yes, it's bin obvious how you and Ricardo felt about one another, Rosie,' the others confirmed, laughing when she started to colour up self-consciously.

'Not that we aren't pleased for you, Rosie,' Mary assured her. 'I'll tell you someone who isn't, though, and that's that foreman. Just look at the way he's watching us. Just because we're having a bit of a chat.'

The foreman *was* watching them, and even though he was standing several yards away, Rosie could feel his anger.

'Pity we haven't bin moved on somewhere else. I hate the way that Duncan looks at us,' Sheila grumbled later on in the day.

'Ian was saying as how His Grace is expected back on leave any day,' Mary informed them, adding teasingly, 'so you'll be able to go and complain to him if you want to, Sheila.'

They all laughed but Rosie didn't feel at all like laughing at the end of the day when the Italians had been driven back to their camp and she and the other girls were still waiting for their own transport. They were in the farmyard, and she had been talking to Mary about the upcoming dance in Nantwich when some sixth sense caused her to turn round to find that the foreman was making his way towards them.

'I want a word wi' you,' he announced sharply.

'What do you think you're up to, encouraging that ruddy Italian? If it's a man you want then there's plenty of English lads around. You don't have to go giving it to some bloody Eyetie. Or are you one of them that likes giving it to the enemy? Is that what it is?'

He was standing so close to her that Rosie could smell the sour stink of his sweat. She wanted to step back from him but there was nowhere for her to go. He had moved so close to her that he had virtually trapped her up against the wall, so that he was standing between her and Mary. Fear spiked through her when she saw in his eyes the lust that was the real reason for his hostility towards her. 'They want teaching a lesson that would mek sure they don't go sniffin' round the likes of you, them bloody Eyeties do – aye, and I know a few handy lads an' all who would be happy to do it.'

To Rosie's relief, Mary pushed her way past the foreman, planting herself right in front of him.

'The Italians are prisoners of war here and have to be treated proper, just like our lads do when they're taken prisoner. That's what we were told before we came here, and Mr Churchill himself has said as how we should treat the POWs with respect.'

The sound of someone clapping their hands and a deep, cultured voice calling out, 'Bravo, my dear. Well said,' had then all turning to look across the yard to where a tall, handsome man in RAF uniform was standing watching them.

It was the foreman who reacted first, his face draining of blood to leave his skin a sickly putty colour as he stammered, 'Your Grace. I didn't know as how you was back.'

'Yes, indeed. I can see that, Duncan. Oh, and by the way, the young lady is quite correct. And even if Mr Churchill had not urged us to treat the POWs as we would want to be treated ourselves, I certainly won't stand for them being treated badly whilst they're working on *my* land. I'll speak to you later.'

With that, the newcomer turned on his heel and left the yard, while Rosie and Mary exchanged awed looks.

'The duke himself!' Mary exhaled excitedly.

'Of course it was, and if you'd not been telling George Duncan what for, you'd have seen him drive up in his posh sports car like the rest of us just did,' said Sheila loftily.

'Truck's here,' Sheila called out excitedly. 'Hurry up, you lot.'

Ian and Charlie had offered to pick up the girls in a truck they were 'borrowing' to save the girls having to ride their bikes into the nearby town, and it was a jolly laughing band of girls that crowded onto the lorry in their finery in the warmth of the summer evening, giggling good-naturedly when they discovered that it was already half full of young men ready and eager to offer them laps to sit on so as not to soil their frocks.

'You never said anything about this lot, Ian,' Mary chided her boyfriend.

'I hadn't planned on them being here, but someone spilled the beans,' he answered ruefully.

Rosie watched as Ian squeezed Mary's hand and the two of them exchanged tender looks. Now she was a member of that magical world that belonged only to two people, and yet to all those who knew what it was to love.

It didn't take them long to get to the town, where, as they discovered, the dance was already in full swing. They were all made very welcome, though, and Rosie was thrilled to see that Ricardo and some of the other Italians were already there. She was almost as thrilled when she saw that George Duncan wasn't, exhaling in relief when she had carefully looked round the dance hall and reassured herself that he was nowhere to be seen.

'Rosie.'

A blush warmed her skin when she looked up and saw that Ricardo was standing beside her.

'Will you dance with me?' he asked.

Unable to speak, Rosie nodded and stood up.

The crowded, dimly lit dance floor was an invitation for couples to make use of the intimacy it offered, and as Ricardo drew her close, Rosie closed her eyes and gave in to her own emotions.

The band were playing 'A Nightingale Sang in Berkeley Square'. Dancing with Ricardo was as easy as breathing; they seemed to fit together so perfectly.

'I feel as though I don't want this evening ever to end,' Rosie whispered an hour later, when they were still on the floor, swaying to the music, lost in their own private world.

'I am hoping that I might soon have some good news for you,' Ricardo told her.

'What? Tell me now,' Rosie begged.

'The duke has said that he would like to have some of us permanently attached to his estate. He will provide us with accommodation and take personal responsibility for our status as internees. He has asked for volunteers, and I have put myself forward.'

Rosie could hear both the excitement and the tension in his voice.

'It will not mean total freedom, of course, but it is a step in the right direction. I want you as my wife, Rosie. I know that at the moment that is not possible. Nor can I even ask you to become engaged to me because I have nothing to offer you as things stand at the moment. But I do love you and the very first moment I can I intend to ask you to be my wife. Will you wait for me, Rosie?'

He sounded so humble that she wanted both to cry and to fling her arms protectively around him and tell him that she would marry him tomorrow. But what he had said was true. She didn't even know if it was possible for an internee to marry. But she did know that it was possible for her to wait. For ever, if need be.

'Yes,' she told him. 'Yes, I will. Ricardo, what

are you doing?' she protested when the moment the music stopped he took hold of her hand and hurried her off the dance floor and out through the door into the darkness of the evening.

Moonlight illuminated the town square, but it could not reach into the narrow cobbled alleyways that led off it, and it was in one of those, in the shadow of the ancient church, that Ricardo took her into his arms and kissed her as a man kisses the woman to whom he has given the whole of his heart.

How different it felt when Ricardo kissed her rather than Rob. How different *she* felt. A shiver of sweet awareness tingled through her. This was why she hadn't been able to give her love to Rob, because somehow, deep down inside, her heart had known that she should save her love for Ricardo.

It was the happiest evening of her whole life. Rosie felt as though she was walking on air, having Ricardo at her side, his arm around her waist as he kept her close.

Towards the end of the evening, Ian called for silence and then announced that he had asked Mary to marry him and that she had accepted. When everyone had finished toasting them, Charlie stood up and said bashfully that he and Peggy were also going to be married. How lucky they were, Rosie couldn't help thinking, a little sadly, even whilst she was so very happy for them. Hers was in some ways a bittersweet happiness. There was her joy in having found love with Ricardo, but there was also her awareness that the road ahead of them was not an easy one. Ricardo was an internee, even if it was not his fault that circumstances had meant that he had not been able to take British nationality before the war. They were at war with Italy, and Ricardo must be anxious about those members of his extended family who still lived there just as she would have been were their situations reversed.

But still, they were here together now, and they knew how they felt about one another. Whilst everyone was shouting and cheering their congratulations to the two newly engaged couples, Rosie and Ricardo exchanged special looks that spoke of their private promises to one another and their hopes for their shared future.

TWENTY-FIVE

'And then Charlie said as how he wants to ask me dad for me hand in marriage proper, like, so I said, and exactly how are you going to do that when me family live in Birmingham and we're up here in Cheshire and you're on duty, you know like you would. And then blow me if Charlie doesn't go and get permission to go home wi' me to see me mum and dad, so that's what we're doing this very next weekend,' Peggy told them all triumphantly, having come to the end of her breathlessly excited revelation.

'Me and Ian won't be able to go and see my family or his on account of him being on duty, but he has written to me dad,' Mary offered when the girls looked expectantly at her.

They were all in the common room, relaxing after a long tiring week helping to harvest corn.

Both Peggy and Mary were proudly wearing their engagement rings, bought from a jewellers in Nantwich where the two young couples had gone just as soon as they could. Peggy's ring had three small diamonds set into a gold band whilst Mary's was a larger single solitaire. It had given Rosie a small pang to see the way their faces were illuminated by the joy of looking at them and showing them off to everyone, but being the generous-hearted girl she was, she had quickly put aside her own longing to be wearing Ricardo's ring, to admire theirs.

Ricardo had told her during the week that he had been summoned to see the officer in charge of the camp and told that his name had been put forward to the duke with a good recommendation that he be accepted to work and live on the estate. Rosie hardly dared to let herself hope that the duke would take him, because if he didn't she didn't think she would be able to bear the disappointment. It would make such a difference to them and their future together if Ricardo were taken on to work on the estate. They would be able to plan a future together, a future that would be as secure and happy as the futures Peggy and Mary were looking forward to.

'Shouldn't Peggy have bin back by now?' Jean asked. 'She told me she'd only got the weekend off and it's Tuesday now.'

'Perhaps she and Charlie decided to sneak away somewhere private like and not come straight back,' Sheila giggled.

But there was no place for giggles later on that

day when a white-faced Mary passed on to them the news she had received from Ian.

'The house took a direct hit, and according to Ian they haven't found anything, only exceptin' Charlie's cap. He must have took it off and left it in the hallway or summat.'

The girls looked at one another in stunned silence.

'She can't be dead,' Sheila burst out eventually. 'They've only just got engaged, her and Charlie. They was going to get married.'

Remembering what Mary had told her about Sheila losing her parents, and sympathising from her own experience, Rosie reached for Sheila's hand and squeezed it comfortingly. She couldn't bear to think of Peggy – timid, gentle Peggy, who had been so ecstatic at getting engaged – now cold and for ever still.

As though the dreadful news was some kind of turning point, within a matter of days of them receiving it, Brenda had decided to leave the Land Army and return home, along with several other girls from one of the other groups. The stark reality of war and death couldn't be ignored.

Rosie found that she was clinging tightly to Ricardo the next time she saw him, her fear for them both and their future bringing a sharp edge of uncertainty and urgency to her love for him.

'I still can't take it in,' she had told him sadly. 'Poor little Peggy. She was so happy, Ricardo, and she had so much to look forward to.' Thinking of Peggy brought back memories of her mother's death, but that wasn't something Rosie could bring herself to discuss with Ricardo. Her shame over her mother's behaviour was still with her, and so tied up with her feelings about her father, and the guilt she still sometimes felt at loving Ricardo, that, like the skin over a newly healed wound, Rosie felt it was safer not to disturb it.

Her love for Ricardo was opening her eyes to so much, including the unexpected strength of her own physical longing for them to be together in every single way.

Even so, she was still shocked when Mary took her on one side when they were alone in the dormitory.

'There's a favour I want to ask you to do for me, Rosie,' she began. 'Me and Ian are going away together for the weekend. I'm not going to tell anyone, especially our Sheila, because of all the fuss, but just in case anything should happen, I wanted someone to know.'

'But why don't you want anyone to know?' Rosie began naïvely and then blushed when she saw the look on Mary's face. 'Oh, Mary.' She took hold of her friend's hand. 'Are you sure you're doing the right thing? I mean, if Ian is pressing you to do this . . .'

'It isn't Ian wot's doing the pressing, it's me,' Mary told her flatly, ignoring Rosie's small gasp of shock. 'See, the way I see it, Rosie, is that after what's happened to Peggy and Charlie, and with

464

me and Ian not being able to get wed for a good few weeks yet, I don't want to wait. We could be dead tomorrow, either of us, and if that's going to happen then I want at least to know what's it's like, you know, being with a man. My man. I love him, see, Rosie, and I want him to know that. I want to hold him close and I want him to hold me in the same way, and . . .'

'But, Mary, what if something should go wrong and you were to—'

'Ian says that it won't, and if it did, well, then we wouldn't be the first couple to be registering their first kiddie's birth less than nine months after the wedding.'

Rosie knew that there was nothing she could say that would change her friend's mind. And a part of her actually envied Mary the chance and the freedom to do what she was doing. She tried to imagine herself in Mary's shoes and knew with a sharp pang that if she were to be offered the chance of being with Ricardo as his wife and then losing him before they could be married, or losing him but keeping her virginity, she would, like Mary, have opted for the former.

But she wasn't going to lose him. As an internee, Ricardo was relatively safe, since he would not be called upon to fight, and neither would he be sent back to Italy in a POW exchange.

'Now, think on,' Mary urged her. 'Not a word to anyone else about this, especially not our Sheila. She's that gobby she'd be spilling it all out back home before she realised what she was doing.'

'I won't say anything,' Rosie assured her.

'Rosie, the warden wants a word with you,' Sheila announced breathlessly, bursting into the common room where Rosie was mending a tear in her dungarees.

Putting down her mending, Rosie got up and smoothed off her clothes. The warden was kind but stern, and had no qualms about fining those girls who broke the rules about smoking in the dormitories, or giving those who came in after curfew a sound telling off, but it was so unusual for her to actually send for a girl that Rosie couldn't help but worry that she might somehow have broken some rule without realising.

Mrs Johnson's office was tucked away off the main entrance, and Rosie knocked on the door and waited to be told to enter.

'Ah, Rosie, you got my message. Good. Come in and sit down.'

The warden was smiling so she could not have done anything too dreadful, Rosie comforted herself, doing as she had been instructed.

'I don't want to alarm you, my dear, but I'm afraid it's bad news.'

Rosie gripped the sides of her chair. Something had happened to Ricardo. She could feel the sick fear clogging the back of her throat.

'We've received a message to say that your aunt

has been taken ill and that she needs you to return to Liverpool to look after her.'

Rosie stared at the warden. 'No,' she protested. In her agitation she had risen to her feet without knowing she was doing so. 'No. I can't . . . I don't . . .' she began, and then stopped when she saw the way the warden's smile was giving way to a frown.

'Mrs Leatherhall is your auntie, isn't she, Rosie?' the warden questioned Rosie sternly.

'Yes, yes, she is,' Rosie admitted. 'But—'

'Well, that's all right then. For a minute I had begun to worry. The poor lady's been very poorly, you see, and she'd put you down as her next of kin. And of course you must go to her. You do understand that, don't you?'

'Yes.' Rosie felt as though the admission was being wrung out of her. She couldn't go back to Liverpool. She couldn't leave Ricardo, not now that they had found one another and resolved all the problems between them, and especially not because of her aunt, who hated her and who did not even accept that they were related.

'You'll be given a travel warrant to get home and as much compassionate leave as you need. It seems that your auntie is not going to get better, my dear. I'm so very sorry. You can leave first thing tomorrow morning.'

First thing in the morning. But that meant that she wouldn't be able to tell Ricardo what was happening. Rosie could feel all her old anger and resentment for her aunt boiling up inside her.

'I don't want—' she began, but then stopped when the warden fixed her with a stern look.

'You don't want to cause anyone any problems; I know that, Rosie. But we all understand that it is your duty to go to your aunt, don't we?'

There was to be no escape for her, Rosie could see that, and yet she still looked despairingly towards the window as though somehow, if she wished for him hard enough she would see Ricardo there and she could run to him, and beg him to hold her and keep her safe so that she would not have to go to Liverpool.

But of course it was impossible for Ricardo to know what was happening and impossible too for her to be able to tell him before she left.

Instead she had to explain as best she could to Sheila that she had been summoned back to Liverpool and that she had no idea how long she would be gone.

'You'll make sure that Ricardo knows what's happened, won't you?' she begged her, wishing as she did so that Mary was here for her to entrust her message to.

But Mary, of course, was with Ian. Lucky, lucky Mary to be with the one she loved.

PART FOUR

Summer 1941

TWENTY-SIX

Rosie had known about the bombing, of course, but knowing about it had not prepared her for the devastation and the destruction of her home city. It caught her by the throat and paralysed her with distress and shock; so much so that every time she came to a fresh place where the building she had once known had now gone, she stood and stared, oblivious to the irritation of those around her, who bumped into her and cursed under their breath.

Lewis's had been bombed out and so too had Mrs Verey's shop. Rosie shuddered as she looked at the blackened shell of the building where she had spent so many hours of her life. If Mrs Verey hadn't planned to close the shop she and the other girls might even have been there when the fateful bomb dropped.

Rosie's pace slackened as she walked up Wavertree Road. The damage was less up here, although still visible in the early evening light. At the end of her aunt's road she stopped. She didn't want to do this. She could never forget her aunt's unkindness to her, and she hated being parted from Ricardo. But she knew it was what her father would have wanted and expected her to do. It was for his sake that she was here, not her aunt's.

'Rosie, it is you, isn't it?'

Rosie stopped to return Molly Dearden's warm smile.

'You'll have come back on account of your auntie, I expect?' Molly asked her sympathetically. 'I am sorry. How have you been?'

'I had a message to say that she was poorly,' Rosie answered her. 'I'm in the Land Army now and they've given me compassionate leave to be with her.'

Molly reached out and gave her arm a small sympathetic squeeze. 'If there's anything I can do, just say the word,' she entreated before going on her way.

The house still looked the same as when she had left it all those months ago, and Rosie still had the same sickly mixture of dread and misery churning her stomach that she remembered from every visit she had made here. It had been a hot day, and the smell of dust and devastation that hung on the city air stung her nose as though she was alien to it after the long weeks of country living.

Rosie lifted the latch on the gate. It wasn't too late. She could turn round and go back; tell the warden that she had changed her mind; lie to her even; fling herself into Ricardo's arms and beg him to let her give herself to him after all.

But she knew that she wouldn't. Because her father would have wanted her to do what she could for her aunt. And as his daughter she had to prove his trust in her had not been misplaced.

Her throat had gone so dry that she could hardly swallow. She lifted her hand towards the door knocker but before she could use it the door opened.

A small middle-aged woman in a nurse's uniform stood in the hallway.

'You're the niece, I hope.' Her voice was brisk and sharp. 'The hospital said that they'd finally managed to track you down.'

Now Rosie thought that an edge of disapproval had been added to the briskness. 'My aunt . . .' she began uncertainly.

'Upstairs in bed. The doctor came earlier. He'll be round again tomorrow so you can talk to him then. She'll be asleep most of the time from now on.'

Now that she was inside the hallway Rosie could smell the carbolic and what it wasn't quite masking.

'What – what exactly is it that's wrong with her?' she asked. As she waited for the nurse's reply Rosie could not quite help looking up the stairs. As though she expected her aunt to appear at the top of them, telling her to leave.

The nurse's lips folded into a tight line. 'That's for the doctor to discuss with you, miss. Now, if you don't mind I'll get me coat and be on me way.'

'No wait . . .' Rosie swallowed against the acid taste of her own panic. 'They said . . . they told me that . . . that it was serious, and that—'

'She hasn't got much time left, although sometimes they hang on longer than you expect. Why, I do not know when you think of the pain they're in. You'd think they'd be glad to let go.'

Rosie shuddered, thinking how awful it must be to be left in the care of someone who was so obviously uncaring. Had she loved her aunt she would have been beside herself with guilt at the thought of this woman nursing her. But she couldn't help it: she could not find any love for her, Rosie admitted. The love that had brought her here was for her father.

'I think you'd better tell me what I have to do for my aunt before you leave,' she managed to find the determination to insist to the nurse. 'I'm not a nurse, of course.'

'That you aren't,' the older woman agreed sniffily. 'And there's nothing you can do for her, except follow the doctor's instructions. She'll be asleep now until he comes tomorrow.'

'But if she should wake up . . .'

'You can sponge her down and see if you can get her to drink some water. Mind you, she won't if she thinks you want her to. Never had such an awkward, disobliging patient, I haven't. Some folk don't know when they're well off and that's a fact.'

It was almost dark by the time the nurse had left. Rosie went round the house putting up the blackout curtains and so putting off the time when she would have to go upstairs and see her aunt. But eventually it couldn't be put off any longer.

She climbed the stairs, tensing as the forgotten stair halfway up creaked, still expecting, despite what the nurse had told her, to hear her aunt calling out sharply, demanding to know what she was doing. But there was only silence.

The sickly smell of decay the carbolic had masked downstairs was stronger up here. Rosie closed her mind to what it meant as she pushed open her aunt's bedroom door. Ignoring the bed, she went first to the window to sort out the blackout before turning back to the bed.

Her first shock was seeing how small her aunt had become, her body barely lifting the bedclothes, as though all her flesh had melted from her bones. Her second was the sight of her aunt's face, with its yellowed skin drawn tight to the bones. One frail hand rested on top of the bedclothes, its fingers curled into a small claw.

Rosie remembered that there had been a woman in the street when she had been a child who had died like this, the flesh falling from her bones whilst her disease ate away at her.

Suddenly she was trembling so much she could hardly stand. She needed desperately to get out of this room but she made herself stay until she was sure that her aunt was, as the nurse had said, deeply asleep and as comfortable as someone in her situation could be.

There was hardly any food in the house and Rosie's first task was to go out and do some shopping. She was standing in a queue outside a greengrocer's in the city when she heard a familiar voice hailing her.

'Rosie!'

'Rob!' She had tensed when she heard Rob saying her name, reluctant to turn round and wishing that he had not seen her. Now, knowing what love was, she felt even worse about having hurt him.

But when she did turn to look at him, Rob was smiling warmly at her and standing next to him, holding tightly to his arm, was a small pretty blonde girl.

'I thought it was you. This is Angela.' Rob introduced the girl proudly, adding in a softer voice, 'my angel.'

'Oh, go on, you,' the girl giggled, but Rosie could see how much in love with one another they were.

They chatted for a few minutes, then said goodbye and turned to leave, but just before they did, Rob told her quietly, 'You were right to do what you did about us, Rosie, and I'm glad you had the courage to do it, especially now that I've met Angela.'

She was pleased for him, of course she was, oh, but seeing another couple so happy together did make her heart ache for Ricardo.

'You'll be the niece, I expect?' The doctor's words might be the same as those of the nurse, but the doctor himself looked far more approachable than she had done, Rosie decided thankfully as she held open the front door to let him in.

She had slept in her old room, finding bedding for its narrow stripped bed, knowing even as she made it up that she wouldn't sleep.

'How is your aunt?'

'She's awake,' Rosie told him, 'but she doesn't seem to know me. I tried to give her a drink of water like the nurse said, but she wouldn't let me.'

'It isn't unusual for patients in her condition to behave that way. She is very poorly, I'm afraid. I don't know how much you've been told . . .'

He was younger than Rosie had expected, and he walked with a slight limp.

'Not much. Only that her condition is . . . that she's dying.'

Would he hear the relief in her voice?

'Yes, she is. The tumour was very large and although she's had an operation to remove it . . . I'm sorry. All we can do now is make her as comfortable as possible. I'll come every day to see her and if you think you might need me in between times, you can send a message to the surgery. I'll go up now and take a look at her, shall I?'

One day slid into two and then three, and Rosie's life became her duties in the sickroom and her care for her dying aunt. Physically her time was occupied, but nursing her aunt couldn't occupy her thoughts or keep them at bay. Guiltily, Rosie admitted to herself how much she longed to be back in Cheshire, with her friends and Ricardo. She missed them all so very much. The girls from Birmingham had become as close to her as though she had known them all her life; her love for Ricardo couldn't have been stronger if they had been courting for years. The bonds she had formed with her friends, and most especially with Ricardo, strengthened and supported her and without them she felt vulnerable and alone.

She had been back in Liverpool four days when the letter arrived. It was lying face down in the hallway along with some others, so she picked it up and carried it into the kitchen, putting it on the table, and that was when she saw the familiar handwriting on it and felt the kitchen floor tilt violently beneath her feet with the shock.

Her father's handwriting. How could that be? It wasn't possible.

The letter was addressed to her aunt. Rosie had never ever contemplated opening someone else's mail nor ever imagined that she might do so, but she didn't hesitate for one second in tearing at the manila envelope. Her hands were trembling as she removed the letter that was inside it.

My dear sister,

Have you heard anything from Rosie yet? I keep hoping that she will have been in touch with you. I know you said you would try to find out where she was for me, and I am grateful to you for that. I am sorry she caused you so much distress, speaking to you the way she did and saying that she wanted nothing more to do with you. That isn't like my Rosie but then she'd had a lot to bear before I left. I think of her all the time, tell her if you should hear from her, and I love her dearly.

I'm getting used to managing on the one leg now, and the doc here says that I'm lucky I didn't lose the other, what with me being in the sea for so long before I was picked up and the frostbite.

I'm a lot better now, though, and now that I've got a bit of a job here in Canada I don't mind so much having to stay here until after the war's over.

Don't forget: tell Rosie I love her if she should get in touch.

With love, Gerry

Her father was alive! Her aunt had known that and yet she had never told her. Rosie remembered how she had been driven by her conscience to slip that piece of paper with her new details as a land girl on it through the letter box of this house before she had left Liverpool. Her aunt could have traced her if she had wanted to do so. But she hadn't. Cruelly, instead she had let her continue to think that her father was dead.

She picked up the letter from her father that

she had just put down, holding it as tightly as though it was his hand. She was still too shocked to feel any joy. Shocked and, yes, angry too. She looked up at the ceiling.

Putting down the letter she went to the door and made her way upstairs.

Her aunt lay unmoving on the bed, her face almost waxen and her eyes closed. What went on inside her head? Did she feel any remorse at all for what she had done? Had she ever lain here at night, tormented by feelings of guilt or regret? There was so much Rosie wanted to say to her, so much anger and hurt within herself that she wanted to rid herself of. But her aunt was dying, and even if she could have heard her Rosie couldn't bring herself to darken the dying woman's last hours with angry words and bitterness. No matter how justified they might be.

Her aunt was barely breathing, and lost to what was going on around her, but Rosie still lifted the blackout blinds, and opened the window to let in the warmth of the sun-scented air – not properly fresh like country air, but still preferable to the sickly, unmoving and heavy sweetness of the air in the bedroom.

When she was satisfied that she had done as much as she could to make her aunt's room comfortable, Rosie went back downstairs. She couldn't leave the house until the doctor had been but she desperately wanted to write to her father.

She went to the sideboard and pulled open the

drawer where she remembered her aunt had kept her writing paper and envelopes.

The drawer wouldn't open properly. Rosie could see the writing paper but she couldn't get it out because of a thick pile of envelopes that were jamming the drawer. It took her several minutes to work them free and remove them. Tied together with a piece of ribbon, which had now come unfastened, the letters had all been opened, and Rosie saw that they were from her father and were all addressed to her.

An hour later she had read them all, from the first, explaining how he had survived the sinking of his ship and been picked up by another ship and taken to Canada, after several dreadful hours in the icy cold sea, to the latest, reassuring her yet again that he had never been in any doubt that she was his daughter.

I'm not denying that I felt very bitter about what your mother did when she took up with that Aldo, and then started taking you round there to that Italian lot, like you was theirs and not mine. Many a word we had about her doing that, but she never paid me any mind. I'll be honest, Rosie. I was glad when they moved away, and I didn't have to see them any more and be reminded of what your mother had done. But that's in the past now. Your mother's gone, but you and me are still here. I keep thinking of you, Rosie, and imagining you marrying that nice young chap of yours. A good decent lad he is that I'd be happy to see you wed to.

Tears misted Rosie's eyes as she put down this last letter. She had been so caught up in the joy of learning that her father was alive that she hadn't thought until now how he was going to feel about her and Ricardo. Her father would never be able to understand or accept her loving and marrying an Italian. If he knew . . . *if* he knew. What was she thinking? That she could keep Ricardo and their love for one another a secret from him? That she could marry Ricardo and not tell her father? That she could let her father go on thinking as he did now that she had disappeared and could not be traced? It tore at her heart to even think of doing any of those things.

But it also tore at her heart to think of giving up Ricardo and their love.

Was this how her mother had felt about Aldo? Had she too been filled with despair and stricken with pain at the thought of living her life without the man she loved? Was she after all her mother's daughter and not her father's? Admitting that she loved Ricardo had opened a door to a part of herself she had not previously known existed. The coolness and lack of response she had felt towards other men, including Rob, had made her think that she simply wasn't a girl who was given to falling in love and passion, but her feelings for Ricardo had told her differently.

Some girls fell in and out of love a dozen times with a dozen different men, throwing off any heartache they might suffer in the excitement of a new love affair, but Rosie knew now that she wasn't like that, and that she would love only once and so deeply that her love, once given, could never be taken back.

But she loved her father as well as Ricardo, and she had loved him first and longest. He had a father's right to her love and she felt very strongly about her daughterly duty towards him.

A firm knock on the front door brought her out of the bleakness of her thoughts.

'How is your aunt this morning?' the doctor asked her when she had let him.

'She was asleep when I went in to her earlier,' Rosie told him as he stood back to allow her to precede him up the stairs.

Previously Rosie had only experienced death in the shocking destruction and violence of war. But she knew immediately she looked towards the bed that her aunt had gone.

The doctor was kind but efficient.

'You must not be too upset,' he told Rosie firmly. 'It is a blessing in many ways that your aunt did not linger.'

Had she slipped away in her sleep, not knowing that her life was over, not knowing that she was dying alone and unloved, or had she roused from her semi-conscious state and felt remorse for the unhappiness she had caused and regret for what she had done?

She would never know, Rosie acknowledged. She was glad now that she had not been granted the opportunity of challenging her aunt over what she had done, for the sake of her own conscience. She could not mourn her aunt's death, but that didn't mean that she couldn't feel pity for her.

By the end of the day Rosie had done everything that needed to be done. It had taken her a long time but she had finally managed to write a letter to her father that she hoped wouldn't betray to him too much of her bitter anger against his now dead sister.

Dad,

I know this will come as a shock to you and cause you sorrow, but I know that you would want to know that Aunt Maude has passed away. She died peacefully at home, with every care from her doctor, and I was with her at the end.

She had named me as her next of kin in this country and so when she was first taken into hospital the authorities were able to get in touch with me. I had no idea until then that you were still alive, and I am so sorry that you have been thinking that I had cut myself off from you. I would never ever do

that, Dad. I thought you were dead. There
was a misunderstanding.

Rosie had thought long and hard about how she
should write about her aunt's deliberate deceit, and
in the end her love for her father had overcome
any desire she might have had for revenge. The
most important thing, after all, was that her dad
was alive.

I had left my details for Aunt Maude when
I joined the Land Army but it seems that she
didn't get them. I am so sorry about that,
Dad. I should have taken some leave from the
Land Army and gone to see her to make sure
she had them when I didn't hear from her. If
I had done she would have been able to give
me the wonderful news that you were alive.
    Please write back to me as soon as you
can.
    All my love and lots of hugs,
    Your loving daughter, Rosie

Once she had finished writing the letter, Rosie read
it several times before sealing it and then hurrying
out to post it, guiltily aware that there was one
thing she had not mentioned in her letter to her
father and that was her love for Ricardo. A love
she would have to deny herself now, for her father's
sake. There could be no other way.
Rosie wanted desperately to find a way to be

both a loyal daughter to her father and to keep Ricardo's love. But there was no way. She knew that. If she were to marry Ricardo, that would be a constant reminder to her father of her mother's betrayal of their marriage and her affair with Aldo. In choosing to marry an Italian she would surely, in her father's eyes, be confirming any secret doubts he might have about her paternity. Rosie couldn't bear to do that. She couldn't bear to take her own future happiness at the cost of her father's pride and peace of mind.

Two weeks after she had arrived in Liverpool Rosie was ready to leave again. The previous week she had stood in silence at her aunt's funeral, along with the other mourners – neighbours in the main. Rosie had done everything as she had thought her aunt would have wanted, including arranging for her to be buried in the same grave as her husband.

She had seen her aunt's solicitor and been informed that she had left everything to her brother, Rosie's father, as Rosie had expected she would.

There had been the house to empty and clean, and Rosie had been only too relieved when one of her aunt's neighbours had asked if they might rent it for some of their family who had been bombed out.

But there was one thing she still wanted to do before she returned to her land girl duties.

*   *   *

There was more damage to the familiar network of narrow streets that led down to Gerard Street and her old home than when Rosie had left, more stomach-jolting gaps in the rows of houses; the gaps the raw jagged wounds of war that spoke silently of lives lost and destroyed. She was still not sure why she had felt the need to come down here unless it was in search of her younger self and that young girl and boy who had met at a wedding and not known that they would meet again or what that meeting would bring. With so many of the houses damaged and the ever-present danger of more bombing driving people out of the city, the once vibrantly busy streets seemed empty and silent.

Lost in her own sombre thoughts, Rosie didn't notice the young woman turning the corner at the bottom of the street, until she heard a familiar voice shrieking excitedly, 'Rosie? Rosie Price? Oh Rosie . . .'

'Bella?' she responded uncertainly, hardly daring to trust either her ears or her eyes as her old friend rushed across the street towards her.

'Oh, Rosie.' Before Rosie could say or do anything, Bella was hugging her excitedly. 'This is so wonderful. What a coincidence. I've so longed to see you again and to tell you how sorry I've been about the way things were when we left here. Oh, Rosie.'

There was a wedding ring on Bella's finger and the gentle curve of her body betrayed the fact that she was pregnant. She looked happier than Rosie had ever seen her, her face softer and aglow with warmth and joy.

'We heard about your mother. I'm so sorry, Rosie. We did write, but the letter came back "Gone away" – with so many of the old families gone we hadn't heard that your house had been bombed. We, Aunt Maria and I, thought that perhaps you didn't want to keep in touch. We had no idea about the damage to the house. It gave me such a shock when we saw it. What are you doing now? Where are you living?'

'I . . . I've joined the Land Army,' Rosie told her. 'I don't live in Liverpool any more. I had to come back to nurse my aunt . . .'

'And, like me, you couldn't resist coming down here to reminisce?' Bella guessed. 'We had such happy times together, didn't we, Rosie? I didn't realise how special a friend you were to me until it was too late and you weren't there any more. I missed you.'

'I missed you as well,' Rosie admitted. It seemed when she said those words that a sadness she had grown so used to carrying that she was unaware it was there, rolled from her heart. Tears filled her eyes when Bella reached out and touched her hand lovingly.

'What happened to our men affected everyone in the Italian community,' she explained, 'and for a while I blamed everyone who wasn't Italian for it. It took Aunt Maria and then my darling Keith to show me how unfair I was being. Can you imagine it, Rosie, me falling in love with and marrying an Englishman – and not just an Englishman but a soldier as well?' Bella laughed.

Rosie was too stunned to be diplomatic. 'But you were as good as engaged to one of the Podestras,' she burst out.

Bella rolled her eyes. 'I know and you can imagine the fuss my mother made, but, Rosie, when I'd gone along with her plans for me, I didn't know what it was to fall in love with someone, and once I did, well, there was no way I was going to give Keith up. I was lucky in a way that we did move to Manchester. I ended up doing some voluntary war work there – that's how I met Keith. He was in hospital with a shrapnel wound and I was working there as an orderly. But apart from that, the family in Manchester have a much more modern outlook on life than my mother, so although she swore that she'd never speak to me again if I married Keith, once she knew she couldn't bully me into doing what she wanted, she accepted that Keith was going to be her son-in-law. Of course, now that there's to be a baby, you'd think that me marrying him was her idea,' Bella laughed. 'Oh, I'm so glad I've bumped into you like this. It must be fate, and to think I only came down here because we're on our way to Aldershot. Keith has been posted there and I'm going with him. We'd got a few hours before our connecting train leaves, so I told Keith that I'd like to come down here and show him where I grew up. He's gone to see if he can find a chippie that's open. Since I started with baby here, all I've done is eat. Rosie, Rosie, I still can't believe that I've actually found you again. Aunt Maria will be so pleased. She talks about you all the time, and I know she'd love to hear from you. She misses you a lot. Of course, she always thought of you as the daughter she had never had, we all knew that. It must have been so hard for her, wanting children so much and then finding out after they were married that Aldo was unable to be a father because he'd had measles as a boy.'

'Aldo couldn't father children?' Rosie repeated, almost stammering in the wave of disbelief mixed with joy that was surging through her.

'Yes. Didn't you know? I thought your mother would have told you, what with her and Aldo being so close.'

'No . . . no . . . she never talked about him to me,' Rosie told her.

A tall, brown-haired man wearing a soldier's uniform was hurrying towards them, and Rosie guessed from the look of love illuminating Bella's face that he must be her husband.

'Keith, this is Rosie, who I've told you so much about,' Bella introduced them happily. 'Oh, this is so wonderful. Rosie, promise you'll keep in touch. Look, I've got a postcard here with our new address on. I wrote them out to give to the family and there were some left.' She dived into her handbag and handed Rosie a carefully printed postcard. 'Promise me,' she insisted.

Rosie nodded, too full of emotion to trust herself to speak.

'We'd better go otherwise we could miss our train,' Bella's husband warned.

Bella gave Rosie another fierce hug and then let her husband take her arm. Within seconds, or so it seemed to Rosie, they had gone, and she was alone in the street, her emotions in turmoil. Of course she was thrilled to have seen Bella and to have mended the rent in their friendship. She was delighted too to know that her friend had cared enough to try to contact her after her mother's death and that she wanted them to keep in touch. But surely most important of all had been the discovery that Aldo couldn't be her father. Yet the joy she should have been feeling was shadowed by the knowledge that Bella had done what she could not do, in that she had married the man she loved. Rosie did so envy her that. Lucky, lucky Bella. But for Bella to refuse to do as her mother had wished was a very different thing from Rosie risking hurting her father. The two just could not be compared. But oh, the look of joy and happiness in Bella's eyes when she had looked at Keith, and the love and pride in his when he had looked back at her. She must not think about what she could not have, nor dwell on the pain of having to end things with Ricardo. She must not think of herself at all but instead she must think of her father. She must and she would, Rosie told herself desperately.

There was nothing to keep her in Liverpool now and no reason why she should not return to Cheshire. But that meant telling Ricardo that it was over between them and just thinking about doing that made her feel so wretched.

It had to be done, though, Rosie insisted to herself, as she walked to the station to catch her train back to Crewe. It had to be done and she must and would do it for her father's sake. She owed him that.

Rosie held that thought to her later as her train made its slow stop-start way to Crewe. Sometimes doing the right thing hurt – very badly – but that didn't make it any less right.

TWENTY-SEVEN

'Has Sheila told you yet about George Duncan?' Mary asked Rosie after she had welcomed her back, and discreetly described her little holiday with Ian as 'perfect'.

'No. I haven't seen the others yet.' Rosie had been up in the dormitory unpacking her things when Mary had come in. 'What's happened?'

'He's only gone and taken a fancy to our Sheila, that's all. Making a right fool of himself over her, he is, following her around and looking at her like a lovesick bull. Of course, it's partly her own fault. She would go flirting with him. She says it were just a bit of a laugh, but she isn't laughing now, I can tell you. Caused a rare old fuss, he did, down at the dance last Saturday night, when he saw Sheila dancing with one of the RAF lads.'

'But George Duncan is married,' Rosie protested.

'Oh, we all know that, but it doesn't seem to make much difference to him. We've heard as how our Sheila isn't the first land girl he's chased after.

Got a bit of an eye for the girls, our George has, apparently. I've warned her that his sort is always trouble and that she should have seen that for herself, but what's done is done and he won't take a hint that she isn't interested in him, no matter what she does. Your Ricardo has bin missing you, Rosie. He asked me only yesterday if I'd heard from you.' She frowned when she saw the way Rosie's face closed up and she turned away from her without saying anything. 'Now what's up?'

'Nothing. It's just . . . well, I've been thinking whilst I was back home in Liverpool, and I've realised that . . . that me and Ricardo, it just isn't going to work.'

'Rosie, what on earth are you saying? That's rubbish. You love him and he loves you.'

'No!' Had she betrayed her real feelings to Mary with the force of her denial? 'I thought I did, but I – I was wrong.'

She had been away only a fortnight but it was surprising just how much had changed. But not as much as she had changed herself. She had gone away one Rosie and come back another. The Rosie who had gone away had been happy and laughing, and so very much in love. The Rosie who had come back couldn't bear to think about that love.

'Oh, no, not the ruddy potato fields again.'

Sheila wasn't the only one who wasn't looking forward to the week ahead, Rosie acknowledged, as they all climbed out of the lorry.

'You'll have to have a word with that foreman admirer of yours, Sheila, and see if he can't give you summat you'd fancy a bit more,' one of the girls teased.

Sheila pulled a face and glanced over her shoulder, obviously wanting to check that George Duncan wasn't around before she told them, 'He gives me the creeps, he really does. Always staring at me and watching me.'

Rosie wasn't sure whether to be glad or sorry when she saw that the Italians had arrived and were already hard at work. She hadn't slept at all hardly last night for thinking about what she was going to have to say to Ricardo. But the sooner it was said the better – for both of them. She wanted it over and done with. Because she was afraid she might change her mind? She forced herself to think about her father, but somehow all she could do was look helplessly across the field to where Ricardo was looking back at her.

It was dinner time before they could speak to one another. The joy Rosie could see in Ricardo's eyes as he came up to her almost destroyed her resolve.

'Rosie, good news. The duke—'

'Ricardo, I'm sorry. There's something I have to tell you.'

'Something is wrong. Your aunt . . . ?'

'She died.'

Another minute and he would take her in his arms, and she couldn't let him do that because once she was there she knew she would never want to leave.

'Whilst I was at home, Ricardo . . . I've changed my mind. I . . . I don't love you after all.'

She couldn't bear to look at him as he absorbed her words. Hurting him was worse than hurting herself. And worse than hurting her father? She must not let herself think that.

'No. You are joking. You do not mean that. You can't mean it . . .'

'I'm sorry but I do.'

'No.' His shock had given way to angry male pride now. 'No. I do not believe you. You were ready to give yourself to me. You wanted me to—'

'There's a war on, Ricardo. People say and do things they don't always mean . . .'

'There is someone else?'

Rosie hesitated. How much easier it would be if she were to say yes. She could already see the jealousy smouldering in his gaze. He was a proud man. He would not want to be second best. But she just couldn't bring herself to speak the lie.

'No, no, it isn't that. It's just . . . The foreman's coming,' she told him, recognising that this was the first and probably the only time she was ever going to be glad to see George Duncan heading towards her.

'It's over, Ricardo,' she told him quickly, before turning round to join the other girls. 'It's over.'

*   *   *

'You've told Ricardo then?' Mary demanded tersely.

Rosie nodded her head, but couldn't bring herself to look at her friend. They'd arrived back at the hostel an hour ago, tired and dirty, and Rosie had gone straight to have a shower. Now she and Mary were alone in the dormitory.

'I don't know what's up with you, Rosie, really I don't,' Mary continued. 'That poor chap. He thought the world of you, he did, and you knew it. I didn't think you were the sort who would treat a decent chap like that—' Mary broke off as she heard the muffled sob Rosie couldn't control. 'Aw, Rosie . . .' Her voice was softer now. 'You do love him, don't you?'

'Yes,' Rosie admitted, unable to pretend or lie.

'Then why have you gone and told him that you don't? Come on, you can tell me.' Mary cajoled her when Rosie shook her head.

'It's my dad,' Rosie told her reluctantly.

'I thought he was dead.'

'So did I. But I found out before my auntie died that he wasn't and that he's been writing to me.' Rosie reached behind herself to the small bedside table and opened the drawer to show Mary her father's letters as Mary shook her head in astonishment. 'He loves me, Mary, and I can't let him down. He would hate it if he knew about Ricardo, with him being Italian, you know, because of my mother.'

'But, Rosie, if your dad loves you as much as you say—'

'He does.'

'Then he'll want you to be happy, won't he? And if he's in Canada then, who knows, by the time the war's over, if Hitler hasn't done for us all, when your dad comes back here you and Ricardo could be married and your dad could be a granddad. I can't see him being too bothered about you being married to an Italian then.'

'I could never do that,' Rosie told her, shocked.

'Well, perhaps not,' Mary conceded. 'A person's got to respect their parents, we all know that, but you'd never catch me letting mine or Ian's mum and dad come between us.'

Rosie shook her head. 'It's different for me, Mary, what with my mother getting herself involved with an Italian and everything. I know what I'm doing is the right thing, but oh, Mary, it does hurt so much.' Tears trickled down Rosie's pale face.

'Well, I don't know as I believe that you are,' Mary told her promptly but she hugged her none the less. 'I do know that I couldn't give my Ian up, and by the looks of you, what you've done is half killing you, Rosie, and I can't think that any loving dad would want to see that happen to his daughter, no matter what your mother might have done. See, you aren't her, are you? You're you and Ricardo is Ricardo. And . . .' Mary shook her head. 'Well, I just think that there's a war on and when you meet The One you've just got to grab happiness together whilst you can. Look at poor Peggy and Charlie.

That's why me and Ian are getting married just as soon as we can.'

'Where's our Sheila?' Mary asked tiredly, sticking her potato fork into the ground and sinking down onto the grassy verge by the hedge. 'Only I've got her sandwiches here as well as me own.'

'She said she was just going to nip behind the hedge for a cigarette,' Rosie answered.

They weren't supposed to smoke when they were working and it had still been ten minutes away from their dinner break when Sheila had announced that she was desperate for a smoke.

'I'll go and get her, shall I?'

'Oh, thanks, Rosie, would you? And tell her to get a move on. I'm that hungry I'll end up eating her sandwiches as well as my own if she doesn't watch out.'

The ground dropped away to a farm lane on the other side of the hedge, and as she climbed over the stile and then slithered down onto the track, at first Rosie couldn't see Sheila for the sweeping branches of the chestnut tree several yards away, but then she saw the back of her blonde head and realised that she must be leaning against the trunk of the tree.

Rosie waited until she had almost reached her before calling out her name, and then came to an abrupt halt when she realised that Sheila wasn't alone and that the reason she hadn't come back to join them was because the foreman, George

Duncan, was virtually imprisoning her against the tree, his arms resting on the trunk either side of Sheila's head whilst she looked up at him in fear.

'Rosie.'

Rosie could see the relief in Sheila's face when she saw her, she could also see the anger in the foreman's, but she didn't think twice about her own safety as she rushed to her friend's side, demanding, 'Let her go.'

She tugged at George Duncan's arm as she spoke, trying to pull it away from the tree so that Sheila could escape, but he shook Rosie's hand from his arm with a roar of fury, and then grabbed hold of her, shaking her furiously.

'You dare interfere wi' me. Why, you little bitch, I'll learn yer to put your nose into my business.'

Rose could hear Sheila screaming but the sound was blurred by the pain in her own head as the foreman pushed her against the tree where Sheila had been, banging her head violently against the wood. Rosie could taste blood in her mouth. She felt sick with the fear that she might faint. When she saw the foreman raise his hand she turned her face to one side to avoid the blow. But the blow never came. Because suddenly the foreman was being wrenched away from her and she was safe in Ricardo's arms.

She was in too much of a state of shock to be able to speak and could only cling to Ricardo in relief whilst he murmured words of love and concern against the top of her head.

'You're all right, *bambina* . . . tell me that you are all right. If he has hurt you . . .'

He sounded so anguished that Rosie had to find the strength to raise her head from his shoulder so that she could look at him and reassure him, 'No, he hasn't hurt me, Ricardo. I'm fine . . . I . . .' Out of the corner of her eye Rosie saw a movement over Ricardo's shoulder. The foreman had picked up the potato fork Sheila had left when she had fled from him and now he was advancing on them, the fork raised.

As she cried out a warning, the foreman flung the fork at Ricardo's unprotected back like a spear.

The speed with which Ricardo moved her, snatched Rosie's breath away. She could hear the sound of tearing cloth and felt Ricardo release her. His shirt was ripped and blood was dripping from his arm but to her relief she saw the fork was buried in the earth and not him.

'Go back to the field,' he told her. 'Go back now, Rosie.' He had turned his back to her and was advancing on the foreman who standing waiting for him, a malicious sneer of anticipation and excitement twisting his mouth.

'Think you're up to it, do you, Eyetie? Well, come on then, let me show you what it means to get a real man. And then afterwards, it will be her turn . . .'

'Ricardo, no,' Rosie begged. He might be taller than the foreman but he was nothing like his weight and nor, Rosie suspected, did he have the armoury of dirty tricks the other man would possess.

She was right. The moment Ricardo got close the foreman reached up and grabbed a branch of the chestnut tree, levering himself off the ground and aiming a kick at Ricardo's body with both his feet.

Somehow, though, Ricardo managed to avoid it and somehow too he managed to drag the foreman down off the branch and hold him with one hand whilst he punched him swiftly with his other hand.

'That's for Rosie,' Rosie heard him saying thickly, 'and this is for me . . .'

The foreman staggered back, clutching his face. 'Get him, lads. Get the bugger and lock him up . . .'

Until that moment, Rosie hadn't realised that other people had come running from the field, alerted by Sheila to what was going on.

'You'll pay for this, Eyetie, by God you will.'

The soldier who was in charge of the Italians had come running up out of breath demanding, 'What's going on?'

'The bloody Eyetie attacked me. I caught him and her here, having a bit of you-know-what, and—'

'That's not true,' Rosie protested, turning to the farm hands. 'Tell him. You saw.'

They were looking away from her, no doubt too afraid of the foreman to tell the truth, Rosie realised sickly, and now the soldier was already taking Ricardo by the arm and sternly marching him away.

'He's lying,' Rosie sobbed to Mary. 'It's all my fault. Poor Ricardo. All he was doing was trying to help me. Oh Mary, what's going to happen? Ricardo was so pleased because he had been picked as one of the men the duke wants to work here permanently and live here, and now—'

'Don't go getting yourself upset, Rosie. Sheila told us what was going on. Them cowardly farm hands might not have what it takes to stand up to George Duncan but me and the other girls know what he's like. I'm going to have a word with my Ian about all of this and, if necessary, I'll go and see the duke meself.'

Rosie sobbed with relief on her friend's shoulder.

'For someone who reckons she doesn't love a certain someone any more, you're getting yourself in a bit of a state, if you don't mind me saying so,' Mary pointed out.

'I never said I didn't love Ricardo, only that we couldn't be together,' Rosie corrected her. 'Is Sheila all right?'

'That one will always be all right. Gave her a bad scare, of course, and no wonder. And she'll have to do summat about the buttons he tore off the front of her shirt. Dirty pig. If I had my way I'd do to him wot farmers do to them male calves they don't want as bulls. Serve him right, an' all. I've told Sheila that she's got to report this to the warden, and I'm going to make sure that she does.'

* * *

Mary was as good as her word, and later on that evening the warden sent for Rosie and told her that she wanted to hear what she had to say about the day's events.

As calmly as she could Rosie explained what had happened.

'I hope this is the truth you're telling me, Price,' the warden told her sternly. 'I do know that you have your own personal reasons for not wanting to see a certain POW getting into trouble.'

Rosie's face burned. 'I wouldn't lie about something as important as this,' she told the warden truthfully.

The warden's face softened. 'No, I don't think you would, Rosie. Now let's go through it all again, shall we, just to make sure I've got everything down correctly?'

'It wasn't Ricardo's fault, really it wasn't,' Rosie insisted desperately when she had finished retelling the story. 'You will make sure they know that, won't you, Mrs Johnson?'

The warden sighed as she put down her pen. 'I understand how you feel, Rosie, but you must understand what a serious matter it is for an internee to attack a foreman in charge of him.'

'But Ricardo was only—'

'I appreciate that he had come to your defence,' the warden continued firmly. 'But none the less he did attack the foreman. Like I said, this is a very serious matter.'

Rosie's fears for Ricardo grew even stronger

when, after she had left the warden's office, Mary came to her to tell her that Sheila was beginning to panic about the foreman taking it out on her later if she got him into trouble.

'If you ask me the silly fool probably started it all by leading him on, even though she swears she didn't, and now she's afraid of what's going to be said.'

'She's probably afraid of George Duncan as well,' Rosie shivered. 'And who can blame her?'

Mary looked at Rosie's white face. 'You did tell the warden about how he hit you and threatened you, didn't you, Rosie?'

'Yes. But I'm not sure she believed me. She knows about me and Ricardo, and she probably thinks I'm just trying to protect him. But George Duncan did try to hit me, Mary, and when I saw him about to throw that fork at Ricardo . . .'

'He's a thoroughly bad lot and I know that Ian agrees with me about that,' Mary said forthrightly. 'Didn't take to him one little bit, my Ian didn't, even though he tried to smarm his way round him.'

On another occasion it would have made Rosie smile to see how partisan Mary was on her fiancé's behalf. But now she felt too worried about Ricardo to even think about smiling.

'It's all my fault,' she told Mary wretchedly. 'If Ricardo hadn't seen me leaving the field he would never have come after me and then—'

'If I was you I'd thank my lucky stars that he did. That daft cousin of mine had no right to run off, leaving you on your own with George Duncan, especially not after what he'd just bin trying to do to her.'

'She only did it because she was trying to get help,' Rosie reminded Mary.

'Did you tell Ricardo about your dad?' Mary asked, changing the subject.

'No, there's no point. It won't change anything. I've made up my mind, Mary; I can't let my dad down. Not after everything he's been through, what with my mother, then being torpedoed and losing his leg, and thinking that I didn't care. I'm all he's got now, Mary, and I just can't.'

'Oh? And what about letting poor Ricardo down? He really loves you, Rosie. Anyone can see that. And if you ask me, he has a right to know why you're giving him up,' Mary told her roundly, 'especially now, after what he's gone and done to save you. He could have got himself in a lot of trouble on account of you, Rosie.'

'It doesn't matter what you say,' Rosie told Mary desperately. 'I can't change my mind. And besides, Ricardo will find someone else. An Italian girl. His family probably wouldn't want him marrying me any more than my dad would want me marrying him.'

She could see from the tight-lipped look Mary was giving her that her friend didn't agree with her. Still, what Mary had said to her had been almost too much for her to bear. She loved Ricardo so very much. So much that she wanted him to find happiness with someone else. Rosie felt as though someone had taken hold of her heart and was squeezing it so painfully that she just couldn't bear the agony. It wouldn't always be like this, Rosie tried to comfort herself. The pain would lessen, and Ricardo would find someone else to marry. A girl from his own country whom his family would welcome.

There was no sign of George Duncan when the girls arrived for work the next day, but any relief Rosie might have felt about his absence was cancelled out by the fact that there was no sign of Ricardo or the other POWs either.

She couldn't help worrying about the warnings both the warden and Mary had given her about the trouble Ricardo could be in for having saved her from the foreman.

'What do you think's happened?' she fretted to Mary at dinner time, unable to eat her sandwiches.

'I don't know, Rosie. I'm seeing Ian tonight so I'll ask him then what he thinks. Are you going to eat them sandwiches?'

'No, I'm not hungry.'

'Well, I am,' Mary told her. 'So pass them over here, will you? Our Sheila was saying this morning that she wants to go home. She says she's had enough of being a land girl and she doesn't want to do it no more. I reckon what's happened has given her a real nasty shock. She said she was going to see the warden tonight and tell her that she wanted to hand in her cards.'

'But what about Ricardo?' Rosie protested. 'What if he's in trouble? If Sheila goes then there won't be anyone to say what George Duncan was doing.'

'Well, the warden won't let her go unless she's satisfied that Sheila's told her the whole story,' Mary tried to reassure her.

But Rosie wasn't convinced and she suspected that in her heart of hearts Mary wasn't either. Sheila had such a pinched, nervous air about her now, and had changed so much from the cheery girl she had been, that it was obvious how terrified she was of the foreman seeking revenge.

All the girls were talking about what had happened and offering their own opinions on the outcome.

'My chap's in the Military Police,' one of the girls from another gang informed them all when they were chatting after their evening meal at the hostel, 'and he says there's bound to be a disciplinary proceedings brought, and that the foreman's bound to be favoured and let off on account of him being British and the Italian foreign and an internee. He reckons that the Italian could end up spending the rest of the war in prison.'

Rosie stood up, her whole body trembling with the intensity of her feelings. 'But it wasn't Ricardo's fault. It was George Duncan's.'

'You can say that as much as you like, Rosie, but

it stands to reason that no court is going to favour a foreigner above one of our own,' the other girl insisted. 'You can bet that George Duncan has already warned them as works with him what they can expect if they don't keep their mouths shut about what he's like, and that wife of his isn't going to tell on him, is she?'

'But that's unfair,' Rosie protested.

'It might be, Rosie, but that's the way things are. There are plenty of folk around who think that it's unfair that the POWs get a better food ration than we do, and plenty too who don't like seeing them being allowed to walk free and go to dances and the like. They won't lose any sleep at night worrying about an Italian internee spending the rest of the war locked up in prison.'

In the uncomfortable silence that followed, Mary gave the other girl a dark look and then said firmly, 'It's just daft folk who think like that. How do they think we'd get the ruddy farm work done without them lads to help us?'

'It's all right for Mary to say that,' Rosie heard one of the other girls mutter, 'but Mabel's got it right: without someone proper to stand up and speak for him, that Italian hasn't got a chance.'

'I'm going to have a word with the warden about Ricardo,' Rosie told Mary, adding passionately, 'He can't go to prison, Mary. It isn't fair.'

'Well, you and me might know that, Rosie, but it isn't us that has the say so, is it?'

Mrs Johnson said much the same thing when Rosie asked to see her.

'I do understand your feelings, my dear,' she tried to comfort Rosie, 'but this is a military affair now and will have to be dealt with accordingly. It seems that the foreman – George Duncan, wasn't it? – has alleged that he was the one who was attacked by your friend and not the other way around. He claims that Ricardo held a grudge against him because of an accident to another Italian, who had blamed him for his own clumsiness.'

'He must mean Paolo, but that was his fault too. Oh, Mrs Johnson, surely people won't believe a man like him?' Rosie was practically wringing her hands together in her despair. 'He is horrible, cruel and unkind, and his wife—'

'That's enough, Rosie. I do understand how you must feel, my dear, but it is up to the authorities now. If your friend has a good record as an internee then I am sure that this will be something in his favour.'

But not as much in Ricardo's favour as having someone like His Grace speak up for him, Rosie realised.

Mary was horrified when Rosie confided her plan to her.

'You can't just go up to the manor and ask to see the duke, Rosie. You'd never be allowed anywhere near, even if you could sneak away from working without being found out. And then what help to Ricardo would it be if you was to get in trouble as well?'

'But I've got to see him, Mary. I've got to see him and make sure that he knows what really happened.'

'Oh, yes, and he'd believe you, of course, you being madly in love with Ricardo and him with you. Look, I'm seeing Ian tonight 'cos we've got some stuff to sort out, what with the wedding coming up soon. I'll ask him if he can find out what's happening, and perhaps have a word with His Grace himself if he can, but you've got to promise me that you won't go doing nothing daft.'

Rosie hesitated and then gave in and promised.

Rosie was waiting for Mary that night when she came in, pouncing on her the moment she walked through the door.

'Did you speak to Ian about Ricardo?' she asked her anxiously.

'Give us a chance to get in the door, Rosie,' Mary complained. When she saw Rosie's stricken expression Mary relented. 'I said I would, didn't I? Ian's said he'll see what he can find out, discreetly, like. He knows a chap who knows someone based at the camp with the internees and POWs so he's going to try and find out what's happening. Do you want him to try and send a message to Ricardo from you?'

Rosie ached with longing to say yes and to send

Ricardo her love, but how could she? She had made up her mind and told Ricardo that it was over between them, and she couldn't go back on that.

'There's nothing for me to say that hasn't been said. But what about the duke, Mary? Did Ian . . . ?'

'The duke's not there at the minute. But he should be back next week, so you see, it's just as well you didn't go rushing off to see him like you was planning. I'm going to have to give our Sheila a bit of a talking-to, I don't want her going rushing off before me and Ian get married. I've got me mum and dad and as many of the family as can make it coming up to see us wed, and Ian's lot as well. The vicar's said we can have the village hall for the wedding breakfast and a bit of a dance afterwards. There, Rosie, don't go looking like that,' Mary urged when she saw the sadness in Rosie's eyes. 'I still reckon that you're daft not telling your dad how you feel about Ricardo. It's not Ricardo's fault, when all's said and done, that your mum got herself involved with an Italian.'

Rosie knew there was no point trying to explain her position to her friend all over again, and she was grateful to her for what she had done. She just hoped that if Ian could get some news of Ricardo it would be good news.

The week ended with wet weather and the unwanted news via another girl that George

Duncan had been swaggering around the village boasting that 'that bloody Eyetie who had a go at me has got hisself in big trouble'.

'He'd got his wife with him,' she added. 'Half scared out of her wits, she looked too.'

'Talking of folk being half scared out of their wits, how's your Sheila feeling now, Mary?' Mabel asked. 'Only my chap was saying that she's bound to be called to give evidence at the inquiry. He said he'd heard talk of how there'd bin a lot of gossip about her and the way she flirts wi' lads, and he reckons that George Duncan will say that she led him on, and wasn't making any fuss until Rosie interfered.'

'But that's not true,' Rosie fired up indignantly.

'Well, it might not be true that she was willing, but it is true that she's allus encouraging the lads to flirt with her, isn't it?' a plain sour-faced girl demanded sharply.

Rosie's heart sank as she remembered that the girl had already complained bitterly about Sheila's behaviour, claiming that she was giving them all a bad name.

'Sheila's pinched her chap off her is more like it,' Mary had said pithily at the time, and Rosie had thought that her friend was probably right.

'Anyone fancy going down the village to the pub Saturday night?' Audrey asked.

'Me and Ian are going to the pictures,' Mary answered her, whilst Rosie shook her head. She didn't want to do anything any more, only hear that Ricardo wasn't going to be unfairly punished for what he had done for her.

It was quiet in the hostel with it being Saturday evening, and those girls who had not gone home for the weekend having either hitched a lift or cycled into the town or gone down to the village pub.

Audrey had urged Rosie to go into Crewe with them to the dance hall, but Rosie had refused. It frightened her to think of how bleak and empty her life now felt. It would be different when her father came home. She would be busy taking care of him and making it up to him for all that he had gone through with her mother. She wondered if he'd received her letter yet and, if so, how long it would be before she heard back from him. It would be a terrible shock for him to read about his sister's death, but at least she had been able to tell him that she had been there with her, and she would make sure that she never let it slip that her aunt had tried to keep them apart and had let her go on thinking that he was dead.

She had always felt protective of her father, but never more so than now.

Ricardo would find someone else, she insisted stubbornly to herself. He was Italian, with a family who would insist on finding him a suitable wife, an Italian girl. She knew nothing really about his family other than that they were distantly related to the Volantes and lived in Manchester. There hadn't even been time for them to talk in detail about such things. But now for some reason she started to torment herself, trying to imagine what they were like.

Ricardo had told her he had returned to Italy on behalf of his grandfather. And what about Ricardo's parents? Was his mother like Maria or was she more like Sofia? If so, she would certainly not welcome a non-Italian as her daughter-in-law. And, of course, it wasn't impossible – far from it, in fact – that once her connection with the Grenellis was known to Ricardo's mother, questions would be asked, and when the answers were received she would be even more inclined to be hostile towards Rosie.

It surprised her a little that Ricardo had not spoken more frequently about his mother. She remembered how, in the Italian families she had known, the sons were always adored by their mothers and adored them in return. No good Italian son would marry a girl his mother had not approved. In Italian households, young brides knew to defer to their mothers-in-law, and if they didn't their husbands took them to task for their failure. An Italian male was a son first and a husband second. When a young Italian couple got married, it was a very important event for both their families and a matter of pride to have a huge and lavish wedding.

She might know the customs of Italian family life but she was still an outsider to that life, Rosie knew, and that was how she would be considered by Ricardo's family and their friends. So really, she was doing him a favour by not putting him in a position where his marriage would cause him to be isolated from his family. And no doubt it wouldn't be very long before he realised that for himself. And then he would look around for another girl to love and marry.

Tears filled Rosie's eyes and spilled down her cheeks. She tried to comfort herself by rereading her father's letters, but the ache in her heart wouldn't go away, not even though she knew she was doing the right thing. In fact, right now, doing the right thing seemed a sorry exchange for the happiness she had felt in Ricardo's arms.

Sunday brought more rain, but Mary's smile was beatific after the church service and the last reading of her and Ian's marriage banns. She went to join Ian straight after, and they went together back to the camp.

Rosie and her other friends were just about to start walking back to the hostel when another land girl came rushing up and burst out, white-faced, 'Oh, Rosie, I don't know how to tell you this. I'm ever so sorry . . .'

'What? What is it?' Rosie demanded.

'It's that Italian you was friendly with. The one that went and got himself in trouble over that foreman.'

Rosie could feel the sick dread twisting through

her stomach. 'Tell me,' she begged. 'Tell me quickly what's happened.'

'Well, he only went and ran off from the camp and tried to escape. He didn't get very far, mind. They soon caught up with him and took him back. But then – I really hate to have to tell you this, Rosie, but you'll hear it soon enough anyway, I reckon – it seems he got himself in that much of a state that he had to be locked up.'

Rosie couldn't speak. All this was her fault. None of it would have happened if Ricardo hadn't come to her rescue.

'And then this morning,' the other girl continued, speaking more slowly now and very uncomfortably, 'well, when they went to take him his breakfast they found he'd gone and hanged hisself.'

'No! No!'

'Rosie . . . Rosie! What did you have to go and tell her like that for, you stupid nit?' Jean snapped.

'I didn't mean no harm. She'd have found out soon enough anyway.'

'What's going on here?'

That was the warden, Mrs Johnson's, voice, Rosie recognised numbly as she stood stiffly, gripped by shock, and unable to say or do anything.

Someone was explaining what had happened and then the warden was saying calmly, 'Come along, Rosie. Let's get you back to the hostel and make you a nice cup of tea. One of you girls help her. She's bound to be feeling a bit shaky.'

'All right now, Rosie?' asked one of the land girls when they got back to the hostel, making Rosie a cup of tea.

Rosie looked blankly at the concerned face of the girl standing over her. How could anything ever be all right again? She had no recollection of the walk back from the village, or indeed, of anything other than hearing the dreadful news of Ricardo's death. How desperate and alone he must have felt to do such a thing. It was a crime against the law and against God for anyone to take their own life. Rosie started to shiver violently.

Why had he tried to escape? Because he feared what would happen to him because he had hit George Duncan? That was her fault. And her fault too that he had died believing that she had stopped loving him.

'Here, Rosie, drink this tea, there's a good girl.'

Obediently she gulped the hot sweet liquid from the cup someone else had to hold for her because she was trembling too much to hold it herself.

Ricardo was dead. He'd taken his own life.

She shuddered violently.

Ricardo. Ricardo . . . how could he be dead, when she loved him so much?

It was all her fault.

TWENTY-EIGHT

'What's going on? What's up with Rosie?'

Rosie heard Mary's voice sharpening with anxiety but she couldn't find the strength to speak to her friend. Instead she left it to the others to explain for her, hugging the numbing protection of her grief to her as their words slid in and out of her consciousness.

'She's heard about Ricardo.'

'What? I didn't think anyone else would know yet. Me and Ian have only just heard and I came straight back from camp to tell Rosie meself.' Mary was sounding very put out, Rosie noticed distantly.

'It's given her ever such a shock, Mary.'

'Mebbe, but I'd thought more of her than to see her looking like this, especially after all the trouble my Ian's been to, and the duke, an' all.'

'Well, you can't blame Rosie for feeling like she does, Mary. I reckon anyone would feel the same, hearing about a chap like Ricardo doing away wi' himself.'

'What? Who told you that?'

'Vera heard it in the village, didn't you, Vera?' Mabel spoke up.

'Yes. Everyone was talking about it. Given everyone a shock, it has. Of course, there's them as was saying that it's all on account of what happened with that George Duncan and that—'

Rosie dragged herself up from the chair she had been given. 'Stop it! Stop it, please,' she begged. She couldn't bear to hear any more.

'Rosie, it's all right,' Mary told her, coming over to her and taking hold of her to give her a small shake. 'Ricardo isn't dead. Vera's got it all wrong.' She gave a small sigh. 'It was that poor lad Paolo who went and did for himself.'

'Paolo? Are you sure?' Hope struggled inside her against her fear and the shame of knowing that whilst she would be saddened to hear of Paolo's death it couldn't cause her the same pain as Ricardo's.

''Course I'm sure. I wasn't going to say anything about it for now. I know you had a soft spot for the poor lad after what you did for him, but it seems that his spirits had got that low there was no reasoning wi' him, and there'd already been a lot of wild talk from him about doing away with himself. All he wanted was to go home but, of course, that wasn't possible. He tried to escape but he didn't get far. Daft lad couldn't speak a word of English and didn't have any money wi' him. You can't help feeling sorry for him. Your Ricardo will be cut up about him, of course, seeing as he'd bin doing his best to try to help the lad learn a bit of English and settle down.'

'He isn't my Ricardo,' Rosie told her, but she couldn't put the vehemence into her voice she knew should be there.

'Oh, so you don't want me to tell you what's going to happen to him then, do you?' Mary demanded, relenting when she saw the pain in Rosie's eyes. 'You are a softie. Fancy thinking that a chap like Ricardo would do himself in. He's got more sense than to do summat like that. And I'm not the only one as thinks highly of him, I can tell you. It seems that the duke himself has taken a hand in what's been going on. I told my Ian that he had to go and have a word with His Grace and make sure he knew all about our Sheila and that, but when he did the duke told him that he'd already made his own enquiries and found out about some of the things George Duncan had been up to. Mind you, I'm not saying that he wasn't grateful to my Ian for putting him straight,' Mary announced smugly, ignoring the teasing comments of those close by. 'Anyway, seemingly the duke has arranged for Ricardo to be released from his internment into his charge on the promise of good behaviour from Ricardo. He's to live in a cottage on one of the farms and take charge of the POWs that are sent to work for His Grace.'

Rosie could scarcely take it all in. To have gone from believing that Ricardo was dead to learning that he wasn't in such a short space of time had left her feeling unable completely to trust in the feeling of relief that had covered her earlier despair.

'Ricardo is to work for the duke?' she managed to question. 'But what about George Duncan?'

'Oh ho, well, he's got his comeuppance and no mistake. He's bin given his marching orders and told to leave. And not only by the duke. His wife has told him that she's going back to her family. Serves him right, if you ask me. Well, aren't you going to thank me?' Mary challenged Rosie teasingly. 'After all that my Ian's done.'

'Yes, Mary, of course I am,' Rosie told her fervently. 'Oh, but poor Paolo. How awful that he should feel so distressed that he . . . I hate to think of anyone feeling so unhappy that they did something like that, though,' she added sadly. 'I felt so sorry for him, Mary. He was so young and so dreadfully unhappy at being here. He wasn't a soldier at all, really, just a boy who had been forced into the army against his will.'

'I don't know how you can be hard-hearted enough to tell Ricardo that you don't want him any more, and then go moping over that lad.'

'You know why I can't be with Ricardo, and anyway—'

'Anyway what?' Mary challenged her.

'Ricardo's Italian and they always marry their own. His family won't want him marrying me any more than my dad would want me marrying him.'

'That's silly talk. It's what you and Ricardo want

that matters. Them old-fashioned ways don't count now that there's a war on.'

Rosie should have been asleep but instead she was lying in her bed wide awake, grieving for poor Paolo and yet at the same time feeling with every beat of her heart her joy that Ricardo was alive.

How different his life was going to be from now on. With a cottage provided on the duke's estate and the duke's confidence in his ability to act as a specially appointed sort of foreman in charge of the other Italian workers, the hopes for his future that Ricardo had shared with her had been not just fulfilled but exceeded. It hurt so much, knowing that she wouldn't be sharing that future with him.

She tried not to picture the cottage, cosy and private, somewhere where they could be alone as a married couple when they had finished work, but her own imagination was deliberately tormenting her. What would have happened if somehow she and Ricardo had actually got married before she had found out about her father?

Rosie's heart bumped uncomfortably. She mustn't think like that, she told herself guiltily.

'Oh, no, not the potato fields,' Sheila, who, once she had been told that George Duncan had been dismissed and that she wouldn't have to see him any more, had decided to stay on after all, groaned theatrically when they arrived at the farm on

Monday morning to be told that it was time to start harvesting the potato crop.

A piece of machinery attached to the tractor would unearth the potatoes – lift them, the farmer told them – and then it would be their job to gather them up.

It sounded a simple enough task but, as the girls soon discovered, if they got too close to the machine when it was lifting the potatoes they ended up sprayed with soil, and if they didn't get close enough the potatoes would start falling back into the furrows before they could get to them, which meant that they had to dig down to reach them.

It was dirty, exhausting work, especially on such a warm day, and those girls who had cheekily cut off the legs of their dungarees to turn them into shorts and get sun tans were very quickly regretting wearing them for potato picking when they ended up spattered with mud.

It wasn't until they broke for dinner that Rosie lifted her head from her work to realise that the Italians were back and working a couple of fields away.

'Ricardo's with them,' Mary told her unnecessarily, for his familiar back had been the first thing Rosie had looked for and focused on, recognising that it was only now that she had seen him that she felt truly able to believe that he was alive. 'Why don't you go over and speak to him, Rosie? I'll cover for you.'

'There's no point,' Rosie refused, but when she

dipped her head and turned her back on the men, her eyes were flooded with tears that she didn't want Mary to see.

'Well, if you won't talk to him then I certainly will,' Mary told her promptly.

'No, you mustn't tell him what I told you about my father,' Rosie began, but it was too late. Almost as soon as Rosie had spoken Mary had put down her sandwiches and was already walking nonchalantly towards the men.

Although she had tried not to do so, Rosie couldn't help but look across the fields to where she could see Mary talking with Ricardo. Was she telling him about her? Was he begging Mary to persuade her to change her mind? Did she want him to do that? It seemed an age before Mary came back.

'What did you say to him?' Rosie demanded urgently.

'I just told him what my Ian had done for him, and I said as how we was both sorry he had such a bad time,' Mary answered.

'You didn't say anything about me then?' Rosie persisted.

'I'm not telling you any more, Rosie, but I have to say that I wouldn't want to see my Ian looking so cast down and not himself. Proper thin, Ricardo is looking, and a bit drawn in the face too, like summat's really upsetting him,' Mary concluded meaningfully.

Rosie could feel her guilt growing by the

heartbeat. At the very least, she ought to go over and tell Ricardo how sorry she was about Paolo. That couldn't do any harm, could it? And it wasn't as though she'd be saying anything personal, if she did that. Not personal like about her and Ricardo and why she didn't want to see him any more. And besides, she had to see him, Rosie admitted, so that she'd be able to set her own mind at rest instead of worrying herself sick now that Mary had started going on about how poorly he looked.

Rosie put down her dinner and stood up, unaware of the small triumphant look Mary gave her as she took a deep breath and then set out across the field.

Ricardo made no attempt to pretend that he hadn't seen her. Rosie saw him throw aside the apple he had been eating, and come towards her, almost running over the furrowed field.

He *was* thinner. Rosie's heart flung itself against her chest wall as though urging her to fling herself into his arms. Now that he was within arm's reach of her, Ricardo was standing still, his brown-eyed gaze fastening on her face so hungrily that she wanted to cry.

'Rosie. My Rosie!'

Just hearing the fervent way in which he whispered her name flooded her with love. But when he came closer, and tried to take her hands, Rosie stepped back with a small agonised moan of denial. She dare not let him touch her.

'Rosie. My little love . . .' How Italian he sounded now as he breathed her name with such intense emotion.

'I just came to say how sorry I am about Paolo,' Rosie told him, using the words to hold him away from her. She shivered. 'Poor, poor boy, to do such a thing. He must have felt so alone.'

She could see her own pain mirrored in Ricardo's gaze.

'None of us had any idea. It was a shock to us all when he left the camp. We had all tried to talk to him and to cheer him up. We knew how much he missed his home and his family, but we never imagined he would do something like this. The war had made him sick at heart inside himself; he felt that he had let his family down by being captured. The elders of his village are strong supporters of Mussolini, and poor Paolo had never really wanted to fight. He was a country boy who loved his family, not a fighter. He should never have been forced to go to war.' Now Rosie could hear anger as well as sadness in Ricardo's voice. 'He has paid the ultimate price for the warmongering pride of others. And he will not be the only one to do so. This war has many different kinds of casualties. Please don't make our love one of them, Rosie. I have missed you so much. Longed for you so much, my Rosie.'

Rosie began to panic. Every word he said was making it harder for her to remember why they could not be together. 'No, no, you mustn't say that,' she told him, and, 'I'm not your Rosie. I – I can't be. Not now.'

'Because of your father.'

Rosie stared up at him, torn between relief and anger. 'You know? How? Mary told you?' she guessed. 'She had no right.'

'But surely as the man who loves you, and who believes that you love him, I have every right to know why you are doing this? You must not blame Mary. I begged her to tell me. If she broke a confidence between the two of you then she did so in the belief that what she was doing was right. She told me as your friend, because she is concerned for you. Concerned that you are mistaken in believing that your father would want you to deny our love for one another.'

'She had no right,' Rosie repeated. 'Mary doesn't understand. My father has bitter memories of . . . of the past and my mother's relationship with an Italian. Seeing me with you would only remind him of what he suffered. I can't cause him that kind of pain.'

'But you can inflict pain on me and on yourself?'

How could she bear this? But somehow she must find a way to do so. 'There's no point in saying any of this, Ricardo, and besides . . .'

'Besides what?'

'You're Italian,' Rosie told him almost accusingly. 'You know as well as I do that your parents, especially your mother, will expect you to marry an Italian girl.'

The look in his eyes made her feel small and mean. 'So, now you want to include my parents in this blame? Well, you cannot do so. I will not allow it. My mother will want me to marry the girl I love.'

Rosie's look was scornful. His own words had proved the point she had just made. 'I've lived in an Italian community, Ricardo. I know all about how much Italian mothers worship their sons, and how they expect those sons to take wives they approve of.'

Ricardo shrugged. 'My mother loves me, yes, but why should you think that she will not approve of you?'

Rosie was losing her patience. 'Because I'm not Italian,' she repeated.

'No, that is true you are not, but then neither is my mother.'

Rosie gaped at him, unable to conceal her astonishment. 'She isn't? But . . .'

'My father also fell in love with an English girl and he married her. It is true that his parents, my grandparents, were not entirely accepting of my mother at first, but in the way of things, once the *bambini* arrived all was forgiven. What Italian *nonna* can ever resist her grandchildren, eh? So my mother was forgiven and truly welcomed into the family. So much so, in fact, that my grandparents chose to live with my father and my mother rather than with one of my father's sisters and their families. You see, Rosie, with love, if you have enough of it, anything is possible. No, don't look at me like that with your lovely eyes full of tears,' Ricardo begged her rawly.

But it was too late, she had already done so, and now she was in his arms and he was kissing her so tenderly that Rosie felt as though her heart was melting with love for him.

'Your father will understand,' he whispered to her.

'No,' Rosie told him brokenly. 'No, he won't, Ricardo, and I can't ask him to. I can't! Please don't make this even harder for me than it already is. If you truly love me you will understand and accept that we cannot be together.' She broke free of his hold and stood back from him.

'Rosie,' he pleaded.

'No. No more, please. I can't bear it.'

'And you think that I can? I, who love you and who want you as my wife, the mother of our children. You are everything to me, Rosie – my love, my woman, my future.'

'No! No!'

Rosie felt as though she were in mortal agony and dying from a thousand wounds. Her tears fell as though they were her blood and she was dying from the pain of having her love ripped from her. But she could not abandon her father. She was all he – a badly wounded victim of the war – had. He had written bravely of losing his leg but he would need her now, not just emotionally but practically as well, once he came home.

Thinking about her father steadied her a little, allowing her to regain control of her emotions. She took a deep breath. 'I'm sorry about Paolo, really I am. And . . . and I'm pleased about . . . about you getting the cottage and everything, and not being in trouble for hitting the foreman, but you've got to forget about me and . . . and look for someone else. It's for the best, for both of us.'

The look Ricardo was giving her told her how little he agreed with what she had said.

'How can giving up our love be for the best?' he demanded savagely.

'It's the best for my dad,' Rosie told him. 'And . . . and I can't let him down like my mother did, Ricardo. I just can't. He needs me now.'

'And you think that I don't? I am not giving up, Rosie. I will find a way for us to be together.'

To Rosie's relief, Ricardo didn't wait for her to answer him, simply turning on his heel instead and walking back across the field.

It was over. For a few sweet, short and precious days she had known love and believed in it. But now the realities of life were crowding in on her, taking root where it should have grown.

The week felt like it was never going to end. Every day that passed was harder for Rosie to get through as she tried to ignore the fact that Ricardo was working only a field away.

On the Wednesday, at dinner time, Mary told her defiantly, 'I know you won't like this but me and Ian are inviting Ricardo to our wedding. I'm just going across to tell him now.'

Rosie didn't want to watch them talking together but somehow she couldn't stop herself from looking yearningly towards the other field. She saw that Mary had reached Ricardo and was handing him something. But when Ricardo leaned down and kissed Mary on the cheek Rosie had to look away.

It lifted her spirits a little bit to find a letter from her father waiting for her when they got back to the hostel after their day's work. She went up to the dormitory to read it, sitting down on her bed and then frowning as she realised that the drawer in which she had put his letters was slightly open. She must have left it like that without realising it, she decided, as she closed it again and opened his new letter.

He was overjoyed to have heard from her, he had written, but shocked and sad to learn of the death of his sister. She was not to worry about him or fret for him, for he was doing very well in Canada and had the kindest of new friends in the couple he was lodging with – a fellow sailor and his wife who had made him feel very much at home.

You would love it here, Rosie. It's a
wonderful country. I wish you could be here
with me to see it. I'm not saying that it's been
easy getting used to the fact that I've had to

lose my leg. It hasn't. But at least I'm still here and alive, and there's many a poor chap who will have worse to face than me when this war's over and he's back on civvy street. Of course I won't be able to sign on under the Red Duster no more – but I dare say I'll be able to get myself a bit of a job somewhere.

Rosie had told him in her own letter that she wasn't seeing Rob any more and he had gone on to write teasingly that he would look around for a nice young Canadian for her.

It's a good place for young ones, Rosie, and maybe after the war you'll be able to see that for yourself. Of course he'd have to be willing to give your old dad a berth, seeing as how I'm likely to be shore bound from now on. I've told Pat and Arthur all about you and how proud I am of my lovely girl and how proud I am to call you my daughter, Rosie. And don't you ever think any different than that, because it's the truth. Your aunt shouldn't have said what she did to you and that's a fact. She didn't mean any real harm. She just got a bit carried away, that's all, and said more than she should have done. Your mum never ever said anything about you not being mine, and knowing her and how she felt about Aldo, it seems to me that if you had bin his she would have told me so. In fact, between you and me now, Rosie, there was times when I worried that she wasn't treating you as lovingly as a mother should and I worried that it was on account of you being mine and not his. It made me feel proper angry, that did. Of course I know she was always taking you round there to them Italians, but if you was to ask me I'd have said that that was on account of her wanting to go round there so as she could see him. And they certainly didn't think you was one of their own. Leastways, that sister of Maria's never did. Told me once, she did, that she was sick of your mother carrying on with her sister's husband and that she'd told Maria to put her foot down and put a stop to it. Had a real go at me, she did, and all, saying as how I should have done something about it. But you know what your mum was like, Rosie. She'd made up her mind that it was him she wanted and nothing was going to stop her from seeing him. I don't want you ever thinking badly of yourself though, Rosie, or thinking that I don't believe you're my own girl. I've bin thinking a lot about how it was when I last saw you. What with the shock of hearing about your mum's death and everything, I didn't perhaps make it as plain to you as I should have done that I've never gone along with your auntie's daft talk. Your mum's gone now, may she rest in peace, and you and me can have a fresh start once this war is over. Who knows, we could even end up living here in Canada. It's a fine country.

I want you to forget about all that silly stuff your auntie came out with and to remember until we can be together again, that you are my girl and you always will be.

And he had signed the letter, 'From your loving dad.'

By the time she had read the letter three times over, Rosie's heart was overflowing with love. If she closed her eyes she could almost see him, his face weathered by the sea's salt-laden winds, his blue eyes warm with love as he smiled at her. He had always walked with a sailor's slightly rolling gait. With the loss of his leg that walk would have changed, and so too, she imagined, would the familiar salt and tar smell she always associated with his return from sea. She didn't know enough about Canada to be able to picture him against a Canadian background in the same way that she could so easily picture him against the backdrop of Liverpool's docks, where she had gone so often as a young girl to wait for him coming off his ship, kitbag over his shoulder, his face crinkling into a wide smile the moment he saw her. Then he would stand there, putting his kitbag down and holding out his arms so that she could run into them and be swung up onto his shoulders.

He had cared for her and loved her unstintingly throughout her childhood, and now it was her turn and her pleasure to do the same for him. His sister's house would provide them with a comfortable roof over their heads, and she could work even if her father couldn't. They would manage – somehow – and she would be happy – somehow.

'Oooh, Rosie, that looks ever so nice, it really does.'

The enthusiasm in Audrey's voice as she studied the flowers and greenery with which Rosie had just finished decorating the church hall made Rosie force an answering smile.

The last thing she wanted to do was in any way spoil Mary and Ian's special day, so she had thrown herself into helping with the arrangements for the wedding and put her own unhappiness to one side. The result was that she had virtually decorated the church and the church hall single-handedly, with the greenery and flowers they had all gathered from the hedgerows, and those kind villagers who had offered them flowers from their gardens, wild poppies, and pale pink dog roses from the hedgerows, ragged robin and verbena. Cultivated roses of every shade, there were, and large white garden daisies, white, blue, lilac and purple larkspur and delphiniums, and many more.

Everywhere did indeed look very pretty, Rosie acknowledged as she pushed her hair out of her eyes before climbing down the stepladder on which she had been perching to go to put the final blooms into place over the lich-gate.

Mary's parents had arrived earlier in the week and were staying in the village, and Rosie, along with the other girls, had oohed and ahhed over the wedding dress they had brought with them. Clothing coupons now meant that Mary could not have a brand-new dress, but one of her cousins had been married the previous year and her dress had been passed on and retrimmed.

Everyone had done their bit to help, and seeing Mary all aglow with excitement and happiness had made Rosie all the more aware of what she had given up. She must not dwell on that, though, she told herself determinedly. Instead she must just think about being happy for Mary and Ian; and remembering poor Peggy, who would now never stand where Mary would be standing tomorrow, being joined in marriage to the man she loved; and of course the end of the war and her own life with her father.

Mary's closest group of friends, which included Rosie, had been given permission to finish work at dinner time so that they could set to and help with the organisation of the wedding. Now with the flowers all finished and the light fading, Rosie came down off the ladder, propped on the lich-gate, and asked Audrey, 'What else is there to do yet?'

'There's still the tables and that to put up in the village hall, ready for the wedding breakfast. Did you say you'd done some flowers for the top table, Rosie?'

'Yes. I left them in the church porch. It's cooler there and, with so many of them being wild flowers, they won't last more than a day at most.'

'Some of Ian's pals have come over from Hack Green to give us a hand, and by the sound of it when I left the hall half an hour ago, some people are celebrating this wedding already.' Audrey chuckled. 'The lads have brought down a gramophone and some records. A bit of music whilst you're working really helps to get things going, doesn't it?'

Rosie nodded, folding up the ladder, which the vicar had loaned her.

'If it stays fine like it's supposed to, they'll have a lovely day for the wedding tomorrow,' Audrey observed, looking up at the clear sky before tucking her arm through Rosie's as they walked down to the village hall.

The village itself might be quiet and peaceful, but inside the village hall it was anything but. The sound of Vera Lynn singing could hardly be heard above the bustle of activity and excitement.

A group of young men in RAF uniform were busily putting up trestle tables, whilst the girls, watched over by Mary's mother, were covering them with sheets to hide the trestles and then with tablecloths.

'It's really kind of the duke to send down them plates and glasses and things to help out,' Audrey commented. 'He's let Mary have a couple of chickens as well, and they've sent down some tins of ham and fruit and that from the NAAFI, she was telling me yesterday.'

'Come on, you two, don't just stand there watching, give us a hand,' Sheila demanded breathlessly, hurrying over to them.

'Oh, you're a fine one to talk,' Audrey laughed. 'The last time I came in here you was dancing with some lad.'

'I was just doin' me duty, that's all,' Sheila grinned. 'On account of him not knowing how to dance close up, like, with a girl.'

'Go on with you. You never fell for that one, did you?' Audrey shook her head. 'I heard the other day about this girl that was that soft that when she was on the train and some young soldier pretended to faint, she was daft enough to get down on the floor to have a look. Of course, the chap was only pretending, and the next thing she knew he was grabbing hold of her and giving her a kiss.'

'I never said that I believed him,' Sheila laughed.

'Just look at her,' Audrey told Rosie when Sheila danced off to talk to someone else. 'You'd never think looking at her now that only a few weeks ago she was all ready to go home because that George Duncan had scared her half silly. You think that would have taught her a lesson she wouldn't forget in a hurry, but then that's Sheila for you.' Audrey had had to raise her voice during the last part of her conversation, due to the sudden surge in the level of excited laughter and jollity behind them, when a couple more men in RAF uniform arrived carrying some bottles of spirits.

Rosie was still nodding in acknowledgement of the truth of what she had said when Audrey called out to her, 'Come on, let's go and get a drink before it's all gone.'

'No, you can't have a drink. This is for the punch,' Ian's best man, Tommy Lucas, refused, mock dramatically clutching the bottles to his chest and calling out to the other men, 'Save me, lads. These girls are after trying to grab hold of me assets.'

'We're not going to let him get away with not letting us have a drink, are we, girls?' Sheila challenged. 'Come on.'

In the play fight that ensued, somehow or other the bottles remained intact and untouched, which was more than could be said for the modesty of the girls who had flung themselves at them, or the airmen's clothes.

Rosie watched from the sidelines. The pressure of war meant that it was rare for healthy young people to get the chance really to let off steam with members of the opposite sex, and although the mêlée of arms and legs that resulted from the free-for-all went a bit further than Rosie would have wanted to go herself, she couldn't help joining in the laughter when Sheila emerged from it, flushed and breathless and laughing triumphantly as she waved Tommy's trousers in the air.

Completely unabashed, once he had struggled

free, Tommy pulled them back on and winked at Sheila, telling her, 'Now that you've had a bit of a look at what's on offer, how about you and me cutting loose from this lot so that I can show you me tattoo?'

'Oh, give over, do,' Sheila laughed back, as un-embarrassed as he was.

Such high spirits were only natural, and an acceptable part of the fun of the pre-wedding proceedings, when you didn't know what tomorrow would bring, and whether or not the young man you had flirted with tonight would still be alive then.

It was dark by the time the punch had been made and sampled. In view of its strength and the effect on everyone's libidos of the alcohol, a wedding and a full August moon, it was no wonder that some of the girls paired up with the airmen for the walk back through the village to the hostel.

Rosie had already seen Mary and Ian slip away hand in hand, a look in Mary's eye that made her own mist with emotion.

Not that she was the only girl to be walking back to the hostel without a partner. Audrey and Jean, who were with her, both commented ruefully that they suspected there would be some sore heads and red faces in the morning.

'Sheila wants to do something with Mary's wedding night suitcase – you know, put a bit of stuff in it for a joke, like, but I don't know as we should. What do you think, Rosie?'

'A joke's a joke, and no one minds a bit of a laugh, just so long as it doesn't spoil her clothes,' Rosie answered her.

'Well, there's no confetti.'

'I've collected some flower petals to throw, but they would stain her clothes. We could put a bit of rice in, perhaps.'

'Yes. Good idea.'

Rosie hadn't been sleeping properly since she had broken up with Ricardo, and when she saw Mary slip from her bed and go over to the blacked-out window, she went after her to ask if everything was all right.

'Oh, yes,' Mary whispered emphatically. 'More than all right, Rosie. I can't tell you how happy I am and how lucky I feel right now to be marrying Ian tomorrow. I'm too excited to sleep and somehow I don't want to. I don't want to waste a second of feeling like this. I wish that I could hold on to it and bottle it in one of them Kilner jars and keep it for ever. I never thought I'd be one to feel this way. Of course, I wanted to get married and have kiddies, but I'm the practical type and it's our Sheila that I've always thought of as more the one who would fall head over heels in love and go mooning around all over the place. But me and Ian . . . I just love him so much.'

She turned her head and Rosie could see the tears filling her eyes. 'I was just thinking about Peggy.'

'I was thinking about her today as well,' Rosie acknowledged.

There was a small silence, and then Mary said softly, 'No matter what happens from now on, Rosie, I shall have had this. I never thought that I could be this happy or this much in love. Me heart feels that full of love and happiness I can hardly believe it.' She gave a soft laugh. 'Just listen at me. I sound more like our Sheila than meself, but I still can't wait for tomorrow, and to be standing next to my Ian in church, exchanging vows with him.'

Rosie couldn't speak. She managed to nod her head, though, and hug Mary back as fiercely as she was hugging her.

As she went back to her bed, the full force of what she herself had given up descended on her, enveloping her in bleak black misery.

There would never be another man she would love the way she loved Ricardo. She knew that instinctively. He had touched something deep inside her she hadn't even known was there, awakening dreams and hopes so precious and private she wanted to wrap them away as carefully as Mary wanted to bottle her happiness. Only Mary's happiness now was just the beginning of her love, whereas her own bittersweet memories were all that she would ever have of love.

It was a long time before Rosie was able to escape from her thoughts into sleep.

*　　*　　*

'They've bin right lucky with the day, and our Mary's bin so lucky with all her friends as well, especially you, Rosie. Why, these flowers you've done for her would be fit for the grandest wedding you could imagine. A real flair you've got, and no mistake.'

'Indeed she has,' the vicar's wife added her own praise to that of Mary's mother as they all waited outside the church where Ian's comrades in arms were lined up, wearing their dress uniforms, to provide a traditional guard of honour for the newly married couple.

'Here they are now,' the vicar's wife warned.

All the guests surged forward, throwing the rose petals Rosie had collected over the bride and groom so that their clothes and those of the guard of honour were scattered with petals.

It was a perfect day for a wedding – blue sky, sunshine, the village picture-postcard pretty, and the bride truly lovely in her glowing happiness as she held on to the arm of her new husband when they walked slowly amongst their guests and then on through the village to the church hall.

Rosie had deliberately kept herself as busy as she could, volunteering for all manner of necessary jobs in her desperation not to have to be aware of Ricardo. But of course that had been impossible. She had no idea where or how he had got the smart suit he was wearing, his thick curly hair neatly slicked back beneath the hat he had removed when they all went into church. He was taller than nearly all of the other men present, and broader too, and Rosie had overheard one of the airmen comment to him knowledgeably that he had the look of a boxer, to which Ricardo had replied that he wasn't a fighting man but that he had grown up with a crowd of boys who had frequented one of the local boxing clubs and gyms that were part of the Italian immigrant social scene. Such clubs, as Rosie knew from her own growing-up, did a lot of good for their local communities, often sponsoring outings and charities, and were often closely linked to a church. Even her father had been heard to say that he would rather see young lads working off their energy at St Joseph's gym, and learning a thing or two about handling themselves with the right sort of person, than hanging around the street and getting into trouble.

Rosie was acutely aware of Ricardo now, even though he was standing several yards away from her and had his back to her. Somehow it was as though her very skin possessed the ability to know when he was there and react to that fact, she admitted wretchedly.

He had been given permission by the duke to whom he was now 'paroled', to attend the wedding, so Mary had told her, and to judge from the laughter coming from the group of airmen and land girls surrounding him, his company was very welcome. Sheila, as Rosie had already noticed jealously, was flirting outrageously with him, but then as chief bridesmaid no doubt she felt it was her duty to go round making sure that everyone was having a good time – just so long as 'everyone' meant all the best-looking men!

Not that Sheila was reserving her attentions exclusively for Ricardo, Rosie had to admit. She had seen her earlier clinging to the arm of the young airman whose trousers she had held aloft so triumphantly the previous evening.

She shouldn't criticise Sheila nor be resentful of her because she was having such a good time with Ricardo, making him laugh in a way that showed how much he was enjoying her company, Rosie told herself. After all, hadn't she herself told Ricardo that he must find someone else? Ricardo and Sheila. Rosie tried to smother the sharp pang that racked her.

It was too soon yet for her to expect to receive another letter from her father – he would probably only just have received her own letter to him – but she couldn't help thinking about him now because although she was in a room that was packed with people, she still felt miserably alone. Sheila might have lost her parents in a bombing raid but at least she had a loving aunt and uncle in Mary's parents, along with the comfort of a large extended family of cousins, aunts and uncles, whilst she had no one apart from her father, Rosie thought sadly.

'Come on, Rosie. Sam here wants to dance with you but he's too shy to ask.'

Politely Rosie suffered Mary's mother's kindly

meant matchmaking as she introduced Rosie to one of Mary's cousins, a bespectacled, earnest-looking young man, so shy that he was inarticulate, his Adam's apple bobbling up and down wildly as he looked at Rosie and blushed, whilst making some strangulated sounds that Rosie guessed must be an attempt at conversation. It wasn't in her nature to be nasty, so she smiled good-naturedly and discreetly managed to steer him round the dance floor.

Not that Sam was her only choice of partner. The young airmen weren't backward in coming forward to ask her to dance and, of course, good manners meant that she couldn't refuse. There might be safety in numbers, she acknowledged later on in the evening when she had returned to her seat after a dance with yet another partner, but a treacherous little voice inside her was telling her that there was something much sweeter and more alluring about having a one-and-only to dance with and be held tenderly by, the way that Ian was holding Mary now as they circled the floor together, lost to everything but their love for one another.

And Mary wasn't the only girl enjoying being held close by her partner as the music changed to a smoochy romantic number. Sheila was dancing with Ricardo – again – her head nestled against his shoulder as she snuggled into him. The lights dipped and Ian took the opportunity to kiss his new wife. Everyone clapped and roared their approval and then when the lights came on again

Rosie saw that Ian wasn't the only man with a smudge of lipstick staining his mouth. Ricardo too had obviously made good use of the dipped lights to kiss his partner.

Rosie stood up, almost pushing her chair over in her sudden frantic need to be somewhere where she didn't have to see Ricardo with someone else. Ignoring the concerned looks she was attracting from the others at the table, she almost ran towards the door, half stumbling as she did so.

Outside, a full moon washed the village in pale yellow light. In the semi-darkness, the scent of the land was so much sharper somehow, and so very different from Liverpool. Here she could smell sun-warmed soil, and the dried stubble from the fields, along with the closer scents of still warm tarmac, cottage garden plants, and even the beer from the local pub. Rosie leaned her head against the stone gatepost in front of the village hall. Almost without her being aware of it, she had grown fond of the country and would miss it when the time came to return to Liverpool. Soon Mary and Ian would be setting off on their short honeymoon, the beginning of their married life together. How must that feel? Being married to the man you loved, and knowing that tonight you would be together in every sense of the word, knowing that what you shared tonight marked the beginning of a new life, knowing that it must be guarded carefully because who knew what unhappiness war might bring?

'Rosie, I have to talk to you.'

She had been so lost in her own thoughts that she hadn't heard Ricardo walking towards her until he spoke her name.

She spun round, her eyes huge with angry pride and pain.

'What about?' Rosie demanded. 'You and Sheila? Well, you needn't bother. I've seen for myself what's going on.'

'Me and Sheila . . . ?'

She could hear Ricardo swallowing a sound that was a mixture of disbelief and a groan.

'Don't be silly. You're the one I want. You know that.'

'I certainly know what I've seen,' Rosie agreed bitterly.

She didn't want to stand out here with him in the moonlight, where she was all too vulnerable to her own feelings.

'I'm going back inside,' she told him, but as she went to walk past him he took hold of her. The feel of his hands on the soft bare flesh of her upper arms made her suck in her breath and give a small low moan of anguish.

'Rosie. Did I hurt you? I'm sorry, I didn't mean to.'

He was rubbing the flesh of her arms gently, having mistaken the cause of her pain, whilst he pressed small pleading kisses on her face, begging her to forgive him.

Rosie couldn't bear it. It was too much. She tried to pull away from him but somehow ended up in his arms, crying against his shoulder whilst he held her tight and begged her to tell him what was wrong.

'I am wrong, we are wrong, this is wrong,' Rosie tried to say but the words just wouldn't come out and when she looked up at him to speak them, Ricardo cupped her face gently and kissed her so slowly and lovingly that Rosie wept even more.

'Go back to Sheila,' she stormed at him. 'And see how she likes knowing that you've been out here two-timing her with me.'

'Rosie,' Ricardo protested, but it was too late. Rosie had taken advantage of his confused distress to pull away from him.

She couldn't go back to the village hall, not with her face streaked with tears, and everyone there to see them and talk about them. Instead, she went back to the hostel, empty and quiet with all the girls and even Mrs Johnson down at the village hall enjoying the wedding celebrations.

Ricardo and Sheila. She couldn't bear it but somehow she would have to.

TWENTY-NINE

September had given way to October and the
weather had turned wet and windy. The gang had
been set to work hedging and ditching, a horrible
job that involved clearing ditches of brambles and
weeds to drain the land. Rosie had developed a
dry nagging cough that hurt her ribs and left her
feeling deathly tired.

She shivered now in the driving rain. Ricardo
and the other men were working several fields
away and Rosie's blurring gaze kept returning to
the distant smudges of movement that were the
men. It should have been impossible for her to tell
which one Ricardo was, but somehow she could.

In contrast to her own despair, Mary was singing
happily under her breath as she worked. She and
Ian had just had three days off duty together in
Ricardo's cottage whilst he had bunked in with
one of the other farm hands.

'It was so kind of Ricardo to let us use the
cottage. Our Sheila told me that it was ever such

a cosy place, but I must admit I was surprised when I saw how nice Ricardo has got it. Given it a coat of lime wash right through inside, he has, and Mrs Graham up at the Home Farm has found him some bits of furniture she didn't want.'

Rosie couldn't muster the smile her pride was demanding. It had been weeks now since she had given him up and yet, if anything, it hurt even more than at first knowing that Sheila and Ricardo were together. Not that anyone talked about it in her presence, but she had seen Sheila walking across the fields in the direction of Ricardo's cottage on several occasions, and now here was Mary confirming what Rosie had guessed was happening.

Soon it would be a year since she had been trapped in the Durning Road Technical College bombing, and then after that it would be the anniversary of her mother's death. Rosie shivered again. It wasn't particularly cold but she felt as though she would never be warm again, as though the damp had forced its way right into the heart of her body and her bones. Several of the girls had commented on how much weight she had lost and her constant cough.

'I suppose you'll have heard – about our Sheila,' Mary told her now, looking slightly uncomfortable.

'I had guessed, yes,' she admitted, her voice low.

'Well, she couldn't have kept it a secret for much longer. My mother wasn't too pleased at having to sort out another wedding so soon after my own . . .'

Rosie felt a surge of sick faintness wash over her. 'They're getting married?'

'They don't have much choice, do they?' Mary told her bluntly. 'Not with our Sheila being in the family way. I've told her that she's lucky that he's prepared to do the right thing by her, and marry her, and that many a lad wouldn't, but then he is a decent sort. I knew that she'd been sneaking away to see him, of course, but I didn't realise she'd let things go that far. And you can't blame him, not with the way she carries on. Rosie? Rosie, are you all right?' Rosie heard Mary demanding sharply before the blackness overwhelmed her and sucked her down into its depths.

'Rosie. Oh, thank goodness you've come round.'

Rosie looked up at Mary. She was, she realised, lying on the muddy ground where she had passed out whilst Mary and a couple of the other girls crouched over her.

'You gave me ever such a shock, fainting like that,' Mary told her. 'Whatever's to do? I know you haven't bin so good recently, with that cough and everything, but it gave me a real shock when you passed out like that. I've sent Audrey across the fields to get Ricardo, but I reckon you need to see a doctor.'

Rosie struggled to sit up, panic filling her at the thought of Ricardo seeing her so vulnerable; Ricardo, who was marrying Sheila because she was having his baby. Rosie couldn't believe there could be so much pain. It filled her and flowed over her, until it totally possessed her and she had no escape from it.

'I'm sure that Ricardo will make a good husband and father for Sheila and the baby.' Rosie didn't know how she managed to get the words out, they hurt so much.

'Ricardo?' Mary was looking at her in astonishment. 'You surely aren't thinking that it's Ricardo that Sheila has got herself into trouble with, are you, Rosie?'

Numbly Rosie looked at her.

'Well, of all the daft things. What on earth put that idea into your head? No. It's Tommy Lucas, Ian's best man, the one whose trousers she took off the night before the wedding. Sneaking off together in the evening, the two of them have bin doing, making use of the blackout for stuff it was never intended for, an' all. But like I said, at least the lad's prepared to do the decent thing by her. Oh, good, here's Ricardo now. He'll know what to do . . .'

It was too much for Rosie to take in, too much for her to cope with right now, when she felt so ill, and too much for her to bear knowing that Ricardo was here. She could hear Mary telling him what had happened.

'She hasn't bin well for a while, Ricardo, and if you ask me she's bin pining for you that badly she's made herself ill.'

'No! That's not true.' Rosie finally managed to

sit up. 'I'm all right, there's nothing wrong with me,' she insisted valiantly, struggling to her feet, even though she had to hold on to the hedge to keep herself upright.

'No, not much,' Mary agreed drily. 'She only went and passed right out because she thought it was you that has got our Sheila into trouble, Ricardo.'

How could Mary betray her like this? But before Rosie could tell her how she felt, a bout of coughing had her doubled over, unable to speak.

'You should see a doctor,' Ricardo announced.

'Exactly what I've bin saying to her, Ricardo, but she won't listen. I've never known anyone as stubborn as Rosie is.' Mary shook her head.

'I keep telling you, there's nothing wrong with me, or at least there wouldn't be if certain people left me alone,' Rosie said sharply. 'Haven't you got some fields to plough?' she asked Ricardo pointedly. She saw the look he and Mary exchanged, but she turned her back on them both defiantly and went back to work.

Beneath her defensive anger, though, she was greedily lingering over the stolen pleasure of seeing Ricardo. Farm work had strengthened and corded the muscles in his arms, and Rosie shivered inwardly at the thought of his maleness. He needed a haircut and there was smudge of dirt on his forehead where he must have pushed his hair out of the way. He still smelled the same, though – of coffee and clean fresh hardworking man, and of himself. It was a scent she would carry in her memory until her dying day.

'That really is a nasty cough you've got, you know, Rosie,' Audrey pointed out as a fit of coughing had Rosie almost bent double. Leaning against the wet hedge, and unable to speak for the pain in her chest, Rosie waited for the discomfort to go.

'It's all this rain,' she told Audrey when she could finally speak. 'It gets on my chest.' The days were drawing in, giving them shorter working hours, which was a relief, but the cold wet conditions in which they were working meant that Rosie felt constantly chilled and unwell. Not that she was one to complain. It didn't seem right to do that when none of the other girls seemed to be as badly affected by the weather as she was.

She could do with a tonic of some kind, though, she admitted tiredly later as she slumped against the side of the truck taking them back to the hostel. She was waking up at night coughing and she was uncomfortably aware of the fact that she was probably disturbing the other girls' sleep as well as her own. Mary, who was on leave with Ian, so that they could attend Sheila's quickly arranged wedding at home in Birmingham, had said to her only the other week that she ought to go to see a doctor, but Rosie didn't feel she wanted to take up a doctor's time when there was really nothing wrong with her.

The first thing she did when they got back to

the hostel was go and have a warm shower, but not even that could drive the cold out of her bones.

'Postie's delivered a whole sack full of letters today. There's one here for you, Rosie,' Jean called out as she sorted through the mail that had been delivered whilst they were out working.

The sight of her father's familiar handwriting on the letter Jean handed to her lifted Rosie's spirits. She went straight up to the dormitory with it so that she could read it in private, impatiently opening the envelope, delighted to see that her father had covered both sides of several sheets of writing paper. He had written,

Rosie, Rosie, oh, love, I am so sorry and I feel so guilty. Your Ricardo has written to me to tell me what's been happening between the two of you and how you've told him that you don't want to see him any more because of me, and him being Italian.

He says that you love him and if that's true, Rosie lass, and something tells me, as your loving dad, that it is, then I feel really bad. I wouldn't for one moment want you to put yourself through any kind of unhappiness on my account, Rosie, and I just wish I was there so that I could speak to you myself and tell you truthfully that all I want is for you to be happy. Ricardo has told me all about himself and his family and he's been straight with me as a man should be when he wants to marry a chap's daughter, but he's also stood up for himself and said how it is for him being both Italian and English, and I respect him for that. I would not want my precious girl to be wed to a chap who doesn't think anything of himself. He sounds a decent sort, your Ricardo, Rosie. A straight-up, honest lad who will do the right thing by you and look after you like he should.

I can't pretend that it wasn't a shock when I first got his letter, especially with you not having said a word, but then when I read what he'd written about you not wanting to hurt me by marrying an Italian, but him believing after what you'd told him about me that I was the kind of dad who would only want his daughter to be happy, I warmed to the lad and appreciated his honesty. He wrote that he could understand my feelings on account of your mother, but that he felt sure that I wouldn't want you to give up the man you loved because he happened to be part Italian. And he's right, Rosie. Oh, my poor girl, I'm not ashamed to tell you, lass, that I cried some tears when I read what he had written to me about you; how much he loved you and what a special girl you are, but most of all on account of knowing the sadness you've been going through.

Rosie love, I would never expect you to give

up Ricardo on my account, and if I was there with you I reckon none of this foolishness would have happened. Being your loving dad I would have seen that something was wrong with my girl and found out just what it was pretty sharpish, and of course, as Ricardo said in his letter to me, he would have been able to come and see me and talk to me man to man about everything. Did I tell you that he wrote that he 'didn't think Rosie could have had a better father' and that when his turn came to be a dad to a little girl he hoped that I'd be on hand to help him learn the ropes, since his dad and mum only had boys?

He sent me some really nice photographs of himself and his family. Would you credit it, his mum looks a proper English rose. He's explained to me how he got to be interned, and it seems to me that this duke is a shrewd chap for seeing the good in him and helping him out.

I don't want to hear about you going through any more unhappiness, Rosie, and I want you to understand that the most important thing in the world to me is you, and you being happy. If you love this lad as he says you do then I promise you that the pair of you have my blessing. I've written to Ricardo too, telling him that you've both got my blessing.

Your always loving dad

PS. Write me soon, Rosie, to tell me how you are. I'll be worrying until I hear from you.

Ricardo had written to her father! How dare he do such a thing? How could he have done it? How had he got her father's address? Rosie frowned as she looked at the drawer where she kept her letters. Mary must have got it for him. She had never felt so angry or so betrayed. I'm not giving up, Ricardo had told her, but she had never imagined he would do something like this.

Her poor dad. What must he have gone through when he had received Ricardo's letter right out of the blue with no warning? Hadn't Ricardo realised how unfair he was being? How cruel? Of course her father would say now that he didn't mind – Rosie had known all along that that would be his reaction. She had never ever doubted her father's love for her and had known that he would put her feelings first. But that wasn't what she had wanted. She hadn't wanted to feel that her father had been forced to accept Ricardo for her sake.

Had Ricardo received her father's letter yet? And if he had, did he think that he had won and that everything was now all right? A grim determination seized her. Putting down her father's letter, Rosie stood up.

'Rosie, where are you going? It's almost supper time.'

'I've got to go out. I shan't be long,' Rosie called

back to Jean before stepping out into the darkness of the wet October evening.

It was just over two miles across the fields from the village to Ricardo's small cottage, by way of a narrow footpath. Not a particularly long walk, on a fine summer's day, but not a walk to be attempted by an emotionally wrought young woman with a bad cough on a cold wet night in October. Rosie had to stop several times to wait as a bout of coughing made it impossible for her to keep walking. The footpath, churned to mud by cows, was slippery and treacherous, and to make things worse the wind had picked up, driving the rain into her. But the heat of her rage was more than equal to the discomfort of the walk.

Thick clouds obscured the moon, making Rosie glad that she had thought to bring her small torch. It was still a relief, though, when she could finally see the cottage. Her impatience to get there and confront Ricardo made her walk faster, which in turn caused her cough to start up again.

The cottage was double-fronted, with a good solid porch and neat little dormer windows upstairs, which might on another occasion have made Rosie smile with appreciation of its prettiness. But tonight she had other things on her mind. She opened the gate and marched up to the front door, raising the knocker and letting it bang down again loudly. Blackout curtains covered the windows so that it was impossible to see inside, and when several minutes ticked by with no sign of someone coming to open the door it suddenly struck Rosie that she might have come here for nothing and that Ricardo could be out. Her heart sank at the thought of her long wet walk back to the hostel without having had the satisfaction of telling Ricardo what she thought of him.

Dispiritedly she stepped back from the front door and was just about to turn and walk away when abruptly it opened and Ricardo was standing there.

'Rosie!' There was shocked concern in his voice, instead of the guilt Rosie felt he should have been exhibiting.

'I expect you know why I'm here,' she challenged him determinedly.

'Oh, my poor little love, what's happened to you? You look so sad and thin.'

'I am not your love,' Rosie repudiated angrily. 'I've come about the letter you sent to my father.'

A huge smile illuminated Ricardo's face. 'You have his letter? He wrote me that he had sent one to you. Oh, Rosie, it is just as I knew it would be. He wants your happiness above all else . . .'

Ricardo had taken hold of her arm and was drawing her into the small hallway, closing the door behind her so that they were enclosed in the cottage's warmth.

'You are wet and cold. Come and sit by the fire. You shouldn't have walked here on a night like this. I had already asked if I could have time off tomorrow to talk to you. Ah, but it warms my heart, my Rosie, to know that you were as impatient to see me as I have been to see you. I have missed you so much.'

This wasn't what Rosie had expected. Doggedly she stuck to her guns. 'You had no right to write to my father.'

Ricardo had opened the door into the cosy sitting room whilst he was talking to her and now she could see the log fire burning in the inglenook fireplace. The room was simply furnished with the bits and pieces he had been given, and immaculately clean and tidy. Her father, with a seaman's habit of neatness, would approve of that. Rosie closed her eyes, squeezing back the painful sting of her unwanted tears. She had not come here looking for ways in which her father would approve of Ricardo.

Ricardo was still holding her arm. Angrily, Rosie wrenched it free. She could see the happiness fading from Ricardo's face along with his smile as he registered her antagonism.

'You are angry with me,' he said quietly.

'Yes,' Rosie agreed. 'I am – very angry. You should not have written to my father.'

'How else could I have presented myself to him and asked for his permission to marry you?'

'I had already told you why we could not be together; you knew about my mother, you knew how my father feels about Italians.'

'I knew certainly how you *believed* he felt,'

Ricardo acknowledged quietly, 'but it seemed to me when I put myself in his place that no matter how much the behaviour of your mother had hurt him, his love for you must mean that he would want your happiness above all else. And indeed, his letter to me confirms that this is so.'

'Of course he's going to say that, but that doesn't mean that it's what he really feels. I'm all he's got. He needs me.'

'When you marry me your father will have a whole new family. He will have a son-in-law and grandchildren, have you thought of that?'

'You say that now but—'

'I say it because it is what I mean. I shall be proud to have your father as my father-in-law, Rosie. I shall honour him as he should be honoured, and so will our children. He will always be assured of a home under my roof. That is the Italian way, you know that.'

Rosie could feel herself weakening. 'What makes you think that he will want a home under your roof?'

'I think it because he has written to tell me it is so,' Ricardo told her simply.

'Can't you see he's just saying that because of me, to make me feel better? But I know how he really feels.'

'Do you? Or is it that you have changed your mind and are using your father as an excuse to end things between us? Is that what this is really all about, Rosie? Are you not the girl I thought after all, but too much of a coward to say what is in your heart?'

'No. It is not that at all,' Rosie denied furiously.

'So you do love me still then?'

How neatly he had trapped her, she recognised. 'It is not my love for you that matters.'

'Your father wouldn't agree with you about that. He says that your feelings, your love are more important than anything else, at least to him. Have you thought, Rosie, how unhappy it would make him to see you unhappy?'

'He wouldn't have known if you hadn't told him.'

'Do you really think he wouldn't have guessed that something was wrong? He loves you very dearly. Think, Rosie, if you had a child and they loved someone but felt for your sake they had to keep that love hidden, think how you would feel. Would you rejoice because they had protected your feelings, or would you grieve for their pain?'

Rosie already knew the answer. 'You mustn't do this to me. It isn't fair.' Her voice broke as her feelings overwhelmed her.

'So what is fair? Is it fair that we should spend our lives apart, each yearning always for the other? You have told me already to find someone else but that can never happen, for no girl could ever mean to me what you do. I am sorry if I have angered you, but I was desperate, Rosie. I couldn't bear to lose you, and when Mary told me about your father, and told me to write to him and throw myself on his mercy, I knew that that was what I must do. Surely you can trust and believe in your father's love, Rosie?'

'Yes, of course I can.'

'Then surely too you can trust and believe him when he says that he is happy to give us his blessing and that the bitterness he holds against Aldo is held against the man and not his race?'

Rosie opened her mouth to answer him but before she could speak she was overcome by a paroxysm of coughing that left her ribs aching with pain.

'You are not well,' Ricardo told her immediately.

'It's just a bit of a cough, that's all,' Rosie told him tiredly, and then shivered so violently that her teeth chattered together.

'Come and sit down by the fire and get warm whilst I make you a hot drink. You should not have walked here tonight in the rain.'

'I'm all right,' Rosie insisted, but she still let him guide her towards the chair closest to the fire and push her gently into it.

'Let me take these boots off and put them on the top of the range to dry them out a bit.'

'I can take them off myself,' Rosie protested, but somehow it was easier to lie back in the chair and let Ricardo remove them for her. This continual coughing left her so wrung out and exhausted sometimes, it was an effort just to breathe.

'Your feet are so cold and wet.'

'My boots leak, and we are not allowed to have another pair because of the shortage of material for them with the war.'

Ricardo had removed her wet socks now and was chafing her cold feet between his hands.

It was so cosy here in the cottage with him, being cosseted like this. She felt so tired that she could fall asleep right here in the chair. Another fit of shivers gripped her body, and then she sneezed.

'You need what my English grandmother used to call a mustard bath,' Ricardo told her, 'but I don't think I have any mustard.'

Rosie managed a weak laugh. 'I'm glad to hear it,' she told him.

'Your breeches are wet and I don't think it is a good thing for you to be sitting in damp clothes, especially when you are not well already.' Ricardo was still holding her feet in his hands. To Rosie's shock he bent his head and kissed them lightly, causing a delicious feather-light tingle of pleasure to warm her body, followed by a sharp surge of anxiety. They were all alone here in the cottage. Ricardo was a very passionate man. He loved her and he knew that she loved him. He had her father's permission to court her. In Ricardo's eyes might all of this mean that he felt he had every right to the kind of intimacy they had not previously shared?

He had released her feet and was standing up. Did she feel anxious or was that tightening

sensation inside her more excitement and anticipation than apprehension?

'I am very conscious of the fact that your father
has put his trust in me, Rosie.' Ricardo's voice had
deepened and thickened. 'We are alone here
together, and there is nothing I want more than
to claim you as my own, but I am honour bound
to think of your father and to act as though his
gaze is upon me and his judgement hanging over
me, for I am not just the man who loves you but
the man who will one day be his son-in-law, and
the father of our children and his grandchildren.
I want you to know this before I say to you what
I am going to say and to understand that my words
and my actions are motivated by my concern for
your health, and that they do not contain anything
I would not want your father to witness. Do you
understand?'

Rosie nodded.

'Good. I am now going to go upstairs and bring
down for you a warm dressing gown. Whilst I am
in the kitchen, making you a hot drink and filling
a hot-water bottle for you, you are to take off your
wet clothes and put it on. I give you my word that
I shall not come in until you say that I may do so.'

'I can't do that,' Rosie protested, although in
truth she was so cold and wet that there was
nothing she wanted more. 'I have to get back to
the hostel.'

Ricardo shook his head firmly. 'No, you cannot
go back there tonight. You are not well enough.

In the morning I shall go and see the warden and explain to her the situation, and I shall ask as well that she arranges for the doctor to come out and see you. There is no point in arguing with me, Rosie. I am acting now not just as your husband-to-be but also in the place of your father,' Ricardo told her sternly. 'This, I know, is what he would want and expect me to do. When your father and I finally meet face to face, I want to be able to meet him as a man of honour.'

'You *are* a man of honour, Ricardo,' Rosie told him in between her increasing bouts of shivers. 'You are the most honourable man I know.'

'You will trust me then? Tonight?' he emphasised. 'In all things?'

Rosie looked up into his face and was overwhelmed by the force of her love for him. 'Yes,' she told him truthfully.

She had removed her damp clothes, kneeling on the rug in front of the fire, stripping right down to her underwear, and now she was wrapped snugly in the large warm dressing gown that smelled so wonderfully of Ricardo.

'Here is some special coffee for you,' he told her, coming in with a mug of rich dark coffee that smelled so strong she wrinkled her nose.

'What's in this?' she demanded after she had taken a sip.

'Brandy,' Ricardo told her. 'It will help to warm you and help your cough, so drink some more.'

Obediently Rosie did so, pulling a face and telling him, 'Ughh, it tastes awful.'

'But it warms the stomach, *sì*?'

'*Sì*,' Rosie agreed and then giggled. She felt oddly light-headed, and somehow almost carefree, as though a huge weight had suddenly been lifted from her shoulders.

'I will take your wet clothes and put them to dry over the range,' she heard Ricardo telling her. 'They are a wonderful piece of equipment for a cottage such as this, provided you know how to deal with them. I confess it took me nearly two weeks to learn how to keep it in without using too much fuel.'

Rosie laughed. 'You've done very well. I've heard that they are well known for being difficult to deal with.'

'You are warmer now?' Ricardo asked her.

'Much. But I don't need a doctor, Ricardo,' Rosie told him gratefully and then gasped as she suddenly started to cough so violently that Ricardo had to hold her mug of coffee. 'The cough gets worse in the evening,' she defended herself. 'But I'm all right really.'

'You are too thin, and whilst, *cara*, I would dearly like to think that you are wasting away on my account, it seems to me that you are not as well as you want us all to think.'

'People have enough to worry about, without worrying about me as well.'

'That is typical of you, Rosie, that you don't want to cause others concern.'

She stood up, careful to keep the dressing gown wrapped tightly around herself, surprised to discover how pleasantly light-headed she felt. 'I think you put too much brandy in my coffee,' she told him solemnly.

'It will help you sleep.'

'Will it? Do you know, Ricardo, I don't think I want to sleep. Dear Ricardo,' she smiled beatifically at him, 'I do love you so very, very much. Do you truly believe that my father doesn't mind about us?'

'Yes. I truly believe it,' Ricardo assured her.

Rosie exhaled on a small happy sigh and then stood on her tiptoes and leaned forward to wrap her arms around Ricardo's neck so that she could kiss him.

'Rosie . . .'

'Don't you want me to kiss you, Ricardo?' she reproached him. 'I thought that you would.'

'Rosie, I do,' he assured her, his voice muffled, 'but . . . Rosie . . .'

But it was too late. Rosie was pressing irresistible and eager little kisses all over his face.

'Rosie . . .' he protested thickly.

'Ricardo?' Rosie whispered back against his mouth. 'Did I tell you how good it feels when you kiss me?'

The logs hissed and crackled in the fireplace as the wind buffeted the cottage. Rosie made a small ecstatic sound as she pressed herself closer to

Ricardo, lost in the wonder of what they were sharing. This was the first time they had truly been alone together, the first time they were free to whisper and kiss and touch, safe in the knowledge that there was nothing between them and no one to see them.

Rosie had stopped hugging Ricardo's dressing gown round herself when she had reached up to wrap her arms around his neck and now *she* was the one to whisper softly to him, 'Touch me, Ricardo . . . properly . . . here,' she emphasised, taking his hand and placing it on the warm swell of her breast.

How was it possible for something as simple as a man's touch to give her so much pleasure? She felt dizzy with delight on the intoxication of it, yearning eagerly for more, but Ricardo was already pushing her gently away.

'This is not what your father would expect of me, Rosie. Not now, before we are married. And besides, you do realise, don't you, my darling girl, that it would be totally wrong of me to take you to bed in your present condition?'

'It's just a bit of a cold, that's all,' Rosie protested.

Ricardo laughed and held her close. 'I was talking about the brandy in the coffee I gave you. Now why don't you go upstairs to bed? I've lit the fire up there for you and put a hot-water bottle in the bed, and then in the morning—'

'Where are *you* going to sleep?' Rosie knew that

the cottage had two bedrooms but only one bed, from what Mary had told her.

'I shall be sleeping down here,' Ricardo told her firmly.

It was hard to leave the warmth of his arms, and even harder not to coax him into going upstairs with her, but Rosie wasn't so strongly affected by the brandy that she didn't realise the wisdom of what Ricardo had said. If her father meant what he had written in his letters, then she and Ricardo had the rest of their lives in which to share the intimacies of being together. Besides, Rosie knew that she didn't want to share the fate that had befallen Sheila, whose condition had caused so much gossip, with some of the other girls saying that her young man would never have married her if it wasn't for her pregnancy. That wasn't the kind of start to married life that Rosie wanted for her and Ricardo.

The bedroom was small and cosy, with its sloping walls and dormer window, but the coldness of the icy bathroom had left Rosie shivering as she got into the old-fashioned high bed with its iron bedstead.

The tot of brandy Ricardo had urged her to drink before coming upstairs had soothed her cough and made her so drowsy that her eyes were closing almost as soon as her head touched the pillow.

It was the pain in her chest that woke her up – that and the sound of her own coughing. At first she thought that she was at home in Liverpool, and she called out for her mother. Then she remembered that her mother was dead, but by that time she felt so poorly, and her thoughts were sliding in and out of her head in such a confused muddle, that she couldn't catch hold of them to think about them properly – and besides, her head hurt too much. She knew, though, that the bedclothes were cold and damp and she thought somehow in her confused state that she must have fallen asleep outside in the rain but then she remembered that she was in Ricardo's cottage, so she felt for the hot-water bottle, thinking it must have burst, whilst she shivered convulsively and her body burned up with fever.

'Rosie . . .'

Someone was calling her name urgently, dragging her back from a place she didn't want to be dragged from. She tried to blot out the voice, but it wouldn't go away. Reluctantly she opened her eyes.

'Ricardo, I'm too hot,' she told him, and then shuddered violently and started to cough.

THIRTY

'Doctor says that you can go home for Christmas, Rosie. Isn't that good news?'

The news she had just been given was even more welcome to Rosie than the cheerful smile Nurse Bradley gave her as she checked Rosie's temperature chart and then poured out a spoonful of linctus for her.

Rosie had no memory of the night Ricardo had bundled her up in his dressing gown and the eiderdown off his bed, and then carried her all the way to the village and the doctor, and no memory either of how Dr Flint had taken one look at her and said immediately that she needed to go into an isolation ward so that her chest could be checked out for TB.

The first memory she had of the events of that night and its consequences was that of waking up in hospital, her bed surrounded by screens, and a doctor and two nurses, all wearing masks, peering down at her.

She had thought at first that she must be dreaming and then when she realised that she wasn't she had been filled with disbelief that a mere cough should have resulted in her being in hospital.

There had then been a week when she had drifted in and out of sleep, feeling too ill to care about anything, crying helplessly because Ricardo hadn't been to see her, not knowing then that he had spent every spare minute he had at the hospital, badgering the staff for news of her, desperate to be with her but not allowed to be because she was in an isolation ward.

Then eventually, when it was realised that she didn't have TB, she was moved to another ward, and she could still remember the joy that filled her when she had woken up one night to find Ricardo sitting beside her bed.

'Sssh,' he had warned her, putting his finger to his lips. 'I'm not supposed to be here and if the nurse catches me, she'll throw me out.'

Rosie was a very lucky young woman, Dr Hood was fond of telling her. Another few hours without treatment and he doubted that anything could have saved her from succumbing totally to pneumonia. It was thanks to Ricardo's prompt actions that she had not done so, he had added. Rosie smiled softly now, thinking how much she had to thank Ricardo for. He had saved her life, she knew that, even though Ricardo himself tried to make light of what he had done.

'I certainly couldn't carry you across three fields now,' he had joked with her, only yesterday. 'Not now you've filled out a bit again, thank goodness.'

Rosie had smiled ruefully at him, remembering the number of times he had sat patiently at her bedside, spoon-feeding her the nourishing foods she needed for her recovery, but had felt too weak to bother eating.

And now she had made such good progress that she was being allowed to 'go home'.

But where to? She didn't have a proper home any more. There was the house in Liverpool, of course, which now belonged to her father, but she could hardly turn out the tenants, especially not at Christmas.

Then there was the hostel. Mrs Johnson had been to see her, as had the girls, and the warden had assured her that there would be a bed for her there, but Rosie was a sensible girl and she knew that, whilst the danger was over, it would be some months before she was strong enough again for land girl work.

Ricardo came to visit her every day after work although, strictly speaking, visitors were not allowed, but somehow he had managed to persuade the nurses to let him see her. Rosie and Ricardo had grown so close these last weeks. She loved him so very much and she didn't know how she could ever have imagined she could live without him.

Ricardo had been making enquiries and it

seemed that they could be married, especially with the duke already standing surety for Ricardo's 'good behaviour'. The duke had also said that he wanted to keep Ricardo on, and that they were welcome to live in the cottage. Mary had come in to see her and had offered her the loan of her wedding dress, assuring Rosie that she wouldn't have to worry about a thing so far as a wedding was concerned, because she and the other girls would see to it all for her.

The future couldn't have looked brighter except for one thing, one shadow, one fear and sadness that Rosie couldn't quite banish. Her father. Oh, he had written – and more than once; telling her how relieved he was that Ricardo had been there to look after her when she had been so poorly, and telling her too that she wasn't to give another thought to his own foolish comments about Italians, made in the heat of the moment when his blood had been up over her mother. But Rosie still worried that she might be taking her own happiness at the cost of her father's pain.

Although it was a Saturday afternoon, Rosie knew that Ricardo would be working. The duke had been very good about him having time off to visit her, but Rosie knew that Ricardo didn't want to take advantage of the duke's generosity.

She was sitting in the convalescent room of the hospital, wrapped in blankets to protect her body from the cold air from the open windows and the sharp fresh air she had been instructed to breathe in to help her lungs. Matron was a firm believer in the efficacy of good fresh air, and Rosie couldn't help laughing when she heard the comments the other patients made about this practice when Matron and the nurses were out of earshot.

Rosie wondered what time it was and how long it would be before Ricardo came to see her. It wouldn't be until it had gone dark and his work was over for the day, she knew. What would he say when she told him what the doctor had said? Although they'd talked about getting married, Ricardo had been disappointingly vague when Rosie had tried to discuss setting a date, and that had upset her although she hadn't let him see it. Had the fact that she had been so poorly made him have second thoughts? If so, he certainly hadn't given any indication of that when he came to see her. He was always so loving and kind to her that she could only agree when the nurses told her how lucky she was.

The door to the convalescent room opened and one of the nurses announced cheerily, 'Rosie, you've got a visitor.'

It must be one of the girls from the hostel, Rosie decided as she turned round to welcome her, but the smile she had been about to give trembled into a shocked exclamation of disbelief when she saw who was standing in the doorway looking at her.

She was still supposed to be taking things carefully and not doing too much, but she was pushing away the blankets wrapped round her legs and standing up unsteadily, blinking hard just in case she was imagining what she was seeing. But no, the two men she loved best in all the world *were* there, standing together in the doorway, Ricardo supporting her father, just as a son should.

'*Dad!*' Rosie didn't know if she was laughing or crying or perhaps doing a bit of both.

Her father hadn't changed at all. His eyes still had the same loving twinkle and he still smelled of salt and tar, even if his familiar rolling walk had ceased with the loss of his leg.

'I can't believe that you're here. I just can't believe it,' Rosie was still repeating half an hour later, unable to find the words to say what she really felt.

'Well, it's your Ricardo who organised it all, writing to me to say as how you were fretting and asking if I was up to coming home. If my girl needs me, I told him, then wild horses won't stop me being there for her. So Ricardo speaks out to this duke chap and asks him if there is anything he can do and, blow me, before I'd got me kitbag packed up, someone was knocking on the door saying as how a berth had been arranged for me. By, lass, but it's good to see you,' her father said in a less jocular voice. 'I've bin that worried about you, knowing that you weren't well. Of course, I knew you'd got Ricardo here to look out for you, and that helped.'

Rosie had to blink away tears as she saw the look her father was giving Ricardo.

'He's a fine lad, Rosie love. I knew that the minute I read his letter, but now that I've met him . . . I couldn't ask for anyone better to take care of you, and I know that your mum would say the same.'

It was too much for Rosie's composure. 'Oh, Dad . . .'

'There . . . what on earth are you crying for? We should be celebrating, shouldn't we, seeing as there's going to be a wedding in the family?'

They were married quietly two days before Christmas in the village church. Rosie's father gave her away, and Ian stood as best man for Ricardo. Earlier in the week Rosie and Ricardo had gone to her mother's grave to place some flowers there. To Rosie's own surprise, her father had struck up a friendship with the landlord of the village pub, who had offered him the job of barman, explaining that, with the extra business brought in by aircrews coming in and the land girls, he and his wife were struggling to manage. It was a live-in job and, as her father had told Rosie happily, it was a snug berth that would suit him down to the ground.

'Rosie, what are you doing?'

'I'm decorating the Christmas tree, what does it look like?' Rosie laughed.

Ricardo had brought home the Christmas tree earlier in the day and Rosie had set to making what decorations she could. Ricardo had come home earlier than she had expected, and now, as she stood on a stool trying to reach to the top of the tree, Ricardo held out his arms to her. When she saw the look of passionate adoration in his eyes Rosie's laughter died, to be replaced by a soft betraying blush.

'Don't look at me like that,' she protested shyly.

'Why not?' Ricardo demanded. 'Surely now I can look at you with all that I feel about you, my Rosie.'

Rosie didn't bother to reply. She was too busy enjoying the way he was kissing her.